KT-362-771

Forced Confessions

John Fairfax

Little, Brown

LITTLE, BROWN

First published in Great Britain in 2020 by Little, Brown

1 3 5 7 9 10 8 6 4 2

Copyright © John Fairfax 2020

The moral right of the author has been asserted.

*All characters and events in this publication, other than those
clearly in the public domain, are fictitious and any resemblance
to real persons, living or dead, is purely coincidental.*

All rights reserved.
No part of this publication may be reproduced, stored in a retrieval system,
or transmitted, in any form or by any means, without the prior permission in
writing of the publisher, nor be otherwise circulated in any form of binding or
cover other than that in which it is published and without a similar condition
including this condition being imposed on the subsequent purchaser.

A CIP catalogue record for this book
is available from the British Library.

Hardback ISBN 978-1-4087-1160-6
Trade paperback ISBN 978-1-4087-1159-0

Typeset in Sabon by Palimpsest Book Production Limited,
Falkirk, Stirlingshire

Printed and bound in Great Britain by Clays Ltd, Elcograf S.p.A.

Papers used by Little, Brown are from well-managed
forests and other responsible sources.

Little, Brown
An imprint of
Little, Brown Book Group
Carmelite House
50 Victoria Embankment
London EC4Y 0DZ

An Hachette UK Company
www.hachette.co.uk

www.littlebrown.co.uk

For Benedict, Jerome and Myriam

Your very silence is your confession

Iphigenia Auliensis,
Euripides

July 1999, HMP Kensal Green

Benson pulled up the sleeves of his grey prison sweatshirt.

'It's the mark of Cain.'

Camberley recoiled.

'Don't say that. You must never say that again.'

'It's the truth.'

'No, it isn't. We both know it isn't.'

'We both know it doesn't matter what the truth is any more.'

Only a few months ago Benson had been in his second year of a philosophy degree. He'd toyed with the idea of tattoos. Something aesthetic; and linked to grammar – an obsession of the logical positivists. He'd thought of an exclamation mark on his chest and a question mark on his back. He'd ended up with a string of full stops on each arm.

'They'll fade,' he said, pulling down his sleeves.

'I'll pay for their removal.'

'The conviction will remain, Miss Camberley. I might as well keep them.'

Four days earlier, Benson had been dragged into a pelly on D Wing. There, with a needle, blue ink and toilet paper, the job had been done. Twelve dots. Four on the inside of one arm and eight on the other, a jab and a dab for each letter in the name Paul Harbeton. 'It doesn't matter if you're innocent,' the screw had said, watching. 'You've been convicted.' There'd been a Zippo as well, to sterilise the needle and light the burns of the onlookers, all of them branded in the same way; all of them lifers for murder, members of the most exclusive club in the prison system.

'No,' said Camberley. 'You cannot keep those . . . mutilations.'

Prior to his trial, she'd leafed imperiously through the witness statements. At times, he'd even wondered if she was glad he'd been charged, for he'd sensed in Helen Camberley QC – silver-haired, with eyes like burning jet – the white-knuckle vanity of the virtuoso. She was going to show Benson how it was done.

'I owe you an apology,' she said, sitting down.

'You gave me a fighting chance. You fought—'

'And I lost. And all I can tell you is that I've never wanted to win a case more than yours; or feel more responsible for . . .' – embarrassed, she focused on the stained walls, then the broken light, and finally the worn-out lino. She held her breath, as if wondering what to do with it, and finally she let it go, as so much waste. 'Perhaps one day you might forgive me.'

Benson blamed her for nothing. In court she'd been cajoling, inquiring, indignant, rousing – he'd been mesmerised. His one fleeting concern – dismissed at the time as ignoble – was that maybe, just maybe, she'd tried too hard. That energy hadn't diminished in the slightest.

'Last week you said you were resolved to come to the Bar?'

'I did.'

'You've reflected on my advice?'

'I have.'

'Good. Because I, too, have given considerable thought to your future. Have you seen *A Man for All Seasons*?'

'No.'

'A pity. It's about the life of Thomas More. At one point, he tries to steer a man away from moral catastrophe. Because his professional ambitions are misplaced. More urges him to abandon them and consider teaching. It's a quiet life, he says; and I say to you—'

'I don't want to teach.'

'Why not?'

'I want to be like you.'

'Me?'

'Yes. I want to question people who think they know the truth.'

'But you can do that in the classroom. The mind, too, can be a prison. You can open—'

'I'd rather keep them out of places like this.'

'And live with failure, like I must?'

'Yes.'

'Well, that's admirable; and of no significance.'

She'd already told Benson why. And she repeated it with agitation. You can't become a barrister without joining one of the four Inns of Court. To do so, you'd have to disclose your conviction . . . and since you pleaded not guilty, you'd have to admit the murder you didn't commit. And she came to a halt, dismayed, guessing – correctly – that Benson had already written to the Parole Board in those terms. He said:

'Is there a law that forbids someone with a conviction for murder from practising at the Bar?'

'No. But—'

'An Order made by the Secretary of State?'

'No.'

'Any rules or regulations published by the Bar Council?'

'No. Will, stop this. You're—'

'Any guidelines restricting the exercise of discretion?'

3

'I don't know and it makes no damned difference. They'll slam the door in your face.'

'But it's possible? Theoretically?'

'Forget the theory. You're not a "fit and proper person".'

'You don't need to tell me that.' Benson tugged up his sleeves. 'The fit and proper person I once was is dead and gone. I'm starting again. But these dots won't define what is fit and proper . . . they won't determine what I do with my new life. I won't forget the theory. It's all I've got left.'

Camberley went to the barred window and looked over the expanse of slate, chipped brick and barbed wire, towards the gas works, and, beyond that, the distant shops and restaurants of Kensington. Turning a bangle round and round her wrist, she stared as if straining to distinguish someone through the summer haze.

'Dead and gone?'

'For ever.'

She became quite still; then she returned to the table with its bent legs bolted to the floor. Although she was short, her voice had an authority that conjured stature. Gazing down at Benson through two half-moons of glass, she seemed far away, in a cold place.

'I'll help you challenge the inconceivable. But on one condition.'

'Name it.'

'Dying isn't enough. There can be no resurrection.'

Benson nodded, but his agreement had come too quickly. Camberley became irritated:

'An advocate must be free. Free from any kind of external pressure or internal distraction. All that matters is the client. *Their* case, as *they* see it, supported or unsupported by the evidence. Not as seen by the Crown, or the media, or pressure groups, or the armchair critic. And certainly not as seen through the eyes of an embittered victim of injustice. Some may have the detachment to look beyond their pain. But not a few don't. They live out their anger finding common cause with those they would help. That is fatal for an advocate. And fatal for the client. Your vocation is to become someone else's voice; not give them your own. This means you must only look forward. You cannot look back in a search for lost innocence.'

'I understand.'

'And neither can anyone else. Not your mother, not your father, not your brother, not your lover. What is dead is dead. If that life is gone, then you must leave it buried.'

'I will.'

He would become a disciple. And it would cost him nothing.

'I'll never look back.'

After a long moment Camberley's expression softened. A warming vulnerability appeared in her eyes, and she said:

'From now on, call me Helen.'

With that she went to the door and gave it a knock to summon a guard. Turning suddenly around, she said:

'We'll never speak of your case again. So let this be the final word: whoever killed Paul Harbeton lives in a hell of their own making. And unless they admit their crime, they'll remain there for ever. You can take some comfort in that.'

A key rattled in the lock and Benson felt the misty onset of panic. His respite was over. He was going to be banged up for twenty-three hours a day with Needles. Through a choking fog of tobacco and anxiety he saw him slouched on the toilet, legs wide open, farting and knitting. The guard shoved open the door.

'How do you know?' said Benson, and Camberley gazed at him, overrun by an abrupt compression of empathy and accusation. Her voice was barely audible:

'Getting away with murder always comes at a price.'

PART ONE

January 2017
Two days before trial

1

'I'm dying, Will,' said Camberley, striking a match to light a cigar.

George Braithwaite, sporting a holly and ivy patterned tie, had just taken his unsteady leave. It was late now, and Camberley had returned to the dining room with a bottle of something special, bought long ago, when she'd planned ahead for those ordinary moments that suddenly turn into a celebration.

'Dying?' Benson repeated, as if it was a foreign word.

Camberley smiled: 'Yes. I suppose I should be frightened; but I'm not.'

Benson felt nothing. Then, very slowly, his chair seemed to tip backwards.

'How do you know?'

'I've got lung cancer.' With a flick of her wrist, she extinguished the growing flame.

'What?'

'Never ask a useless question.'

'You're having treatment?'

'There's no point. It's everywhere.'

'But surely—'

'I mean everywhere.'

'It can be slowed down, Helen. There's—'

'Not mine.' She paused to adjust her paper crown. 'It's in my lungs. My lymph nodes. My bone marrow. My organs.

My brain.' She sounded like a pathologist reading labels on a row of glass jars. Savouring the brown aroma of Cuba, she said, 'I'm banjaxed.'

Benson felt the beginnings of a headache.

'How long did they give you?'

'Oh, I wasn't listening. A few weeks or so.'

They were quiet together – as they'd often been in the past after they'd talked themselves dry, dissecting trials and witnesses; scoundrel advocates and rising stars; shrewd judges and the odd dimwit who should never have been appointed. Arching a brow, she appraised the hot, creeping ash at the end of her cigar.

'I would have liked to go in late spring, with the wisteria out of control. Pull another cracker, will you?'

That conversation had taken place on Christmas Day. A wet and cloudy Sunday. It was now mid-January. Another cloudy Sunday, and even wetter. Camberley's paper crown had been replaced by a transparent PVC ventilation helmet that reached down to her neck. Glowering at Benson she said:

'Stop moping and tell me about the Limehouse case.'

Her decline had been rapid. Within a week of pulling that cracker, she'd lost weight. Her breathing had turned short. She'd coughed up specks of blood. After ten days' resistance, a chest infection spreading, she'd said goodbye to her rambling home with its dormant garden and taken a room at the Royal Marsden Hospital.

'You told me it's about family secrets,' she said. 'I'm intrigued. Especially when they end in death.'

The riddle in the cracker – 'Why is it getting harder to buy Advent calendars?' – had foxed Camberley; and Benson had refused to read the punchline. He took her hand:

'Jorge Menderez is a doctor from Spain.'

'What kind?' she snapped.

'Medical. Works for years in a maternity clinic and then becomes a GP. Decides to take a sabbatical. Comes to London, seeking distance.'

'From?'

'Memories. Problems with his parents. Childhood confusion. So when he gets to London he checks out various therapists and finally settles on Karen Lynwood. Like him, she's in her fifties. And she speaks Spanish.'

'I assume he spoke English?'

'Yes. He did his medical training at Cambridge.'

'Think pilgrimage.'

'Sorry?'

'A return to the place that put him on the road to the rest of his life.'

'Well, it's an odd pilgrimage, because, according to the police, he never went to the shrine.'

'Meaning?'

'He rents a house by Limehouse Cut and just stays there. Never went back to Cambridge – at least not to his college – and made no attempt to contact any of his contemporaries.'

'Very interesting.' Camberley had closed her eyes and was frowning; breathing was hard work. 'Did he know anyone nearby?'

'No.'

'Colleagues from Spain?'

'None of them were in the UK.'

The police investigation had shown that Menderez only made connections with people who'd got some link to his homeland and its culture. And none of them had ever crossed his path before. He'd sought them out, wanting, it seemed, a place to anchor his identity; and, having found them, he'd been at pains to maintain his privacy. He'd dropped into the Instituto Cervantes; he'd attended a few cultural events organised by the British Spanish Society; and he'd eaten fairly often at El Ganso, a Spanish restaurant in South Hackney. The only people who'd got anywhere near him were the chairman of the Limehouse Photography Club, a witness for the prosecution with nothing much to say, and, of course, Karen Lynwood, his therapist. Who had a great deal to say but wouldn't be saying it. And that, said Benson, was the heart of the case.

'The Crown says she fell in love with Menderez. And he with her.'

'There's evidence of a relationship?'

'Overwhelming.'

Camberley could no doubt imagine the rest: the husband finds out and, driven to despair, he kills the man who'd exploited the rift in his marriage. She'd seen it many times before.

'The person I'd most like to have questioned is Dr Menderez,' said Benson. 'He came to England with a secret . . .'

Benson felt a flush of sadness. He'd turned, to see Camberley's head had fallen to one side. She was sleeping, a pained frown upon her face. With each uncertain respiration, a piece of shiny blue plastic moved in a tube at the side of the helmet, rising and falling no more than a centimetre. Benson watched it, holding his breath: up, down, up, down, up, down . . . the blue disc always fluttering at the high and low point . . . up, down, up, down, up, down . . . Unable to watch this quiver on the edge of life, he tiptoed towards the door, but then, just as he was about to leave, he heard a soft cry:

'Will, come back.'

Benson quickly obeyed, but his mind fled elsewhere. He couldn't forget the Camberley he'd known since his own strange death, the woman who'd brought him to another life and who, only recently, had sported a crown, worn aslant above a mischievous grin. She'd worked out why it's getting hard to buy Advent calendars. Their days are numbered.

'I want to talk about the trial,' she said hoarsely.

'We will, Helen. I'll come when I can, after court, but you've got to rest now, there's no—'

'Not the Limehouse case, Will. I mean yours . . . your trial.'

'Mine? That's dead and buried.'

She shook her head.

'There are things you must tell me; and there are things I must say.'

Benson had taken her hand once more. They were looking at each other through a shroud of PVC. She was going to die in there. Her skin was sallow and her hair was tangled; but for a moment her pupils became sharp.

'Our journey's almost over, Will. And I've one last step to take. Help me finish what we began.'

Before Benson could reply, she slowly closed her eyes. All he could hear was the rasp in her lungs and the uneven passage of the plastic disc. Up, down; up, down; up, down . . .

On the way home, Benson popped into a newsagent's and bought a keyring torch. While the manager rooted in a box for some batteries, Benson heard the news, coming muffled from a radio in a back room. A body had been found in Nine Elms. But Benson couldn't engage with someone else's death. He could only think of Camberley, who'd shortly leave him . . . wanting, first, to return to the beginning of their relationship. The apposition of beginnings and ends had thrown him, making that inevitable parting all the more significant. Back on board *The Wooden Doll*, his barge moored at Seymour Basin, off the Albert Canal, he stood in the darkness, sending a blade of light along the curved walls, oiled floorboards and beamed ceiling. He drew patterns, cutting left and right, slashing at the night; and tears ran down his face like never before, save once, when a screw had told him his mother was dead.

2

'Bless me, Father, for I have sinned. It's been twenty-one years since my last confession.'

'You must have come with a skip.'

'No, Father, I've come with a mistake.'

'Well, I hope it's a corker.'

'It's about doubt. The breaking of a promise. And betrayal.'

'That's fairly Petrine, actually.'

'Petrine?'

'Like Saint Peter. Do you remember? The denial by the fire? He made three mistakes in less than a minute. But, to be fair, he was scared out of his trousers. What about you . . . are you all right?'

'Yes . . . I'm just tense. And confused. And it's been such a long time, Father. I can't remember what comes next.'

'It's forgiveness. You can tell me anything. Anything at all.'

Tess de Vere hadn't planned to enter the confessional. Throughout a wet Sunday, she'd stayed warm at home in Ennismore Gardens Mews reading a trial brief, preparing for tomorrow's client conference with Benson. Then, to clear her head, she'd ambled through Hyde Park into Marylebone. She'd stared at a display case in Shipton's, the jeweller's; and then, not quite thinking, she'd followed her feet into a church off Spanish Place. She'd seen the glow of torchlight on worn-out black Oxfords peeping out from beneath a curtain on one side of the booth. She'd heard a page turn, and then a soft laugh. Moments later she'd been on her knees.

'As an undergraduate I went on work experience with a solicitor,' she said suddenly. 'And I attended the trial of a student charged with murder.'

The priest's head remained perfectly still. And Tess thought of her father in Galway, motionless in Barna Woods, listening for redwings.

'This student, a man, went to a pub on a Saturday night. He ended up outside, challenging another man about his behaviour. This other man floored him with a headbutt. That's it. Only this other man was found dead in a back street forty minutes later.'

Benson had been arrested, because he'd been seen in Soho, and the question of his guilt or innocence had been born.

'When this man got life, Father, I watched him go down . . . and it was traumatic.'

'Why?'

'Because I was powerless. And because he'd sworn to me that he was innocent.'

'You believed him?'

'Yes.'

'Why?'

'I don't know.'

'You do.'

Tess closed her eyes and knotted her fingers.

'He told me he was going to be convicted, he could sense it, but he needed at least one person he didn't know to accept that he was innocent. He didn't want pity, Father; he wanted belief . . . and it was like he was giving me his soul, and I had to look after it, because once he was taken away in a prison van his life was over.'

Tess opened her eyes to find the priest had moved closer to the grille.

'And when you saw him again?' he said.

'I felt bound to him. Bound to who he'd been, to who he might have been, and to who he'd become . . . I'd been left with his true identity, only no one accepted him any more, and he didn't accept himself . . . and he still doesn't . . . and there was I, holding on to something important that he didn't want back, because he'd changed . . . It's complicated, Father.'

'It could only be complicated.'

Alone in the tense moments before the verdict had been delivered, Benson had told Tess he would have liked to come to the Bar, and she'd thrown back hope like a life-guard: go for it, she'd said. Don't give up. Sixteen years later Tess had sat in a restaurant, eavesdropping on two hacks as they mocked the ex-con no-hoper who'd opened his own chambers from an old fishmonger's in Spitalfields. Clerked by a former cellmate with convictions for tax fraud, he'd landed a murder trial that he couldn't possibly win.

'Are you frightened?' said the priest.

'Yes, Father.'

He waited.

'Of yourself?'

'Yes. Because I don't know what I feel. The man who came out of prison is so different from the person I'd met in the cells. That guy was simple. He was desperate, but . . . his desperation was transparent.'

'Which is why you trusted him?'

'Probably, yes.'

'What about the man who was freed?'

After leaving that restaurant, Tess had resolved to help the no-hoper defy his critics. She'd parked her classic Mini near Benson's barge, waiting for him to come home. He'd appeared, head down, checking his pockets for his keys, talking to himself, seconds before a passer-by coughed, gathering mucus in his mouth.

'Freed?' she asked. 'He can't shut doors, or lock them. He can't look anyone in the eye. He's still desperate, but it's clouded now. He can't tell you what he feels, because he doesn't know what he feels. I watched someone spit on him, Father, and he accepted it without complaint. I gave him my handkerchief and he just wiped his face.'

And that had been the beginning. For when Tess had run across the road, she'd no longer been a powerless bystander. She'd been a solicitor with Coker & Dale, a top London firm. Despite opposition from the partners, she'd stayed at Benson's side. They'd become 'Benson and de Vere', with Archie Congreve in the clerk's chair and Molly Robson on the throne of chambers administration. They'd become a team like no other. The priest drew a deep breath.

'Isn't this compassion?'

'Yes. Only . . . I'm frightened I might love him.'

'What's wrong with that?'

'Nothing. It's just that . . . I came to doubt him.'

'What's wrong with doubt? I graze on the stuff.'

'I mean serious doubts, Father.'

'So do I.' The priest paused, as if to read the label on a packet of laxatives from hell. 'They clear the mind. Wonderfully. And they lead to action.'

The last time doubt had brought Tess to her knees, she'd been with Fr Kennedy. He'd dished out the penance before Tess had described the wrong turning. He couldn't restrain a longing to forgive. She said:

'I tried to deal with these doubts. I asked this man to help me prove his innocence. And he begged me not to.'

'Did he say why?'

'He said if everything was resolved he might lose the flame.

You see, Father, something takes over when this man walks into a courtroom. His deadened life is left behind . . . he says he comes alive . . . and it's electrifying. So I promised to leave his past alone.'

'And is this the mistake that weighs upon you?'

'No, Father. My mistake was to break that promise.'

'And why did you break it?'

'Because in public he says he's guilty and in private he says he's innocent . . . and it harms him and his family and the family of the man who was killed. They're all ghosts in a twilight world of confusion and anger and grief.'

'So you did what you promised you wouldn't do?'

'Yes. Helped by my oldest friend, I began a secret investigation into this man's trial.'

Urged on by Sally Martindale, Tess had pored over the witness statements, seeking leads that may have been missed. The priest leaned closer.

'Did you uncover anything?'

'Yes. And if we act on what we now know – which, for him, would be an act of betrayal – there's a chance he'll be vindicated.'

'You don't sound especially pleased.'

'I'm not. Because I'm scared of making a second, bigger mistake. I'm wondering if it might be better for people to live without the truth, because, if the truth comes out, the confusion and anger and grief won't go away. It'll only increase. The twilight world will only get darker.'

'How so?'

'Someone out there will be arrested, and their life, and the lives of those closest to them, will be changed, utterly and for ever. And as for the man who's declared innocent . . . what does he gain? He can't get back the life he once had, and he might lose the one he's built upon injustice, which helps so many people . . . because he's different. He listens

differently. He acts differently. And all that might disappear
. . . because of the truth. Come on, Father. Let's face reality.
The truth? Who needs it?'

The priest leaned back and the light – a gap between the
curtain and the booth – fell upon Tess. She squinted, for
even weak light is bright in the dark.

'What have you found?' said the priest from a shadow.

'A bracelet.'

3

'An investigation?'

'Yes.'

'Into Rizla's trial?'

'Yes. That's what I said.'

'And you've found a bangle?'

'No, a bracelet.'

Archie dropped the sock that he'd been filling with
breadcrumbs onto his desk.

'Take me through this again.'

At that moment the door opened and Molly bustled in,
clutching a wicker basket.

'Stand well back,' she said. 'I've got the oranges and the
sugar. Oh . . . hello Miss de Vere. Is everything all right?'

Archie pointed to the chairs in front of his desk.

'Miss de Vere has something to tell us.'

Talking about her dilemma in the darkness of a confessional had nudged Tess into a kind of daylight: she had
to tell Archie and Molly what she'd been doing. Knowing
the two of them had planned to meet in chambers to
continue 'preparations for the next trial', Tess had gone

there, but on entering the clerk's room she'd found Archie preoccupied, crumbling sliced brown bread into a bowl. Bemused, she'd watched him transfer the crumbs into a sock. But when he'd looked up, mischief in his eyes, she'd blurted out the beginning and end of what she wanted to say. And now, with tea made by Molly, Tess went back to her point of departure. They listened intently, each sitting on the edge of their chair.

'The man who found Paul Harbeton's body was a motor-cycle despatch rider. A guy called Mickey Lever.'

'He's the one who called the police?' said Archie.

'Yes. But that's not all he did.'

'What do you mean?'

'He robbed Benson of a line of enquiry that might have led to his acquittal.'

While talking to the emergency operator, Lever had seen something twinkling a few yards from the body: a platinum bracelet with nine small diamonds. Rather than hand it over to the police when they arrived, he'd put it in his pocket.

'You're kidding,' said Archie, squaring up for some sort of backstreet reckoning.

'I'm not.'

'What did he do with it?'

'He gave it to his girlfriend as a present.'

'And what did she do with it?'

'She sold it to a shop in Victoria.'

'Which one?'

'Evington's.'

Tess hesitated. Do I tell them I lost faith? That it was Sally who'd carried on the investigation and not me? That it was Sally who'd gone looking for Mickey Lever and found Tracy Patterson, his girlfriend? That it was Sally who'd brought Tess back on board when she'd sensed a breakthrough? No, she couldn't. Some secrets had to be kept, because neither

Archie nor Molly would have understood Tess's doubts. For them, Benson's innocence had always been beyond question.

'Why sell it?' asked Molly.

'Because she got married to someone else.'

'You went to Evington's?' said Archie impatiently.

'Yes.'

'And?'

'They'd sold it to an old lady who lived in Pimlico, and yes, I went there. And when I got there, I took photographs of the bracelet. One of them shows who made it.'

'And who's that?'

'R. J. Shipton in Marylebone. And I went there, too.'

This was the jeweller's before whose empty window Tess had paused earlier that afternoon. A few months earlier, the owner, Anthony Shipton, great-grandson of the founder, had dug out an old ledger. And Tess had taken another photograph, this time of a copperplate entry from 1918.

'The bracelet was made by a master craftsman, Manny Brewster. The work had been commissioned by Arthur Wingate.'

'For himself?'

'No, Archie, for his daughter.'

'And who's his daughter, and why the hell would it matter now?'

'Because this is where it gets interesting. The bracelet was an eighteenth birthday present for Elsie Wingate.'

Archie looked at Molly, and then back at Tess.

'Who, might I ask, is Elsie Wingate?'

'The grandmother of Richard Merrington. Who happens to be . . .'

'The Secretary of State for Justice,' said Archie under his breath.

Tess didn't need to say any more. The autopsy on Paul Harbeton had identified a fatal head injury, along with a vertical bruise to the right leg. The prosecution had argued that Benson had attacked Harbeton from behind, with a kick and a blow to the skull. Camberley had countered with an explanation for which there'd been no evidence: that Harbeton had been struck by a car or motorcycle, causing him to fall and strike his head on the kerb.

Molly spoke:

'Is Elsie your prime suspect?'

'No, she died when Benson was in nappies. So the question becomes, who might have been wearing her bracelet on the night Paul Harbeton was killed?'

'Do you know?'

'Not for sure. But I've a good idea. Only I daren't follow it up.'

'Why?'

Tess repeated the worries that she'd disclosed to Fr Winsley; but Archie, roused from a trance, seemed to shoulder his way into the confessional.

'Sure, tons of crap might hit the fan, and Rizla might like feeling guilty, but, sorry, there comes a time when leaving the truth untold becomes wrong. You've got to shake things up. Do what's right. For everyone.'

'That's what the priest said.'

'What priest?'

'I went to confession.'

'When?'

'Earlier today.'

'But you've done nothing wrong.'

'He said that, too.'

The priest had wondered whether the true mistake was to have promised not to investigate Benson's conviction, which, given his claim to innocence, was tantamount to leaving a truth untold.

'So why did you go?' said Archie.

Tess wasn't sure. A longing, perhaps, for that childhood encounter with wonder, which had always happened with Fr Kennedy, the go-between who dispensed God's forgiveness before you'd named the wrongs you hadn't committed yet. But this other priest hadn't survived the Somme. He wasn't half-deaf. And he was in no rush to offer peace of mind. He'd said you can hesitate about whether *now* is the time to tell the truth, and *how* and *why* you should tell the truth, and to *whom*, but a situation can arise when ongoing silence becomes as evil as the wrong it conceals.

'I went because I wanted someone to tell me what to do,' said Tess.

'Did he?'

'No. But he helped.'

'How?'

'He said I'd know soon enough what to do and when to do it.'

He'd said once certain events spring into motion nothing can stop them; even the person who started the process. He'd told her to be vigilant. Evil, he warned, has a way of creeping up on people trying to do their best. It leaves everyone else alone.

'You should have come to me, Tess,' said Archie. 'I'd have told you straight. You need to find out who the bloody hell—'

'No, Mr Congreve.'

Molly, too, could square her shoulders.

'What are you on about? Rizla did eleven years for a crime he didn't commit. There are people out there – and that Merrington is one of them – who want to see him back in jail, and the sooner—'

'Miss Camberley is dying. Mr Benson is all over the place. And we've a trial starting the day after tomorrow.'

Tess, grateful for the support, nodded and said:

'And if I bring the truth – whatever it might be – into the open, Benson's world will change. It's a world he built with Camberley; and it rests on his murder conviction and what he's done with it in court . . . and if I change the ground rules to his life . . . he might fall apart.'

A heavy silence grew between them; a silence with content: Tess had begun something. It would lead either to a dead end or Benson's vindication. All their worlds would change. In ways that were difficult to imagine. And even the imagining became a sort of temptation, because Molly was right. The real matter of the moment was the impending trial. Nothing could distract any of them from their respective roles. And, as if returning to a task that couldn't be delayed, Archie went into the kitchenette, returning moments later with a bowl of warm water . . . into which he gently lowered the sock filled with breadcrumbs, while Molly produced a knife and began cutting the oranges in half. Tess watched them uneasily.

'What are you doing?'

'Preparing to blow our brains out. Yours, too. And Rizla's.'

'What with?'

'You'll see.'

'When?'

'After the trial.' Giving a clue, he nodded towards a jerrycan on the floor. 'It's the best way to mark a win . . . or a loss.'

The silence grew strong again, because Archie's comment was ambiguous. He'd referred to the stakes in the Court of Appeal as much as those in the Old Bailey. Lifting the sock out of the water, he said:

'Tell me something, Tess.'

'Yes?'

He looked up and his jaw hardened.

'Who do you think was wearing Elsie's bracelet?'

4

Tess hadn't been home for ten minutes when Sally turned up. She'd responded immediately to a text sent by Tess: 'I couldn't be bothered to put the kettle on.' So Sally did; and she made the tisane. And she listened to Tess confess to her double confession, first to a priest, and then to Benson's closest friends.

'That's three times in one day,' observed Sally with her bevelled Home Counties vowels.

'And I'm still confused,' replied Tess. 'I just know now is not the time.'

Sally looked at Tess over her cup.

'You're not on your own, you know. Whatever you do, and whenever you do it, I'm here. We're in this together.'

Tess reached out a hand; as Sally took it, she said:

'Give yourself a break. Tell me about the Limehouse case.'

When Tess first met the Lynwoods she was convinced they were hiding something. That there was a bigger story, greater than themselves, and they were trapped and needed help . . . maybe to handle a mess that the trial would bring into the open, but in the end, after hours in conference, first with one, then with the other, and then together, she'd realised they were just another unhappy couple. That was the big secret. And things had spun out of control.

'Benson's representing them both?' asked Sally.

'Yes.'

'So what does he think?'

They sat in facing armchairs. The curtains had been drawn and a fire flickered in the grate.

'Well, he's part of the problem. He thinks that there is, in fact, a bigger story, only we can't see it. He thinks they're trapped—'

'And need help?'

'Yes. Even though there's no evidence to ground his belief.'

'There must be something.'

'There isn't, Sally. It's an open and shut case.'

A youth breaks into a disused warehouse by Limehouse Cut and finds a body. The police are informed and it turns out the dead man is Jorge Menderez, a Spanish doctor taking a sabbatical who'd rented the adjoining house. His computer is missing. Along with the SIM card from his phone, which is in his coat pocket. The science shows the killing took place in the sitting room and that the body was moved to the warehouse, which was then swept clean of footprints. But something's been left behind. Close to the body, a Scene of Crime Officer finds a tiny screw from a pair of glasses.

'Why move the body?' asked Sally.

'A preliminary step. It would have been visible from the path by the Cut.'

'So the killer planned to come back?'

'Probably. After working out what the hell he was going to do. Which is why they took the keys. But then the youth turned up.'

Menderez had no relationships to speak of, said Tess. Save one, with a therapist, Karen Lynwood. By the time the police investigation is over, it's clear they'd become involved; and John, her husband, had found out. Karen had been paralysed with indecision and Menderez had refused to back off.

'And John?'

'Lost his head. Went to where Menderez lived and stabbed him with a pair of kitchen scissors . . . probably after a row gone wrong.'

In pre-trial hearings it had been accepted that John had threatened to kill Menderez; that he'd gone to Limehouse Cut to confront him; that they'd argued in the sitting room;

26

and that the screw found by the body had come from his glasses. None of these admissions had been volunteered. They'd all been forced out of him. The threats had been overheard; CCTV footage showed him fleeing the crime scene; and a forensic expert had linked the screw to John's glasses.

'And what about the wife?'

John had obviously told her about the killing. Because the very next day she deletes her emails, voicemails and texts. All of which are retrieved by the police. And taken together they present two desperate people – Jorge Menderez and Karen Lynwood – struggling to contain what's happened between them, and how to handle a husband who can't see sense, because he's blind to what his wife really needs and wants. That his marriage is over, and has been for years.

'That's terribly sad,' muttered Sally, 'but there's no crime in what the wife did. She must have been beside herself . . . and frightened . . . and confused.'

'She was. But she also offered money to her best friend, begging her to withdraw her evidence. That's attempting to pervert the course of justice. Because Karen had told her about this wonderful man she'd met, and what she felt for him.'

'Oh dear.'

The rest of the evidence had fallen into place like a jigsaw. Menderez's computer had eventually been found by divers searching the Cut; and it didn't take a leap of the imagination to see why John, like his wife, might seek to destroy anything that evidenced the relationship which had pushed him over the edge. The case, said Tess, was impossible to defend.

'Then why don't they admit what happened?'

'Because they have a son. And all this floundering around

is just an attempt to hide the truth, that love had died at home. They're not even in step on that one. He wants to change the past, make it into something different, something the son would want, but she can barely look her husband in the face. It's all so human, and so understandable. But someone's ended up dead, and now it's in the hands of a jury.'

Sally frowned.

'But if there's to be a trial, how does the wife explain herself?'

'She says Menderez was stalking her.'

'And the husband? What can he say?'

'That's credible? Nothing.'

According to the defence statement drafted pursuant to section 6A of the Criminal Procedure and Investigations Act 1996, as amended, Menderez must have been killed by someone with a grudge against him, or someone intent on silencing him, or paid on either score to do so. The notion of a grudge had been left as a logical possibility, because the defendants couldn't possibly know who may or may not have held a murderous intent towards the deceased. As to the alternative, a silencing, it had been maintained that an unknown third party may have been concerned to keep secret whatever the deceased had planned to disclose to his therapist. That Mrs Lynwood had been left alive was, of course, an obvious flaw in the argumentation: if you kill the messenger, you also kill whoever might have got the message.

'And Benson credits these explanations?'

'Yes, he does. And what's mystifying is that we needn't have put this nonsense on the form. It's up to the Crown to prove their case, so all we were obliged to say was that we don't know who killed Menderez or why. Which is, in fact, John's defence. But Benson wanted on record the explanation given, even though nobody on the witness list could possibly know about any grudge, or some secret Menderez might have intended to reveal, or a third party who stood to be compromised. The fact is, John Lynwood is in a desperate position, and Benson has made him look even more desperate.'

'Unless he drags something into the open.'

'I just said it couldn't be done.'

Sally's belief in Benson had riled Tess.

'Look, this isn't about whether Benson is innocent or not. It's about court craft. And he's made a mistake. And it's not the only one. He's insisted on calling two witnesses who've got nothing to say. Their evidence could have been read in court, but no, Benson's insisted on his right to question them.'

'Point taken,' said Sally. 'It's just that he always seems to pull off the unexpected.'

'Sure he does, but the trial hasn't even started and he's making things difficult for himself, and for the clients. He's *mishandling* the clients . . . we have conferences tomorrow, one with the wife, the other with the husband. He didn't want a joint conference. That's his call. But he wants to see the wife at home, and in her consulting room – the one place she's been avoiding since Menderez was killed. The place is locked up. She told us that, early on – said she can't imagine opening the door again – and now Benson wants her in there the day before the trial begins. It's as though he *wants* to dismantle her, and to do it when there's no time for emotional reconstruction . . . I can't understand him.'

Sally didn't say anything in reply. She looked at her watch, as if to say tomorrow has almost arrived, and then took the empty cups into the kitchen. The sounds of washing up, and Tess saying 'Oh leave it', filled the air, but the real noise,

29

for Tess, came from within: she felt accused – for doubting, yet again – and she was annoyed that in the competition of loyalty, Sally, a stranger to Benson, kept taking pole position. The discovery of the bracelet had insinuated a rivalry that neither of them wanted, or could avoid. Tess sought words to edge ahead, but Sally got there first:

'You're the specialist,' she said, shrugging on her long blue coat. 'But I wouldn't second guess Benson, if I were you.'

5

'She paid for the lot,' said the Rt. Hon. Richard Merrington MP, Secretary of State for Justice. His wife, Pamela, pushed her plate to one side. Having battled with the timer on the Dualit, she'd lost her appetite just when she'd got the colour of the toast right.

'How much, did you say?'

'A hundred and sixty thousand pounds sterling, give or take a few coppers.'

'But that's insane'

'She did it. While of sound mind.'

That someone had spent a significant sum on the rehabilitation of William Benson was not itself a surprise. For those with any interest in his case, it was well known that he'd enjoyed the patronage of a secret benefactor. There'd even been discussions around the dining table as to who it might have been. A lefty philanthropist, perhaps, or a tycoon with a past. Or – Merrington's preferred option – a crime lord yet to be arrested. That this person turned out to be Annette, his own mother, had come as a shock.

'But it's not even possible,' said Pamela, her eyes flickering. 'She didn't have that sort of money.'

'True. But I did. In a trust set up by my reverend father, who saw fit to make my mother a trustee with near-unlimited powers. She exercised them to the almost total detriment of yours truly. There's five grand left in the pot.'

'She wouldn't do such a thing.'

'Wouldn't? It's done. Shelled out in instalments from the moment he went to prison.'

'Spent on what?'

'Student fees, living costs, books, a houseboat – you'll remember that bijou residence, darling. The *Telegraph* did a spread showing the wages of sin aren't always disagreeable.'

Pamela seemed to inspect the list of disbursements. 'There has to be some mistake.'

'There isn't. My source works in the lion's den.'

'Lion's den?'

'The solicitor who handled the payments. A Methodist lay preacher, would you believe. George Braithwaite. He's one of only two people who knows what's going on – even Benson has no idea. The other is Braithwaite's secretary. The delightfully disloyal Mrs Purdy. Bradley bought her candour.'

'Oh, how cheap.'

Pamela's face had soured. She didn't like Bradley Hilmarton. A former detective, he earned his living carrying out discreet investigations into persons of interest to his clients. Off the books, he specialised in the acquisition of compromising material by undisclosed means and its dissemination without traceability. Such services had unconventional price tags.

'What did he want in return?'

Merrington gave a prophet's smile.

'To be remembered when I come into my kingdom.'

'Oh do stop, Richard. It's irreverent.' The glance of

reproach became a frown. 'But that's a fortune. It could have gone to David.'

'It *should* have gone to me. And *I'd* have given it to David. He's still intent on coming to the Bar, you know, and that'll cost us an arm and a leg.'

He removed a piece of shell from the egg white, a culinary solecism he wouldn't normally associate with his wife's cooking, but he made no complaint. Pamela, however, did:

'How long have you known about this?'

'A few months.'

'Why not tell me earlier?'

'I hoped to preserve your high feeling for Mr Benson.'

'Rubbish. You'd got your hands dirty with that slimy Hilmarton again and you didn't want me to know.'

'I'm sorry. You're right. *Mea culpa. Maxima culpa*, in fact.'

Pamela released a delicate snort.

'Why did you put that slug onto Benson at all?'

'Because I wanted to ruin him, darling. Didn't you know?'

If Pamela hadn't been enthusing over Benson's next appearance at the Old Bailey – while cracking that egg – Merrington would have kept Hilmarton's findings a secret. But he'd decided to extinguish her fervour once and for all. And what a delicious moment it had been.

'Instead, I've flushed out my mother's iniquity,' intoned Merrington. 'And it's mind-boggling. She chose to fund Benson's indecent ambitions over my interests. What the hell did she see in him? I mean he's a—'

'Stick with your mother. It doesn't make sense. Where on earth did the money come from? I thought your father was broke . . . in a worthy sort of way.'

'Oh absolutely. Not every High Church vicar has money, you know. There's a respectable tradition of penury. My father's distinction is that it was *thought out.*'

Gilbert Merrington had been a theologian of note – conservative, of course; none of that *Honest to God* nonsense – differing from his peers in that he was inspired as much by Tolstoy as by Holy Writ. And, like Tolstoy, he'd embraced poverty with gusto, sharing it generously with those closest to him. The fly in the unction had been a large endowed vicarage in Lewes, East Sussex, which he'd endured with touching patience. Merrington gave a shrug:

'Well, I suppose he stored up treasures in heaven . . . but kept a barn on the side, stacked to the rafters.'

'Oh, for heaven's sake, stop.'

Merrington laid his knife and fork on his plate.

'In a way, it's rather moving. He stacked it up for me, to ensure that I'd be all right.'

Merrington had not required any financial assistance. With surprising ease – he put it down to talent – he'd built a twenty-year career as a political journalist and pundit. By the time the funds were paid out to Benson, Merrington had been a new face in Parliament and – again by his own modest assessment – a brilliant future beckoned. Money had been the least of his problems.

'Why on earth did she do it? I can't help but feel I've done something to upset her. That she knows something about me and disapproves.'

'I've always said you're so awfully bright and know all the answers, but now you are talking rot. You haven't done anything, have you?'

'Well . . . to get where I am, I've had to stretch the odd moral boundary – the more elastic ones – and occasionally they've snapped, and a few bystanders have got hit in the face . . . but I've done nothing that would remotely affect her; or you, or the family.'

'There you are, then.'

'Maybe it's because I dropped journalism and went into politics. She's never approved, you know. Within a year of winning my seat she's saying I ought to do charitable work. Do you remember? Give unto Caesar and all that?'

'Vaguely. But you're barking up the wrong tree, darling. She'll have read about Benson's trial and felt sorry for a boy who'd messed up his life . . . that's just like her, in fact. Helping someone that no one else would notice. She's a good person, too, Richard. A true Christian.'

'Who's made a mistake.'

In a way that he couldn't quite grasp – founded upon endless tiny happenings, witnessed as a child, absorbed but not understood – there was something obscurely vengeful about his mother; but it had been resisted, and deeply repressed, only to emerge in good works that annoyed her neighbour.

And astonishing acts of generosity.

He suddenly visualised her. She was crying, turning the pages of a photograph album by the light of a Christmas tree. Pausing, she identified herself with the wavering finger of a ninety-two-year-old. A young woman was holding out her arm with embarrassed reluctance. On her wrist was a bracelet.

'Do you remember that bracelet of my grandmother's?' he said, nudging his cup. 'The one passed on to my mother when she turned eighteen?'

'Yes . . . the catch was broken.'

'That's right. Well – I'm revealing a state secret here – she wanted to give it to you.'

'Me?'

'Yes, as a birthday present. Back in '98, not long after I got elected.'

'Dear God, that's almost twenty years ago.' Pamela had left the table to fetch the coffee pot. 'Why did she change her mind?'

Merrington held out his cup.

'She didn't. I lost the damned thing. She asked me to get it repaired. And I kept forgetting. Remember? She was staying with us while the central heating was being redone at her place. She'd put it in my briefcase, my trouser pocket, my coat . . . and I just brought it home again. I don't know why she didn't deal with it herself,' – he reached for the milk – 'damned silly thing to do, putting an heirloom in my pocket, because it could so easily fall out – which is precisely what must have happened.'

'What on earth made you think of that?'

'I saw a photograph of her wearing it.'

Merrington was struck by an odd thought.

'You don't think there's a connection, do you?'

'Between what?'

'Well, me losing that bracelet and her funding Benson?'

Pamela took a long, slow breath. Then she said, 'You've gone potty. That can't have anything to do with it.'

'I'm elected in '97, I lose the bracelet in '98, and in '99 she starts forking out the readies.'

'You're suggesting she punished you for losing it?'

'I'm trying to understand her, my love.'

Pamela examined his face, blinking impatience. 'I've already told you: she'll have felt sorry for him. There's no other reason. You've done nothing wrong . . . dropping journalism has nothing to do with it; and neither has losing a bracelet.'

'How do you know?'

35

JOHN FAIRFAX

'She rarely wore it. For heaven's sake, she hasn't even noticed it's gone missing.'

That last observation arrested Merrington, and he smiled in agreement . . . and then, like sunlight striking a forgotten ornament – something like porcelain, so delicate it was transparent when held up to the light – he saw his wife of twenty-three years with sudden surprise. She was dressed in a blue and white striped Breton dress, bought years ago in Carnac. Her eyes were dark and earnest, lined carefully, to match her black hair which, these days, was dyed. She was ageing; as was he. There was tiredness in her glances; she fretted easily; she wore colourful scarves to hide the wrinkles on her neck. He loved her, and the changes she didn't want.

'Those are good points, Mrs Merrington,' he said, stroking the blue veins on her hand.

'I worry about you sometimes, Richard,' she said, indulgently, but drawing away. 'You're so terribly bright, what with your Cambridge first and so on, and yet – quite honestly – you entertain positively loopy notions as to why people do what they do. You shouldn't be Secretary of State for Justice. You're a risk to yourself and the nation.'

'Well, perhaps things are about to change on that front. Brexit is an absolute godsend. We're in total disarray . . . and you appreciate that ultimately Caesar had back problems—'

'Oh God. Not now, darling. I'll be late. Your mother's due an injection at Moorfields and I said I'd take her. Shall I ask her what in blue blazes she's been up to?'

'Absolutely not.'

Merrington folded his napkin; and he spoke to himself, because Pamela had quickly left the room:

'That's a question I reserve for myself.'

36

6

Tess dropped a gear and turned into Cornfield Road, Islington, and immediately saw Benson. Wearing his old blue duffel coat, he was standing by a lamppost near the Lynwood family home, a study in concentration and loneliness. His hood was down and rain was gently falling on his short black hair. Rubbish bins and green refuse sacks, slumped and fat with neat yellow ties, lined each side of the road as if they were commuters waiting for the bus. She parked her cherry red Mini Cooper, flicked off the wipers, and shook open the door. Benson spoke before she'd closed it:

'This is a very important conference, Tess.'

'Good morning, Will.'

She'd been thinking of the priest at Spanish Place; the one who fed himself with uncertainty. He'd seen no reason why she shouldn't love a man with a murder conviction; a man whose innocence she'd once doubted.

'This is our last chance to find out what really happened between Karen and Menderez,' said Benson. 'If I can show her how much I know, then maybe she'll give in.'

Tess smiled, but sadly. Benson couldn't know anything that she didn't; and, in the attempt to winkle out the truth, there was nothing in the brief that hadn't been used already.

'And how will you do that?' she said.

'By asking questions.'

'Just questions?

'Yes.'

Tess was no longer smiling; his grip on the case was in question. Again.

'And if she gives in?' she said, looking at the water running down Benson's face. 'We'll have a guilty plea tomorrow?'

Benson's gaze flickered in the rain. 'No, Tess. We'll have a defence.'

He swung on his heel and pushed open a glossy black gate.

Mrs Lynwood's consulting room was situated in an annexe to the family home. It was cold and airless, but something of past encounters had survived the abandonment: a trace of stale incense. Behind her chair was a spot-lit alcove. And on a shelf was a plaster statue of a boy in rags carrying a water jar on his shoulder. Though small, and despite a wall of books, and a large oil painting depicting a dreamy silver forest, he dominated the room.

'Why have you brought me here?' said Mrs Lynwood, on the edge of her seat.

'Because this is where your relationship with Dr Menderez began,' replied Benson. 'When you get into court, this is the place you will find yourself. You can't run away from what happened here.'

'But there can't be anything more to discuss.'

'There is.'

Mrs Lynwood had shoulder-length dark hair with gatherings of grey, like natural stripes. Agitation had removed the routine crumpling of empathy around her eyes. She'd lowered herself reluctantly into the therapist's chair. Benson sat facing, and Tess, an observer with a notepad, took a seat to one side. She sensed in this unprecedented arrangement, chosen by Benson, a tactic: to compromise the absolute secrecy of Karen Lynwood's professional world. As if bracing herself for the challenge, Mrs Lynwood held her head high.

'At the outset of your work together, Dr Menderez filled out a questionnaire in which he confessed to suicidal ideation,' said Benson.

'Yes, that's right.'

Tess recalled a ticked box. She glanced at Benson, seated, legs crossed, one hand folded inside the other. As usual, and in breach of good practice guidelines, he'd come without the brief.

'The reason for this suicidal ideation was never given,' he went on.

'I've told you before, Mr Benson. He said he wanted to tell me his story first. Beginning with his childhood. He wanted to put everything in context . . . and then explain why he'd wanted to end his life. I thought that was a sensible way to proceed, so that is what we did.'

Benson had raised this issue at the first client conference. It was of capital importance, because the reason Menderez wanted to kill himself had become, for the Lynwoods, the reason why *someone else* might want to kill him; either because of a grudge, or to prevent him revealing whatever he'd planned to say. It was pure conjecture. And unconvincing, because Menderez had gone on to recount stories about his *parents'* childhood, not his own. Stories about the Spanish Civil War. Horrors that could have no possible bearing on their son's mental health struggles seventy-five years later.

'I'd like to take a closer look at the mechanics of this imagined self-destruction,' said Benson.

'I don't quite follow.'

'Literally *how* did he imagine killing himself, *where* did the imagining take place, and *when* did it start.'

'Well . . . it began in July 2014.'

'And the how?'

'He fantasised about shooting himself . . . in the head. Holding a gun under his chin and pulling the trigger. The thoughts were constant, beginning as soon as he woke up. Then he'd get to work, but as soon as there was a moment of quiet he'd find himself closing his eyes and reaching for an imaginary revolver.'

'And the where?'

'This was in Spain . . . his village, Candidar.'

'We know that prior to being a GP in Candidar he'd worked at a maternity clinic in Madrid. Did he mention Madrid as being in any way relevant to what he was feeling?'

'No.'

Benson thought for a moment. 'A bullet in the brain is a particularly violent way of ending your life.'

'I agree.'

'He was evidently struggling with high levels of negative emotion?'

'Absolutely.'

'Which, rather than building up over time, had a fixed starting point?'

'Yes, though a sudden onset isn't uncommon when feelings have been repressed.'

Benson accepted the point as if it didn't matter.

'Either way, there seems to have been an event of some kind in July 2014 that induced a sudden deterioration in his well-being?'

'Yes, that was my conclusion.' She frowned impatiently. 'Using the word "event" isn't helpful, Mr Benson. It sounds dramatic, which needn't have been the case. The smell of a cake can release a flood of memories.'

'People rarely want to blow their brains out over a Victoria sponge.'

Mrs Lynwood's face went blank.

'No, I suppose they don't.'

'He could have read something, or heard something, or seen something, but a desire to kill yourself, beginning at a specific moment, points to a graphic encounter. I suggest he met someone. What do you think?'

Mrs Lynwood didn't answer immediately, so Benson repeated the question, only more slowly.

'I agree,' she said irritably. 'But I can't be certain, because we didn't get that far. He never told me.'

'It doesn't matter what he told you. I'm considering his behaviour. You did consider his behaviour?'

'Of course, yes.'

'And to have affected his behaviour in the way that it did, the encounter in question must have involved Dr Menderez becoming aware of something?'

'That's possible.'

'It's axiomatic.'

'All right, it's axiomatic.'

'Something about which he'd previously been ignorant or had hoped to keep secret. You must have considered these options?'

Mrs Lynwood thought about the alternatives, hands working each other.

'I did.'

'And?'

'And yes, I agree.'

'The outcome was an imagined gun to the head. Which implies self-disgust, regret or a fear of exposure. Given that Dr Menderez was a man of the highest moral rectitude, I'd go for all three. What do you think?'

'I don't see how this is relevant to—'

'Someone came to see Dr Menderez in July 2014. Whatever they said shattered the status quo. We can forget cake.'

'Yes, I accept that.'

'Cake won't do as an answer, Mrs Lynwood. I suggest someone brought Dr Menderez face to face with his past, and he didn't like what he saw. And he probably didn't want anyone else to see it either. I'm asking you to assess the behaviour of Dr Menderez with a clinician's eye.'

'Yes,' she said, suddenly petulant. 'I agree with everything you've said. But he never confirmed anything I might have thought. So I fail to see why—'

'I'd like to focus on who this person might have been.'

'I haven't the faintest idea.'

'I have, and I'd like to know what you think. The police in Spain investigated Dr Menderez's clinical and personal relationships in and around Candidar. There'd been no incident to provoke his departure for the UK. He was held in universal high esteem. So, unless this person didn't speak to the police, or was hiding something when they did, I think we're dealing with someone he'd known in Madrid. Did Dr Menderez ever mention anyone he'd known in Madrid?'

Mrs Lynwood snapped back:

'No. Never. You've read my notes: he mainly talked of his parents. And towards the end of our time together, we talked of their effect upon him. How their fears had influenced his view of the world. We never discussed his work, either in Madrid or Candidar.'

'I'd like to return, if I may, to the suicidal ideation.'

'But there's nothing else to be said. I never found out what—'

'Did you ask him when it began to diminish?'

'Yes.'

'Well?'

With a flick of the hand she brushed off the question's importance.

'As I recall, it was December 2014.'

'Which was when he made his first move.'

'Sorry, you've lost me.'

'He contacted Redgrave Estate Agents on the sixteenth of December, looking to rent a property.'

'I really wouldn't know.'

Benson fell quiet. Tess watched him; so did Mrs Lynwood, only she'd paled and a nerve jerked the corner of one eye.

'This, then, is the probable picture,' said Benson, rising to his feet. He went to the window, which looked onto the quiet street of waiting detritus. 'In July 2014 someone came to Candidar. Someone who'd probably known Dr Menderez in Madrid. Whatever they said was shattering. After six months of suicidal thinking he decides he has to get away, not just from Candidar but from Spain. In December he settles on London, and at last the symptoms begin to withdraw. We know from the police investigation that he spends the next two months organising a locum for his surgery. He arrives at Heathrow on the second of March 2015. Towards the end of May he contacts you seeking help. Your first session takes place on Monday the first of June.'

'That's right.'

'You described him as "buoyant". The suicidal thinking, it seems, was over.'

'Yes. Because he was resolved "to face the past with honesty . . . and look to the future with integrity". Those are his words,' – she gave a sigh. 'They're in my notes.'

Benson turned around.

'There then followed fourteen other sessions, once a week, every Monday, until the seventh of September. That's four months. And he never mentioned the past that needed facing?'

'No.'

'Four months of dialogue. And he gave no hint of his deepest secret; the reason he left Spain and came to see you in the first place?'

'No, Mr Benson.' A curtain of hair fell forward. 'We never got that far.'

43

7

Benson stayed at the window, not speaking. His tenacity, combined with Mrs Lynwood's resistance, had produced an uncomfortable silence, shared, Tess felt, by a fourth person, a ghostly presence whom Benson had conjured into the room through logic: the individual who'd made the journey from Madrid to Candidar with something important to say. She envisaged a man leaning over a GP's desk, pointing angrily. Outside, a bin lorry heaved along the road, stopping and starting. Bins scraped across the pavement and lids banged.

'I want to talk about your policy on ethics,' said Benson, an issue he'd never mentioned to Tess, never mind Mrs Lynwood. 'Your website states that it was your practice to breach confidentiality in order to assist in the prevention and detection of crime?'

'Yes.'

'And yet Dr Menderez wished to discuss the matter?'

'Yes, he did.'

Mrs Lynwood raised her head and drew back the curtain of hair. She looked exhausted. Still on the edge of her seat, her shoulders had slumped and her eye no longer twitched.

'Your contemporaneous notes on this are brief,' said Benson. 'You only jotted down key words. I'd like to fill in the gaps.'

'I understand.'

Tess felt a chill run down her spine. Those gaps were the reason for the conference. Mrs Lynwood's eyes had the brightness of grief, that childlike shining that precedes tears. The bin lorry was approaching, revving and braking. Voices cried out.

'You wrote "silence, victim, harm",' said Benson.

'I told him that I could never be put in a position where, through silence, I would deny a victim justice or expose someone else to harm.'

'And should either circumstance arise?'

'I would call the police.'

'You also wrote "grey".'

'I said there could be no grey areas.'

'Why did you write "integrity, reason"?'

Mrs Lynwood stared back, blankly. Benson repeated the question and she turned from his voice, pinching her lower lip.

'Was he referring to yours?' said Benson.

'Yes,' she said at last.

'He was praising you?'

'Yes.'

'Did he give your moral integrity as the reason why he'd approached you rather than anyone else?'

'Yes, Mr Benson, he did.'

Benson waited for the truck to pass; there were shouts of laughter between workmates. Someone yelled 'You must be joking.' Then Benson said:

'The last entry is difficult to read, so I need your confirmation: did you write "report self BACP"?'

'Yes, I did.'

'What did you mean?'

Mrs Lynwood now tugged at her upper lip. 'He wanted to know whether I'd go so far as to report myself to the British Association for Counselling and Psychotherapy if I crossed a professional boundary.'

'What was your reply?'

'I said I would, though I couldn't imagine the circumstances ever arising.'

'It seems to me that he wanted to know if you'd ever be prepared to compromise. In respect of a client or yourself?'

'Yes . . . that's true. And I said I wouldn't.'

None of these replies had come as a surprise to Benson. He'd listened like a teacher correcting an aural examination. He'd known the answers already. He was just ticking the boxes. After a pause, he came away from the window and returned to his seat. This time, like Mrs Lynwood, he sat on its edge.

'Mrs Lynwood, have you ever wondered why Dr Menderez was so concerned about the strength of your moral convictions?'

'No, Mr Benson.'

'Are you sure?'

'Yes.'

She was lying: it was obvious; and, having a very specific sound, Tess realised she'd been listening to the same strained notes since they'd taken their seats beneath the gaze of the boy in rags carrying water. When she spoke again there was a plea in her voice:

'I can't help you any more, Mr Benson. I don't know why he chose me. I don't know why he questioned me on the law. At the time, I just thought here was someone who cared about what was right and wrong, and now that he's dead I can't bear to recall him as he was on that day . . . someone setting out to do something good.'

'I'm afraid you have to.'

'But why, Mr Benson? He's gone. How can we know what was in his mind? And why would it matter?'

'It matters because his interest in your ethics policy goes to the heart of what he expected from you.'

'I don't understand.' Mrs Lynwood lowered her head and covered her eyes with one hand. 'Why do you say that?'

'It was only after he was sure you'd contact the police in certain circumstances that he said he wanted to face the past with honesty. Am I right?'

Mrs Lynwood nodded, tightening her hand around her forehead, massaging her temples. Benson watched her carefully, seeming to pity her with a surgeon's determination.

'Mrs Lynwood, at some time in the past I think Dr Menderez committed a grave crime. He got away with it. He left it behind. He got on with his life.'

Tess waited for Mrs Lynwood to respond, but her thumb and fingers just grew whiter.

'Someone, however, confronted him. They brought him face to face with what he had done. We don't know what they said, but we know the result. He wanted to die.'

Almost imperceptibly, Mrs Lynwood began to fold, bending at the waist, her hand still working her temples. Benson said:

'Mrs Lynwood, I think Dr Menderez came to the UK in an attempt to escape his conscience. But guilt ate away at him until, after three months, he decided to stop hiding . . . only he daren't go home because his crime was a big crime, and he feared the outcry . . . so he came to you, because he knew he lacked the courage to confess what he'd done. He was relying on you to help him take the one step that scared him most: going to the police.' Benson paused, and the effect was excruciating. 'Am I right, Mrs Lynwood?'

She continued her minute tipping-forward.

'Did Dr Menderez tell you what he'd done?' said Benson. 'Did he finally explain himself on the seventh of September 2015, your last formal session together?'

Mrs Lynwood became perfectly still, and Benson's words came in a murmur.

'Is that why you didn't note up what he'd said? Because the unimaginable had happened? Because you'd come to understand this very lonely man . . . a good man, who, long ago, had done something terribly wrong? And you couldn't reach for the telephone because—'

Suddenly Mrs Lynwood dropped her hand; she slowly raised her head. Tears were running down her face. And Tess was transfixed.

'If you tell the truth you can handle anything,' said Benson; he was like a crouched figure approaching a butterfly. 'It's strange, Mrs Lynwood, but to speak the truth is always a liberating experience, even if no one believes you. And, stranger still, one can always live with the consequences. Unlike a lie. A lie brings a kind of death, and—'

'Mr Benson, I am very much alive.'

With a jolt from the neck she flung her hair back, and something fragile in her voice flew off. The shine in her eyes had been replaced by a cloudy glaze that reminded Tess of cruelty.

'For the last time: I did not have a relationship with Dr Menderez. He told me he'd once been suicidal. He never told me why. He never mentioned any criminal conduct on his part. Otherwise I would have called the police. Our professional relationship came to an end because he'd become fixated on me. He then stalked me for weeks. I didn't know what to do. I handled things badly. And now I'm in trouble. Because my best friend has lied. And John's in trouble. Because someone killed Dr Menderez. They killed him on the night John went to see him. I know the prosecution say that no one else had access to the property, and I know a screw from John's glasses was found by the body, and he can't explain these things, and neither can I, but what I've said is the truth: the only possible reason John might have had for taking this man's life is because of this so-called relationship with me, and it never happened. But this is how it all appears, and it did so from the moment his body was found. I deleted everything on my phone and computer because I was ashamed. I'd let my dealings with a patient spin out of control. But now I'm frightened.

Because if I was on that jury I'd find myself guilty. I'd find John guilty. But we're innocent, Mr Benson. Completely innocent.'

Tess had heard this impassioned speech before: it had been delivered at the beginning of the first joint conference with her husband. She'd spoken for herself and John, and Tess had written it all down, just like she'd written it all down again, not knowing which elements to believe and which to cast aside as anxious fabrications. But this time, as predicted by Sally, Benson had dragged something new into the open. Menderez had told his secret to Karen Lynwood. It had been hidden while he was alive, and it was being hidden now that he was dead.

'Noted,' said Benson.

8

'She knows everything, Will. She knows what Menderez did. She may even know who killed him.'

Seymour Basin was only a short distance from the Lynwoods' home. At Benson's suggestion they'd gone there, to *The Wooden Doll*, for lunch. But upon arriving neither of them felt hungry. They sat on either side of the small table in the kitchen, still in their coats, drinking coffee. Traddles, Benson's cat, came through the open port door and moved between their legs, leaning and purring.

'She's keeping quiet,' said Tess. 'Even though her husband is charged with murder.'

Benson nodded. He was slowly stirring his coffee, though he'd added no milk or sugar.

'That is a huge step to take, Will. She'd already decided what to do if anyone ever confessed to a crime. She'd made a stand. She'd put it up there on her website. It's what Menderez wanted.'

Benson carefully laid down his spoon.

'What's the crime, Will? What did Menderez do?'

Tess spoke as if addressing a magician, resigned not to understand how he did things. She'd thought Benson had been mishandling the case. She'd thought there was no bigger story. But he'd drawn one out from a single box on a questionnaire. She'd watched, amazed.

'You're right, it must have been a very serious offence,' she went on. 'No one leaves their country because of an unpaid parking fine. So what did he do?'

Benson shook his head in troubled ignorance. Dreary light slipped through a round window, falling on his shoulder like a long-fingered hand.

'I mean, what kind of crime does a doctor commit?' said Tess.

She'd been sifting possibilities during the silent drive to Benson's refuge.

'Sexual assault?' she suggested without conviction. 'Organ theft? Misappropriation of funds? Clinical malpractice? Something to do with drugs? None of them rings true.'

Because no one had come forward to volunteer any criticism of Menderez's conduct. The police had dismantled his past, from birth to death, and found nothing but attestations of moral stature. Which had led Tess to another conclusion.

'It's a secret crime, Will. There's nothing out there for anyone to find. No clues. No forensic. No witnesses . . . or at least none who are prepared to speak out.'

Benson nodded; he'd arrived at this conclusion before he'd even questioned Mrs Lynwood.

'It might be a closed circuit,' said Tess. 'Where only those involved know anything.' She watched the fingers of grey light play on Benson's ear and hair. 'Do you think there are others, Will? Or do you think Menderez did whatever he did on his own?'

'There are others,' he said.

'How do you know?'

'Because one or more of them killed him.'

'But how?'

'Ask Karen; she's the only one who knows.'

Tess felt the giddy impulse to object – the prosecution case remained impregnable: the only person who could have killed Menderez was John Lynwood; he, alone, had the opportunity; and his behaviour in the aftermath was that of a guilty man – but, just as quickly, the feeling subsided. Tess was unsure of herself now.

'What are you thinking, Will?' she said.

He looked up.

'I scared her off.'

Tess replied at once:

'Maybe she's stronger than you realised.'

'Yes, maybe.'

He became absorbed again; and then he said:

'We were this close to the truth, Tess,' – he was showing a few millimetres between his thumb and forefinger – 'and then the light went from her eyes.' He paused. 'I don't know how she copes with the strain of secrecy . . . it's not normal to cope. Not with this kind of secret. It's a learnt skill. It takes years. And she hasn't had years; she's had months.'

'So what does that mean?'

'It means her situation is extreme. Whatever she's hiding is extreme. Her refusal to cooperate is extreme. It's a problem for her; and it's a problem for me. Because if I've not been told what's happened, I can't defend her properly; and I can't defend John properly. I'm left without proper instructions.'

51

Tess's objection resurfaced, this time as a tentative question:

'Will . . . Menderez could have done something awful way back and someone involved could have killed him. All that is possible. But there's a simpler explanation. Karen began a relationship with Menderez. She denies it, but we know for sure that John went to confront him, having threatened to kill him. Isn't that enough?'

'Yes, if we're only concerned about the evidence.'

'But isn't this the case we have to defend?'

'It is. And, somehow, we will. But fighting a case according to the evidence without worrying about the truth is a sure way to lose. And anyway,' – Benson glanced to one side; and the pale light brushed his face – 'I don't want to be that kind of barrister.'

'What kind?'

'The kind who wins without caring if he got it right.'

Traddles pushed against Tess's leg, and for a brief moment she thought it was Benson; she returned the pressure and Traddles, easily seduced, leaned in, bending round her ankle.

'I spent eleven years inside,' said Benson. 'I've met countless people who were convicted of murder. Most admit it. But some don't. And of those who don't, you get a feel for which ones are lying. It's not evidence, I know. But in prison, you're with people for whom the game's over. They're branded. Nothing can change the record. There's a kind of hopeless desperation in their voice when they tell you they're innocent . . . and I hear the same sound when I listen to Karen and John Lynwood. It doesn't matter what else they say – it could all be rubbish – but when it comes to the killing of Menderez, I believe them.'

'But what about the Crown's case?'

'There'll be a counter-explanation. There has to be. That's

why I tried to break Karen down. She knows what it is. John certainly doesn't.'

'Why do you say that?

'Because he's been left with no defence. He wouldn't share a secret about Menderez when the risk for him is a life sentence for murder.'

Tess agreed, and she said so, watching Benson. His slightest actions were charged with energy and lost honour. It pulled at her recklessness like a magnet. As if to clear the way, Traddles emerged from under the table and sauntered out the way he'd come.

'Why wait?' she said, after clearing her throat. 'Why confront her at the last moment?'

'We need the truth up front. In the first conference, I asked for it. In the second, I pleaded. So this time I made it clear that I had a good idea already.' He leaned back into shadow. 'She might be in an extreme position, but she has to know that I'm not going to help her cover up a murder. That would make me part of the crime.'

Tess thought of a quiet laugh and a pair of battered black Oxfords. She recalled a warning about how silence can turn into evil; and she remembered some consolation: that she'd know soon enough when to act.

Tess swung into Pentonville Road, heading west to HMP Kensal Green for the conference with John Lynwood. Benson was at her side. Once again, they didn't speak. The only sounds were the clunk of the gears and the drone of the engine and the thud of the wipers. While she saw the brake lights ahead and the jostling umbrellas to one side, her attention lay with Benson's every movement: the restive hand on his thigh; the intake of air; and the warm exhalations. But then, as if nudged from behind, she thought of that indistinct presence summoned into the secret history of Dr

Jorge Menderez. An unknown person, central, now, to the outcome of his life.

'I wonder who went to Candidar,' she ventured at last. The prison lay ahead, its barbed wire black against the sky like badly stitched lacerations. 'Someone involved in the crime?'

'Possibly.'

'What about the killer?'

'Possibly.'

'Who do you think?'

Benson's face grew dark as Tess drove closer to the high Victorian walls with their dirty bricks and the splatter of graffiti. He'd begun his brutalising incarceration on the other side. While they'd never come to an arrangement, he'd expected Tess to visit; she knew it; and she hadn't done. Mr Braithwaite had forbidden any future contact. Regret stirred like fire in ash.

'I said, who do you think went to Candidar?'

Benson didn't hesitate:

'A victim.'

9

A white swan emerged out of the mist in St James's Park. It must have cut across the lake, floating into view opposite the bench upon which Merrington was sitting. They looked at each other through the haze until footsteps sounded on the path; measured footsteps that Merrington recognised and had been waiting for. They belonged to Jos Fowler, a leading member of the 1922 Committee, the body that represented backbench Tory MPs' interests; the body that handled any challenges to the leadership.

'Everything's in place, Richard,' said Fowler, sitting down.

He meant he was sure at least 15 per cent of Conservative MPs were ready to write a letter to the Committee chairman expressing their lack of confidence in the Prime Minister. He meant that once those letters had been received, a vote of no confidence would have to take place. He meant he was sure the PM would not survive the ballot, which would then trigger a leadership election. He meant that the plot they'd hatched to ensure Merrington won the ensuing contest had been approved by other key players.

'You know what to do?'

It was hardly a question; but Merrington replied all the same.

'Yes, Jos.'

Sarah Appleton, the Education Secretary – a close friend of Merrington – had been encouraged to declare herself as a candidate. Merrington was to support her in exchange for being appointed Foreign Secretary. What Appleton didn't know was that information had been obtained concerning her husband, Rex, and a secret love-child . . . Merrington had stopped listening. He was captivated. Midday sunlight was trying to break through the mist. And by some quirk of physics the swan seemed to shimmer in the air. All Merrington could do was look on in awe, as if he was a boy again.

'Richard, I said I need to know everything.'

'Sorry, what was that?'

Fowler, wrapped in a black overcoat and a crimson silk scarf, turned to Merrington.

'I do hope I'm not talking to myself.'

'No, no. I was just thinking of Sarah. She's always been good to me. And she wouldn't do to me what I'm about to do to her.'

'Which is why she'll never make the hard calls. Now, tell me everything.'

Merrington had expected this inquisition months ago. That it hadn't taken place was a strong demonstration of Fowler's trust, and of those to whom he'd spoken. But the moment had now arrived. Fowler wanted to know Merrington's secrets. Anything he'd said, done or failed to do that might compromise his position once he declared himself as a candidate. He meant anything *at all*. From a fling to an injudicious email. Even those known to Merrington alone, for such things can emerge years down the line like the reaper with his scythe.

'Tip it all out and I'll decide what's important,' said Fowler. 'You'll feel immeasurably better afterwards.'

And so Merrington trawled through his past, his eyes on the bright swan. There'd been no flings or ill-advised emails. No love-children. Just the odd unconscionable manoeuvring required to realise his political ambitions – which didn't trouble Fowler in the least, for such things, while attracting short-term censure if exposed, never harmed anyone's career.

'Anything else?'

'No, Jos, that's everything.'

'Are you sure?'

The swan had turned its long neck to one side and was gazing elsewhere.

'Don't hold anything back.'

Merrington thought of the conversation that had taken place over breakfast with Pamela that morning. He'd only told her half the story – the half concerning his mother; he'd said nothing about Hilmarton's other discovery.

'I organised an investigation into William Benson. You appreciate who Benson is?'

'How could I not?'

While Benson couldn't be described as a national figure, the controversy surrounding his coming to the Bar had become associated with Merrington, who most certainly was. Shortly after his appointment as Justice Secretary, the family of Paul Harbeton had demanded the enactment of 'Paul's Law', banning anyone with a serious criminal conviction from any kind of employment in the legal profession. They'd been backed by the tabloid press and an online petition. Merrington, seizing the opportunity to advocate high principle, had vowed to shut Benson down. But then another petition had appeared: 'Everyone Deserves a Second Chance'. A slow burner, it had gathered strength in tandem with Benson's first appearance at the Old Bailey; a remarkable performance in defence of a woman deemed guilty by the very papers that were out to destroy him. Pity for her and respect for Benson had coalesced into indignation, for the high principle of fairness had been breached. To calm the growing dispute, Merrington had postponed any immediate legislative action.

'You backed down, Richard,' said Fowler. 'Which made you look weak. I've spoken to Spellow and Hardy in Soho and they think that is something we may need to address. As they like to remind us, image is everything. But why investigate Benson?'

'Because he made me look weak; and I considered it something I may need to address.'

Fowler smiled.

'What have you learned?'

'Do you want the good news or the bad?'

'The bad.'

Merrington hesitated. The swan was drifting away, gradually turning its back towards him.

'My mother paid for Benson's rehabilitation.'

'Jesus Christ.'

'He might have something to do with it, actually.'
'How much are we talking?'
'A hundred and sixty grand.'
'Bloody hell.'
'Given out of compassion, just after I was elected.'
'Who knows about this?'
'No one except Benson's solicitor, George Braithwaite . . .
and a Mrs Purdy, his secretary. There's no chance of a leak.
I'm not worried either way.'
'Well I am.'
'No need, Jos. I said there was also good news.'
'I'm waiting.'

Merrington strained to make out some plumage, the
curved neck, or the black unfeathered skin between the eyes
and the yellowy-orange bill. But the swan had become a
fading smudge of dirty white, overwhelmed by the encroaching
mist. Merrington felt a peculiar, distant sadness.

'Benson lives a lie. To everyone except himself.'
'Enlighten me.'
'He wrote out his confession. Or perhaps I should say
confessions. Multiple times. Valiant attempts to catalogue
his many sins. He then shredded his efforts and put them
out with the rubbish. My investigator retrieved them.'
'And?'
'He put them back together.'

The swan was almost invisible now; a stain in the grey
air.

'What have you learned?'
'More than enough. Fear not, Jos: I have Benson's soul
in the palm of my hand. When he's ruined – and we can
choose the moment – people will remember that I once
opposed him.'

Fowler nodded slowly; he looked gratified, as if a wrinkle
had been ironed out of a handkerchief.

'You never disappoint me, Richard.'

'I aim to please.'

Fowler stood up. The pale sunlight was still trying to break through the mist; but it was weak now, to the point of indifference.

'Over the years I've quizzed three former challengers, Richard,' he said. 'When they'd finally emptied their pockets, I always asked if they'd told me *absolutely* everything. And on every occasion, each candidate had kept back a little something, hoping it wasn't that important.' He turned, looking down. 'Take a leaf out of Benson's book. Go the distance. Is there anything else?'

Merrington sighed.

'My son, David.'

'What about him?'

'He's thinking of coming to the Bar.'

'So what?'

'He wrote to Benson. Asking to spend a week in his chambers. On work experience.'

Fowler grimaced.

'What is it with your family and Benson? First your mother and now your son.'

'I know. But the problem resolved itself. Benson slapped him off.'

Fowler placed his hands deep in his overcoat pockets. He was straining to see across the lake. There'd been a dip in luminosity. Above the mist, there was low cloud; and the sun must have moved behind that second veil. Fowler rocked on his toes, crunching the gravel.

'There's something else, isn't there?'

Merrington appraised his interrogator. He didn't like Fowler. Fowler was self-important, a hypocrite and a liar. Three vices that he'd never learned to gloss with seeming virtue. But he was powerful. And gullible. Merrington played on it:

'Well, Jos, I suppose there is one last act of wickedness. More like carelessness. I've hidden it for years. And if it gets out, I'm in serious trouble.'

'What did you do?'

Fowler wasn't smiling. Merrington looked for the swan but it had vanished . . . and for a moment he imagined he could just make out the haunting elegance.

'I lost my mother's antique bracelet,' he said.

10

For the greater part of his life John Lynwood had worn suits made from distinctive cloth and cut with his luncher's paunch in mind. He'd lost weight now; and the prison-issue maroon T-shirt and grey jogging bottoms, washed until they were limp and faded, had thrust him into a world of anonymity. There were greenish rings under his eyes.

'How are you doing?' asked Tess.

'It's hell. But I'm keeping out of trouble,' – Mr Lynwood tapped his chest and agony appeared in his blue eyes – 'I'm building a wall in here, where no one can reach me.' He leaned forward and his voice changed colour. 'How's Karen? Is she coping?'

'As well as can be expected.'

'She didn't come, then?'

'No, I'm sorry. She was tired out after this morning's session.'

'I wanted to see her one last time . . . before the ordeal begins.'

Tess thought of another excuse:

'This isn't the place for Karen, not the day before trial.'

Once she'd spelled out John's defence, and her own – at

that first joint meeting – Mrs Lynwood had never willingly attended another conference. Compelled to do so, she'd sat woodenly in this very room while John, at every opportunity, had touched her arm, always framing his replies to Benson's questions in the plural; always glancing at her for some sign of affirmation. She'd left him hanging. Granted bail, she'd never gone to visit her husband on remand. Tess had said, he must be guilty and she knows it. Benson had said, this is what a trial does to a family.

'What about Simon, Mr Benson? Did you speak to him?'

Mr Lynwood was cradling his chest as if his ribs might fall apart.

'No.'

'But you said that you would.'

'I said I'd try. And he won't answer my calls.'

'Or mine,' said Tess.

'Then go and see him. Tell him to give us a chance. Tell him to come to the trial . . . If I'm to get through this, I need him to believe in me.'

Whatever his parents might have said to explain themselves, Simon Lynwood hadn't been persuaded. His mind was made up. His mother had begun a relationship with Dr Jorge Menderez. His father had found out, lost his head and killed him. And now they wouldn't face up to what they'd done. And, faced with that, he'd cut them off. There'd been no contact since they'd entered not guilty pleas in the Magistrates' Court. Tess had said his behaviour, by any standards harsh, implied . . . but Benson had shut her down. He'd said this is what a trial does to a family.

'Will you do that, please, Mr Benson?'

'Yes, I'll go and see him.'

'And will you tell Karen that I'm okay? I call, but I never seem to catch her . . .'

'I'll contact her.'

'Thank you.'

He spoke like a man delivering his last words, sending them to someone who probably wouldn't listen. And again Tess wondered why his wife had abandoned him, if he was innocent. And why she'd made no effort to conceal her antipathy. She glanced at Benson. Knowing he'd get Mr Lynwood alone, he'd insisted on this last conference. She didn't know its purpose. He said:

'There's one last matter I wish to examine, Mr Lynwood. It may be central to your wife's defence. I'd like to know who met—'

'Before we get to that, can I say something?'

'Of course.'

Mr Lynwood paused, tightening his hold on himself.

'During the last conference, you told me I didn't have to prove my innocence, but that the jury still needed an explanation as to how Dr Menderez was killed . . . a credible explanation that would make them unsure about the prosecution case against me.'

'That's right.'

'I've come up with something.'

Benson didn't react; but Tess could sense he was more circumspect than confident. Together they'd racked their brains trying to find arguments to undermine the facts; and they'd failed.

'Let me take it from the beginning,' said Mr Lynwood, hands gripping his elbows. 'I threatened to kill Dr Menderez, I accept that. I said crazy stuff because I was angry. He rang me up that night, saying he was in love with Karen and that she was in love with him, that my marriage was over, and I went over there to try and talk some sense into him. Karen had failed, so I had a go . . . because the threats hadn't worked. This is what happened, Mr Benson . . . now, that's credible, isn't it?'

'Yes. But your problem lies elsewhere.'

'I'm coming to that.'

'I want precision,' said Benson. 'Those threats to kill took place at two p.m. At six-fifteen Karen met Menderez at the Grapes in Limehouse. At six forty-five they left. Karen went to the theatre with Narinda Hassan. Menderez went home. He must have got there by seven p.m.'

'I know, Mr Benson. And I get the phone call from Dr Menderez at eight thirty-one, an hour and half later. That's when I thought, right, this isn't working, I'll go and see him.'

'The conversation lasts nine minutes. You then drive to Limehouse. You arrive at nine-twenty p.m.'

Tess had watched the CCTV footage multiple times. It recorded the car pulling up on Upper North Street and Mr Lynwood heading down the steps onto Limehouse Cut. Street lighting reached part of the footpath captured on film, illuminating, of necessity, anyone using the Cut. And from 9.20 p.m., right through to 6.03 a.m. the following day, when a jogger appeared – who'd been traced and excluded from the inquiry – it fell on no one except Mr Lynwood. Benson said:

'The estimated time of death is between eight and ten p.m. You're filmed running back to your car at nine forty-four p.m. You'd been with Dr Menderez for twenty minutes.'

'And when I left him, he was alive.'

'Which means, on your account, he was murdered in the fifteen minutes following your departure.'

'Exactly. By someone who wanted to silence him.'

'Forget the reason for now. Because we've come to the central problem with your defence. No one had access to the property within that fifteen-minute window. The prosecution can prove this.'

The property rented by Dr Menderez, 59 Limehouse Cut, was situated on a section of the canal that runs between Upper North Street and Burdett Road. On the night of the killing, anyone using the Cut would either have been filmed by the CCTV camera on Upper North Street or seen by witnesses having a boat party near Burdett Road, a party that had kicked off at 8 p.m. and fizzled out towards two in the morning. The rear of Number 59 faced a yard with a gate onto Ropemaker's Way, where, on the night in question, Alan Wilcot was working on his car between 8 p.m. and midnight. And Mr Wilcot had seen no one enter or leave the relevant premises. The cul-de-sac, as usual, had been absolutely deserted. Benson underlined the point:

'The prosecution can prove that you're the only person who went to Number Fifty-nine within the time frame for the killing.'

'No, Mr Benson, they can't. The explanation is obvious . . . and it came to me only this morning.'

'Go on.'

'Whoever killed Dr Menderez was already in the premises when I arrived. They could have come along Ropemaker's Way before Mr Wilcot started working on his car; or they could have come from Burdett Road before the boat party got underway. That's why no one saw them arrive.'

These were the two approaches not covered by CCTV cameras. Benson thought for a while.

'So they'd come to the house at some time after seven p.m., when Menderez got home, and before eight p.m., when witnesses were present on either side?'

'That's right.'

'But there was no forced entry to the property.'

'So whoever it was knew him, Mr Benson. Menderez let them in. And they were in the house when he called me. This person knew I was coming.'

'Something doesn't make sense, Mr Lynwood. Why would Menderez call you to discuss his relationship with your wife if this other person was there, possibly right in front of him?'

'I don't know . . . but the facts are I didn't kill Dr Menderez; and when I left the property, he was alive. So the murder must have taken place afterwards. It all comes down to logic.'

'And the killer then left by Ropemaker's Way some time after midnight, after Mr Wilcot had gone indoors. Or by the Cut some time after two a.m., when the party was over?'

'Exactly, Mr Benson, that's it. And whoever it was waited until I'd come and gone, knowing that I'd be picked up by the CCTV, or the boat party people.' Rage and impotence tightened his mouth. 'Whoever it was framed me.'

They were silent, Mr Lynwood looking at Benson desperately, like a child seeking approval. Tess waited for Benson to say he'd already thought of this explanation. And that it foundered on at least two grounds. First, the incredible coincidence that Mr Lynwood, a man with a motive to kill, would visit Dr Menderez at the very time someone else was planning to kill him. And secondly, the tiny screw found by the body. The screw from Mr Lynwood's glasses. Benson said neither of these things. In truth, Tess didn't know what Benson might be thinking. He rose and went to the window that overlooked the exercise yard, the dirty brick walls and the jagged black wire. Almost imperceptibly, he began to shake his head. Was he doubting – like Tess – Mr Lynwood's ability to survive a life sentence? Because he was going to get one. Or was he simply watching himself, recalling the kid who'd walked in circles, head down, keeping out of trouble?

'Who met Narinda Hassan first?' he said quietly. 'You or your wife?'

11

'I did.'

'When, exactly?'

'During freshers' week.'

'That would be September 1976?'

'Yes.'

Benson had been picking away at Narinda Hassan's name in every conference. Throwaway questions only. Nothing systematic. Tess had put that down to his preoccupation with Camberley's illness. She now realised he'd been storing the answers away.

'A lot of relationships are formed during that week,' observed Benson. 'Usually the clinging kind. Would you agree?'

'Not necessarily.'

'Really? You're all away from home for the first time. You're all desperate to fit in. Hormones are fizzing like Alka-Seltzer. At least, that's my story. Wasn't it yours?'

'Well, dear God, I can't remember. It's a lifetime ago.'

'Have another try.'

Mr Lynwood gave a shrug. 'I suppose you're right. But so what? I'd found my feet by the time I was in my second year. That's when I met Karen. In October. Everyone finds their feet in their second year.'

'Not everyone, Mr Lynwood. By November, I'd been charged with murder. In another age, I'd have been hanged by Christmas. Not unreasonably, my girlfriend dropped me. Thing is, she probably would have anyway. You see, it was one of those frantic attachments from the first week that faithfulness had kept alive, long after the kicking had stopped. Where, precisely, did you meet Narinda?'

'A nightclub.'

'Which one?'

'God. Rosters, I think. Or some other flea-pit.'

'One of those hideous fresher outings?'

'Yes.'

'Is that how you met Brian?'

'No, I met Brian later . . . through Narinda, actually.'

Tess tried to link the answers with what she'd noted previously. John Lynwood went to Bristol University to study maths. There, he met Karen Robinson, another second year, reading psychology. They later married. Narinda was Karen's best friend; Brian Unwin was John's. Together they formed a foursome. This much was on file. For the first time, Benson was going back in time, to the period of nervous flux, before ties had been formed; ties that would get tighter and stronger, to the point you'd think they could never break.

'So it was through Narinda that you met Karen?' said Benson.

'That's right.'

'She's an important person in your life, isn't she, Narinda Hassan?'

'Why do you say that?'

'Well, if it wasn't for her, you'd never have met the woman you married or the best man at your wedding. It's all thanks to Narinda.'

'Yes, put like that, you're right.'

'Put any way I'm right.'

'But it's Narinda who now wants to tear us apart. So I'd be slow to thank that two-faced liar for anything.'

Raucous voices burst onto the exercise yard. Benson stepped back, turning a dark, concentrated stare upon Mr Lynwood.

'You met Karen in October 1977 . . . through Narinda, whom you'd met in September 1976?'

'That's right, yes.'

'So you'd known Narinda, by then, for a year?'

'Correct.'

'You knew her well?'

'Sort of. It turned out we were in the same hall of residence, so, yes, we saw a lot of each other.'

'Shared life stories?'

'Meaning?'

'Helped each other through the ups and downs?'

'Probably, yes.'

'Which is good, because some people have more downs than ups.'

'I suppose so.'

Benson gave a rare look of compassion: 'In my experience, John, it's the downs that bring people closest, not the ups.'

'Possibly . . . I never gave the matter much thought.'

Benson meditated on his own point; then, with a certain firmness, he said: 'Your own story is tragic, if I may say so.'

'I survived.'

Tess had taken down the history in her first client conference. In 1975, when John was seventeen, his parents and godfather had been killed in a car accident on their way to Edgbaston. They'd been going to watch the cricket. England against Australia. John had stayed at home on account of a broken ankle. Benson had never referred to this episode before.

'It takes time to survive, I think.'

'Sure, I accept that.'

'You went to university only a year after your loss.'

'And?'

'You must have been vulnerable.'

'What are you getting at, Mr Benson?'

'I'm wondering if you shared your story with Narinda Hassan.'

'I imagine I did. So what?'

'Pain brings people together.'

'Sure . . . we became friends. Good friends. We're not now. I still don't see your point.'

'Did Narinda share her story?'

'Probably. We lived in the same building.'

'I know. Rutherford Hall. First floor. Room fifty-one.'

'How did you—'

'Narinda was in forty-eight?'

'Sorry, I can't remember.'

Watching Mr Lynwood squinting at the past, Tess was quite sure Benson was – as usual – onto something. Coming away from the window, he returned to the metal table, hands tapping behind his back.

'I get the impression – and do correct me if I'm wrong, Mr Lynwood – that your friendship with Narinda Hassan wasn't the frantic kind. Not one of those freshers' week limpet mines that blow up when one of you meets someone else . . . say, in your second year. It was serious.'

'Yes, Mr Benson. It was. And I know where you're going with this and you're wrong.'

'Where am I going?'

'You're wondering if we ever went out together. Whether Narinda and I were a couple, before I met Karen.'

'Were you?'

'Absolutely not. And I never felt that way. I was a friend, Mr Benson. Nothing more.'

'Then why hide her role in your life?'

Mr Lynwood made a grimace, as if he couldn't see properly. 'I've hidden nothing. I've just *forgotten*. We're talking ancient history, you know. I was *eighteen* back then. I didn't even shave every day. Dear God, I'm sixty next year. My bum's dropped three inches. My hair's gone white. How could all that teenage stuff possibly be relevant?'

'Narinda Hassan was your close friend. She became your

wife's best friend. Forty years later, she's determined to tear apart the life that you and Karen have built together, a life that she has shared. Mr Lynwood, you spent your life working with numbers. And these don't add up. Unless there's some hidden—'

'Mr Benson, there was nothing between Narinda and me. Nada. And even if there was, I can't see how that would make her lie about Karen.'

'Well, Mr Lynwood, something has done. And I need to know what it is. So think again. Narinda's evidence, unchallenged, will put your wife in a hole like this for two years. Is there anything you've not told me? Anything that might undermine her reliability?'

'Nothing. Absolutely nothing.'

'Anything that might explain her animosity?'

'No. I'm as lost as you are.'

'Okay,' said Benson, after a pause. 'We're done.'

They all shook hands and Benson gave his usual encouraging words: that the pressure of the trial fell on him alone; that Mr Lynwood wasn't to worry; that surprises always happen once the evidence shifts from paper to the courtroom.

'You'll visit Simon?' replied Mr Lynwood, not comforted, a fresh desperation coming with the approach of the guard outside.

'I'll try.'

As the door swung open, Benson hesitated, and then he drew Mr Lynwood to one side. His voice was gentler and Tess only just caught his words:

'That wall you're building, the one in here . . .' – he tapped his chest – 'if you want a relationship with Simon – if you want a relationship with anyone – then be careful. I'm talking about height and length and breadth. And cement. Because one day, you'll have to take it down. Brick by brick.'

12

'It's listed as "a charming bolt-hole", Mr Benson,' said Stuart Redgrave, the founder of Redgrave Estate Agents.

Going by ads online, his business had a firm grip on rental property from the docks at Wapping to the wharves along the Isle of Dogs, which, thought Benson, might explain the navy-blue jacket, the tie sporting a yellow anchor, and the crisp grey trousers. He exuded yacht-club bonhomie and the confidence of a wealth management specialist. They'd met at the mouth of Ropemaker's Way. Having arranged to join Tess that evening for a final case review, Benson had gone back to the crime scene.

'Most of my clients are waterfront,' said Redgrave, closing his Redgrave-branded umbrella with a flourish, 'by which I mean the Thames, but he couldn't afford the going rate. And I had this little place by the Cut in Limehouse, Number Fifty-nine, a caretaker's property attached to Foxton's Warehouse. It was only on the books because I manage the real estate portfolio of the owner. He lives in Abu Dhabi, actually, a chap from Brighton who—'

'But you advised against rental?'

'Eh? Who told you that?'

'I'm guessing.'

'Why would I do that?'

'Because Number Fifty-nine is not charming, and because you seem to be a decent man.'

The compliment unsettled Mr Redgrave; an inner argument ensued, and caution lost out; he lowered his voice:

'Okay, off the record, I told him not to bother. The damp wasn't serious, but the place attracts break-ins. Youths with nothing better to do. And there's a connecting door between the warehouse and the kitchen . . . and since there's nothing in the former, I've always been worried they'd turn their attention to the latter.'

'Couldn't they anyway?'

'Yes, but there's bars on all the windows and every door has a top and bottom lock . . . except the connecting door, which is secured with a bolt. Abu Dhabi wouldn't pay for anything more sophisticated.'

'That's why he's rich.'

'You got it, Mr Benson.'

'And you warned Dr Menderez?'

'More than that. I suggested he look elsewhere, where it was cheaper and safer, but he wouldn't have it. He insisted on Limehouse.'

'Did you get the impression he knew the area?'

'No, because he didn't. But he still insisted.'

'Did you ask him why?'

'Certainly not.'

'Did you ask him why he'd come to London?'

'Mr Benson, please, I'm a professional. My middle name is discretion. Shall we?' Mr Redgrave pointed with a set of keys towards a large wooden door into the warehouse. Beside it was a boarded-up window. 'Given what happened inside,' he said, 'I won't be joining you.'

Which was as well, because Benson wanted to be alone. He'd come to the *locus in quo* once before, with the police and the prosecution, following the route taken by Mr Lynwood along Limehouse Cut. This time he wanted to track the movements of the youth who'd broken into the warehouse. He'd come from the opposite direction, and behind the building, heading up Ropemaker's Way. According to his statement, Karl Ambrose had prised open a ground-floor window, climbed inside and looked under a large open staircase. He'd seen a dead body and then fled the way he'd come.

'There you go,' said Mr Redgrave, standing well back. 'It's all yours.'

A long column of daylight fell on the old stone flags. Benson stepped inside, closing the door behind him.

He was in almost total darkness. Moments later he'd lit the keyring torch – the kind used by Karl Ambrose – and its thin beam of light struck a staircase immediately to his right. The only other objects of note were the connecting door and another door, on the far side, that opened onto the wharf.

I want to talk about the trial, your trial.

What the hell for? You told me never to look back. Benson went quickly past the staircase. But Camberley's urgent whisper followed him, and the blade of light, as he went towards the connecting door. On reaching it, he turned on his heel and directed the torch along the route he'd just taken, the beam finding – instantly – the confined space beneath the staircase where the body had been found. Benson slowly retraced his steps, recalling the crime scene photographs.

Dr Menderez had been laid under the stairs, his hands crossed upon his chest. He'd then been part-covered with a piece of sacking. The screw from Mr Lynwood's glasses had been found fifty-three centimetres from the right foot, lodged between two flagstones. As to the provenance of the sacking, it must have been found in situ by the killer – a remnant of the days when coal had been unloaded from barges onto Foxton's Wharf . . . a wharf that was accessed by the door on the far side of the room.

There are things you must tell me; and there are things I must say.

About what? There's nothing to be said. We moved on, together. Again, walking briskly, Benson followed the pencil of light across the flags to the other door. Then, after examining the lock, he went back outside.

*   *   *

Mr Redgrave quickly hid his hand. He'd lit up, and, being caught, he gave an embarrassed smile. Smoking in public, it seemed, was an attribute befitting a lower class of estate agent. Benson came to his assistance:

'Could I possibly have one?'

Once Benson had taken his first, grateful intake they were joined in the happy silence shared by social outcasts. Then Mr Redgrave gave a conspiratorial cough.

'He did say something unusual, come to think of it.'

Benson watched a blue cloud disperse in the breeze.

'I might be discreet,' Mr Redgrave continued, 'but I still ask questions. Getting to know the client, you appreciate. Well, I'd asked him all sorts, how long he'd be staying, when he'd be going back, whether he might want to extend the lease, and he'd sidestepped every enquiry – he wasn't a bundle of laughs, I can tell you – but then, just when I was about to give up, I says, "Are you in London on business?" . . . and that word, "business", he liked it – it made him smile. I don't mean happy. I mean bitter.'

'Did he say anything?'

'He did. We were standing by the Cut, and he was just staring into the canal, and he says, "Yes, it's business. Unfinished business."'

Benson took another long pull of smoke.

'Did you tell this to the police?'

'No.'

'Why not?'

The outbreak of honesty had taken away Mr Redgrave's sheen. He was holding his cigarette between his thumb and index finger.

'I wanted to say as little as possible. You see, Abu Dhabi didn't want the attention. And he wouldn't want me on the witness stand.'

'Then why tell me?'

'Because you seem to be a decent man who wouldn't draw me into things unless he has to.'

'And?'

Mr Redgrave took a final drag and then flicked his stub into the gutter.

'I felt guilty, Mr Benson. Do you know what I mean?'

13

Benson was despondent. He'd tried to crack both Lynwoods and he'd failed. They were hiding something out of fear. From Benson; and from each other. Different fears that were similar in magnitude. Because both of them were prepared to risk conviction rather than speak about what they knew. Which meant Benson would go into court the next morning with empty hands. He'd been banking on a joint collapse, followed by a reappraisal of the evidence. But they'd both shown extraordinary strength; and resistance to Benson's attempt not only to defend them . . . but help them. They didn't want helping. They wanted a miracle. And to keep their secrets. He looked up, over the trial papers. Archie was staring at him. So was Tess.

'There's nothing else you can do, Rizla.'

'That was my prison name, Archie. I no longer answer to it. And I don't even smoke roll-ups any more. I don't buy the papers. I haven't bought a pack of Rizlas since I left HMP Lindley.'

'You've done your best, Chief – how about that? – and when they both go down, they've only got themselves to blame.'

They'd gathered in the Gutting Room, Benson's study, for a final review of the case. It was here that Archie's four sisters had cleaned the fish for selling out front. The alcoves were now lined with books and journals. Framed prints of old Spitalfields hung on the walls. Two worn leather armchairs – occupied by Archie and Tess – faced a ship captain's desk, the only fitting in chambers that hadn't been culled from a charity shop.

'But if you want my opinion . . .'

Archie waited; but there was silence, soon followed by a rattling of crockery, for Molly had brought the tea. She served everyone and then quietly left. As the door closed, Archie said:

'Let me get this right. Menderez commits some sort of crime. Years later someone rumbles him and he wants to top himself. He comes to London instead but his conscience won't let go and he ends up seeing Karen Lynwood, hoping she'll help him face the music. He eventually tells her what he did, but then someone kills him; someone involved in the crime who wants things kept quiet. Is that what you think?'

'Roughly,' said Benson.

Archie knitted his fingers together, resting them on the strained buttons of his black waistcoat. He'd rolled up the sleeves of his white shirt, and his pinstriped trousers were hitched for the fight.

'I'm not convinced.'

Benson didn't ask why. But Archie persisted:

'Once Menderez was dead, why doesn't Karen tell the police everything?'

'Because if she admits to having got close to Menderez, she'll give the police the motive they need to nail her husband for murder.'

'Okay. But why not tell them what Menderez had done . . . whatever it is that got him killed. By someone who wasn't her husband?'

'Because she's scared, Archie. Whoever killed Menderez could just as easily kill her. Or her husband. Or her son. So she says nothing. Not to the police, not to Tess, and not to me. That's why she's still alive.'

Archie glanced at Tess but he got no support. She was looking at Benson . . . like she'd looked at him on his barge; her eyes were feeling their way around his face. The nerves to his mouth and cheeks were flaring.

'Let me get this right,' said Archie. 'The Lynwoods are only saying that someone must have killed Menderez because he was about to reveal some secret to Karen?'

'Yes.'

'Well, I'm no lawyer, but I'm the sort of bloke that sits on a jury . . . and it's cobblers. They've obviously made it up. There's no evidence for what they say, except Karen herself, which is convenient, and – forgive me, Rizla – there's no evidence for the rest, the stuff you've worked out from that questionnaire. It's all imagination.'

'It's imagination that fills in the gaps, Archie. And there are a lot of gaps in this case. I'm after a comprehensive account. Something that explains why Menderez came to the UK, why he picked Karen as a therapist, why Karen denies any involvement with him . . . and why John claims to be innocent.'

Archie wasn't impressed.

'But you said so yourself: there's no evidence that anyone except John went to see Menderez on the night he was killed. No one's seen arriving at the house, and no one's seen leaving it.'

'I know, Archie. It's a problem.'

'John Lynwood is with Menderez at the very time the pathologist says he was killed.'

'I know.'

'And he said he was going to kill him. Narinda Hassan

will tell you why. Karen had fallen for him and her husband didn't like it.'

Benson didn't reply.

'These are hard facts, Rizla. They're not going to shift. And all this stuff about a crime in Spain and a tortured conscience . . . you can't prove any of it.'

'I know.'

'Even Karen Lynwood doesn't agree with you.'

'So she says.'

'If she did, she'd have told John. And she hasn't.'

Archie took a breath.

'Someone took Menderez's SIM card and chucked his computer into the Cut.'

'Correct,' said Benson.

'Why would this other killer do that?'

'I wish I knew, Archie.'

'Why isn't there a screw from *their* glasses by the body?'

Benson sighed. Archie placed a large hand on each large knee, and said:

'And what's all this about "unfinished business"? What does that mean?'

'I don't know.'

'Well I do. It contradicts your idea he was on the run. You see, Rizla, to my mind . . .'

Benson turned away. And not just from Archie and Tess, but from the Gutting Room. He vanished behind the wall he'd built in prison – he'd laid the first course in HMP Kensal Green, just like John Lynwood; only Benson had carried on the work, brick after brick, year after year – but all at once he heard a whisper, over Archie's distant grumbling:

Getting away with murder always comes at a price.

Benson felt sick. He'd lied to Tess. He'd lied to Archie. He'd lied to his own mother and father. They'd all been unsuspecting. He'd depended on them ever since, drawing their trust like water from a well . . . he heard the rasp in Helen's lungs and he—

'Rizla?'

Benson gradually brought into focus a crop of silver hair, bristling eyebrows and large red cheeks.

'Yes?'

'I'm only saying you mustn't blame yourself. They were finished anyway.'

Tess finally spoke:

'They're not finished until the jury delivers a verdict.'

She'd hardly blinked since arriving. She'd hung up her red coat and green velvet hat, and then, turning around, her attention hadn't strayed once from him.

'What's to be done, Will?'

'Go see the priest.'

'What priest?'

'The one at Spanish Place. Father Winsley. He's mentioned in the unused material. Menderez went to his church regularly. I'd like to know if he asked God for help before he turned to Karen.'

Tess shifted in her seat.

'Well, if he did, we'd know by now.'

'Not necessarily. Secret people encourage other people to be secret. Even without saying anything. It rubs off . . . so let's see what he says.'

'Okay.'

'While you're at it, ask him if Menderez ever mentioned Cambridge. He never went back. I'd like to know why.'

'Sure.'

Benson turned to Archie.

'Get the Tuesday Club onto Narinda Hassan.'

'Again?'

'Yes. I need more.'

'Done. But I haven't changed my mind, Rizla. They're both guilty and you won't find anything to show—'

The Tuesday Club: a group of ex-cons who met once a week to solve the world's problems; men and women who trusted each other like they trusted no one else; skilled outcasts, humbled by failure or injustice; Benson's investigators; his closest friends. He'd lied to them, too.

'Will, are you okay?'

Tess was standing by the door with her coat on, hat in hand, frowning. Her affection broke through the pollution of memories: she wanted to prove his innocence; she wanted to set him free; and he wanted to tell her everything . . . but he couldn't span the distance between his first, impulsive lie in a police station and this simple moment of concern, the endpoint of so much calculated deception.

'I'm fine, really. And Archie: you've got to stop calling me by my prison name. Remember, it's "Mr Benson". Or, my favourite: "Sir". The clients want the old deference. And roll your sleeves down.'

Archie was standing, too. And, like Tess, he was frowning at him, those huge hands thrust into huge trouser pockets. He didn't believe him; neither did Tess. And because they cared, they wouldn't be deflected: the conversation wasn't over, but then Molly broke in, pushing her trolley. She stopped, glancing first at Archie and then at Tess.

'Is everything all right, Mr Benson?' she said.

'I'm fine, Molly.'

She left the tea things where they were, for Benson's voice had trembled with the kind of anger that springs from fear.

14

'You can't imagine what it's like,' said Annette, dabbing the tears on her cheeks.

'I'm quite sure it's awful,' said Merrington.

'I lie there, and he comes at me with a needle.'

'Dreadful.'

As was usual on the days that Annette had a hospital appointment, Merrington and Pamela went to her flat in Hampstead for supper. They'd just finished eating. Pamela was washing up. Merrington sat with his mother in the living room.

'And he sticks it right in my eye,' said Annette, bony hand lunging forward.

'Horrific.'

'And I just have to stare ahead and think of England.'

That the procedure was painless, and that his mother had undergone it many times before, did not detract from Merrington's sincerity. The very idea of a hypodermic needle made him feel faint. It was the primary reason why he'd never given blood. He'd tried, because he fancied the idea of the gold donor's badge, but, on that first and only morning, the nurse couldn't find a vein in either arm. Smiling gaily, she'd prodded around until Merrington, with a saintly groan, had passed out. He'd never gone back. And, of course, he'd never got the badge.

'I'm ninety-two,' said Annette. 'I'll be dead before too long. So why bother with the treatment?'

'Nonsense, Mother. You have the springing limbs of the Queen of Sheba's gazelle.'

'Dicky, the Queen of Sheba's gazelle is extinct.'

'Oh God, yes, sorry, I forgot about that.'

The royal gazelle had featured in many of his father's

sermons as a symbol of wisdom, and instinct had brought
it to mind. But Merrington meant what he'd tried to say.
Annette was extraordinarily strong and it was only the
onset of age-related macular degeneration that had reminded
him that his mother was, in fact, mortal. The eye condition
had developed quickly, over a matter of months. A small
part of her vision had become blurred and distorted; then,
most disorientating of all, straight lines had looked crooked
– her reverend husband would have had a field day with
that one, make the crooked way straight, etcetera – and so
the trips to Moorfields had begun. To an observer, the only
noticeable side effect was bleeding in the eye. For Annette,
she had this feeling that there was something there, a tiny
splinter that she couldn't shift . . . the Reverend would have
loved that one, too.

Just then, the doorbell rang.

'Oh hell, that'll be Mr Orchard,' said Annette, rising.
'Checking that I'm all right. Or so he says.'

'Be careful, Mother. He seeks forbidden fruit.'

'Don't be ridiculous. It's you he wants to see. Can't you
give him five minutes?'

'Absolutely not.'

She went towards the hall.

'I wish he'd just sod off – to quote your father.'

As soon as Annette had gone, Merrington made straight
for his mother's bedroom and flipped open the lid of her
jewellery box. Frantically, his fingers raked through bangles,
rings, lockets and pendants . . .

'What the hell are you doing?'

It was Pamela, hunched at the door, yellow-gloved hands
upon her hips.

'I'm looking for that bloody bracelet,' said Merrington. 'I
just wondered if she took it back. Can't damn well ask her,
can I? I'm hoping it's here . . . and it bloody well isn't.'

'I thought we'd been over this,' whispered Pamela testily. 'It's all in your clever head, darling. She didn't shovel all that money into Benson because you lost her bracelet.'

'I know, I know.'

'Then forget about the bracelet.'

'I can't.'

Merrington was opening drawers now, carefully checking the contents.

'Richard, this is really not on. You're acting like that oily Hilmarton fellow.'

'That bracelet was important to her, Pam, even if she never wore it. I thought about it this afternoon. It was made for her mother. Her mother gives it to her. If David had been a girl, she'd have given it to him. The damn thing is all she's got from her mother's side of the family . . . and I've gone and lost it. There's no way round it. I'll have to buy a new one, regardless of this Benson business.'

'Oh, for heaven's sake, leave well alone.'

'It's a matter of principle, Pam.' He slid shut a drawer and turned around. 'I do have them, you know.'

Pamela tugged off her washing-up gloves.

'Don't get me wrong, darling, but she'll be—'

'Dead before she can wear it? Yes, I know. But we can't live like that, can we?'

'You'll embarrass her.'

'Nonsense. It tells her she has a future.'

The thud of a door closing reached their ears. Instantly, Pamela went to the kitchen, and Merrington made a dash for the living room. He was in an armchair, legs crossed, when Annette stepped back into the room; as she did so, Merrington suffered a stab of pity. The problem with complicated relationships is that there's so much that's been left unsaid, so many rows and reconciliations that never happened. Until you come to this, a son looking at his mother standing within arm's reach of death, one hand on the door handle, another on the back of a chair. Her eyes were gashes of red. Her cheeks were stained. She looked immeasurably sad.

'He says we should remain in Europe.'

Merrington's reply was heavy with regret. He barely knew his own mother.

'There's no going back.'

Of late, she'd been more tearful. She'd begun to review her life in a way she'd never done before. At Christmas, she'd talked of dear Gilbert's funeral, wiping her eyes, recalling their first meeting in Lewes, shortly after the family had moved from London. She'd been seventeen. Merrington has seen the photographs. Annette had dug out the album. There, on his mother's wrist, was the bracelet. She'd been given it that day, for her eighteenth birthday. Flanked by her proud parents, she was holding out her arm as if to get her wrist slapped.

'He thinks we need another referendum.'

Her transferred distress was too painful to be comic; Merrington didn't laugh:

'That will never happen.'

'He thinks the French will try and stuff us.'

'They've already started.'

'Along with the Germans.'

They'd flicked back through the album, to earlier years, and Merrington, watching his mother cry as she identified herself, realised the smiling girl who'd grown up in Kensington was a stranger to him. She looked radiant and funny and mischievous . . . not the woman who'd moved to Lewes and become his mother.

'He thinks we need a change in leadership.'

'For once, I agree with Mr Orchard.'

Pamela sailed into the room.

'No more politics. We're going to have some fun.'

She brought out the Scrabble, and the search for words began. But Merrington couldn't find any. At least not the right ones. Only that lunchtime he'd bristled with excitement, knowing he could finish Benson's career, along with all his relationships, at the drop of a hat.

'"Stumped",' said Pamela, laying down the tiles.

Me too, thought Merrington. He'd wondered what his mother might say after reading Benson's secret history in his own words. But seeing her by the door, bleeding, squinting and soon to die, he knew he couldn't do it: blast and damn it, he couldn't ruin Benson. Not while she was still alive. The jab of pity had weakened him. Despite the longing, he couldn't tarnish her protégé.

'C'mon, Dicky,' said Annette. 'We haven't got all night.'

'Sorry, Mother. I was just thinking of the morrow.' Merrington couldn't stop himself: 'I understand the infamous Mr Benson goes into action once more.'

'That's right,' said Annette, brightening slightly. 'It's the Limehouse case.' She checked her letters. 'You really should give him a chance, Dicky. Your father would have.'

'Perhaps he has.'

'What on earth do you mean?'

'Well, only a few years ago Benson was in a cell, and now he runs his own chambers. I'd say he's backed by a fallen angel.'

Annette smiled. 'Why fallen? That's a terrible thing to say.'

Merrington savoured every word:

'Only the fallen would help the malign.'

'That was very naughty,' said Pamela, in the taxi on the way back home to Highgate.

'Darling, she glowed with pride,' said Merrington. 'And the

way you looked at her, I'd have thought you wanted some of the glory.'

'Don't talk rot. I was just pleased to see her happy. She's been down recently.'

'Yes, she has.'

The memory of her bloodied eyes remained with him to Pond Square, where Merrington tipped generously, hoping the driver might one day talk glowingly to the press. But his attention had been caught by a light flickering on the dark sitting room wall. Moving briskly, he opened the front door and strode towards a confrontation that would unquestionably seize the front pages and the lead slot on every news channel. Fearless Justice Minister Grapples With . . . but he needn't have been worried. Splayed on the sofa watching Netflix – or some such – was David. He was meant to be at Oxford. Hilary term had only just begun.

'I'm sorry, Dad, I know you're going to disapprove.'

Merrington paled instantly. 'Oh God, have you been sent down?'

'No.'

'You're going to be a father?'

'No, Dad, I'm—'

'You're gay?'

'No. Stop. I'm back because I want to go to the Old Bailey.' David ran a hand through his untidy black hair. 'I'm following the Limehouse case.'

15

Tess drove Benson to Putney. She'd offered to take him to Simon Lynwood's house and share the embarrassment of doorstepping the son who'd refused to answer the letters and calls of his parents' legal representatives. Benson was staring out of the passenger window. Tess was rehearsing a conversation that had just taken place in the clerk's room.

'You're the lawyer, Miss de Vere,' whispered Archie. 'And I'm just an ex-con watching from the side-lines.'

'You're so much more than that, Archie.'

'And you're not helping Mr Benson.'

'What do you mean?'

Benson was still in the Gutting Room; he'd called the Royal Marsden to enquire after Camberley.

'He's not himself. Not since he found out she's dying.'

'I know. That's why he's distracted, but—'

'He's not seeing the case flat on, Miss de Vere, and you aren't helping by supporting his crazy thinking.'

'It's not crazy, Archie. You should have been there when he—'

'He's pushing aside the obvious. His imagination's in overdrive. And if he goes on like this, he'll make a fool of himself in court . . . and there are too many people out there who want to laugh at him.'

'Archie, trust me. I know the case. And I know Benson. And—'

'Do you see him flat on, Miss de Vere?'

'I beg your pardon?'

Archie shuffled his bulk, scratching the back of his head. His whispering dropped lower.

'Look, I know my place, and it's nothing to do with me, but I've got eyes in my head. And whatever you feel for Mr Benson, it can't—'

At that point Benson had backed out of the Gutting Room, pulling the brief, all three boxes of it, on a luggage trolley.

*   *   *

Tess turned to look at him.

He was still gazing out of the window; probably avoiding her attention; out of reach. He'd always been like that. In the past, she'd felt his interest in her, and, being scared, she'd rebuffed him; but even when she hadn't, even when she'd been careful not to respond too quickly, to reassure him, he'd retreated, forever drawn to the safety of loneliness. If only he'd forgive himself, she thought, turning off the wipers and then the heater and then the engine.

She didn't move. Neither did Benson. The windscreen and side windows gradually misted with condensation. The outside world disappeared behind a curtain, so fine it could be wiped away with the back of one's hand. Tess turned and breathed in to speak, her heart racing.

'Let's get this over and done with,' said Benson.

'Yes, let's . . .'

And he jerked open the door.

'You're Mr Benson, aren't you?'

An elderly woman in a black dress looked over her shoulder, down the corridor; she then pulled the door to and stepped outside, leaning on a stick.

'And you're Miss de Vere?'

'I am.'

Her face was the colour of old olive wood. Deep lines spread out from her eyes and mouth as if she'd been squinting at the sun all her life. There was a hint of a foreign accent, smoothed away by years of speaking English.

'Speak to Simon, will you?' she said, her dark eyes flashing between Benson and Tess. 'Tell him he must come to the trial. I'm Isabel, Isabel Tindale, John's godmother. More of a mother, after his parents died, along with my dear husband . . . I've known Simon all his life, I'm the grandmother he lost and I—'

The door suddenly swung open and a tall man with sandy hair appeared. This had to be Simon. Behind him, in the kitchen doorway, stood a woman holding a small boy by the hand. The boy was in rumpled pyjamas. He, like his mother, had been crying. They were Emma and Jack. Their names were on file.

'Isabel, please, leave this to me.'

Mrs Tindale dropped her stick and grabbed Simon's arm with gnarled hands.

'Listen to Mr Benson, I beg you,' she said. 'Give your father a chance, and your mother.'

'They've had their chance.'

'They love you. They've given you a wonderful life. Give them your—'

'I've given them some honesty.' Wresting himself away, he picked up the stick and drew Mrs Tindale back inside. 'Wait in the sitting room, please. I'll be with you in a moment.'

'Listen to them, Simon, listen,' she cried.

He closed the door on her pleading and then ushered Tess and Benson back along the buckled path, through the gate and onto the pavement. There, beneath a broken streetlamp, he tugged at his hair.

'You don't smoke, do you?' he said, finally.

'I do, actually,' said Benson. 'But I'm trying to stop.'

'Blast.'

'I buy them . . . and then I take one and throw the rest in the bin.'

Simon was shaking his head

'Half the time I retrieve them,' – tapping his pockets, Benson had found a box of matches – 'I'm sorry, this is all I've got.'

Tess spoke:

'Here you are.'

She held out a packet of Sobranie Black Russians, a brand she'd seen Benson destroy with pain in his eyes. She'd planned to give them to him later that night. For a grateful moment, he blinked at her uncertainly.

'You normally read out the warnings of death,' he said. 'And point at pictures of shrivelled organs.'

'I know. For once, I thought they might come in handy.'

Simon took the packet and ripped off the cellophane.

'If I'm ever in trouble, I'm coming to you.'

After they'd lit up, he looked at Benson, and then Tess, and then Benson again.

'I'm not coming to the trial.'

'Why not?' said Tess.

'Because my mum and dad are guilty. I know they're guilty. There's nothing they can say that will persuade me they're innocent.'

Benson had a go:

'Simon, a trial is the place where evidence is tested. Where—'

'I've got my own evidence. If my parents had any sense, they'd recognise I've not been blind these last twenty years . . . I've seen through their best efforts. Saw through them years ago. My mum's tried hard, she really has; and my dad's a good guy and he loves her . . . but something happened, way, way back. My mum went into therapy and she found out she wasn't happy. And hadn't been for a long time. Found out that this was one situation she couldn't change by burning incense and lighting candles and putting Dead Sea salts in the bath. So she chose to lie. Not to her therapist – to me.'

Benson stood motionless, his head angled as he listened.

'In my line of work, I meet a lot of people who are forced to lie,' he said. 'People who live with secrets they'll never be able to tell anyone. And it's very easy to misread them, to think they can't be trusted. But believe me—'

'In my line of work – social work, child protection – we meet lots of liars, too. But, unlike lawyers, we don't try and make the truth fit what we've been told. We challenge people. My parents don't want to be challenged. So I'm not playing ball. If they'd dodged some tax, I might have gone along with it. But someone got killed, Mr Benson. Doesn't that make you uncomfortable?' He paused, but only briefly. 'Thanks for the smoke.'

Waving away any argument, he turned and kicked open the garden gate, resigned to have another row with Isabel, who loved his dad as if she were his mother.

After dropping Benson off at *The Wooden Doll* – another stilted journey, ending with a wave at her rear-view mirror – Tess went home, made herself a stiff vodka and orange, and rang Sally.

'I know what I want to do; and when I want to do it.'

'Really?'

'Yes. And that when is now.'

'You're talking about Benson? And the investigation?'

'Yes. Let's get it over and done with. Benson said that about something else; but it applies to us, and what we've begun.'

'Is that all it took? The right form of words?'

'No.'

Tess could almost see Benson leaning into a shadow.

'I'm not going to help him cover up a murder. That would make me part of the crime.'

Neither of them spoke; for a moment Tess wondered if the line had dropped. Then Sally said:

'What do you want me to do?'

Tess visualised a family tree she'd drawn. And the person

who might have inherited a bracelet made in 1918 by the great Manny Brewster.

'Look into Annette Merrington,' she said.

16

Benson had lingered on the pavement as Tess struggled with the door of her Mini. Moments later, its rear wheels had churned up the drizzle, and she'd been waving. He'd barely noticed her hand; all he'd been able to think of was the spray of orange confetti on her nose, and the dirt on his soul . . . freckles and sin that the rain would never wash away. As she'd turned into Wenlock Street, he'd set off immediately for Bethnal Green, to see Dr Abasiama Agozino, a clinical psychologist who specialised in war-related mental health problems.

Benson had been Abasiama's patient, on and off, for about six years. Bouts of crippling depression aside, he'd had problems with closing doors. When she'd said, 'Keep your coat on, then,' he'd thought he'd struck gold. She'd always been there for him, day or night. He never intended to consult her again.

'When I first came to see you, we never worked on those open doors. You were more interested in my relationships. And the fact I couldn't feel anything . . . for anyone, or for myself. Do you remember?'

'Yes.'

'You said I could leave all the doors in the world wide open and it didn't matter. You said what mattered was an authentic life, with myself and with other people.'

'I did.'

'And you told me an authentic life – not necessarily a happy one – was like a fruit in a tree. It was up to me to pick it. That question of choice became the subject of our time together. Because in my case, of course, being authentic was a problem. And it still is.'

Abasiama nodded. Her eyes were fixed on him.

'We began with being authentic to myself. We didn't get very far, did we? Because speaking about things didn't change how I felt. I remained numb. And so, after years of talking, you suggested I write down my confession.'

Abasiama was expectant; and wary. Benson had never spoken like this before. He was in control.

'Writing is so different to talking – you knew this. Looking at the page, I saw myself for who I was, and I *felt* something: horror . . . and, at the same time, relief at not having to hide . . . at least until that delicious moment when, like an act of suicide, I ended that honest life. I fed it into an electric shredder that cost me fourteen ninety-nine from Argos. It was great.'

Benson appraised Abasiama in her wheelchair. She'd lost a leg in an accident of some kind, and the other had been damaged at the ankle. Forgoing prosthetics, and explanations, she'd chosen to celebrate her appearance. She always decorated her long hair with silk or ribbons or beads or coloured threads. She went in for dyes, too. And cheap jewellery: bangles and rings and necklaces bought from Cancer Research or the Red Cross. Apart from these surface details, he knew nothing about her. She knew everything about him.

'All that integrity just went out with the rubbish, week after week, and I got on with the day-to-day. Thing is . . . I'd changed.'

Benson fixed Abasiama with an accusing stare.

'That was the trick, wasn't it? You knew that once

I'd been honest with myself I'd want to be honest with other people, that once I'd felt something about myself, I'd feel something for others. You knew, in time, I'd find the old existence unbearable . . . that I'd want to unburden myself to those I cared about, and that I'd suffer if I didn't.'

Abasiama didn't reply. Benson stood up, shaking.

'Well, you forgot something.'

Abasiama was impassive.

'And what might that be?'

'I'm in control. Not you. I don't give a damn about fruit in trees.'

'I know.'

The reply angered Benson.

'All I ever wanted from you – all I ever needed – was help in closing doors. And would you believe it? After everything you put me through, I still leave them open.' He paused, flushed with a desire to wound. 'Goodbye. I won't be coming back.'

Benson strode past Abasiama; when he was behind her, she spoke:

'Will?'

'Yes?'

'Would you do me one last favour?'

'Of course.'

'Shut the door on your way out.'

Benson opened a locker and grabbed a neatly folded handkerchief. It was trimmed with lace. The initials 'T de V' had been embroidered in one corner. Tess had offered it to him after a man had spat in his face – someone paid to provoke him so he'd end up back inside. She'd thrown it in the bin, but later, after she'd gone, Benson had retrieved it. That had been the day she'd walked back into his life.

He now went into the kitchen, stamped on the pedal bin and got rid of it.

She, like Abasiama, wanted to save him. Unlike Abasiama, she didn't know the half of it. And it was going to stay that way.

He was moving on. The squirming around in the Gutting Room was over. Along with the quick glances, the brushing of feet and shoulders and hands, and the lingering outside court. It was all over. Because these tentative forays towards intimacy were simply a pretext to scout around the past. As if they could both go there, pull up a few weeds and move on, hand in hand . . . singing songs by the Proclaimers. Benson had toyed with that idea for years. He'd imagined every detail. He'd even walked to the edge once, here on *The Wooden Doll*, late one night. He'd started telling Tess about Eddie, because Eddie was the key to everything, and he'd broken down, and she'd come towards him, she'd touched his neck, and . . . and thank God, ten-ton Archie had crashed through the cabin door wanting sausages. Bacon, too. And an egg.

The farce was over.

Benson was moving on.

And what about Abasiama, who did know the half of it, and more? She was out of his life. It was as though he'd told her nothing, because she'd never repeat it. Her ethics policy had been widely drafted to accommodate soldiers who may have killed outside the rules of engagement. She believed they needed a certain moral leeway if they were to get help. It was why Benson had chosen her in the first place. At the time, his reasoning had troubled him. It thrilled him now.

'I'm moving on,' he said out loud.

But what of Helen? She wanted to talk about his trial.

There were things she wanted to hear; there were things she needed to say. At the time, the declaration had confused Benson, and worried him. The basis of their relationship rested upon her insistence that they never look back. And they hadn't done. Ever. Helen had then devoted herself to his reconstruction, not in ordinary life, which had been changed, irrevocably, but in court, the arena of other people's lives. Why, then, would she want to interfere with the foundations of what she'd achieved?

The answer was morphine. Or the delirium of pain. Or a shortage of oxygen.

Her mind had been loosened. She'd strayed. That's all. Benson would gently lead her back, to a trial. This trial. He'd bring her to the uncharted territory she'd taught him to live for: the endless contest for innocence.

The Wooden Doll rocked lightly. Benson's court robes were by the open door. His black shoes had been polished. His dark blue pinstripe had been spot-cleaned with a toothbrush. He'd selected cufflinks with a design appropriate for a man out to catch something as slippery as the truth: leaping fish, etched in silver. The brief was flagged and marked. He was ready for the trial; and he went to bed.

Turning out the light, he was conscious that Karen and John Lynwood were writhing in the dark, alone with their fears. But, for the moment, there was nothing he could do to help them. That was tomorrow's task. For now, he was in a sort of limbo. All at once, he pictured Dr Jorge Luis Rafael Menderez on the 1st of March 2015. He, too, was alone; and scared; and in a sort of limbo. He was walking along a quiet ravine. The evening sun had begun its slow decline behind a grove of olive trees. Shadows among the branches moved like threatening hands. The next morning he'd board a flight to Heathrow.

'Did you really think you could escape yourself, Jorge?' said Benson. 'Or have I got it wrong? And if I have,' – for Benson now had doubts; he'd been brooding on the notion of unfinished business – 'why did you leave paradise for a damp house by Limehouse Cut?'

PART TWO

The case for the prosecution

A week after the tattoo ceremony Mr Braithwaite turned up. A donor had come forward, offering Benson the necessary funds to study any subject of his choosing. Further monies would be made available to help him establish a career. All that was sought in return was a promise from Benson, endorsed in formal undertakings, that he would never seek to discover the identity of his benefactor. The ink hadn't dried on the paper before Braithwaite produced a thick folder of trial transcripts from his battered briefcase. He'd been instructed to bring them by Helen Camberley QC. They demonstrated the art of asking questions. This, she'd said, was to be the true object of his study; the rest could be forgotten.

Nevertheless, Benson had to learn the rest before he could forget it. And so he registered as an external student at the University of London for an undergraduate degree in law, to be completed over six years. A few days later, Mr Braithwaite arrived with an articled clerk pushing a trolley. On it was piled textbooks, stationery, a printer and a laptop. After the clerk had stepped outside, Braithwaite said:

'I had great difficulty remembering the contents of this one.'

He flipped open Barnes and Hawks, On Equity.

'It contains maxims about the general principles of fairness. One of them springs to mind: Ubi jus ibi remedium . . .'

Benson's Latin went little further than 'Et tu, Brute!' and Braithwaite guessed as much.

'The general idea is that where there's a wrong, there must be a remedy. You might find hope in that.'

When Camberley next visited, Benson wondered whether to step over the undertakings and just tell her he knew already: that she was his benefactor and that he was immensely grateful. But her expression silenced him.

'I want to tell you a story,' she said, her eyes averted. 'It's a tragedy.'

And Camberley recounted the story of a woman who'd come to the Bar during the sixties. It had been a man's world, she said. But this woman had shown talent. And she'd been determined to join the list of fabled advocates associated with the struggle for justice. She'd been so driven that she'd failed to notice the onset of cancer that came to grip her husband. After his death, she'd worked even harder, and she'd failed to notice that her sixteen-year-old son had gone astray. When she'd finally opened her eyes, it had been to identify his body in a morgue.

'It was with Christopher's suicide that my life ended,' said Camberley. 'Friday the fourth of July 1986. I had no claim to innocence, so I went home to a prison cell. I have never left it, except to go into court.'

Benson was cold to his bones It was common knowledge that Camberley's career had soared after the death of her son. Pity had played no part in it; neither had hard work. Something had changed in her court presence. And she was feared.

'Are you prepared to learn from someone who has only one lesson to teach?' she said, looking up.

'Yes,' said Benson.

They were both silent, vaguely aware of the distant

profanity, the clang of iron slamming into iron, and the jangle of heavy keys. The sound that had seized their attention, however, was very quiet. They were listening to the echo of their own voices. Helen's had been like a mother's; Benson's had been like a son's.

17

The fact that David was missing lectures and tutorials during the last term before finals, just to watch Benson, had left Merrington incandescent. But he'd shown little feeling, confining himself to a sharp aside about his son's hair, which was, as usual, a mess. After a fitful night – for this venture was all about David's admiration for Benson – Merrington came down to breakfast resolved to have a calm discussion that would culminate in David taking the first train back to Oxford. The first part of that resolution went out of the window as soon as Merrington entered the dining room.

'What the hell do you think you're doing?'

'You know, Dad.'

'I don't.'

'I've told you before.'

'Tell me again.'

David did, and Merrington stared into the garden. When he'd bought the house he'd been a journalist and pundit, planning a move into politics. At the time he hadn't been married. Hadn't even met Pamela. He'd thought his worst problems would be enhanced versions of a plot gone wrong at school. Crippling anxiety about a son had never entered his mind.

'He's not even listening,' said David, addressing his mother, who sat opposite with eyes closed.

Merrington fired back:

'For you Benson is unlike any other barrister. He's an outsider. He has no interest in money. His only concern is justice. He's contemporary. He's free from all negative associations with power, privilege and class . . . which I took to mean the class to which you belong, the privileges you've enjoyed and the power that came with both. Either way, you're forgetting something.'

'What's that?'

'He killed somebody, David.'

'And he's paid the price.'

'Tell that to the Harbeton family.'

'The Harbeton family would like to see Benson hang. Which is why their say only goes so far.'

Merrington remained standing, not wanting to diminish his authority. But there was no point in rehearsing the argument. They'd had it so many times before. His concern was how to make Paddington Station the morning's destination, and not the Old Bailey.

'Dad, I just want you to understand. I believe in second chances. Imagine if Mum had killed someone.'

'Leave me out of this.'

'No, Mum, it's a good example. What would you do?'

'I'd go with her to the police station.'

'That's not what I mean. I'm asking, would you give her another chance?'

Merrington glanced once more at the garden. In that first year of ownership, he'd filled it with perennials. He'd built his own picnic table – the kind with integral benches on either side. It was still there, as precarious as the day he'd finished it.

'Dad?'

He looked at David with affection. The lad had combed his hair and shaved. He'd put on a shirt and tie. And then it struck him with the force of a wet dishcloth. The change in appearance was for the trial; not for him.

'Yes.'

'Just look at it from a personal point of view. I'm not talking about torture and mayhem. I'm thinking of mistakes. A night gone wrong. Stepping over a line because emotion takes over . . . it can be a split-second, and then it's too late. Don't you think someone like that should get their life back once they've done their sentence? Once they've changed and they're no longer the person who—'

'No, David, I don't. Because someone remains dead. And the person who killed them remains a killer.'

'I don't think you'd say that to Mum.'

'I said leave me out of this.'

'I'm afraid I would, David. And I'd tell her she can't even think about joining the legal system that examined her conduct. The system that must remain above the terrible mistakes . . . and the torture and the mayhem.'

David paused as if to weigh the argument; then he said:

'Dad, do you still go to church?'

'Of course.'

'But why?'

Merrington couldn't answer that one easily.

'Because I need to.'

'But you don't belong, Dad. Any more than Benson, for you, belongs at the Bar.'

'And why is that?'

'Because you don't believe in redemption.'

A spasm of love shook Merrington's soul. David was looking at him with uncluttered sincerity. Merrington had forgotten what it must feel like, to be like that . . . but David, mysteriously, had retained it; this treasure from childhood that Merrington had mislaid somewhere between the onset of pubic hair and his first cigarette. Or perhaps it was the other way around. Abruptly, he was arrested: David so reminded him of his father. He, too – unlike the tells-you-as-it-is-psalmist – had never seen the downside of virtue.

'If the Bar could accept someone like Benson, it would send a message that mercy—'

'Had come down from heaven,' said Merrington. 'But it hasn't and it can't. Not the kind you're talking about. Because the English legal system doesn't claim to offer final justice. We deal in the interim. Now, when's the next train to Oxford?'

'I'm not taking it, Dad. I want to follow the Limehouse case.'

'What is it with you about Benson? Fine, you think he deserves a second chance, and he's a rock star, or whatever, but—'

'Things happen in his trials, Dad. And whether you like it or not, he's sensational to watch . . . and this time he's against one of the best-known silks in the country.'

'You make it sound like afternoon television, David. I suggest you turn it off.' He paused. 'You forget, he rebuffed you.'

'Only because I'm your son. He saw my surname and that was enough. You see, Dad, the fact is, you're my problem, not him.'

David instantly regretted what he'd said; but only because he'd named a truth he'd rather have kept to himself. In the wounded silence, he quickly left the room, leaving Merrington staring at his wife, who'd finally opened her eyes.

'This is your damn fault,' he said.

'Don't be ridiculous.'

'It is, Pam. You and my bloody mother. You've drawn him into this foolish elevation of the outcast. And now he's putting his future at risk. Because the thing about outcasts, my dear, is they're outcasts; and those who join them are cast out, too.'

Pamela said nothing. She was sitting bolt upright. She closed her eyes again.

'I said this is your damn fault.'

'I know you did, darling.'

Pamela pushed herself away from the table. She went to the window, looking at the perennials that Merrington had planted back in the early nineties. Shortly afterwards, upon their marriage, she'd become responsible for their welfare. Along with Merrington's mother, who'd moved to London from Lewes at much the same time. The newly wed and the newly widowed had spent hours together in the garden. It was glorious now. Mature, as estate agents like to say.

'Who could have foreseen all this?' she said sadly.

She hated these rows between father and son. Merrington took a step towards her and then halted.

'What do you mean?'

Pamela gave a low moan, reminding Merrington of the family cat when he wanted meat over pellets.

'All this. You. Benson. Your mother. David . . . and me. How was anyone to know?'

'Know what?'

'That we'd become divided over . . . something that happened so long ago.'

Pamela turned around. She'd plumped for a red scarf this morning, arranged around her neck for a striking contrast with her black dress. Her face seemed red, too, the morning light bouncing upwards from the scarf.

'When your mother decided to help Benson, you'd only been in Parliament for a year or so. Who could imagine you'd become Secretary of State for Justice? Or that Benson would actually make it to the Bar? Or that he'd open his own set of chambers a few months after you'd been appointed? Or that you'd try and shut him down and fail? No one.'

Merrington bridled.

'And who could have imagined the mother, wife and son of the Secretary of State for Justice would become Benson's claque? Not me, I can tell you.'

'How could it be otherwise for your mother?' said Pamela, her voice strained with emotion. 'The person she decided to help – someone nobody else would have given a second glance, a kid who'd messed up his life – that sad case has turned into a sensation. David's right: Benson is associated with the struggle for justice for justice's sake. Things do happen when he's in court. And this is your mother's achievement.'

Merrington let his eyes drift from Pamela's rosy, lined face to the dormant garden; and, for the first time, he wondered what she and his mother might have spoken about while they'd been on their knees, dirtying their hands.

'Achievement?' he whispered.

Just then the front door opened and then shut. Merrington and Pamela both heard the familiar tug and thud. David had gone. But not back to Oxford.

'Would like you like a cooked breakfast, darling?' said Pamela brightly. 'I've got some organic mushrooms.'

18

'Rizla, are you in there?' said Archie.

Benson spat and coughed into the toilet bowl. Still sweating and feeling dizzy, he wondered why this awful rite of passage awaited him before every trial. Then he retched again.

'Rizla?'

Guts turning, Benson had swapped the robing room for

the toilets, which now held a reflective pause; then Archie spoke again:

'That's you, isn't it?'

'It is,' said Benson. 'And will you ever learn? I am now a barrister. You call me—'

'The prosecutor wants to see you. Now. She says it's urgent. Are you all right?'

'I'm just fine, Archie, just fine.'

'You know she's famous.'

'Who?'

'The prosecutor.'

'I do.'

The door closed, and then opened again:

'So are you, Rizla. So are you.'

A few minutes later, Benson rinsed the acid from his mouth, washed his face and put his wig back on. Then he went looking for Tess – and Janet Forde QC, an advocate of such standing that her memoirs had just been serialised in the *Guardian*. As Archie might have observed, Benson's name had appeared in the same paper, and closer to the front.

'I spent the weekend checking the disclosure schedule,' said Forde.

Born in Kingston, Jamaica, she'd come to the English Bar before Benson had drawn his first breath. She'd taken silk before he'd dreamed of shaving.

'Unfortunately, a police officer's notebook hasn't been listed,' she said. 'I've had it produced. It contains material that may be of interest to you.'

Benson, Tess and the prosecutor were standing in a conference room near Number 3 Court. Forde explained that the officer in question, PC Rudge, had been one of the uniforms doing house-to-house enquiries on the day the body had been found. Leaving the crime scene, he'd met a homeless woman called Harriet Kilbride, who often slept on Caxton Green.

'By Ropemaker's Way?' said Benson.

'Yes.'

Forde opened the notebook.

'She tells him, "I saw a man coming out of Ropemaker's Way at about a quarter to one in the morning." There's no description and no age estimate.'

Forde looked up.

'But she's referring to the night of the murder. That's almost three hours after the latest estimate for the time of death. And it's forty-five minutes after Alan Wilcot said he went indoors.'

Benson glanced at Tess. This was the one piece of evidence they needed. It was critically important. Because this man could have been with Menderez, from 7 p.m. onwards, as John Lynwood had surmised. Forde may not have considered the possibility; but she certainly appreciated the significance of the timing: it meant someone other than John Lynwood had had the opportunity to kill Menderez. And they could have left the crime scene along Ropemaker's Way at roughly 00.45 a.m.

'I've spoken to Rudge this morning,' said Forde. 'He arranged to take a statement but Kilbride didn't turn up. Shortly afterwards, he went on the sick and he took his notebook with him. He can't remember anything else.'

'We need her,' said Tess, addressing Benson. 'This changes everything.'

Forde spoke:

'It's William, isn't it?'

'Yes.'

'May I suggest a way forward?'

Benson faked a nod between equals.

'You could make an application to stay the proceedings as an abuse of process, but you'll fail. We both know the evidence against the Lynwoods is robust, and won't, on its own, be undermined by Kilbride's contribution, because there's nothing linking this man to Number Fifty-nine.'

Benson nodded again. Forde continued:

'I've asked the police to find her. If they do, we can take things from there. If they don't, I'm prepared to make an admission limited to the entry in Rudge's notebook. In the meantime, we can warn the judge and get the case underway. What do you think?'

'Agreed. But I think we can advance matters further.'

'Really? How?'

'There are fifty-nine properties that back onto Ropemaker's Way. The occupants of Fifty-eight have been interviewed. None of them saw this man. Which leaves number Fifty-nine as the sole premises he might have visited. I don't ask you to admit that much. But would you admit he didn't visit numbers One to Fifty-eight?'

Forde was expressionless.

'I'll take instructions. In relation to this morning, I propose calling the two witnesses you wanted to cross-examine. We'll get them out of the way, and then I'll press on with the Crown's case. Is that acceptable?'

'Perfectly.'

Benson's own trial had been listed in Number 1 Court. Sixteen years later, he'd returned, this time as counsel, to represent Sarah Collingstone in the Hopton Yard killing. It had been his first homicide trial; and his opponent had been Rachel Glencoyne QC, chair of the Inns of Court Conduct Committee, which had declined his application to become a barrister. She'd taken Benson's successful appeal as an affront to decency. His second homicide trial, the Blood

Orange murder, defending Grant Stainsby, had taken place in Number 2 Court. Now, instructed by the Lynwoods, Benson found himself pushing open the heavy door to Number 3 Court. For the third time, the issue for the jury was the gravest crime known to the law. The sequential listing was, of course, coincidental. But Benson couldn't escape a sense of destiny; of having overcome insuperable obstacles. Camberley had warned him that, very rarely, this, the flimsiest of straws, might appear on the wind. He was to grab it with both hands.

Benson edged his way past reporters and clerks towards the dock. His clients were seated side by side, but a universe apart. They couldn't take in Benson's reassurances, because they'd been awed by the shocking intimacy of the court. The worn oak and classical design couldn't disguise the purpose of the room. It was an arena in which people might lose their lives. Literally, not so long ago; figuratively now. Either way, it was a kind of death. To the right of the jury box, within arm's reach, was the dock; to the left, within arm's reach, was the witness stand. Whichever way the jury turned, nothing would escape their attention.

Benson, too, felt the threat of coming scrutiny. In the public gallery he'd glimpsed Mrs Tindale, John's godmother, and Simon's putative grandmother. He looked at her again: she was leaning forward, both hands clutching the brass rail, her dark eyes large with anguish.

'You were once the subject of an online petition, weren't you?'

Benson turned. It was Forde. She'd come from behind.

'I was.'

'A great truth was stated.'

The 'Paul's Law' petition to put Benson out of business had garnered over four hundred thousand signatures. The denunciation of his character had been ruthless. There'd been abuse, too, and it had been vicious. Benson had been traumatised.

'I'm sorry you feel that way,' he said.

Forde's expression hardened. Then she said:

'I'm referring to the second. "Everyone Deserves a Second Chance". I signed it.'

She then moved away, congratulating a stenographer on her recent marriage.

To hide his emotion, Benson looked down at his feet. He was overwhelmed. So much so, that he barely reacted when Judge Stanfield, the Recorder of London, and the Old Bailey's senior judge, appeared on the bench; nor when the jury were summoned; nor when the indictment was put by the clerk first to John Lynwood and then to Karen Lynwood; nor when the tense hush fell on the court as Forde came solemnly to her feet. He remained adrift. For once his identity as a murderer would not interfere with the fight for a verdict. He'd been accepted – if only by this opponent, for this trial, in this court. He glanced at Forde. She was speaking, but he was still struggling to concentrate so he missed her opening words. He caught, however, the final sentence, a formula containing descriptions of character and standing which, until now, had never been uttered with sincerity:

'The gentleman on my left, nearest to you, is my learned friend Mr William Benson. He appears for the defence.'

19

Fr Charles Winsley, it transpired, was a jurist in his own right. The canon law kind. After studies in London, Washington and Paris, he'd taught for thirty years at the Gregorian University in Rome until his return to London some three years ago, a profile which had persuaded the Archbishop of Westminster that he was a fitting candidate to run a parish with a long and illustrious association with the Spanish Embassy.

'I don't even like tapas,' he said. 'And as for burritos—'

'They're Mexican, Father.'

'You see, I don't know what I'm talking about.'

Fr Winsley had shown no sign of recognising Tess's voice. But he'd been pleased to see her. Leading her down a low-lit corridor, he'd disclosed his own interest in the law: Church law, a particular interest being the circumstances in which sacramental acts can be deemed valid and illegal at one and the same time. A confession that should never have been heard; or a penance that should never have been given. To be effective, even mercy needs the law, he'd observed. By this stage, they'd reached a musty parlour, and he'd quickly turned to the puzzle of his appointment.

'I am, however, fond of Rioja,' he said.

'Me too.'

'And sherry. Being English, you'd think I'd go for the sweet kind. But I like it dry. Dry as dust.'

Their eyes had locked on to each other at the mention of 'confession'. It was a type of conversation between priest and penitent. Its content could never be repeated. And without needing to ask, Tess realised that she was sitting in a chair that had once been occupied by Dr Menderez.

He'd come seeking forgiveness.

'Manzanilla is a favourite,' said Fr Winsley. 'I'm told I must visit Sanlúcar de Barremeda. And I'll go there, one day; but not for the sherry. It's the horse racing that—'

'I'm here to talk about Dr Menderez,' said Tess.

'Well, I doubt if I can help you.'

'Let's see, shall we? He came here regularly?'

'Yes.'

'How many times did you meet him?'

'Face to face?'

'Yes.'

'Once.'

'Where?'

'Here. In this room.'

'How would you describe the encounter?'

'Visceral.'

'Do you recollect when it took place?'

'The fourth of March, 2015. A Tuesday.'

'Do you recall the time?'

'About eleven o'clock.'

Menderez had landed in London on the Monday. He'd come to Spanish Place the very next day. Before he'd even settled in at Limehouse. Evidently, certain things couldn't wait.

'He made an appointment?'

'No. He just turned up. People do that, you know. Particularly when they have something on their mind.'

'He was troubled?'

'Profoundly.'

'You mentioned this to the police?'

'I made a general observation.'

But DC Trent had failed to note it down. Presumably because troubled people are always talking to priests. Tess had read Trent's notebook entry that morning. It contained one line: 'Introduced himself. Agreed to meet in the future. Never came back.'

'How do you know he was troubled?' said Tess.

'It was written all over his face.'

'Like it's written all over yours?'

Fr Winsley allowed himself a smile. He clearly wanted this conversation, while intending to limit precisely what he was prepared to admit. A true lawyer, he'd handled himself well with the police, but Tess sensed he viewed her differently. He wanted her to know that little bit more. She said:

'Father, I represent the man charged with the murder of Jorge Menderez. As we speak, the prosecutor is opening her case. And it may, in fact, be true, in every detail. But the truth, in its entirety, isn't being told today and it won't be told at all unless I find out why Dr Menderez left Candidar and came to London.'

Fr Winsley gave a nod.

'John Lynwood will be convicted for killing a man who'd fallen for his wife, and his wife will be convicted for trying to cover up the mess and save her family. But that isn't the full picture.'

Another nod.

'And I'm concerned the full picture may be relevant to the defence.'

Again, Fr Winsley nodded. And, like the others, it was ambiguous. Tess couldn't work out if he was simply acknowledging what he'd heard or was agreeing with what she'd said. Obliged to choose, however, she'd opt for his agreement. He was rapt. Tess said:

'We, the defence team, have concluded that Dr Menderez committed a serious crime in Spain, probably when he was living in Madrid, and probably a long time ago. We don't think he acted alone. So whatever happened is what we lawyers call a joint enterprise. As to the nature of the crime, we think, at a push, it may have a commercial dimension. Of this we are sure: Dr Menderez and his associates got away with it.'

Fr Winsley chose not to react.

'The past, however, didn't lie still. We think someone went to see him in Candidar in about July 2014. We don't know what they did or said, but they clearly brought this crime to life. This was one of those visceral encounters, Father.

Because afterwards Dr Menderez nearly killed himself. Ultimately, he found another way forward. He came to London six months later on a mission of some kind. "Unfinished business", he called it. That's the one remark he let slip. To an estate agent. We think he turned to Karen Lynwood for help. Ethical, therapeutic and practical. He wanted to involve the police, but only when he was ready to cope with the consequences. She's refusing to confirm what we think. Which means she'd rather watch her husband get life for murder than say what she knows – not to mention do time herself and shatter what's left of the family unit. Which is odd, because we sense it's her family she's most concerned to protect.'

Fr Winsley seemed to have stopped breathing. Tess continued:

'If she won't help us, we have to look elsewhere. We're hoping you know more than you've given the police reason to believe.'

Fr Winsley spoke quietly. 'Who told you such things?'

'No one.'

'But that's not possible.'

'Can you confirm what I've said?'

'Absolutely not.'

'Because you heard his confession?'

'Who said I heard his confession?'

'Well, did you?'

'It makes no difference either way. Heard or not heard, I can't help you.'

That Fr Winsley wouldn't reveal what he'd been told came as no surprise; that he refused to admit he'd heard anything at all was remarkable. He was disassociating himself from Dr Menderez, perhaps in advance of some later disclosure of what he'd done. Which suggested wrongdoing of no ordinary character.

'I'm not sure absolution should come that easily, Father,' said Tess.

Father Winsley returned her challenging stare.

'Who said anything about absolution?'

20

'I'd like you to picture a street in Kolkata,' said Forde, half-moons held in one hand. 'And imagine a foreigner sitting on a stool beside an open suitcase. The destitute have formed an orderly queue. They are his patients and the street is his clinic. The man is Dr Jorge Menderez. His case is full of medical supplies. He's been coming to Kolkata every summer since 2010. This, ladies and gentlemen, is his annual holiday.'

That's some opening, thought Benson, circling 2010 with a red pen. Forde had evoked the spirit of Mother Teresa. She'd implied that the man in the dock had killed one of her kind, and every member of the jury had turned to see what the monster looked like. Forde gave them a second's uneasy appraisal and then continued:

'His working life is spent in Candidar, a small village in the south of Spain. He's something of a loner, without a partner and without children. In March 2015 he tells his patients he needs a longer break than usual. And this time he comes not to Kolkata, but to London. On the fifth of October 2015, shortly before nine forty-four p.m., while standing in the sitting room of a rented property in Limehouse, a pair of kitchen scissors was thrust into the back of his head. He died almost instantly.' Forde paused; then she put on her glasses. 'How – you might ask – could such a dreadful thing happen to such a good man? Why would anyone want to kill him? This trial will answer those questions.'

A holiday? Beginning in March? With therapy thrown in? Benson was sure that Forde didn't believe that for a moment. She had no idea why Menderez had really come to London, and she probably wondered why the hell he'd never gone back to Cambridge. And the not knowing bothered her. Because – as Camberley liked to say – what you don't know can only hurt you. Forde didn't want the jury asking those questions, so she'd framed a story about a saint on the move, assuming, correctly, that no one questions a saint. Not about his travel arrangements.

'Dr Menderez read medicine at Kenwyn College, Cambridge,' said Forde. 'After qualifying he returned to Spain where, in 1985, he secured a full-time position at the Clinica Lorenzo in Madrid, a maternity facility where he remained for twenty-five years. Then, in 2010, aged fifty-two, when some consider the prospect of early retirement, he went back to Candidar, his childhood home – a poor rural community in a mountainous region, where he opened a general practitioner's surgery, serving not just Candidar but numerous surrounding villages. He covered a vast area. It was exhausting work. And it was solitary work.'

More cunning, thought Benson. And more saintly travel. He circled 2010 again.

'This was no ordinary holiday,' said Forde. 'Having changed job and shifted location – and perhaps this is not surprising – Dr Menderez struggled with depression. He'd even thought of suicide. The reason why is of no real importance, because by the time he came to London he was buoyant. All he needed was a guiding hand to help him "face the past with honesty and the future with integrity". Those are his words. Jorge Menderez had reached that moment in life when it was time – to use the words of

Robert Frost – "to rake the leaves away". A time, ladies and gentlemen, that comes to us all.'

Benson glanced at his watch. And he was impressed. Within a minute Forde had addressed all the features about Menderez's history that had caused Benson concern. She'd got there first, just in case Benson found a way of exploiting them. With a sigh, he underlined the quotation from Frost. He was grateful to Frost. He'd brought woods and fields into various HMP Hell-holes. Benson had walked there, along quiet lanes, hearing the crunch of leaves beneath his feet.

'Dr Menderez rented Fifty-nine Limehouse Cut, a former manager's residence adjoined to disused premises known locally as Foxton's Warehouse. Three months later he made contact with the second defendant, Karen Lynwood, a therapist who spoke Spanish, and who specialised in the management of mid-life crises.' Forde paused, as if to look back from a vantage point. 'She was, you might think, an ideal choice for Dr Menderez. Neither of them could have known they shared something primitive. And, being primitive, it was powerful: loneliness.'

Forde's eye now fell on John and Karen Lynwood. They'd met at university and married in 1981, when their careers were established. John was an accountant with Hutton Pryce and Karen was an advertising creative with Glisters. Five years later, when Spain acceded to the EEC in 1986, John was sent to Barcelona to help clients implement Community accountancy procedures. Karen left Glisters. Returning to London in 1989, John fulfilled a dream. He became a partner. Which meant long, long hours. Karen, too, was working hard, because she was now a homemaker, with their young son. And it's only in 1997, aged thirty-nine, after years of parenting, with school now a part of the routine, that Karen, a psychology graduate, thinks of *her* dream. Following intensive training, she becomes Karen Lynwood BSc MA, accredited with the British Association for Counselling and Psychotherapy. She opens a clinic at home. Her practice grows rapidly. She creates a website. And this is the website that Dr Menderez discovered in May 2015, three months after he came to London. In June he became Karen's patient.

'At this stage, ladies and gentlemen, Karen and John have been married for over thirty years. But there is a great distance between them. It's absolutely normal. It's not a crime. And I deeply regret having to bring their private life into this public court. But I have no choice. Because Karen Lynwood and Dr Menderez fell in love.'

The court would shortly hear how that relationship unfolded; and how John reacted when he found out. Because find out he did.

'On the fifth of October 2015 Dr Menderez came to the Lynwoods' home. To speak with John. And John threatened to kill him. The confrontation was over. But not the crisis. Because later that day, before heading off to the theatre, Karen met Dr Menderez at the Grapes, a pub in Limehouse. She claims she was trying to deflect a patient who'd been stalking her ever since she'd brought his therapy to an end. We say they'd met to discuss their future. You will have to judge. To help you decide, you need only consider what happened next. Dr Menderez rang John Lynwood at eight thirty-one p.m. Mr Lynwood will say – and we accept his account – that Dr Menderez declared he was in love with Karen, and that she was in love with him. That his marriage was over. There's no dispute that, following this call, John Lynwood drove to Limehouse Cut. Shortly afterwards Dr Menderez was dead.'

Benson opened the file of autopsy photographs. He lingered on the first, examining the expression caught by death. There were deep lines in the brow, not from age but worry; the mouth sagged at the corners. All that service to the poor had changed nothing. He'd remained a troubled man, and a sad man.

'What took place while the two men were together?' asked Forde. 'Only one person knows. John Lynwood. He insists there was nothing but an exchange of words. But we point to a tiny screw that was found by the body, after it had been laid beneath the staircase in Foxton's Warehouse. This screw came from John Lynwood's glasses.'

Forde had finished, and Judge Stanfield thanked her for such admirable brevity. They spoke like old friends, because they were. He appeared in her memoirs.

'Are you ready to proceed?' said Judge Stanfield.

'I am, my lord. I call Karl Ambrose.'

A few minutes later, Ambrose, a youth aged seventeen, was standing in the witness box, twitching with discomfort, his gaze flashing from the judge to his grandmother in the public gallery. Benson caught his eye on a return flight; and in the brief moment of snagged attention, Benson sent him a message: you're a liar.

21

'Why didn't you call the police?' said Benson.

'I was scared.'

'Of what?'

'Them.'

'Meaning?'

'The police. They'd blame me. Because I've been in trouble . . . and I'm black.'

Forde had spent considerable time on Karl Ambrose's background. The foster homes. The bullying. The racism.

And, sympathy gained, the string of convictions. She'd then turned to his evidence. The murder had taken place on Monday evening. During the night of the following Tuesday, Karl had forced open a window of Foxton's Warehouse and entered the building; he'd then switched on his torch and tiptoed past a large open staircase. Looking sideways he'd seen a pair of legs sticking out from under a sack. Terrified, he'd scrambled through the window and gone straight to his girlfriend's. She'd called the police. That was it. Forde had then surrendered him to Benson.

'Your girlfriend is Hayley Townsend?'

'Not any more.'

'But she was?'

'Yes.'

'Did you dump her?'

'Yeah.'

'Any particular reason?'

'Nah.'

'Why did Hayley call the police?'

'Because someone was dead, right. I mean, it was serious.'

'You're leaving something out, Karl.'

'Am I?'

'Yes. She called the police because she thought you'd killed him. And that's why you dumped her. Because you think she's a snitch.'

'Well, she is.'

'Not really, Karl. She didn't tell them you'd spent ages in the bathroom washing your hands. That you were hysterical.'

Forde looked up quickly. These incriminating details had never made it into Karl's statement, or Hayley's. They had been given to a member of the Tuesday Club.

'I'd touched the body, right? I felt he was on me and I couldn't get him off.'

Benson glanced at the judge, who glanced at Forde.

123

'You moved the body?'

'No, no, I just touched him.'

'Why?'

'I wondered if he was asleep.'

'Under a staircase? In an abandoned warehouse? Half-covered with sackcloth?'

'I wasn't thinking, right . . . I just saw him, and I . . .'

'What did you touch?'

'His foot.'

'Which one?'

'I don't want to think about it.'

'Which foot did you touch? Left or right?'

'The one nearest to me . . . his right.'

'That would be his shoe?'

'Yeah.'

'Did you remain standing?'

'No, I crouched down . . . and reached over.'

'Which hand?'

'My right . . . this one.'

Benson picked up a photograph of the crime scene and handed it to a court usher. It showed the body as it had been found, beneath the staircase.

'Look at the photograph, please. Mark your exact position with a cross.'

After he'd done so, with a red biro given by the usher, and after the photograph, now Exhibit 1, had been shown to the jury, the judge and Forde, Benson said:

'When interviewed, you told Detective Inspector Harvey that you'd been nowhere near the body. That was a lie.'

'I told you, I was scared.'

For two weeks – until his alibi had been confirmed – Karl had been Harvey's prime suspect. And, as Benson well knew, fear breeds lies. Karl had lied over and again. After providing him with the transcripts of all four interviews, Benson went through every single untruth, seeking an explanation and obtaining, each time, the same answer: I was scared. To Benson's eye he remained scared. And the fear was growing. Because Karl wasn't stupid. And he sensed where Benson was heading. Which was more than could be said for his lordship or Forde, who were becoming restive. Just when Forde was about to interrupt, questioning the relevance of this public dismantling of character, Benson said:

'I'd now like to give you a chance to tell the truth, first time around. Do you understand me?'

'Yeah . . . but I've nothing else to say.'

'Let's find out, shall we?'

Benson described one of the first things Karl must have seen when he'd switched on his torch: the door into the adjoining house; a door that was found by the police to have been left open, almost certainly by the party who'd moved the body from the sitting room. And he described what Karl must have seen if he'd put his back to that door, for the torch light would have illuminated the space beneath the stairs. Referring to photographs in the trial bundle, he described the simple Yale lock on the exit to Foxton's Wharf. Judge Stanfield and Forde had become restless once more; and once more Benson spoke before either could intervene. Karl, alone, looked worried.

'This is now your chance, Karl. You broke into Foxton's for one reason. And that was to get into the house?'

'That's true, yeah.'

Benson glanced at the list of previous convictions.

'You've got seventy-three offences for burglary, Karl.'

'Yeah, that's true.'

'I am going to ask you once, and once only: are you telling this jury that, having broken into Foxton's, you didn't enter the house . . . through an open door?'

Karl hesitated; Benson offered a helping hand:

'Karl, tell the jury: the first time you saw the body was on your way out of the house.'

Benson waited. And Karl nodded.

'Is that a yes?'

'Yeah.'

'Thank you.'

'And what was under your left arm when you stepped back into the warehouse?'

'A laptop. I nicked a laptop.'

'And cable.'

'Yeah, and the cable.'

'Mobile phone?'

'Nah. Couldn't find it.'

Benson then reconstructed the actual sequence of events: how Karl had tiptoed straight past the body on his way to the house; how he'd tried the door, found it to be open and had entered; and how, on leaving it, his torch had lit up the body; and how, having touched that right foot, he'd panicked.

'I've been in a lot of trouble, you know.'

'You have.'

'And I knew no one would believe us . . . so I got this brush out of the house and cleaned up the floor and then I went out by the Cut . . . I wasn't going near that body again. I mean, it was like he was watching me.'

'What happened to the brush?'

'I threw it in the Cut.'

'The laptop?'

'Same place, I just threw it in and ran.'

'What about your shoes?'

'Chucked 'em when I got home.'

'The brand?'

Karl shrugged.

'They were boots. Levi's.'

'Okay, thanks, Karl. Is that all you've got to say?'

'Yeah. That's the truth.'

'Are you sure?'

'Yeah.'

'Well, that's strange. You see, Dr Menderez was a member of a camera club. And one of the oddities of this case is that the police never found his camera. You didn't take it, by any chance?'

Again, Karl needed a helping hand. Asked to speak by Judge Stanfield, he said he'd found the camera on a shelf. What had he done with it? He'd slung the strap over his shoulder. Had it ended up in the Cut? No, he'd given it to Hayley. And what had Hayley done with it? She'd binned it.

'Thank you, Karl,' said Benson. 'You've been very helpful.'

Before letting him go, Benson asked him to mark his movements on a floor plan of the crime scene. And it was a tragic sight. For a brief moment, Karl Ambrose, crouched over a piece of paper with a biro in his hand, looked like a kid in art class at school. He was drawing to the best of his ability with what could have been a crayon. His work became Exhibit 2.

22

Fr Winsley had heard Menderez's confession, but he'd held back absolution.

'You *sent* him away?'

'All you can conclude, Miss de Vere, is that he *went* away.'

Tess could only guess what must have happened: Fr Winsley had told Menderez that divine mercy worked hand in hand with human justice. He'd told him to confess, in the first instance, to the police. But Menderez hadn't. For three months he'd been paralysed by fear. Benson had been right: Menderez's conscience had eaten away at him. At a loss, he'd joined the Limehouse Photography Club and traipsed around London taking pictures. He'd tried looking at life through a neutral density filter. That's what Tess's father had used when the light got too bright. She said:

'Did you expect to see him again, one to one?'

'We made an arrangement.'

'Specific?'

'No, loose.'

'And he never came back?'

'To see me, no. I waited impatiently. And then I heard about his murder on the news.' Fr Winsley shook his head. 'I accuse myself now.'

'Why?'

'I should have chased him. Instead, I left him absolutely free.'

And it had all gone so horribly wrong, thought Tess. Menderez had finally contacted Karen, and then everything had fallen apart, because love had got in the way – as it often did. He'd never made it back to the parlour at Spanish Place.

'Don't blame yourself, Father. Your door was open. You gave him a choice.'

'An open door isn't enough. Sometimes we need help with our choices, and I left him alone. I'm afraid that was a mistake. A grave mistake.'

Fr Winsley rose, bringing the meeting to an end. He'd done what he wanted to do: share with Tess that he carried a burden of knowledge he could never reveal; and that by mishandling what he'd been told, he was responsible, in part, for a disturbing outcome: he knew of the crime, but the police didn't. And, with Menderez dead, they'd never know. Tess offered him some comfort:

'A trial is a strange thing, Father.'

'In what respect?'

'Each side fights for a version of events that might have nothing to do with the truth. But somehow or other, nine times out of ten, the truth emerges.'

'Nine times out of ten?'

'It's the best we've got.'

But Tess felt unnerved. Because Fr Winsley's gaze said that wasn't good enough, that the secret he was obliged to carry had sickened him, and it sickened him now.

'Let's hope for the best, then,' he said, opening the door. 'I'll pray for that.'

Fr Winsley showed Tess the church. And she pictured Menderez sitting in the gloom, hearing the shuffle of feet, made melancholy by the scent of melted wax . . . struggling with unfinished business. Outside, in the bracing air, she remembered Benson's other question.

'Do you know why Dr Menderez never went to visit Cambridge? We find it odd, given that he lived there for years.'

'Actually, I do,' said Fr Winsley, pleased, at last, to recall a conversation that wasn't governed by the promise of secrecy. 'He was stopped by shame.'

'Shame?'

'Yes. I asked him what he meant – this was within minutes of our first meeting; you might call it the preamble to his leaving – and he said he'd made the biggest mistake of his life while he was a student. For him, Cambridge was the place where he'd lost his way.'

'Did you mention this to DC Trent?'

'Yes. He didn't seem particularly interested. I got the impression he thought university was the place where mistakes happen.'

'Did Dr Menderez say what he'd done?'

Fr Winsley nodded.

'He'd missed an entire course of lectures.'

'You're joking.'

'I'm not, and I must say, I hoped there were people out there punishing themselves for having missed mine. But I wondered which subject an aspiring doctor might throw aside, believing it to be of no importance.'

'Did you ask him?'

'I did.'

'What was it?'

'Ethics, Miss de Vere. Medical ethics.'

23

Tess slipped into the bench behind Benson, next to Archie, just as Forde called her second witness, Bob Graynor, chairman of the Limehouse Photography Club and coordinator of the Limehouse Basin Neighbourhood Watch Association. He'd served in the Royal London Rifles for five years, and then founded Heart of Spain (Imports) Ltd, a company 'specialising in Spanish food and wine since 1971'. In 2004, after thirty-three years travelling the length and breadth of the country, he'd retired to the boardroom. He was now a sprightly sixty-nine. As with Karl Ambrose, Tess had no idea why Benson had insisted on Graynor being called. Neither had Forde. And neither had the judge, who, at a pre-trial hearing, had proposed that his evidence be read to the court. Benson had politely demurred.

Forde took Graynor through his evidence-in-chief:

He'd first met Dr Menderez on Friday the 7th of March 2015. He'd telephoned two days earlier wanting to join the photography club. He'd subsequently attended every Friday meeting for the next seven months, right up until the Friday before he was murdered. As a beginner, Dr Menderez had sought instruction; Mr Graynor had been more than happy to help. They'd met a few times during the week. There'd been a lot to learn. About exposure. Depth of field. The rule of thirds. On Fridays, after everyone had gone, Dr Menderez had often lingered. He'd spoken of Candidar; and of his parents, who'd been children when the Civil War broke out in 1936. They'd lived through the Red Terror. His mother had seen a priest being crucified to the door of his church. When General Franco had won in '39, restoring order and decency, they'd viewed him as their saviour. But they hadn't been saved. They'd never shaken off the fear that civilisation could easily fall apart, and they'd passed that sense of potential collapse on to their son. While such details were fascinating, it was difficult to see how the Menderez family history, and its effect on Dr Menderez, could have anything to do with his subsequent murder. Or his secret crime. Or John Lynwood's defence. Tess, wondering how things had gone with Karl Ambrose, was impatient to find out why Benson thought differently.

'Did he tell you much about himself?' asked Forde.

'He spoke more about his family. As I said, he was a very private chap. He'd make these references to his parents and then he'd fall silent.'

'Are you an enquiring man?'

'No, ma'am. Which is why I can't really help the court.'

It was, Tess thought, a monumental pity. Because this very proper moustachioed gent in a camel blazer and striped tie had been the last person to see Dr Menderez alive. John Lynwood aside, of course. Mr Graynor had popped by Ropemaker's Way at about 3.30 p.m. on Monday the 5th of October. He'd brought some *jamón ibérico*, a ham from south-west Spain. They'd discussed the pig in question – a descendant of the European wild boar – and then they'd parted at about 3.45 p.m. Mr Graynor had never seen Dr Menderez again. The first he'd known of the murder was when he saw it in the local paper.

'I was absolutely stunned,' said Graynor. 'We'd been together on the day he'd been killed. We'd talked of the good things in life. We talked of the dehesas—'

'Dehesas?'

'Oak forests, ma'am. It's where the pigs forage for acorns.'

'Thank you, Mr Graynor. Please remain there. My learned friend Mr Benson may have some questions for you.'

24

'Pigs? You talked about pigs?'

'Black Iberian pigs.'

'And their eating habits?'

'Yes. He was very interested.'

'You spoke of . . . acorns?'

'And roots and olives. Herbs, too, actually. And grass.'

'Mr Graynor, are you aware that John Lynwood had threatened to kill him an hour or so before that conversation?'

'I know now, I didn't then.'

'Did he look worried?'

'Not in the least.'

'At the time you were discussing the dehesas, were you aware Dr Menderez – according to the prosecution – was in the throes of a relationship in crisis?'

'No, not at all.'

'Did you get the impression he was preoccupied?'

'Absolutely not.'

'Agitated?'

'On the contrary, he was in fine spirits. In fact, I only left because I was chairing a company meeting later that day. Now I wish I'd cancelled it.'

Benson paused to think. Then he leaned on the wooden backrest, arms folded.

'His mother's trauma. The memory of a priest crucified. That's an horrific evocation.'

'I agree, Mr Benson.'

'And he volunteered it without prompting from you?'

'Looking back, he gradually approached the subject. From stories of village life and festivals . . . to the Civil War and its impact.'

'How?'

'Well, during the first few weeks I'd ask him a question about himself and he'd answer with a story about his parents. There was an overlap, of course, because he was touching on his childhood. But inevitably, if someone tells you something about their parents—'

'You ask another question?'

'Exactly. And slowly but surely – while I knew next to nothing about him – I had a sense of his upbringing.'

'A vivid sense?'

'Yes.'

'It sounds as if he was building up an atmosphere of trust between you.'

'I'd accept that.'

'And when the time was right he shifted from the memory of a festival to the memory of a killing?'

'Yes, that's true.'

'Do you recollect when that shift occurred?'

'I do. It was early June.'

'Three months after his arrival in London?'

'Yes. We'd gone, as a club, to the Imperial War Museum.

I mentioned there was a collection on the Spanish Civil War and he said he couldn't face it. A week or so later, he told me why . . . with this story about his mother.'

'So for three months he's getting to know you – without you getting to know him – and then he becomes, in effect, very personal indeed?'

'Yes. But he remained something of a mystery.'

'Not quite a mystery.'

'What do you mean?'

'He told you the one thing you needed to know, if you were to understand him.'

'And what was that?'

'His parents had passed on to him a fear that an ordered, decent world can easily fall apart.'

Graynor pondered the point.

'You're right, Mr Benson. I certainly got the impression that while he'd been born years after the Civil War, he saw himself as one of the victims.'

'Nineteen years afterwards,' added Benson.

'As much as that?'

'Yes. Did he tell you anything else? About this fear?'

'He said he'd put it to good use. It's why he'd become a doctor. So he could save people. Especially children.'

Benson came off the backrest and straightened himself.

'Mr Graynor, as far as we know, the only other person he spoke to with comparable candour was his therapist.'

'I can only say I find that humbling.'

'You knew he was seeing a therapist?'

'No, I didn't.'

'Did he ever mention Karen Lynwood's name?'

'No.'

'Her husband's, John Lynwood?'

'No. The first I knew of them was after they'd been charged.'

Benson reached for the file containing Karen Lynwood's notes.

'My lord, I'm looking at page three.'

'Thank you, Mr Benson.'

And Benson traced his finger across the page: Karen Lynwood, he said, had noted up the crucifixion memory on the 8th of June. Burning churches were mentioned on the 15th and, on the 22nd, we read the finding – by his father – of a bone pit, with shreds of green and black uniforms. In each case, the entries were put to Mr Graynor; he was sure he'd been told the same story, and probably on the preceding Friday. In each case, they'd been snippets, given at the end of the evening, when the other members had gone, just before Mr Graynor had turned out the lights.

'It seems Dr Menderez saw you on a Friday and rehearsed what he planned to tell Karen Lynwood the following Monday.'

Mr Graynor was taken aback.

'That's extraordinary.'

'It is, I agree.'

Mr Graynor adjusted his tie.

'I don't know what to conclude.'

'I do,' said Benson. 'He may have been a very private chap, but he trusted you.'

'So it seems.'

'Which is why I believe you can help this court.'

'How? He told me nothing that might explain why anyone would want to kill him.'

'I'm suggesting he would have done.'

'I don't follow.'

'If someone had threatened to kill him, and he knew they meant it, I'm saying he would have mentioned it to you. Rather than quiz you about olives and acorns.'

Mr Graynor's mouth was tight as he gave the question serious consideration.

'I think that's correct, sir.'

'Similarly, if he'd fallen in love with a married woman – with all the fear that brings – I suggest he would have told you. If only in passing, on a Friday night, before you hit the light switch.'

Mr Graynor's face remained stiff with concentration.

'I agree. I have to agree.'

'Thank you, Mr Graynor. No further questions.'

Once Benson was seated, Tess leaned forward and tugged his gown. She was about to tell him that Menderez had missed some very important lectures when Mr Graynor, released by Forde, asked if he might address his lordship:

'I'm heavily involved in our local Neighbourhood Watch Association,' he said, smoothing back his silver hair. 'I attend meetings with the police and the local authority. And I have made it clear on numerous occasions that there have to be more CCTV cameras in this area. There's only one, on Upper North Street. Had there been others, I believe the court's knowledge of those who had access to Ropemaker's Way and the Cut would have been considerably improved. And I think it unfair that a man stands in the dock when affordable technology might have come to his aid.'

Judge Stanfield pointed out – courteously – that CCTV footage only ever formed part of the evidence. He then thanked Mr Graynor for his public service. So did Forde. And so did Benson. But Benson, with his lordship's permission, went a little further. He'd been struck by an afterthought:

'Did Dr Menderez have a camera when he first contacted you?'

'He didn't. But he'd bought one by the Friday.'

'Upon your recommendation?'

'Yes.'

'The brand?'

'A Canon EOS M5. It's a good all-rounder.'

'The lens?'

'Eighteen to a hundred and fifty millimetres.'

'That's a zoom lens, isn't it?'

'Yes.'

'Thank you again, Mr Graynor.'

25

'Well done, Rizla,' said Archie, returning from the bar with three bottles of Spitfire ale. 'Like I said, you've surprised everyone.'

Tess watched Benson carefully. Ordinarily, when Archie started showering compliments, Benson would frown and shrug them off, but his time there'd been no reaction. He hadn't seemed to hear. And yet there was cause to smile: he'd seen into the minds of witnesses he hadn't even met; he'd made the opening of a strong prosecution case seem fragile.

'It's early days,' said Benson.

'Days that belong to the defence,' added Tess.

After the court had risen, they'd gone to Grapeshots, a few doors along from chambers. Forde had spent the afternoon presenting the crime scene: diagrams of Limehouse, Foxton's Warehouse and 59 Limehouse Cut – two of which had already been appropriated by Benson. (That, thought Tess, had been a stroke of genius. In these critical opening moments of the trial, first moves mattered. Benson had shown the defence to be more rigorous than the prosecution, flushing out evidence they ought to have discovered for themselves.) Forde, retrenching her position, had shown the CCTV footage of John Lynwood's arrival and departure, and then concluded with a reading of agreed witness statements that effectively closed down access to and egress from the *locus in quo*: Alan Wilcot, with respect to Ropemaker's Way, and the boat party people, in relation to Burdett Road. With Benson's agreement, nothing had been said about the sighting of a man by Harriet Kilbride.

'If Kilbride is found, and she's convincing, everything could change, Will,' said Tess.

Benson drank to that. Archie cleared his throat.

'To put John Lynwood in the clear, this man she saw . . . he'd have to have been in the house from seven p.m. onwards, after Menderez got home from seeing Karen?'

'Yes,' said Tess, 'leaving by the back door and coming out of Ropemaker's Way at a quarter to one in the morning. After Wilcot had gone indoors.'

'So he's in there almost six hours?'

'Yes.'

'Having killed him some time between nine forty-five and ten, after John had legged it . . . for no obvious reason?'

Tess looked at Benson; he drank to that, too.

'All we need is someone there, Archie,' she said. 'Someone who might have killed him.'

'But it's got to make sense, Tess. I mean, this guy is with Menderez for three hours before he stabs him in the back of the head? Why not kill him earlier?'

'I don't know.'

'What were they doing between seven and half-eight, when Menderez gives John a ring to tell him how much he loves his wife?'

'I don't know.'

'Giving him advice?'

'I don't know, Archie, we don't need to know. All we

need is another candidate for the murder. Someone Will can point to.'

'I'm sorry, Tess: if I was on that jury I'd need more than a sighting of a man who may have just gone into Ropemaker's Way for a quick leak.'

Benson stirred.

'Did you get anywhere with Father Winsley?'

'Yes. And it's interesting.'

Tess explained how Menderez had turned up at Spanish Place the day after his arrival in London, and that a meeting had ended in confession, but no absolution; how Fr Winsley had sent him off to see the police first. Benson's intuition had been right again. Menderez hadn't had the nerve. Three months later, he'd turned to Karen Lynwood for help.

'Just before the conversation turned into confession, Menderez told him he'd made the biggest mistake of his life while he was at Cambridge.'

Benson looked up.

'And that's why he never went back?'

'Yes.'

'What did he do?'

'Dropped a course on medical ethics.'

'Ethics?'

'Yes. So, given what we know, it looks like Menderez's crime was a violation of his oath as a doctor . . . and that suggests whoever confronted him in July 2014 might have been a patient.'

Archie cleared his throat again.

'And how would a breach of medical ethics by Menderez tie in with a man caught short in Ropemaker's Way?'

'I've no bloody idea,' said Tess.

Benson laughed, but it was mechanical. An effort.

'You'd make a good barrister, Archie. You're good at asking annoying questions.'

'I'm serious, Rizla. Deduce what you like, but don't get your hopes up. I'm telling you. The killer is in the dock. And his wife knows it.'

'That makes two of you.'

'Very funny. Soon there'll be another twelve.'

Benson gave Archie a shove – and again it was a forced gesture, doing what he usually did with good old Archie.

'Has the club come up with anything on Narinda Hassan?' he said.

'Not yet.'

'Tell them we're running out of time. Hassan is important. She's the only person Karen spoke to – the rest is inference.'

'I'd say strong inference.'

'I know you would.'

Benson finished his beer and unhooked his duffel coat from the back of his chair.

'Tess . . . Hayley Townsend. The girl Karl Ambrose ran to when he was scared.'

'Yes?'

'How about you pay her a visit?'

'And ask about that camera?'

'Exactly.'

'Sure.' She felt his coming absence and rebelled. 'Where are you going?'

From the moment they'd left court, Benson had been abstracted. She'd wanted to reach him with confidence about the trial; but she'd failed. His expression had been locked . . . and lifeless.

'I'm off to see Helen,' he said. 'To tell her why Archie Congreve should have come to the Bar.'

With another shove to his clerk – once more an effort – Benson made his way between the tables and shortly vanished into Artillery Passage.

'Something's not quite right, Archie.'

'I know. He's different.'

They both looked at their bottles.

'It must be Helen's dying,' said Archie, turning his.

'Maybe.'

Only Tess wasn't convinced. Sure, Benson was destabilised – she'd spotted that herself, in the build-up to the trial, and even then she'd misread the signs. But this inward sinking, which she'd seen many times before, had never happened once a trial was underway. The opposite occurred, in fact. The life he discovered in court spilled out into his daily existence. That's why he lived for his work. Or his work lived for him. But for once, while he'd performed brilliantly in court, the old alchemy wasn't taking place.

'Do you know what I think, Miss de Vere?'

'No.'

'The sooner you find out who was wearing that bracelet, the better.'

26

The blue plastic disc quivered and then fell. Then it rose, quivered again, and . . . Benson looked elsewhere. But he could hear it travel that centimetre, measuring Helen's hold on life. And he could hear the scrape in her lungs.

'She could go at any time, Mr Benson,' the nurse had said.

'Literally?'

'My feeling is days or weeks. She's a fighter.'

The nurse, who'd witnessed many struggles at the edge of life, had smiled.

'She refuses to go.'

And I know why, Benson had thought.

He stole a glance. Her eyes were closed and her mouth

141

lay open, but the plastic disc moved a fraction more quickly. He took her hand and felt a slight pressure from her fingers. Her lips formed a faint smile.

'I'm against Janet Forde.'

The smile grew firmer.

'I was scared stiff. So I did what you said: I looked at the end of her nose.'

Helen opened her eyes.

'Did you blink?'

'No.'

Helen slowly came round, and Benson began relating the day's proceedings. The key witness, for Benson, had been Graynor. Because he'd shed more light on the background of the victim. Or rather he'd confirmed what had already been troubling Benson. Here was a man who'd fled his conscience, not his country; fled someone he'd met in 2014, and not the police. And what did he speak of when he finally began to open up? Where did the emotional terrain lie? Not his own adult years, when he'd committed a crime of some kind. But the consequences of the Civil War. For his parents, and for him.

'Whatever he did must be connected to that time. But I can't imagine how that would be linked to his killing. Or how John—'

'Tell me about your father, Will.'

Helen was sharply present now. Her eyes were dark holes in the reflections of fluorescent light . . . and Benson felt a sudden wave of confusion: she wasn't blinking.

'Tell me about Jim.'

'Sure,' he said. 'What do you want to know?'

'Tell me what effect your conviction had upon him.'

Benson would have looked away if those black eyes hadn't seized him, tighter than any hand grip.

'Tell me the truth,' she said. 'I must know. I ought to know.'

'But why?'

'Because it's what happened.'

'That was then . . . and so much has changed since. It can't matter.'

'It matters a great deal. Please tell me.'

Benson swallowed hard.

'It broke him,' he stammered.

'Go on.'

Benson saw his dad . . . reaching for his mum when she collapsed in the public gallery, surrounded by the chanting Harbetons; he saw his dad staring into the dock like an exile; he saw him on the other side of armoured glass, in the basement of the Old Bailey, longing to switch places; he saw him in the visitors' hall, cheery and smiling, but with distress gouged into his face; he saw him, as Benson had imagined him when he'd gone back home to Brancaster Staithe, head in his hands . . .

'Tell me,' said Helen.

'He had to hold everyone else together.'

'And?'

'There was no one there for him. He couldn't let anyone know that he'd broken down. He had to be strong. Keep life going for my mother, and my brother. And me . . . he tried to do that for me, too. Show me I had a family. Show me nothing could come between us. From the moment I was convicted, he was there for me. He's never gone away. Even though . . .'

'Tell me, Will.'

'Even though he thinks I might be guilty.'

Helen had become a blur. Benson pulled loose his tie, but the release around his neck made no difference: he was being strangled. At the same time, he felt a heady recklessness. He'd never spoken about this darkness with Helen. She'd forbidden it. Now she was insisting.

'He still does,' said Benson, embarrassed by tears. 'He won't admit it to himself, but he can't escape the doubt. Whenever I go and see him he tells me he knows . . . knows that I'm innocent. When I set up on my own, with Archie, the press turned up outside his house. Rather than hide, he went out there and gave it to them: my son is innocent. He said it over and over again: my son is innocent.'

Benson sought Helen's eyes through the harsh reflected light. She didn't blink, and neither did Benson.

'My conviction broke him, and he's broken now.'

Helen slowly withdrew her hand and turned her face towards the wall.

'Thank you very much,' she said.

When Benson got home he was so tired he could barely move. He sat slumped on a chair in the kitchen, unable to think, unable to feel. He didn't have the energy to eat, never mind cook. Dragging himself to his desk, he tried to work, but his mind couldn't function. It was a silent wasteland. He stumbled out on deck and looked over the water, as he often did, but even the ripples looked slightly different tonight, and he didn't know why; he didn't know what was happening.

You cannot look back in a search for lost innocence. And neither can anyone else. Not your mother, not your father, not your brother, not your lover. What is dead is dead. If that life is gone, then you must leave it buried.

Benson had done. And, in return, she'd helped him build a new life in the courtroom. A rich life that meant some-thing to people – people in distress, people who'd lost hope, people with nowhere else to turn – and now, after years of looking forward and never back, Helen, not Benson, was disinterring the past. She was pawing over the bones – his father's bones, and Benson's bones – leaving them exposed

144

to the air, making him look and weigh the loss. Why was she doing this? Why would she break the condition of their working together?

With effort he undressed and went to bed. Within seconds he entered the deepest sleep he had ever known. But in those seconds, slipping away, Benson had a final thought: this is what dying must feel like.

27

'What do you mean, I'm not the only one who's shown interest in the piece?' said Merrington. 'It was made for my grandmother. Who else but a member of my family would want to know anything about its history?'

'She was a solicitor, sir.'

'A solicitor?'

'Yes. She'd come with a colleague. Another woman.'

'I'm sorry, Mr Shipton, I find it hard to understand on what basis they had the right to dig around in my family's private affairs.'

'She said it was a criminal matter, sir.'

Merrington gave a start.

'A criminal matter?'

'Yes, sir.'

'I've changed my mind: I'll have a coffee after all.'

'Of course, sir. I'll get the original ledger, too.'

Merrington was still smarting from the conversation with David and Pamela. It had ruined his breakfast, his day and his evening. For David had returned to the argument enthusing about Benson's extraction of evidence from witnesses who'd seemed to be of no importance. 'Like I said, with Benson,' – and Merrington had finished his sentence:

'things happen.' Frustrated, he was determined to accelerate the confrontation with his mother. As a preliminary, he'd order a new bracelet, made by the very people who'd crafted the one he'd lost. And so Merrington had come to R. J. Shipton in Marylebone, only to find he wasn't alone in his concern for an heirloom.

A criminal matter.

A girl in black tights, patent leather shoes – also black – and a lime chiffon dress appeared with a cup of coffee.

'Can I have your autograph, Mr Merrington?' she said, the cup rattling on its saucer.

His eyes flickered. This had never happened before.

'Well, of course.'

It was a sign of things to come. And she had no idea. With a flourish he endorsed the back of an envelope.

A criminal matter.

Why would a solicitor be interested in his grandmother's bracelet? And he saw his mother – her daughter – again, one hand on the back of a chair, the other gripping a door handle, her eyes bloodied by injections. She would die, but would he weep? Would he lament her passing? Or would he be secretly relieved? He didn't know, and that had to be a tragedy. It had to be a judgement on their relationship. And the many years that had passed so very quickly, especially after she'd left Lewes for London in '93. She'd wanted a house in Hampstead – a place she associated with artists and lefty intellectuals – and had finally settled for a flat not far from the Heath. A twenty-minute walk from Pond Square. He'd imagined seeing more of her, and he'd done so with enthusiasm because – and this had only dawned on him after the death of his father – he didn't really know his mother; for all her sprightly conversation, and a ready interest in other people's children – a great asset in a vicar's wife – she said very little about herself. To this day,

Merrington knew next to nothing about her childhood and teenage years.

'One simply doesn't talk about oneself, Dicky,' she'd say when, as a child, Merrington had tried to make penetrating enquiries. But that was another era; now, in the age of self-disclosure online, he'd hoped she might change; and talk of her early life in Kensington . . . before her father had left the Bar to become the Deputy Coroner for East Sussex. But she'd maintained her reserve. She'd come for lunch every Sunday, full of questions for Pamela and her only grandchild, David. She'd worried about Merrington's career, taking no pride in his rise, fearing, it seemed, a fall on the home front. That David would grow up without quite knowing his father. That Pamela would be old before Merrington realised he was no longer young. Will I weep? Yes – Merrington wanted to hide his face – I think I might.

A criminal matter.

'Here we are, sir.'

Merrington looked up.

Mr Shipton – a tall, thin man with round spectacles – had placed a heavy ledger on a glass table. He'd already found the page and he pointed at the line of copperplate that recorded the original commission by Arthur Wingate in 1918: an eighteenth birthday present for his daughter, Elsie. The bracelet had been crafted by one Manny Brewster.

'The solicitor came with photographs of the item, sir.'

'Photographs?'

'Yes, sir. That's how I identified it.'

'She came with photographs of my grandmother's bracelet?'

'Yes, sir.'

'Who took the photographs?'

'She did, sir.'

Merrington felt like there was sand in his eyes.

'You mean the bracelet has been found?'

'So it would seem, sir. And this solicitor had tracked it down and taken photographs. Sir.'

'Who has it?'

'I'm afraid I don't know. The solicitor also took a photograph of the original order,' – his long finger tapped the yellow page – 'and she told me I should on no account destroy the ledger. Not that I would, of course, but these days, we put everything in Excel and . . .'

A criminal matter.

Merrington's mind went blank. What had happened to the bracelet after he'd lost it? Had someone picked it up? Mr Shipton's drone grew louder:

'. . . as you can see,' – he nodded at the leather chairs, the antique cabinets and the old skewed mirrors – 'things haven't changed here since your great-grandfather Arthur stood where you are, asking—'

'This solicitor. What was her name? Do you remember?'

'I made a note of it, sir.' He pointed to a loose slip of paper placed like a bookmark in the ledger. 'That's who came, sir. Tess de Vere. From Coker and Dale, Solicitors.'

28

'So far, things are going well, aren't they?' said Mrs Tindale, raising her stick.

Benson remembered how she'd described herself: John's godmother, though more of a mother; the grandmother Simon had never had. He'd thought the claims remarkable. She'd placed herself at the heart of the Lynwood family, even though she'd never been mentioned in a client conference.

'Am I right, Mr Benson?'

'Well, the jury now knows John didn't try to destroy any evidence on the computer; and they know that Dr Menderez didn't take John's threats seriously. So, yes, we're not in a bad place. But there's more evidence to come.'

Benson, Tess, the Lynwoods and Mrs Tindale were in a conference room. They'd met first thing in the morning. So far, Mrs Tindale had done all the talking. Benson placed her at eighty-something. She was a mother to John, she'd said. Had she been a mother-in-law, too? Karen, silent, arms folded, staring into space, hadn't greeted Isabel; hadn't looked at her; and had purposefully avoided the chair beside her. John had taken it, filling the gap between them as if it was his calling. Benson said:

'I have some potentially good news. The prosecution has informed me that a homeless woman saw a man coming out of Ropemaker's Way at a quarter to one on the night of the murder. This means, logically, that—'

'I told you, Mr Benson,' said John, slapping his thigh. 'I was right.'

'We have a sighting, nothing more.'

'No, Mr Benson. This is him. This is the man who killed Dr Menderez. I know it. Where is this homeless woman? Is she here? Will she—'

'The police are trying to find her. She—'

'What do you mean, find her?'

Benson explained what had happened. While fielding Mr Lynwood's angry questions, and noting Karen Lynwood's lack of indignation, his mind worked quietly on the aged, olive-skinned Mrs Tindale, whose English had inflections from another land. She would be the same age as Menderez's parents, had they been alive. Which is to say, she, too, would have been a child during the Civil War. If she was Spanish.

'No, Mr Lynwood, there's been no deceit,' he said. 'At worst, it was incompetence.'

149

'But I need her, and she's missing.'

'And the police are doing their utmost to find her.'

Benson turned to Mrs Lynwood.

'Did Dr Menderez ever mention Mr Graynor?'

'No, Mr Benson. And if he had done, I would have noted it.'

'I see. It's very interesting.'

'What is?'

'Dr Menderez tells Mr Graynor what he intends to discuss with you. But he never mentions you. He then meets you and he never mentions Mr Graynor.'

'That's hardly surprising, Mr Benson. When people embark upon a journey of self-disclosure, they often keep things compartmentalised. It's a defence mechanism.'

'There was nothing to compartmentalise. What he told you, he'd already told Mr Graynor.'

'He told me a great deal more, Mr Benson. I didn't just get the facts. I got the emotion. I got the tears. I got the distress.'

Bothered by an itch, Benson adjusted his wig.

'2010,' he said.

'What about it?'

'That was the year Dr Menderez left Madrid for Candidar. It's the year he started going to Kolkata.'

'I know.'

'Did he discuss those two decisions with you?'

'No.'

'But they're significant.'

'Mr Benson, if they touched on whatever he planned to tell me, he'd have said so, but he didn't. And if he'd said anything that I thought might become important, I'd have noted it down. And I didn't.'

Mr Lynwood intervened, tentatively.

'I think Mr Benson is trying to get inside Dr Menderez's history, Karen . . . further than the police. You know, root out anything that might explain why he was killed.'

'I appreciate that.' Slowly her face crumpled. 'But you keep expecting me to have answers, Mr Benson. And I don't.'

'She doesn't,' added Mrs Tindale, as if she'd been there, at Karen's shoulder. 'She's told you everything she knows.'

Pointedly, Benson did not correct her. And, gently, he applied some pressure.

'Remember, Mrs Lynwood: I said the trial would put you back in your consulting room. Questions will continue to arise. And all you have to do is help those of us who weren't there.'

'Us?'

'Yes. Because Miss Forde will question you. And the judge may have his own concerns.'

Mrs Lynwood seemed not to have thought of that. And then she spoke, as if to the floor that wouldn't open up and swallow her.

'When will this ordeal be over?'

'When the jury has heard all the evidence,' said Benson. 'Which is why I need to know everything. Before Miss Forde or Judge Stanfield find out for themselves.'

Seated in court, Benson surveyed the empty jury box. He listened to Forde opening her file, chatting amiably with the CPS representative. He looked at the radiant stenographer, newly wed, a haggard usher, who smiled, and then, finally – turning around – the public gallery. Mrs Tindale had found her place. Once again, her eyes were on him. She'd probably had words with Simon that very morning. Urging him to come and support his parents. Benson slowly lowered his gaze to Tess, who was seated behind him. He leaned over to whisper:

'John's parents were killed in 1975.'

'Yes.'

'They were on their way to the first Test at Edgbaston.'

'That's right.'

151

Benson had never known anyone to have such restless eyes. He'd noticed them upon first meeting, when her attention had darted between Helen and Braithwaite and himself. She'd lingered on Benson; and for those drawn out seconds he'd thought of the brightening sea at daybreak. And then she'd look away.

'Mrs Tindale's husband was killed in the same accident,' he said.

Tess nodded.

'There should be a newspaper report. Would you check it out? See if it gives you a handle on the Tindales.'

'What do you want to know?'

'Anything about Mrs Tindale. She's my way in to the world Menderez kept talking about.'

29

Forde called it the countdown to murder.

She began by reading an agreed statement of facts. Karen Lynwood, the second defendant, practised as a psychotherapist from 17 Cornfield Road, Islington ('the clinic'). Dr Menderez became a patient of the second defendant on the 1st of June 2015 and attended the clinic every Monday at 2 p.m. until the 7th of September 2015, a period of four months. It was further agreed that Dr Menderez had turned up four times at the clinic, on every subsequent Monday, at the usual time. On each occasion John Lynwood, the first defendant, had refused to grant him access to the clinic. The murder had taken place on the evening of the fourth visit.

Forde then turned to File B, page 16, and drew the court's attention to an agreed list of emails and texts, all of which had been deleted by the second defendant and retrieved by an expert instructed by the police. It was headed 'Emails and text messages from Dr Menderez to Karen Lynwood'. Once the judge and jurors had found the page, Forde began reading out the entries in a slow and measured voice. The sense of a relationship – formed over four months, getting stronger with each passing week, becoming significant to the point of no return – was irresistible. Benson, his eye fixed on the text, felt he was snooping:

07.09.2015 Monday (last therapeutic session):

11.58 p.m. Email:
'Don't worry, Karen. Everything is going to be all right. Just try and get John to see sense. He can't stand in our way. I know this is difficult for you. But you're not alone. I am here.'

14.09.2015 Monday 1:

8.56 p.m. Email:
'Did you speak to John or not? You said you would. This is what we agreed. There's no other way forward. Please find the courage.'

21.09.2015 Monday 2:

10.04 a.m. Text message:
'Did you get my emails? You feel the same as me. Let's get on with the future.'
4.35 p.m. Text message:
'What is happening? We need to make progress. For all our sakes.'

28.09.2015 Monday 3:

11.04 a.m. Text message:
'Have you spoken to John? Have you told him how you feel?'

Having reached this point, Forde called Corrine Tugby to the stand.

Tugby lived at 15 Cornfield Road. She was the defendants' next-door neighbour. A diarist on a Pepysian scale, her bid to record life's fine details extended to the quality and frequency of her bowel movements. It was not surprising, therefore, to learn that little, if anything, had escaped her attention. She'd heard the Lynwoods rowing throughout the whole of September. Two incidents stood out.

On the 28th of September (Monday 3), at 2.05 p.m. – i.e., a few hours after Dr Menderez had asked Karen if she'd spoken to her husband about how she felt – Tugby arrived home to see Mr Lynwood shoving Dr Menderez away from the clinic entrance. Mr Lynwood had said: 'Leave us alone. Don't go near my wife again. That's a warning.' Dr Menderez had replied, 'You don't understand Karen. But I do. Listen to what she has to say. I'll be back.' Mr Lynwood had responded, 'If I see your face again, I'll fix it.'

Forde paused there to draw the court's attention to the next entry in the list, a text sent the following day, Tuesday the 29th of September:

9.03 p.m. Text message:
'Tell him how you feel. You can't let John hold you back. I can't endure this waiting any longer.'

Forde then returned to question Tugby, because at 9.08 p.m. – five minutes after this text, according to her diary – Tugby had gone into her back garden. She was taking out the recycling when, through an open bathroom window, she heard Mr Lynwood shout, 'Have you completely lost your mind? Have you given any thought to me? To Simon?' And Karen shouted back: 'You? What about me? Did you ever

154

even think of me? And what I feel, and continue to feel?' At that point, a door had slammed.

Benson began his cross-examination after lunch.

Tugby had been the Lynwoods' neighbour for over twenty years. Did she consider Mr Lynwood to be a violent man?

'No.'

Did she view Karen's marriage as a sham?

'No.'

It was brief, desperate stuff. Tugby was then replaced by Dietrich Fischer, who lived opposite the Lynwoods.

Chronologically, Forde had now come to '05.10.2015 Monday 4. The day of the murder.' On that day, shortly after 2 p.m., Fischer had been repairing a broken curtain rail. Standing on a stepladder, he'd seen John Lynwood advancing upon Dr Menderez, stabbing his finger into his chest, and yelling, 'We're a happy family. Only a total bastard would try and break us apart.' Dr Menderez had said something, which Fischer hadn't caught. John Lynwood had then bellowed: 'Leave. For good. Or I'll kill you.'

Fischer didn't know the Lynwoods, so Benson's attempt to tone down the description of a frightening confrontation got no further than a reluctant concession: that 'prodding' was a more accurate term than 'stabbing'.

'If Mr Lynwood had been holding a knife,' asked Forde in re-examination, 'do you think the "prodding" would have broken the surface of Dr Menderez's coat?'

'Indubitably.'

'And his skin?'

'Incontrovertibly.'

'Thank you, Mr Fischer.'

After he'd left the courtroom, Forde turned once again to

page 16 in File B, and a text message sent by Menderez some two hours after the confrontation:

4.08 p.m. Text message:
'I'm at the Grapes in Limehouse. Please come.'

'My lord, the Grapes is a public house,' said Forde. 'Its manager is Norman Oakworth. He witnessed the writing and sending of this text. He'll now tell the court what subsequently happened.'

Having been sworn, and confirming what Forde had just said, Oakworth recounted how, an hour or so later, 'let's say five-ish', the second defendant had entered the premises 'in a right state'. She'd gone straight to the table occupied by Dr Menderez. They'd spoken earnestly, heads close to each other. At one point, Dr Menderez had taken the second defendant's hand.

'And how did Karen Lynwood respond?'

'She didn't mind.'

'Why do you say that?'

'Because she put her other hand on top of his.'

'How long did they remain like this?'

'About ten minutes. Until they left.'

'And when was that?'

'About six p.m.'

Benson declined to ask any questions and Forde, still standing, then addressed the judge:

'My lord, at this point, Mrs Lynwood goes to the theatre and Dr Menderez goes home.'

'Arriving at seven p.m. or so?'

'Correct. At which point, at seven o-four, he sends Mrs Lynwood another text.' Forde read it out. '"I mean it, Karen. I want your decision by eight p.m. We have to do what is right for everyone."'

Judge Stanfield, nodding, examined the list.

'And at eight o-five, no response having been received, Dr Menderez sends his final text, saying, "If you won't tell him, I will."'

'Yes, my lord. And, of course, we know that Dr Menderez then rang John Lynwood half an hour later—'

'Declaring his love for Mrs Lynwood, and Mrs Lynwood's love for him.'

'Yes, my lord.'

'At which point Mr Lynwood sets off for Limehouse Cut.'

'Precisely, my lord.'

The judge gave a low sigh.

'Is there anything you want to add, Mr Benson?'

'Only this, my lord: there are two emails and seven text messages. Mrs Lynwood replied to none of them.'

'I'll note that, Mr Benson. All right. I think that would be a good place to stop. It's been a long day.'

The court cleared. But Benson lingered. Tess came and sat beside him. They didn't speak. They seemed to be gazing at the same barren terrain. Forget the dates and times. None of that would remain in the jury's memory. But the effect would. A therapist had become heavily involved with a patient. And the therapist's husband had lost his head.

Was Archie right? Had Benson's imagination gone into overdrive? What did it matter if Menderez had fled Spain with a tortured conscience? What did it matter if Harriet Kilbride had seen a man at the mouth of Ropemaker's Way? Karen Lynwood could still have fallen for Menderez; and her husband could still have killed him. Why resist the obvious?

Because Benson knew the sound of innocence.

'I'll wait for you outside,' said Tess.

*　　*　　*

When Benson came out of the Bailey the wind came funnelling down from Newgate, shoving Tess towards him.

'Do you fancy a quick Spitfire? Or something stronger?'

Benson stepped aside, but their elbows brushed.

'Sorry. I have to go and see Helen. I promised.'

They parted. But Benson went nowhere near the Royal Marsden. He went home and sat on deck, wrapped in his duffel coat, smoking a Sobranie. He saw the demand in Helen's eyes; and another in those of Tess. And he listened to the water lapping against his boat; a boat that could sail here and there, but would only ever come back to this mooring, a landing stage by a clump of trees and two rubbish bins.

30

They were dressed in workmen's overalls. Blue ones, acquired in France when they'd been students – the same year Sally had bought a restaurant table in Montmartre and dragged it back to London. The material was faded now, and spotted with paint splashes and crusts of Polyfilla – evidence of decorating and small repairs, joint ventures, often judged a success by the fun they'd had together rather than the quality of what they'd accomplished.

'This is hell,' said Tess.

Standing on a stepladder, she was tackling the ceiling rose with a palette knife.

'It just takes patience,' replied Sally.

Her task was a cupboard beneath a windowsill; she was working on a jammed hinge, applying paint stripper with a small brush.

'It's still hell,' said Tess.

Sally had decided to renovate the drawing room of her house on Chiswick Mall. All the furnishings, paintings, prints, curios and rugs had been moved into the corridor. The space left behind felt immense. The state of the wood-work and plaster ornamentation was a testament to how the previous occupants had lived. As things had lost their shine, they'd covered up appearances, and cracks, with layer upon layer of paint. Sally was determined to recover what had been lost. With Tess's help.

'How did things go today?' asked Sally.

'Badly.'

She was referring to Benson, who, having sunk into himself, was now ignoring her. Just as she'd cast aside her hesitations – her many hesitations – he'd drawn down the shutters. They'd always moved up and down, but this time there was a sense of a lock at ground level; that they'd never be raised again.

'I caught a roundup on the news,' said Sally. 'It sounded pretty grim. Tell me what I missed.'

First thing in the morning, following on from her 'count-down to murder' the previous day, Forde had called Brian Unwin. He was part of the foursome that went back to university days in Bristol – the others being Karen, of course, and Narinda Hassan. A history teacher now, Unwin had known Mr Lynwood – John – all his adult life. He'd given evidence very, very reluctantly.

'Everything he said was absolutely credible,' said Tess, sitting on the stepladder platform. 'He could almost name the day the problems had begun in the Lynwoods' marriage. And that was when Karen had begun training as a therapist. John had been against it. He'd been scared Karen would change, that she'd start questioning their past . . . see him differently.'

And none of this had been surmise. John had said it all to Brian.

'Within months of starting the course, Karen had changed. She'd stepped back . . . she was looking at them as a couple . . . as a family.'

'Asking questions?'

'Of course. It's natural. It's good. Uncomfortable, maybe, but it can lead to a fresh start – only for John it was just psychobabble. West-coast American crap. And he was getting angry. I mean, he said it outright: he thought these stupid lecturers – and especially her therapist, because Karen had to go into therapy herself as part of her training – were out to pull down everything he'd built with Karen. Which is fair enough, actually, because they probably were, in one sense. They were helping Karen find herself. Helping her uncover anything that compromised her integrity, her true identity. Only John didn't want to be involved.'

'And then Jorge Menderez came along.'

'That's right. After twenty years of drought. He walks through the door and starts talking about facing the past with honesty and doing what's right and looking to the future with integrity. He spoke her language. He understood where she was; and she understood where he was.'

Sally placed her brush on a plate and sat down.

'Did John talk to Brian about this?'

'In detail. Said he thought she fancied him. Can you imagine? John's best friend, fidgeting in the witness box, spilling all this stuff out, not wanting to but having to, because it happened?'

'Jeez.'

'Honestly, it was excruciating. He said John was really upset. Couldn't refer to Menderez by name. Had to use some racist slur. In general, he called him Manuel.'

'As in *Fawlty Towers*?'

'Yes. And Forde is just brilliant. You wouldn't know she's there. Somehow or other she effaces herself, so all you've got is the witness . . . Unwin, doing what's right, being honest. Telling the jury John wanted this bastard to bugger off and die.'

Benson had been powerless to reduce the impact of the testimony. For most of the time, he'd paddled around asking questions about Narinda Hassan. She'd been very vulnerable as an undergraduate. So what? Hassan had nearly dropped out within months of starting her course. So what? Unwin hadn't known why. Again, so what? She'd finally become settled, which, said Benson, was good to know. The judge and Forde had exchanged glances.

'And it was just as bad in relation to Karen,' said Tess.

Forde had called Dr Gerard Evington. He was Karen's supervisor. She'd seen him every month to discuss how she was coping and any issues that had arisen with the handling of her clients. He'd fulfilled this role for twelve years. And between June and September 2015, Karen had spoken about one client only. Dr Jorge Menderez. She'd called him 'captivating'. She'd been fascinated by his family history and intrigued by him.

'And, come August, he warns her to be careful.'

'Why?'

'Because he thought she was at risk of getting over-involved. Losing her detachment.'

'And in September?'

'He'd asked about Menderez and she'd been evasive. Said there was nothing to discuss. He'd thought she was being disingenuous. Wondered if relations between Karen and her husband were under strain . . . I'm telling you, it was a disaster. Remember, the defence argument is that Menderez was stalking her. There was no relationship. But the word never gets mentioned. Not by Karen to her supervisor and not by John to Unwin. Because – and it's painfully obvious – that's not what happened.'

'What did Benson get out of Evington?'

'Very little. All he could do was extract some general principles about human relations. That someone can form a deep attachment and keep it a secret, even from the person to whom they're drawn. That it can become a sustaining thing, for years on end, and the person concerned would never know. Same for friends and family. They wouldn't have a clue. He was doing his best to present Karen as a professional, despite everything Evington had said, and he had to keep it abstract because Karen won't admit what Evington was saying. Really, it was a bad, bad day.'

'For the defence,' added Sally.

Tess thought for a long moment.

'Yes. You're right,' she said at last. 'Maybe it was a good day for the truth.'

Sally picked up a scraper and began lifting the layers of bubbled white paint off the hinge. Almost immediately the brass beneath began to show through, catching the light. Tess looked up at the ceiling rose. She'd drawn the short straw. One false move, one impatient shove of the knife, and she'd break the moulding.

'Shouldn't we leave well alone?' she said.

Again, she was thinking of Benson.

'No. It's all or nothing.'

Tess looked at the years of emulsion slapped on without thought of the future. Some of it was so thick it was crumbling.

'This is hell.'

Sally wiped the hinge with an old rag. The metal gleamed like new. She smiled.

'Aren't you going to ask?'

Tess came down the stepladder. She'd had enough.

'About what?'

'How my day went.'

'How did your day go?'

Sally threw the cloth into a bucket.

'I received a photograph. An important one.'

31

They cleaned up and went to the Old Ship in Hammersmith. And though it was cold, they sat outside, hats pulled down and with scarves wound tight around their necks. They were alone. The heat and the rush of conversation was around the bar and the open fire. Only a hum reached them.

'What's all this about a photograph?' said Tess.

'Be patient.'

Sally was methodical. She liked to work forward from first principles. Even if that involved stating what was already known. She said:

'The bracelet found by the body of Paul Harbeton was made for Richard Merrington's grandmother, Elsie. Our working hypothesis is that the bracelet made it from Elsie to Annette, Merrington's mother. She's now ninety-two.'

There were other features of interest. Like the fact that Annette's father had been in the same chambers as Helen Camberley's father. It was a striking coincidence. And one that needed to be explored. But in the first instance Tess wanted to focus on the person central to the hard evidence they'd obtained: Annette.

And her immediate family.

'As you know, I've been digging around. And there's something about Wilfred Baker, Annette's father, and Annette herself, that intrigues me.'

'Which is?'

'Something joins them apart from blood.'

Sally had started research into the Merrington family some while ago. She'd spent hours in the British Library and the archives of Gray's Inn. She'd read articles and reports in *The Times*. She'd plundered a couple of memoirs from the forties. After Tess had told her to look into Annette, she'd followed her targets to Lewes, via the internet, tracing names in multiple local papers – a *Herald*, a *Chronicle*, an *Argus*, a *Graphic*, an *Examiner* and a *Gazette* – and she'd winged off emails to various historical societies. A number of replies had come back, one of which – from the offices of the *Eastbourne Examiner* – had a photograph attached.

'Tell me about Wilfred,' said Tess.

Sally sipped her hot chocolate.

'He was a high-flyer,' she said. 'Throughout the thirties he's briefed in major case after major case. He's a fixture on the London legal scene. Often pitted against Norman Birkett. And a socialite, too. Throws big parties in the family home in Kensington. He's a rising star in the Labour Party, and a friend of Attlee. He's expected to launch a career in Westminster.'

'Then all at once, in 1942, he drops everything and goes to Lewes.'

'He leaves the Bar?'

'He leaves everything. Surprising everyone. He becomes a Deputy Coroner . . . it's a different career. The year before he's prosecuting the Camden Knifeman, the next he's ruling on a woman killed by a horse in Brighton. It's a huge downward shift in status. And he makes the move when his expectations couldn't have been higher. When he was poised for great things.'

'He made some kind of blunder. Something spectacular . . . and personal.'

'That's the rumour in the papers. Hinted at, not stated.'

'What could it be?'

'My view? Sex. If it was money or power – the other great spoilers – there'd have been a public scandal. It's the intimate stuff that always gets covered up.'

'And when he gets to Lewes?'

'It's the quiet life. No grand soirées. No politics. No board memberships.'

Tess frowned.

'How old was he? When he left the Bar?'

'Forty-two.'

Tess tried to imagine the decision. Sally was right: it was momentous. He'd started his new life just when he'd established the old one.

'What about Annette?'

'There's a parallel. She was a high-flyer in her own right.'

'What do you mean?'

'Even at sixteen she's in the papers. She's a member of the Kensington Light Operatic Society. At school she's a year-on-year prize-winner – for science and maths. She's a potential head girl. All that kind of thing. She wants to be a surgeon. And then, all because of her father, she has to start again in Lewes. But she never gets back into her stride.'

'Meaning?'

'There's a music society in Lewes. She doesn't join it. She wins no prizes at school. She doesn't even go to university. She just vanishes off the scene, only reappearing in the *Lewes Gazette* years later, when her engagement to the local vicar is announced.'

'Gilbert Merrington.'

'Yes.'

Tess didn't know a barrister who'd content themselves with a regional identity. Their sense of purpose is large. It might expand; but it never contracts.

'It wasn't listed in *The Times*?'

'No.'

Tess tried to imagine the upheaval. She pictured Wilfred explaining to Annette that he'd thought it was a good idea to change his career; that he'd always had a soft spot for Lewes. She must have stared back in disbelief.

'How old was Annette when she left Kensington?'

'Seventeen.'

'And when she married?'

'Nearly thirty.'

'And there's nothing in between, in the local press?'

'Nothing. Ever. Until her engagement. She married Gilbert in 1954. Richard's born in '56. And from then on, we see Annette's name beside her husband's. She's at a fête or a tombola or a memorial service. She's your regular vicar's wife.'

'And Wilfred?'

'He chugs along from one inquest to another.'

Tess gazed over the Thames. The river flowed darkly, absorbing splashes of street light all the way towards Barnes Bridge.

'What did she share with her father, apart from blood?'

'Disappointment.'

The word seemed to hang in the near-freezing air. Sally said:

'I know this is all imagination, but if you look at the newspaper entries – there are several references to Wilfred, and always because of some event to do with his son-in-law – he looks sad. He's never standing by his daughter. And she, too, looks sad, though in her case there's a hardness to her smiles. As if she'd paid a price.'

Sally finished her hot chocolate; it was cold by now.

'I can't prove this, but I sense Wilfred left his soul in London, and so did Annette. Wilfred's exile was his daughter's prison.'

166

Tess suddenly remembered why they were talking about the Merringtons at all.

'You've got a photograph,' she said. 'Can I see it?'

Sally took out her phone and tapped the screen. She then held it out towards Tess.

'Look at her left arm.'

The image was of a cutting from the *Brighton Herald*, dated the 4th of May 1990. An ageing Annette was standing beside the mayor of Eastbourne. While it was a grainy picture, it was a close-up. Mayor and vicar's wife were waving. And on Annette's left arm was the bracelet made by Manny Brewster.

'Elsie gave it to her daughter,' said Sally. 'This isn't a working hypothesis. It's a fact.'

32

'My lord, I call Narinda Hassan,' said Forde.

Tess had rung to say she was off to doorstep Hayley Townsend. Archie would take her place, she'd said. But Archie was still chasing the Tuesday Club. Benson turned, hoping to see the big man slip through the door with a report in his hand, but only Hassan entered, a slight figure about whom Benson had suspicions but no knowledge.

It was too late. Karen Lynwood was finished.

Here was Karen Lynwood's best friend. She'd suffered a severe crisis of conscience, whether to remain loyal and silent, or honour her public duty and speak out. In the end, she'd chosen to contact the police.

Benson listened from afar. Hassan was recounting how she'd met Karen during freshers' week in 1976; and how they'd become the closest of friends. Upon graduation, they'd found jobs with the same advertising agency in London. They'd worked on the same accounts. And when hard times had come along, they'd been there for each other. The most significant moments? Karen's three miscarriages. The struggle with depression afterwards . . . and her unhappy relationship with medication.

'I like to think I helped her,' said Hassan. 'The tablets made her feel worse. So we just talked. She'd call, often during the night . . . and I'd listen. That's all she needed, actually.'

'But what about John?'

'I'm afraid he was just too busy to appreciate what was happening.'

'Is that your opinion?'

'It's what Karen said to me at the time.'

'Do you remember the year?'

'Yes, 1983 . . . through to '85. Karen lost a child each year.'

'And what did Karen feel towards John?'

'She was angry. Very angry. But at the same time, she understood his situation. He was aiming for partner, and Hutton Pryce wanted his soul.'

Forde paused. And Benson, like the more attentive jurors, did the calculation. For John – according to Unwin – the problems had begun when Karen had begun that damned master's in psychotherapy. But for Karen – if Hassan could be trusted – the rot had set in within two years of getting married.

'How would you describe Karen's view of you, back then?'

Hassan didn't answer. Forde urged her on with a compassionate smile.

'She couldn't have made it without me.'

'She said that?'

'Yes.'

There was no doubting it. If Karen had any secrets, she'd told them to Narinda Hassan. And now she was telling the jury about Karen's near obsession with a patient. A doctor from Spain. She'd never met anyone who'd been so aware of his inner life; someone who'd listened to his deepest feelings and then tried to make sense of them. She said that most of the time she just let him speak, and she listened, not needing to prompt him or guide his thoughts. She couldn't stop thinking about him. His voice roused something deep in her.

'I asked her if she fancied him.'

'And?'

'She said she'd run off with him tomorrow – but I think she was joking.'

'We'll leave that to the jury, Miss Hassan.'

After the death of Dr Menderez, Karen had been shattered. For the first time, she wouldn't confide. She didn't call. She didn't seek support of any kind. In fact, she'd avoided Hassan. Ordinarily, they'd have gone out once or twice a month, but they hadn't seen each other since the day of the murder, when they'd gone to watch *Sunny Afternoon*, a musical about the Kinks. Hassan had discussed the situation with Brian Unwin.

'And that became the first of many conversations,' said Hassan. 'Because Brian had noticed that John was behaving oddly, too. We'd both been wondering why our best friends were suddenly unavailable. We'd begun to think the unthinkable. That Karen and John had been involved in a murder.'

If Hassan needed any confirmation that the unthinkable might, in fact, have happened, it was when Karen arrived at her flat in Kilburn late one night, a few weeks after Hassan had given her statement to the police.

'She was like she'd always been.'

'In what respect?'

'Very friendly. And apologetic about not having been in touch. But I felt very uncomfortable.'

'Why?'

'There was nothing to be friendly about. Not after I'd spoken to the police. And she wasn't meant to be in contact with me. She'd been told to leave me alone, and here she was, as if nothing had happened; as if there wasn't going to be a trial . . . and I wasn't going to give evidence for the prosecution.'

Hassan had said as much; and she'd referred to her statement. At which point Karen had said that's why she'd come. And, for friendship's sake, thinking of the old and better times, would she just hear her out?

'She swore she'd felt nothing for Dr Menderez. That she'd simply been fascinated by his story, and his desire to find the truth about himself. It wasn't often you got patients like that, she said, and she'd only been drawn along by his strength of character, which had disarmed her.'

'To which you replied?'

'That we shouldn't be talking to each other.'

'Go on.'

'And she said we had to talk to each other, because if I didn't qualify what I'd said—'

'"Qualify". Was that the word she used?'

'Yes. And others. She said if I didn't change . . . take back . . . what I'd said, she was going to spend years in prison and John would be convicted for a murder he hadn't committed.'

Hassan breathed in, and its stagger could be heard across the courtroom.

'I said I couldn't do what she was asking. All I'd done was repeat what she'd told me.'

Forced Confessions

'And then what happened? Please go on.'

'She said, "How much do you want?"'

Forde paused, her eye on the judge as he wrote down these critical words.

'What was your reply?'

'I said, "Nothing." And she said, "Ten thousand? Twenty thousand? We've got savings. You can have the lot. But please, please help us . . . help me survive this. Help me keep our family together."'

'And what did you say?'

'I told her to leave.'

'And did she?'

'Yes.'

'Saying anything?'

'Yes. That she'd never forgive me.'

'That's a lot to remember, Miss Hassan. How can you be sure of Karen's words?'

'I wrote them down after she'd gone, on a gas bill, and then I rang the police. Immediately.'

Forde handed a sheet of paper to an usher, who gave it to Hassan.

'Is this the document to which you're referring?'

'Yes.'

'My lord, you'll find a photocopy on page fifty-six of File B.'

'Thank you, Miss Forde.'

'No further questions.'

33

'I didn't keep it, right? I chucked it.'

Hayley Townsend sat on the other side of a coffee table in a high-rise flat in Stoke Newington. Her mum, Jane Ryman, was on her left, and Danny Beaumont, her stepfather, was on her right. They sat on the sofa, in a line, facing Tess. They were all chewing gum. Above them, on the wall, was a glossy picture of Manhattan at night. Skyscrapers. Bright lights. The Big Time.

'Where?'

'In a skip.'

'Where was the skip?'

'In the street.'

'Which street?'

Danny leaned forward, massaging his hands.

'She doesn't have to answer your questions, right?'

'No, Danny, but she'll have to talk to the police.'

'Police?'

'Yes. They'll be here, too, soon enough. I'm just faster off the mark. Maybe I can help you. Which street?'

'Down there.' Hayley waved in the direction of North London. 'I can't remember which one.'

'Did you try to use the camera?'

'Nah.'

'Why not?'

'It was too complicated, like.'

'Did you manage to turn it on?'

'Yeah.'

'Did you see any of the images . . . you know, the pictures that had been taken?'

'Nah. Never. I just pressed a few buttons and thought, I better shift this. Get rid of it. So I went out and—'

'Binned it.'

'Yeah.'

'Why not throw it in the—'

'You're calling her a liar, aren't you?'

'No, Danny, I think Hayley is scared. I understand why. Jane, can I have coffee? White no sugar.'

Mother and daughter were both in black leggings. Both wore large T-shirts. Both had their hair held up with clips. Both had strong make-up round their eyes. Danny wore spotless white trainers. The loose tracksuit bottoms reminded Tess of prison clothing. He'd gelled his hair back.

'Did Karl bring the camera here, Hayley?'

'Yeah.'

'She was alone, right?' said Danny.

The kettle whistled and clicked.

'We' – he nodded towards the kitchen – 'was out, okay, and when we got back, Karl had gone, and I told her to throw it, and she did, the next day. She's clean.'

'We're on the even, Miss de Vere,' said Jane, coming back into the room. 'We don't want no trouble.'

She handed Tess a mug, filled to the brim. She'd brought a biscuit, too. A digestive.

'I just want you to understand why I'm here,' said Tess. 'A man's in more trouble than you've ever dreamed of. So's his wife. The two of them are staring jail-time in the face. And the man who's dead, well, he's a mystery. If he took some pictures, and those pictures helped us understand him better, well, we might be able to help the people charged with his murder. We're talking serious trouble, Jane. And these people say they're innocent.'

Jane looked over at Danny, and then she sat back down on the sofa. They were in line again, all of them chewing and watching and saying nothing. When Tess had finished her biscuit, Jane looked at Danny again, and then she said:

'Do you do landlord stuff? You know, against the council?'

'Yes.'

'Do you do it for nothing?'

'Now and then. What's your problem?'

173

Danny jigged a thumb towards the light.

'The windows.'

'What about them?'

'They're shagged.'

34

Sarah Appleton was paying.

She'd invited Merrington to lunch at the Goring in Belgravia. When in public, some primitive impulse to protect and preserve his interests always led him towards a corner, from where he could look out on everyone else. On this occasion he'd plumped for the chair by a wall, at its intersection with a heavy curtain. He felt comfortably safe. Sarah had her back to the hotel's sumptuous dining room.

'I'm so very lucky,' she said.

A waiter leaned forward and poured some Chablis into Merrington's glass. He swished it around, tested the nose, and then nodded. Not tasting it showed he knew his onions. He'd seen that on telly. The waiter withdrew.

'Rex is completely behind me. Always has been. Like you and Pamela.' Her eyes caught Merrington's. 'We wouldn't be where we are without them.'

'You can say that again.'

Sarah cleared her throat.

'The two of us are lucky. But we're going to need more than luck if we're to take this country forward, in the direction we need to go. Do you take my meaning?'

'I do.'

'But first off, we're going to need loyalty. And solidarity. A shared vision. At the highest level. We can't make the necessary changes unless we're all pulling in the same direction.'

'I couldn't agree more.'

Why the hell would Tess de Vere, a solicitor, and a solicitor linked to Benson, be taking photographs of my grandmother's bracelet?

'We have to act.'

'We do.'

'The PM is finished. We both know why. Brexit has brought the kiss of death to a passionate European. A fresh approach is needed.'

But where did I lose it? And how would that tie in with a crime?

Sarah was looking at Merrington earnestly. She really cared. This was her chance to make a difference. She'd weighed up the likely impact on herself, Rex and the children. She'd listened to those closest to her. She'd been urged on by Jos Fowler. The difficult task was persuading people like Merrington to stand aside. That was why she'd picked the Goring. Sarah was more of a bistro girl. But needs must.

'There are other contenders,' she said. 'They're not like you. They're not like me.'

She moved her glass to one side.

'They're clever. They've got ideas. They're hugely talented.'

'But?'

'They're in it for themselves. Sometimes, I wonder if politics is, for them, a glorified playground. With playground glories to be won. That's not what we need. Not now, not ever. We need the old sense of public service, without thought of reward.'

Crimes are investigated by the police. Not solicitors. So what the hell was going on? If de Vere is on to a crime, it's with a view to informing the police. She's building a case. But against whom?

'As I say, we have to act. And quickly. Because if we don't, they will.'

'I agree.'

Sarah moved the glass back to where it had been.

'You are an obvious candidate.'

'Me?'

'Yes.'

'Well, obvious isn't necessarily what we need.'

'Come now, Richard, we have to—'

Sarah held her breath. Merrington had raised his hand as if to stop advancing traffic. He pointed at Sarah's glass.

'That wine is like you.'

Sarah smiled. She liked Merrington's jokes. His puzzling openers.

'Go on.'

'It's mature. Sharp on the edges, with a deep and promising allure.'

'Stop being silly.'

'The aftertaste is fresh and clean. It sings all the right notes.'

'You haven't even tried it.'

'I don't need to. I know its quality from a sniff and glance. And I've known you for ten years. No, stop, Sarah, I want you to listen to me. You're junior, I accept that. You've not held one of the top jobs. And I admit, I've been approached.'

'I'm not surprised.'

'And I'll also admit I thought about it.'

'Again, I'm not surprised.'

'But . . .'

'Tell me, please.'

Merrington frowned. He glanced over Sarah's shoulder as if to check the horizon.

'Do you know the psalms?'

'I love them.'

'Well, I don't know which number it is – and I wouldn't

say this to anyone else, and I want this to remain between you and me . . .'

'Of course.'

'Well, there's a line somewhere about, Lord, my heart is not proud, nor haughty my eyes . . . I have not gone after things too great for a wretch like me. Or is that a hymn? I can't remember. But the point is, I don't want the cup. I wouldn't like the taste. If it came in my direction, I'd let it pass.'

Crime? What kind of crime? And who was the victim? If de Vere had gone to Shipton's she must know that it was made for his grandmother. Why hadn't she contacted Merrington's office? Why the secrecy?

'I don't know what to say.'

'I do. This is your chance. Now is the moment. Don't let the bully boys decide what happens to Britain.'

Sarah moved her glass again.

'I have been approached too,' she said quietly.

'Good.'

'I'm told I'll garner support.'

'You have mine already.'

'Truly?'

'Look, we're at a pivotal moment in history. I can't think of a comparable time since Churchill said, "We shall fight them on the beaches." He wasn't the obvious choice to lead either, by the way. They all thought he was past it. And you haven't even started.'

And by the time this business is over, Sarah, you'll be finished. As will Rex. The existence of his secret child – a boy, apparently – will be revealed. Your in-laws, who never much liked you, will say it's your fault. And your own two children will never be the same again. They'll be bullied in the playground and no amount of vigilance by the staff will protect them. For playgrounds are nasty places, actually. There's not much glory to be found, infant-ile or otherwise.

'Richard, if I put myself forward . . . If I can survive the criticism and scrutiny, and win, I'd want you in the Foreign Office. You'd show Britain's best face to the world. Is that a cup you'd take? For me? For the country?'

Merrington raised an eyebrow, and slowly.

'Let me think on it. This is not a conversation I expected to have.'

He picked up his glass.

'As I said, this moment is bigger than all of us. We have to get it right. In every way. Shall we drink to that?'

'With pleasure.'

The crystal clinked two notes, perfectly in tune. They were still singing when Sarah said:

'It's psalm one-three-one, by the way.'

35

'Miss Hassan, how long have you known Karen Lynwood?'

'Forty-one years.'

'You mentioned a conversation in which Karen asked you to change your testimony for money.'

'Yes.'

'How long did that exchange last?'

Hassan gave a shrug.

'Less than a minute.'

'Could you guess the number of seconds?'

'Forty . . . fifty.'

Benson wrote the numbers down.

'I want to make something clear, Miss Hassan. The personal history you have revealed about Karen Lynwood today is true – subject to two matters. The first is the nature of the attachment you had discerned between Karen and Dr Menderez, and we'll deal with that now. Did Karen tell you she was having an affair?'

'No.'

'Did you ask her if she was having an affair?'

'No.'

'Did you suspect her of having an affair?'

'No.'

'The most we can conclude is that Karen had become fascinated by a fascinating man with a fascinating story to tell?'

'Yes, I accept that.'

'Thank you. That leaves the second matter. The alleged offer of money. And I'll be blunt with you, Miss Hassan: I will say to this jury that you have told forty-one years of truth and forty seconds of lies. Maybe fifty. The question is to what end.'

'I did not lie.'

Benson felt a tug on his gown. He turned, and there was Archie, leaning forward with an envelope in his hand.

'One moment, my lord.'

'Take your time, Mr Benson.'

Archie whispered: 'They've found barely anything. I wrote down the bones of it.'

Benson read the brief notes.

'My lord, may I take instructions?'

'Please do.'

Benson went to the dock and summoned Mr Lynwood. He came forward, frowning, and Benson spoke slowly and quietly, ensuring Karen heard nothing.

'You've got a choice to make about which secrets you're going to keep.'

36

His Honour Judge Stanfield politely intervened. Now was an appropriate time to rise, he said. The witness could do with a rest, and Benson's cross-examination could commence after the lunch break, which would also give him time to discuss matters with his clients. The case was adjourned until 2 p.m. Tess caught all this on entering Number 3 Court. But she didn't catch Benson. And he didn't discuss matters with his clients. He left them alone, vanishing into the Bar Mess. Instead, with Archie heading back to chambers, Tess drafted a letter to the Hackney Council Housing Department and she sent an email to Larry Pickering, the founder of EmCheck Ltd. At 1.45 p.m. she went back to court. Benson was standing at the dock. Mr Lynwood gave a quick nod – one of consent. So did Mrs Lynwood. Then she looked away, head held high.

'I've taken instructions on this, Miss Hassan, and I understand Karen has literally told you all her secrets. Do you doubt her?'

'No, I don't. We were very close.'

'Does she know yours?'

'Yes.'

'All of them?'

'Well, as I stand here, I can't think of anything I've hidden.'

'Try again. There's no rush.'

Hassan looked at the judge and then at her hands. She'd raised them to show there was nothing there.

'Yes, I told Karen everything.'

'Did you tell her about your father's illness?'

'Yes.'

'The small tumour in the posterior fossa? And the haemorrhage that killed him two weeks after the diagnosis?'

'Yes, Mr Benson, I shared that with Karen.'

'By that stage, you were already the best of friends?'

'Yes.'

'This tragedy – and I'm sorry to mention it – it happened in 1976? During your first term at university?'

'That's right.'

'When you were also friends with John?'

'Yes.'

'Did you share it with him, too?'

'I did.'

'And he told you about the death of his parents the year before, in 1975?'

'He did, yes.'

'That was a remarkable coincidence, wasn't it? This shared experience of brutal, sudden grief?'

'It was.'

'He supported you and you supported him?'

'Yes.'

'Had Karen met John at this stage?'

'No.'

'So – as I understand it – you knew John and Karen, but Karen didn't know John.'

'Correct.'

'Did you tell Karen about John?'

'I don't think so . . . not in the early days.'

'You didn't tell your best friend about this guy who'd lost his entire family? And that he was helping you get by?'

'No, I didn't.' Hassan turned to the judge. 'These aren't secrets. This is just how things were. We were all getting to know each other.'

Benson said:

'Did you tell Karen that John was your boyfriend?'

'No. Because he wasn't. We were just friends.'

'Did you sleep with John?'

Forde rose instantly.

'My lord, I'd like to know where this line of questioning is going.'

'My lord, I'd like to show my learned friend. The issue is Miss Hassan's credibility.'

'Proceed, Mr Benson. But I warn you, do so carefully.'

Benson instantly resumed his questioning:

'Did you sleep with John?'

Even before she spoke Narinda Hassan seemed to lose her dignity. That's what happens, thought Tess. In a courtroom, all questioning about sex is a kind of theft.

'Yes.'

'Did you tell Karen?'

'No. And I don't see why I should have done, or why you present what I kept private as some kind of secret. John and Karen weren't going out with each other . . . at the time they hadn't even met.'

'When did you last sleep with John?'

The question, delivered quickly, struck Hassan like a punch. Her mouth opened slightly, but there was no sound, as happens with blinding, unexpected pain.

'Did you tell Karen all your secrets, Miss Hassan?'

She'd begun to breathe again, in quick snatches. Benson said:

'According to John, you last slept together in 1985. Is that right?'

Hassan looked down. After a moment, Judge Stanfield said:

'Please answer the question.'

'Yes, that's true. And I didn't tell Karen.'

'And who would blame you?' said Benson. 'Karen was reeling from a sequence of miscarriages.'

Hassan nodded.

'I wanted to, but I felt so terribly guilty.'

'Because you were having an affair with her husband?'

'It wasn't an affair . . . it was . . . a sequence of mistakes. Dreadful mistakes.'

'When did they begin?'

'1984.'

'Where did they take place?'

'At my flat. During his lunch hour.'

Benson's voice was a reluctant monotone.

'By day you were sleeping with John and by night you were comforting Karen. Is that a fair description of '84 to '85?'

Hassan swallowed hard.

'May I have some water?'

'Of course.'

But she didn't touch it. After a pause Benson put the question again, with an inflection of regret.

'It is. And I'm not proud of myself.'

She covered her face with both hands. 'I'm so sorry, Karen. I'm so sorry.'

The words were muffled by her fingers. Her shoulders began to heave. And the judge suggested a break.

'Miss Hassan, I have no intention to humiliate you,' said Benson, twenty minutes later. 'And I am not in any way suggesting what happened was thoughtless or cheap. On the contrary, I'm pointing to another tragedy. For the Lynwoods, and for you. A tragedy that I have to bring to the attention of the jury. Because the truth of the matter is this: you've never stopped loving John Lynwood.'

Tess felt sick. For Hassan. Benson had her trapped. Deny she loved John, and she'd been an alley cat. Accept it, and . . . well, where would that lead?

'I did feel for something for John.'

'You've felt something for John from the moment he started going out with Karen.'

'It's all too long ago.'

'*You* turned John down and then *he* turned to Karen. That's what happened, isn't it?'

'Yes. That's why I said we never went out.'

'But that was your big mistake, Miss Hassan. You had the chance. And you let John go. Face it: you were struggling with a crisis, and when it was over you realised what you'd done.'

Tess, like the jury, remembered the evidence of Dr Evington: that we are all capable of forming deep attachments that can endure for years on end; that friends and family wouldn't even know; even the person to whom we are attached. They can thrive on secrecy.

'And in 1984 to 1985, only three years after John and Karen were married, you found yourself where you longed to be, only it was too late now.'

'Yes.'

'And John – let's be clear – he wasn't going to leave Karen, was he?'

'No.'

'Things couldn't last. You were picked up, and you were dropped. By John Lynwood. While his wife was indisposed.'

Hassan nodded.

'And as much as you were confused, you were angry. You were angry then, and you're angry now.'

'Yes.'

'And you were angry when Karen – your best friend, who knew absolutely nothing – was standing in your flat, begging you to save her marriage. And her family. The family you didn't have.'

'Yes, Mr Benson.'

'She didn't seriously offer you money. It was just an expression and you know it. She said take our savings, take every penny we've got, but take back the lies.'

Hassan didn't reply. Benson left her to think, but the judge, eventually, required an answer:

'Is that how it was, Miss Hassan?'

She opened her hands again – the hands that had held no secrets from Karen – and she looked over to the dock, at the friend who was staring resolutely at the floor, her hair hanging forward to hide her face.

'I'm sorry, Karen,' she said. 'So very, very sorry.'

'Miss Hassan, please answer my question,' said Judge Stanfield.

'Mr Benson is wrong.'

'In which respect?'

'I *am* cheap. Dirt cheap.' She addressed Forde. 'Mr Benson is right, too. I told forty seconds of lies. Maybe fifty. Can I go now?'

37

On his way into the Royal Marsden Benson passed an elderly woman with bloodshot eyes. A few yards down the corridor, he turned around because she'd smiled at him, as if in recognition. The woman had stopped to turn, too; as had the younger woman with her. By younger, Benson thought late forties, early fifties. She didn't smile, however. On the contrary, she looked disturbed, and was urging her charge to get a move on. Moments later, they were outside on the pavement, their backs to him. A taxi had pulled up and the driver was opening the passenger door. An image flickered in Benson's mind, but then it vanished. There was something about that younger, troubled woman. Benson had seen her before, but he couldn't place where, or when. He shrugged and bought himself a chicken sandwich.

*   *   *

Helen was crying.

Benson sat at her side and took her hand.

'I don't want to die,' she said. 'I want to live.'

'And I don't want you to go.'

Benson felt the bony attempt at pressure around his fingers. She was weakening. Her spirit was ebbing away. He looked at the floor, as if expecting to see a large pool of fight and fluorescence spreading around her bed, its glamour slowly drying. How could all that vitality simply disappear? Where was it going? He looked back at what was left – a face in tears. He moved to wipe them away, calling for a nurse to help him with the breathing helmet, but Helen spoke emphatically:

'Leave them. They'll dry.'

She was looking at him with shining pride, and it was agonising, because this was part of the farewell.

'You're early,' she said.

'Stanfield sent us away for the weekend. Forde's experts aren't available until Monday.'

Helen gave another weak squeeze.

'As a rule, I'd rather you came later . . . is that all right?'

'Certainly. I'm sorry.'

'No, no. It's just . . . I'm tired. And I want to be ready for you. You don't look well. What's wrong?'

What's wrong? Benson couldn't bear to look through that plastic dome, to see Helen on the other side, out of reach, already in a place where no one else could go. He couldn't look at her knowing she'd soon be gone, and that these desperate moments together, these horribly simple times, were all that was left to them. And to think, only a few days ago he'd thought her going would be his release. She tugged his hand.

'Tell me.'

'I feel cheap and dirty, that's all.'

'Narinda Hassan?'

'Yes.'

Helen nodded.

'I heard about that.'

'Who from?'

'Oh, one of the nurses . . . and on the news. Tomorrow, she'll be torn apart. Just as you'll be elevated.'

'I know.'

Benson had suspected there'd been some history between John Lynwood and Hassan. That he'd denied even going out with her – when it was the most natural thing to have happened – suggested their association hadn't been entirely Platonic. Archie's people had found someone from their Bristol days who'd known them as an intense couple always talking about death and Dostoevsky. That's all Benson had needed to contradict John and make him choose whether to help his wife or not.

'You made a very difficult decision. Not many would have gone there.'

Helen didn't mean the destruction of Hassan. She meant bringing down John Lynwood in the eyes of the jury. By forcing Hassan to admit she felt dirty, Benson had revealed that John was filthy, too. And now his wife stood accused of having cheated on her husband.

'It was the only way to give Karen a chance,' said Benson. 'I might be able to save her.'

'I agree. But you've made it even harder to save John. Maybe you can't.'

The blue disc rattled in its tube. Up it went; and down it came.

'Soon, we won't be able to do this,' said Helen.

'I know.'

They didn't say any more. And Benson wanted to shout out in protest. With one hand he held on to Helen; with the other he gripped his chicken sandwich. Where was the dignity in that? The alignment of moment?

'We won't play billiards.'

'Or poker.'

'We won't slag off new appointments to the Bench.'

'Or the fools who should never have taken silk.'

Helen smiled.

'We won't drink too much.'

'Or walk too little.'

She'd never been one for exercise. Her idea of urban callisthenics was heading out to buy cigars from a corner shop.

'We won't argue any more.'

'Don't, Helen.'

'We won't worry over our cases.'

'Stop.'

'I won't be here to help you.'

This time it was Benson who shared some pressure: he brought her knuckles together, and they held on to each other like two people waiting to jump from a bridge. Only there was no elastic to bring them swinging back, laughing at the spurt of terror transformed into excitement. With a kind of deliberation, Helen took back her hand.

'Tell me about your mother,' she said. 'Tell me what your trial did to Lizzie.'

38

Friday night was, of course, Monopoly night. So Benson went to the old people's home off Old Nichol Street where Archie's father, CJ, aged ninety-eight, presided over the game, and the bank, from his wheelchair in a roasting-hot parlour.

Archie's sisters, Betsy, Dot, Eileen and Joyce, were already at the table, as was Molly, and Archie was pouring the tea. Benson took his place, but his mind was trapped in the Royal Marsden.

Camberley had been relentless, drawing out of him details he'd never been able to mention, save once, to Abasiama.

'Hide nothing, Will,' she'd said.

At the time of Benson's trial, his mother had already been a shattered woman. Ever since Eddie, his younger brother, had suffered a traumatic brain injury. That had been ten years earlier. He'd just turned nine. A bike accident. He'd been left in a wheelchair, unable to remember what had happened.

'She developed a kind of shake,' Benson had said of his mother. 'Her hands trembled and her head made this tiny nodding motion. It looked like she was agreeing with everything you said, but her nerves were just shot.'

She'd blamed herself for Eddie's accident. For letting him play too far from home. She'd say that, nodding and trembling, telling his dad it was her fault, and not his. She'd been the same during Benson's trial: he'd seen her nodding at the prosecutor's speech, knowing she couldn't stop herself. And then, after the verdict, she'd collapsed.

'I heard this noise, and my dad was leaning over . . . she'd just fallen onto this woman, a tourist or something.'

Archie nudged him.

'It's your turn.'

'Try and keep out of jail,' said Eileen.

It was an old joke, cracked every Friday. They all prayed fervently that Benson would land on GO TO JAIL. They clapped and whooped when he did. They'd only ever sell a 'Get Out of Jail Free' card for a fortune.

Benson threw the dice. They tumbled and bounced.

'I can still see her in the public gallery, hyperventilating in the arms of this stranger,' he'd said. 'The Harbetons are

189

punching the air. Her hands are flapping and my dad's trying to catch them. The judge is calling for order and the guards are holding me back . . . three years later she's dead. Cancer.' Benson had pulled at his collar. 'Eddie's accident? It took her mind. The trial? It killed her.'

Benson felt a kick under the table. From Betsy.

'Pay up,' she said, biting into an almond slice.

The girls were all laughing. CJ was asleep. And Archie was frowning.

'That'll be two hundred quid,' said Joyce.

He'd landed on INCOME TAX.

Benson looked at the dice and then the board. He surveyed the opportunities and the hazards, the squares reserved for luck, good and bad. He picked up his token, the boot.

'You got a right old kick in the teeth there, didn't you?' said Dot.

Benson stood up and reached for his duffel coat.

'Yes, I did. Goodnight.'

And he left them to it.

What was Helen doing?

She hadn't been high on morphine. She'd hadn't been confused by pain. She'd had plenty of oxygen. But for the second time she'd insisted on visiting the past; not the trial, but Benson's former life, the life that he'd lost. But why? The question ate away at him, through the night and into Saturday. It was there while he read the papers, skipping past the photographs of Narinda Hassan, head bowed with a hand shielding her face. It was there, biting hard, while he rummaged through a green sack of waste – pushing aside empty tins, sticky eggshells, a broken cup, pizza crusts, burnt porridge and tea bags – in search of Tess de Vere's handkerchief. It was there while he washed and ironed it. And it was there on Sunday evening as he prepared to cross-examine Dr Grace da Costa, the lead scene of crime officer, and Dr Tariq Masood, a highly experienced pathologist who'd written extensively on sharp force injuries. On Monday morning, heading up to Number 3 Court, and a possible tussle with da Costa, Benson still had no answer, only a certain dread that these excursions weren't over. Which was why he'd kept away from the Royal Marsden.

Where were they leading? Towards his own deceit? Had she glimpsed his lies? Was the endpoint his own confession?

Oh God, don't let that happen, thought Benson.

Da Costa – wiry, with large glasses – was telling the jury where the murder had occurred and where the screw from the first defendant's glasses had been found. She was pointing at diagrams and nodding at photographs.

Don't do this, dear God, I beg you. Don't let Helen's last words to me be words of disappointment.

'Mr Benson?' said Judge Stanfield. 'The witness is waiting.'

'Would you look at Exhibit one, please?'

Da Costa did.

'This is a photograph of Dr Menderez as he was found, beneath the staircase in Foxton's Warehouse.'

'Yes. I took it.'

'Do you see the red cross?'

'Yes.'

'That's where Karl Ambrose stood when he reached over to touch the body.'

Da Costa adjusted her glasses and checked one of her own diagrams – Exhibit 10.

'This is where the screw was found. Exhibit five.'

'It is, Doctor. Would you now consider Exhibit two? This is a floor plan of Fifty-nine Limehouse Cut and Foxton's Warehouse.'

'I see that.'

191

'The lines drawn in red indicate the route taken by Karl Ambrose, from when he entered the warehouse to when he—'

'Oh dear, he literally walked all over the crime scene,' said da Costa, grimacing.

'He did.'

'Including the spot where the killing took place.'

'And where my client admits to having stood when he argued with Dr Menderez.'

Dr da Costa readily accepted that while the screw could have fallen to the ground in the warehouse – as the prosecution maintained – it could also have happened in the house, where the argument had occurred, and then been transferred by Ambrose to the place where it had been found.

Theoretically.

Shown a photograph from the unused material of a partial footprint left behind in the warehouse – of a Levi's boot – she agreed the tread pattern on the sole could easily pick up the screw and drop it elsewhere.

Like a pair of tweezers, she said.

And what about a pair of scissors, asked Benson, just before he sat down. Had any been found at the premises?

No. Da Costa had looked. And her team had checked bins in the surrounding area. Without success.

39

There is something unsavoury about defence work, thought Tess. Exhilaration can come at a moment when you ought to weep. If justice mattered. But Tess couldn't conceal her delight. For all she knew, the Lynwoods were guilty, but Benson had brought a double acquittal within reach.

'We're in a good position, Will,' she said.

'You can say that again,' added Archie.

The court had risen for lunch. They were in the Viaduct Tavern on Newgate, a former prison and gin palace, at a table with a view onto the street. The room was a palace of etched mirrors and arched windows and Victorian wall lamps.

'You're putting distance between John and Menderez,' said Tess. 'And Karen's almost in the clear. If Harriet Kilbride can remember—'

'She hasn't been found yet,' said Benson flatly. 'How did you get on with Hayley Townsend?'

Tess accepted the rebuff with a glance at Archie.

'I came away with a case for breach of covenant to repair.'

'And a camera?'

'No. But I doubt if Hayley binned it. I think her stepfather's got it. He knows what we're after, which suggests he might have seen the pictures, and can tell us what he saw, otherwise—'

'He's taking you for a ride, Tess,' said Archie. 'He just wants something for nothing.'

'I'll sort out the ingress of wind and rain, and we'll see what happens.'

'What about Tindale?' said Benson.

They were surrounded by light and reflected light. But Benson sat in his own private darkness. His features were impossible to read. There was no emotion there: no pleasure at the progress of the case, or discomfort for having wounded Hassan, or anxiety for exposing John Lynwood's betrayal or distress at the thought of Helen's dying, or gratitude for the devotion of Archie. Tess was sure he felt these things, but they were lost to the world. The rise and fall of feeling happened somewhere behind the wall he'd built in prison. The place from which a trial usually freed him, if only for a few days.

And there was no awareness of the person opposite, sipping a double gin and tonic. He'd once begged her to look after his soul.

I can bring it back to you, she thought; but she said:

'You were right. Her husband's name was mentioned in the press. And that gave me a lead.'

Tess had pursued it over the weekend. Edward Tindale, along with John Lynwood's parents, had been killed on Thursday the 10th of July 1975 on their way to Edgbaston for the first Test between England and Australia. The accident had been covered in many papers because Edward had been a journalist of note during the fifties, reporting on Franco's Spain. He'd tracked the changes with a sensitive eye, but he'd been partisan. Which was how he'd met Isabel Delegado, herself a journalist on *El Testigo*, a paper considered to be the mouthpiece of the government.

'They moved to London and Isabel got a job at Senate House Library. But she kept up the writing, here and in Spain. Remember, this is the Cold War. And Franco might have been a dictator and a fascist, but he was anti-communist. So he's backed by the West. And papers like *El Testigo*.'

Tess had found a biographical sketch of Mrs Tindale, prepared for a conference organised by the Spanish Embassy. It transpired she'd been a speaker at various symposia dedicated, in effect, to the rehabilitation of Spain after the Second World War, during which, of course, Hitler and Mussolini had been Franco's political friends, rather than Churchill or Roosevelt. She'd been a living witness, recounting her experience of events that had scarred the national memory. She'd been a strong supporter of the regime. For Mrs Tindale, the Generalísimo had saved the nation from the horrors that had befallen Poland and Czechoslovakia and Romania – all those great, ancient cultures whose people had found themselves staring at Soviet concrete Realism. And the Gulag.

'That's about it,' said Tess. 'She's a child during the Civil War, she marries Edward – who is friends with John Lynwood's parents – and she builds a life in the UK. She's widowed in her mid-forties and then becomes the mother John had lost, and the mother-in-law Karen would rather not have had. Nothing much there to help you, I'm afraid.'

'There's a little,' said Benson.

He looked onto Newgate and the passers-by. Bankers, secretaries, wideboys, tourists. He viewed them as he viewed Tess. They were just there, crossing his line of sight.

'Which is?'

'Mrs Tindale sees things the same way as Menderez did . . . or rather how his parents did. Not everyone viewed Franco as their saviour. Ask the families of the exiled and the disappeared. Or the hundred thousand dead. Avoiding the Gulag came at a price.'

'How does that advance our case?'

Benson's monotone was almost eerie:

'We have a stronger sense of the world Menderez and his family came from. He grew up with people like Mrs Tindale telling him about a real and terrifying past. Telling him what had been done and why. This was the winners talking. The side that went the extra mile to make sure Spain stayed a safe place to bring up a family. That's what Menderez did, remember. He spent twenty-five years in a maternity clinic.'

Archie spoke:

'Look, I left school at fifteen. I don't know much about history. We only ever did the Tudors and Stuarts. And I haven't even been to Tenerife . . . that's Spain, isn't it? Right. Well, help me understand what you're on about. Because, to be honest, I'm lost.'

Tess leaned back. A waiter had brought toasted sand-
wiches to the table. After he'd gone, Benson turned his plate
around, as if to view things from another angle. Then he
said:

'If Karen didn't get involved with Menderez—'

'But she did.'

'Archie, if she didn't – that's called a premise; and it's our
instructions – if she didn't, then all this background material
is a factor we can't ignore. Menderez had some very dark
memories passed on to him. He flew in from Madrid and
he passed them on to Robert Graynor and he then passed
them on to Karen Lynwood. And during their final session
together, I think he disclosed whatever he'd done in Spain
. . . it flowed out of all this inherited suffering and confusion;
for Menderez, it was the climax. But we're not simply dealing
with an aftermath. He came to London because of unfinished
business—'

'And you think it might have something to do with this
Civil War? Nailing priests to doors and that?'

'What I think doesn't matter, Archie. What matters are
the facts that come our way. We have to make sense of them,
see if there's any connection to what happened. And in this
case, Menderez was killed—'

'Because he got fresh with Karen Lynwood.'

'I give up, Archie.'

'Don't, Rizla. I'm just getting started.'

He'd done it: Archie had made Benson laugh. And then
Benson ate something. A glance found Tess and he smiled,
but from far away, and then Archie got stuck in, giving his
view about the next witness, the last in the case, the pathologist Dr Tariq Masood. He didn't think he was that
important. Neither did Tess. But Benson, once more considering the world as it passed him by, said they were both
quite wrong.

40

'How do you know the injury was caused by a pair of scissors?'

'It's the "Z" shape, Miss Forde. Which is what we find when the blades are closed. Had they been open, the wound would have been hard to distinguish from a knife attack.'

'How many blows were struck?'

'One.'

'Where was the point of entry?'

'The nape of the neck, so the assailant probably came from behind.'

'The depth of the wound?'

'Six centimetres.'

'Striking?'

'The medulla oblongata.'

'Which is?'

'Part of the brainstem: the inferior portion that blends into the spinal cord.'

'Its function?'

'There are many, Miss Forde. We're talking Clapham Junction. Multiple nerve tracts come together, ascending and descending, so this small area controls heart rate, breathing, swallowing . . . numerous vital processes.'

'And if it's compromised?'

'You die.'

'How quickly?'

'In this case, I'd say within a minute. But the victim would have been incapacitated immediately.'

Benson, taking notes, underlined that last word. If John Lynwood arrived at the house shortly after 9.22 p.m., and there was no argument between him and Menderez, just a rapid, violent confrontation, then he had plenty of time to move the body, pocket the scissors, access the SIM card, snatch the house keys and run . . . which is what the CCTV showed at 9.44 p.m. The footage was damning, communicating the swiftness of everything that must have happened, and the panic that had gripped a man who was wondering what the hell to do next.

Benson frowned.

'When two people have an argument ending in a fatal stabbing, we ordinarily find multiple wounds, some deeper than others, along with defensive injuries to the hands?'

'Yes.'

'And the nature of those injuries can tell us a great deal about the emotional state of the killer?'

'Certainly.'

'An angry man is likely to stab his victim more than once, and aim for the thorax or neck?'

'Usually, yes.'

Benson looked at one of the autopsy photographs. A thick bundle had been prepared for the trial. They portrayed the gradual and almost total reduction of Dr Menderez, from a naked man to his constituent elements. When preparing the case, Benson had stared at them, sickened at the destruction and the irony. This minute investigation into the brain of Dr Menderez got no one any closer to the one thing the court needed to know: what he'd been thinking.

'How long was the medulla oblongata?'

'Three point two centimetres.'

'A very small target?'

'Indeed. But I never said it was a target.'

'We'll come to that. It was struck once?'

'Yes.'

'With considerable force?'

'Yes.'

'And with speed?'

'Yes.'

'In relation to the track of the wound, did you find any evidence of hesitation?'

'None.'

Benson flicked through the bundle of glossy images, pausing halfway through.

'There were no defensive injuries, active or passive, to the hands?'

'No. Which supports my view that Dr Menderez was struck from behind.'

'Which suggests he didn't expect the attack.'

'That's a fair assumption.'

Benson flicked towards the front.

'The angle of entry. Does this tell us anything about the position of Dr Menderez's head?'

'Yes, I think it does. He was looking down. Assuming a horizonal thrust, I'd say about forty-five degrees . . . as if reading a book.'

'Or making a telephone call? In the circumstances, that's more likely.'

'Yes. I'd accept that. But we don't know, do we?'

Benson put the photographs down with a sigh.

'At the time he was killed, Dr Menderez was wearing a heavy woollen overcoat?'

'Yes. Along with a casual jacket, a shirt and a vest. Which is quite peculiar, really, because I understand he'd got home at seven-ish . . . so I don't know why he kept his coat on.'

'It's even more peculiar that whoever killed him aimed for the head, and did so with a single thrust.'

'Yes, I agree, Mr Benson. I know of only three cases in the reported literature.'

'The killer must have known that attempting to penetrate

several layers of clothing would increase resistance to a blade.'

'That's a very good point, Mr Benson.'

'And it was an impulsive attack, I suggest, because it appears the killer used scissors found in the house. There were three knives and a meat cleaver in the kitchen. But they remained in the drawer. This killer reached for an object close at hand when Dr Menderez turned his back, perhaps to make a call. Is there anything in your report that would contradict such a scenario?'

'No.'

'Dr Masood, you didn't use the word target. I did. And I did so because whoever killed Dr Menderez knew what they were doing. As Dr Menderez turned his back – to make a call, or cry, or drop his head in despair: as you say, we'll never know – this individual made an informed, snap decision. Assuming it was a man, he aimed for a specific anatomical target, and he acted with precision, speed and force.'

'What are you suggesting, Mr Benson?'

'I'm saying whoever attacked Dr Menderez was experienced. They'd been trained. This was a professional killing.'

41

A professional killing. Tess turned the words over in her mind. This is what Benson had been planning to argue from the moment he'd read the autopsy report. It was why he'd insisted on a detailed defence statement: he was capitalising on the little evidence they had.

He was extraordinary.

But there were certain problems that even he could not

overcome. For the remainder of the day, and well into the next morning, Forde guided Detective Inspector Sue Harvey through her evidence. Like a duo presenting a three-act masterpiece from the theatre of the absurd, they read out John Lynwood's interviews. If Benson had dismantled Karl Ambrose with his litany of lies, John Lynwood demolished himself. His culminating denial descended – or ascended – into pantomime. Having denied he'd lost a screw from his glasses, he was confronted with evidence from the Specsavers trainee who'd carried out an on-the-spot repair, and a forensic scientist who'd not only matched the thread of Exhibit 5 to John Lynwood's glasses, he'd found chemical traces commonly associated with chewing gum on the frame. The first defendant's final, mighty confession was that yes, on the way home from Limehouse, his glasses had fallen apart. He'd nearly driven off the road and hit a lamppost, so he'd pulled up and spent ages trying to get the lens back in, but couldn't and, barely able to focus, and in the dark, because the interior light kept going off, he'd used mashed-up Dentyne. Had it worked? Not very well. The jury had laughed.

This struggle to see where he was going contaminated all the evidence that had gone before. The idea that one of Karl Ambrose's shoes had functioned like a pair of tweezers seemed laughable. As did the idea that John Lynwood had driven all the way from Islington to have a conversation man-to-man with someone he'd threatened to kill a few hours beforehand. As did the idea that he'd only run back to his car because he was worried he'd left his lights on.

The overall effect, when Forde and Harvey had finished their recitation? John Lynwood had struggled with his glasses; and he'd struggled ever since; and he'd struggle to persuade the jury that he hadn't killed Dr Menderez.

Karen Lynwood's interviews had a different ring to them, especially in the light of her husband's duplicity. It now seemed far more likely he'd lied to her again; Karen's denials sounded plausible. She'd deleted her text and email history out of shame, for having mishandled a troubled client who'd become obsessed with her. Why had she met him at the Grapes? To urge him to leave her alone. It had been a spectacular mistake. She'd hoped that by speaking to him in a social context, away from the clinic, she might be able to reach him. Showing warmth by touching his hand had sprung from the same misguided impulse. Her biggest mistake? Failing to be honest with Dr Evington. He'd have known what to do.

The overall effect? What did it matter if she was lying about what she felt for Dr Menderez? Hell's bells, it was understandable. She'd met a sensitive, honest, caring man whose idea of taking a break was to serve the poor of Kolkata. She deserved better than this, sitting in the dock at the Old Bailey. And why? Because of her fidelity.

Benson's cross-examination could never have dinted these strong, lasting impressions of the two defendants. He knew it. So instead he came at Harvey from the angle she was dreading, berating her for a decision made within hours of the body being found. She'd gone after Karl Ambrose when she should have been taking a witness statement from Harriet Kilbride – about whom the jury would hear in due course. Benson was impressive. He made no reference to Ambrose's allegation of racism, allowing it to seep of its own accord into the back and forth. He then picked away at Harvey's case management. And multiple breaches of the Criminal Procedure and Investigations Act Code of Practice. Her failure to notice that PC Rudge's notebook was missing became a failure to work efficiently with the disclosure officer, a failure to record and retain material, and a failure to reveal material to the prosecutor.

The overall effect? A man facing an allegation of murder had been ill-served by the officer charged with investigating the crime. The word 'failure' hung in the air like a clash of cymbals. And on that confused and unpleasant note, Forde rose to close her case.

'My lord, I make an application in relation to Karen Lynwood.'

Benson had asked for the jury to be sent out.

'Of no case to answer?'

'Yes, my lord. From what we've heard, the *Galbraith* test hasn't been satisfied.'

The question was simple: given the evidence, could a properly directed and reasonable jury be sure of the defendant's guilt? Benson argued that they could not. It was of no importance that Mrs Lynwood may have begun a relationship with Dr Menderez. Or that she'd lied about it, which, of course, wasn't admitted. She was charged with an attempt to pervert the course of justice. A key element of that offence had disappeared with Hassan's retraction of her testimony.

'And what about the deletion of emails and texts?'

Forde rose.

'My lord, I think we can advance matters expeditiously. I'm not surprised by the application. Neither, I'm sure, is your lordship. I've taken instructions. The application is unopposed.'

A cry, very like pain, came from the public gallery. Tess looked behind her. Mrs Tindale was leaning forward, her gnarled hands gripping the brass rail. An usher came threading towards her, whispering a warning, and she clutched his arm, too, nodding frantically and gasping something about justice, but then a door thumped and the jury

203

were back in court, and Judge Stanfield was explaining what
had transpired in their absence, and he was instructing them
to return a verdict of not guilty with respect to the second
defendant, and again a cry came from the gallery.

This time Tess didn't turn around.

Her eyes were on Benson. He was endorsing his brief as
if nothing had happened.

42

'Don't think for a moment that she was being fair,' said
Benson. 'Forde was doing what any sensible prosecutor
would do.'

'Which is?'

'Letting the little fish go so she can catch the big one.'

Tess followed Benson into the conference room. There,
Mrs Tindale came at Benson with both arms raised, fingers
splayed, almost knocking over a chair.

'Oh Mr Benson, I don't know what to say, thank you,
thank you.'

She reached for him, but Benson stepped aside, took an
arm and guided her back towards the table where Karen
Lynwood was sitting. Her eyes were closed and she clutched
herself as if the room was freezing.

'I knew you would do it,' said Mrs Tindale, still standing.

'Do what?' Benson's tone had an edge.

'Do what is right and proper. It's your reputation, Mr
Benson.'

'My reputation has nothing to do with it.'

'You've done it again. You've—'

'Isabel?'

Mrs Lynwood had spoken quietly.

'Yes?'

'Shut up. Sit down. And shut up.'

She raised tormented eyes to Benson.

'Am I free?'

'Yes.'

'For ever?'

'The case against you is over. It's not on a shelf. It's gone. You've been found not guilty.'

'I won't be questioned by Miss Forde? Or the judge?'

'No.'

'The police?'

'No. No one. You'll only be questioned if you give evidence for your husband. We'll discuss that later.'

'I'm not doing it. I'm not going into that witness box. I'm never going to talk about this terrible business again, never, never, never.'

She closed her eyes again, this time tightly.

'I didn't know this could happen . . . I didn't see it coming.'

She was referring to the procedure as much as its outcome. Tess had been surprised by the application, too. But not because of its merits. Benson hadn't said he was going to do it. He hadn't shared his many thoughts. He'd just looked out on Newgate.

'You're free, Karen,' said Mrs Tindale triumphantly.

And Mrs Lynwood began to shudder . . . just like Narinda Hassan, after she'd said she wasn't proud of herself. She quickly covered her face with both hands, and Benson reached for the jug of water.

'Have something to drink, Mrs Lynwood.'

He filled a glass and placed in front of her, but she left it untouched. Like Hassan.

'Now you'll do what is right for John, won't you?' said Mrs Tindale.

She was staring at Benson out of gaping dark sockets.

205

'It's the jury who try to do what is right, Mrs Tindale.'

'No, it's you. It's you who leads them . . . to the truth. And now John must be freed. What will happen now?'

'I'll tell you what will happen now.'

Mrs Lynwood had spoken, rising from her seat. She went briskly to the door and opened it.

'You'll wait outside.'

'Karen, I'm here for you, I've always been here for you, you know that. I've only ever tried to—'

'Outside. Now.'

'Let me be a—'

'You've done enough. I don't want any more of your help . . . your guidance. Your support.'

'We've been over this, Karen, and I'm sorry if I—'

Mrs Lynwood's voice became suddenly deep:

'Not here. Not now. Not ever. Please . . . just take a seat outside. Or I will call the police.'

Mrs Tindale hesitated, but finally, with a bow of the head to Benson, she did as she was told. After she'd gone, Mrs Lynwood kept her back against the door, with her hands behind her, holding on to the handle. She was ashen; and the corner of one eye began to flicker.

'Do you need me for John's defence?'

Benson didn't think long.

'You denied getting involved with Dr Menderez in interview. So the jury knows what you're going to say. But if you don't say it to them, to escape cross-examination, they'll think you've got something to hide.'

'And if I do give evidence?'

'There's no boundary to the questions Forde can ask. And if you do have something to hide – I'm speaking theoretically, of course – and Forde finds it, then—'

'They might not believe me.'

'No, they might not.'

Benson's sharp reply surprised Tess as much as Mrs Lynwood. But then Tess understood: he was urging the most important witness in the case to speak out. Again. He wanted to know about Menderez. What he'd said; and what he'd done.

'Your husband's best defence is the truth,' said Benson. 'At the moment, in relation to the murder, we're pointing to abstractions. Someone with a grudge . . . or someone who didn't want Dr Menderez to reveal his secrets to you.'

'That's right. I can't know it's true, but I think it's true.'

Benson took off his wig and threw it on the table.

'May I call you Karen?'

'Yes, do.'

'I could have asked you this question a long time ago. But I've not wanted to unsettle you. Not until I knew you were beyond the reach of the court.'

'What is it, Mr Benson?'

'Are you frightened?'

A hand went to her neck, covering her throat.

'No, why should I be?'

'Are you frightened that whoever killed Dr Menderez might kill you, or Simon, or John if you tell me everything you know?'

She was absolutely still.

'Don't worry,' said Benson. 'What we speak about here remains between us. We can decide what to do afterwards. But I need to know everything if I'm to help John. He's facing conviction, Karen.'

Her mouth opened slightly; her bottom lip moved, as if to form a word; her tongue appeared, rising behind her back teeth; and then she swallowed.

'Mr Benson, I've told you over and over again, if Dr Menderez—'

'Had said anything you would have noted it down. You're right, Mrs Lynwood. I'm obtuse. Forgive me.'

'I didn't say that. It's just . . . you evidently don't believe me.'

'I'm not the one who matters, Mrs Lynwood. It's the jury. They're the ones who need to believe you. If you give evidence.'

The nerve at the corner of her eye wouldn't be tamed, and she stubbed it with a finger.

'When must I decide?'

'You have tomorrow to think things over. I suggest you talk to John.'

Judge Stanfield had adjourned the opening of the defence until Wednesday morning. Forde had a case in the Supreme Court and efforts to trace Harriet Kilbride were still underway. The judge had also opined that a break in the proceedings might be put to good use. Which Tess had understood to mean a guilty plea from John Lynwood might be a sensible way forward.

'Mr Benson, I've forgotten my manners,' said Mrs Lynwood, coming away from the door. 'I've not thanked you . . . I'm sorry.'

She held out her hand. It was still trembling, and when Benson took it he said:

'Mrs Lynwood, a trial is a crisis that can yield good fruit or bad. It might never happen again. Don't let it go to waste.'

If Mrs Lynwood had forgotten her manners, Mrs Tindale had forgotten her stick and Benson had forgotten his wig. Tess returned both items to their owners and then, leaving Benson to smoke in a back alley, away from the press, she went to Ely Place, and her office at Coker & Dale. She'd imagined something of a night out with Archie and Benson. After all, a victory of sorts had been won. It would fill papers, screens and radio airtime. Benson, the errant star, had done it again. But the star, hiding his light behind the

Bailey, had apologised mechanically: Helen had been waiting, he'd said. And so Tess, alone in the kitchenette, made herself a coffee while musing on a new arrival.

The usual crowd of reporters and photographers had been outside court. Tess knew them all. She knew the outlets they serviced or worked for. But this time there was a journalist from Spain. For *El Mundo*. A young woman. She'd sent various messages, asking to speak to Benson, and he'd refused. So, when confronted, had Tess, who now mused on a departure.

Ordinarily, when Benson appeared in a high-profile trial at the Bailey, the Harbeton family positioned themselves on the other side of the road. They'd stand there, Maureen and her four sons, beneath a banner with blood-red lettering: WE HAVE NOT FORGOTTEN. This time, they hadn't turned up. Somehow, it didn't feel right, though Tess would never have said that to Benson. Their protest was as much a cry for the truth as Tess's secret investigation.

Back at her desk, she rang Larry Pickering at EmCheck Ltd.

'Have you got anything for me?' she said.

And Larry's team, the most efficient background-checkers in the business, had come up trumps.

'Would you believe it?' he said. 'Annette Merrington's father has a criminal record.'

43

'The wife got off,' said David. 'But she's still in trouble.'

'Why?' said Pamela.

'Because she obviously got very involved with the guy who was killed.'

Pamela looked bewildered. She served the sprouts and sat down, and David tried again.

'The involvement is the motive for the murder. She has to go into the witness box to deny it. And if she does, Forde will chew her to pieces.'

'And if she keeps out?'

'Her husband will be convicted.'

Pamela thought about the dilemma.

'So this accountant is finished either way?'

'Yes. It's a really tragic case.'

Merrington came out of his torpor.

'Tragic case? What about the man who was killed? Justice delivered is not a tragedy.'

'I didn't mean that, Dad. I meant what happened to the wife. The therapist.'

'Enlighten me.'

'She's living with this guy who's lied to her for years . . . all of their married life. And she only finds out he'd been knocking off her best friend because he's been forced—'

'Knocking off? Chew to pieces? Got off? You speak as if a trial was a damned game.'

'Unlike politics?'

'That was uncalled for, David,' said Pamela, and, turning to Merrington, 'are you all right, darling? You're not quite yourself. Is it this leadership business?'

'I'm sorry, yes. It's troubling. I got a call from Jos.'

'And?'

'If the Committee receives one more letter of . . . let's call them complaint, there'll have to be a vote of no confidence.'

'Who in?' said David.

'The PM.'

'And then what?'

'It depends.' Merrington frowned. 'If the PM loses, there'll be a leadership election.'

There was a drawn-out busyness, of serving plates colliding, a spoon hitting crockery, wine being poured, a napkin flapping.

'You're not thinking of throwing your hat in the ring, are you?'

When they'd first met, Pamela had handled Conservative Party business at Spellow & Hardy, the advertising company specialising in political branding; getting the message right, and getting it across. She'd sat with Merrington in many a bar, drawing up a hit list . . . like that family pariah in *Kind Hearts and Coronets*, planning eight murders so he could inherit the dukedom. They'd worked out what Merrington would need to do if he was to have a chance of leading the party – the goals he'd need to achieve and the people he'd need to undermine. Step one had been to find a safe seat.

'I barely see you as it is,' said Pamela. 'If you run and win, well—'

'Don't worry, my love, I've been thinking.'

And Merrington had – broadly speaking – stuck to the plan. He'd stabbed and jabbed his way towards the front of the queue. He'd jumped red lights. He'd done all the metaphors. Easily eight of them. And Pamela had watched with increasing dismay. She must have thought he'd been joking.

'And what have you been thinking?'

'My hat stays on my head.'

'What do mean, Dad?'

'We don't need another man. We need another woman.'

David looked astonished, so Merrington corrected any misunderstanding.

'I'm not talking gender and power. I'm referring to talent. And the challenges we face. And I'm not the best candidate.'

'Who is?

The admission silenced Pamela. She became immobile.

And then, slowly, her skin – her wonderful ageing skin – flushed. She could hardly contain her . . . dear God, it was joy. She's actually jubilant. Merrington rumpled his brow.

'I've told Sarah Appleton she has to put herself forward. I'm backing her. To the hilt.'

'Sarah?'

'Yes.'

'But you're far more experienced.'

'That's not what matters. She has the mark of greatness. I don't.'

'Oh darling, you are so right . . . I mean, you have, too, of course, in spades, but so has Sarah. She's . . .' Pamela stemmed her flow. 'You've bowled me over, Richard. You've talked of nothing else for the past few months, you've dreamed of this for years, and now, when the crunch approaches . . . you've stepped aside. I don't know what to say.'

'Thank you, darling.'

David was troubled; he put down his knife and fork.

'Hang on, Dad, are you sure? You'd be a fantastic leader.'

'That's very kind, David, but yes, I'm sure. I'd only consider it if I was being pushed and pulled by the great and the good . . . along with the not so good and the not so great. And that, I assure you, is not going to happen.'

'Really?' said Pamela.

'Yes dear, I've as good as said I want to take a back seat from here on in.'

'You're not serious?'

Merrington made a pained grimace.

'It was in talking to Sarah that I realised, yes, she's the better candidate . . . but also that I am tired. That – quite frankly – I've done my bit for Britain.'

Pamela's face shone with pride.

'You're exceptional.'

'I am.'

'Sarah Appleton,' said Pamela, turning to David. 'My oh my. Do you realise, she only went into politics because . . .'

Merrington tuned out.

He hadn't enjoyed laying that seed, the tiny grain from which his glorious ascent would spring. He'd be watering it day after day, now, and Pamela and David would think how wonderfully selfless he was. That wasn't an entirely agreeable prospect. But needs must, and . . . All at once Merrington felt a rush of anxiety. He'd felt the same influx on the night he was first elected, waiting for the count to end; he'd felt it three times afterwards, when ministerial appointments were being considered, when he was pacing up and down the sitting room. And he felt it now, because – *Oh God, turn the other way, don't look, just for the next week or so* – Sarah Appleton would soon fall by the wayside – *You'll look after her, won't You, along with the kids? Stuff Rex* – the road would be open . . . the highway had been made straight, and Merrington would be pushed and shoved – *bugger the not so great and good* – all the way to Downing Street, and . . . Tess de Vere was investigating a criminal matter.

A criminal matter?

Related to his grandmother's bracelet?

Things were serious. De Vere had taken photographs. She'd insisted on evidence being retained. She'd . . . told Benson?

She must have told Benson.

And the two of them were planning some act of revenge. Which is why they hadn't been in touch with his office, or his mother, to say what they'd found, and why Merrington might want to seek legal advice.

Benson would love that.

This was the same Benson whose reintegration to society had been financed by his mother.

Was that just a coincidence?

Merrington's anxiety swirled. These were not phantom fears. Something was underway.

The bracelet. The damned bracelet . . . where the hell did I lose it?

'Dad?'

'Yes?'

'You're not upset, are you?'

David's clear gaze was upon him. Merrington blinked and looked around. Pamela had left the room and was clattering about in the kitchen. She'd prepared an apple crumble. All their married life, no matter what he'd done splashing around at the trough – he'd done good things, of course, and he wanted the best, and he'd bust a gut to help his constituents, to the point of needing Zantac, but let's face it, he was no Sarah Appleton – he'd come home to find Pamela smiling, with organic mushrooms on offer. Or shepherd's pie. Or a crumble. Made with Bramleys. Emblems of purity for a muddied husband who'd finally made it home. He returned his prickling eyes to his son.

'No, not at all.'

'I'm sorry for what I said, Dad.'

'Dear God, what for?'

'The other day, when I said you were my problem. You're not.'

'Oh forget it.'

'And for just now. I'm sorry. You're right: I was being trivial. A trial is a very serious thing. And I want you to know that I admire you. That I'm proud of you. You play around with words, and it's funny . . . but I know you'd never play around with people's lives.'

Merrington didn't know what to say; so he said nothing.

That night Merrington made vigorous love to Pamela. And then, with her shout, he rolled over, all sweaty. The decision had come to him like a flash, just before he'd scored. The only way to protect himself from Benson and de Vere – if he could – was to gather as much information as possible. And that meant answering outstanding questions. Question singular, in fact. There'd be a quid pro quo. He'd tell his mother he'd lost her bracelet (though it had now been found), and in return he'd want to know why in the name of God she'd shoved £160,000 into Benson's lap.

44

'I'm trapped on the Circle Line,' muttered Benson.

He fished a scrunched packet of Camels out of the pedal bin. They were still wet. He threaded one out, being careful not to tear the paper, placed it in the microwave, and punched the start button. Watching the countdown, he checked his pockets for matches.

After Tess had gone back to Coker & Dale, Benson had taken the District Line, heading east, from Mansion House to Whitechapel. And from there he'd walked to Selby Street, where Abasiama lived and worked. He'd reached for the buzzer.

Ding.

Benson took the cigarette out of the microwave and went on deck.

'I'm trapped on the Circle Line,' he said. 'And I want to get off.'

He'd gone back to Abasiama because he'd felt the approach of a depression. Not the heavy cloud variety that hides the sun, but the leg-cutting kind, the ones that not only blocked out the light but stopped him moving. He'd noticed the warning signs over the weekend: a distance between his mind and his eyelids; a sense of being far off, inside his head; and being tired. Too tired to talk. And, out there, in real life, not bothering to cook. Recycling the unwashed clothes. Leaving the dishes in the sink. He'd tried to reclaim that sense of destiny which had nudged him towards exhilaration at the opening of the trial, but he hadn't been able to rouse the memory. Even Forde's quiet endorsement of who he was, a man who deserved a second chance, had seemed an illusion, and unimportant. And, as if it was part of the routine, he'd thought of Abasiama.

But he hadn't pressed the buzzer. Because of a sickening realisation.

There was nothing new to say. There never would be. It had all been said. He'd run out of words years ago. And the ones he'd been using – the ones he'd planned to use again, including 'Sorry' – had all been rubbed smooth until they didn't mean anything any more. He was broke. And then, like the sun rising in the middle of the night, and shocked by the wonder of it, he'd suffered a jolt of excitement, a kind he'd never felt before – except once . . . maybe . . . on the wooden rollercoaster at Great Yarmouth, when his heart had pounded and his hands had turned oily, just before the plunge, knowing there were no brakes on the line, just a brake man, who could make a mistake, and the sun, shining in Benson's eyes, had blinded him.

'I can end all this,' he'd said.

He could hand in his travel pass. He could join Helen out west.

Which is exactly what he'd done. He'd taken the District Line, westbound, from Whitechapel to South Kensington. And from there he'd walked to the Royal Marsden. He'd walked up the steps. And then he'd walked down them. Dizzy with the idea that he needn't exist, he'd forgotten something. Helen had her own travel plans: she had a season ticket to the place Benson had left behind – his past. Which included Eddie.

And so Benson, not wanting to talk about Eddie – because Helen was bound to ask how he'd been affected by the trial – had come home, taking the Circle Line to King's Cross, followed by another quick walk.

He'd literally gone round in a circle.

And he'd been going around in circles for years, he'd thought, groping for a cigarette, still damp from when he shoved the packet under the tap that morning. He'd lurched from depression to depression, from the Old Bailey to Selby Street, and from depression to depression again. That wasn't many stations. And he'd had enough.

'I'm trapped on the Circle Line,' he'd said.

Only that hadn't been true. He'd already broken the cycle. He'd dropped Abasiama.

So – he wondered – what do I do now?

Benson pulled in the smoke, holding the poison until the quiver of tension became nausea.

As it happens, he'd thought of Eddie earlier that day.

Throughout his trial, Benson had glanced frequently at the public gallery, hoping to see his brother. But he'd never turned up. The only person he'd seen, beside his mother, was a stranger, one of those regulars who sit through the whole proceedings. Which, at the time, had meant nothing.

Until today.

Because when Benson heard that cry from Mrs Tindale, he'd turned around instinctively, thinking of his family, and the empty seat that his brother wouldn't take. And for a few incinerating seconds, he hadn't seen Mrs Tindale gripping the rail, or the usher coming towards her, he'd seen his mum – she'd only become 'mother' when he'd started talking to Abasiama – he'd seen his mum had keeled over, on to

217

that stranger. Harrowed, she'd been helping his dad get her upright, while the Harbetons had jumped around. He'd often wondered who she'd been and where she'd gone, because he would have liked to have thanked her.

And Benson, reliving that moment, had recognised her.

She was the woman he'd seen coming out of the Royal Marsden, helping the granny with the bleeding eyes.

PART THREE

Threads can unravel

Benson obtained a simple pass in his law degree, for there were no honours with a part-time course. On the day the results were published, he filled in an application to join the Inner Temple, declaring, as he was obliged, his conviction for murder. Summoned to appear before the Inns of Court Conduct Committee, he was brought by two screws to a recreation room in the basement of HMP Denton Green, where two senior criminal practitioners and a lay person were seated at a ping-pong table. The tribunal had generously agreed to meet there, because the prison governor had refused to grant Benson an SPL – a special purpose licence – which would have enabled him to leave the prison. Vexed, no doubt, by this unexpected gesture, the governor had passed his own judgement: if Benson wanted to play games, he'd let him. The committee, however, listened carefully to Benson's argument; but they refused his application.

'By the nature of your offence, you are not now, and you never will be, a fit and proper person,' – Rachel Glencoyne QC, a Bencher of the Inn, paused to glare at the screw who'd laughed – 'to become a barrister.'

Undeterred, Benson sought redress from the Bar Standards Board Review. Declined an SPL again, he made his submissions in writing; and they were rejected in writing. The *board had been unable to improve upon Glencoyne's pithy reasoning.*

Benson then lodged an appeal with the Visitors to the Inns of Court, a tribunal made up of Appeal Court judges who, when convened, sat in the Royal Courts of Justice. Mysteriously, Benson had no problem obtaining an SPL this time. And so Benson took the train to London, accompanied by the same two screws. And this time, when he'd risen to his feet, there'd been no sniggering.

Benson had one argument. Helen, who couldn't attend, had told him to keep it brief.

'My lords, is it appropriate for the legal profession, of all professions, to restrict, a priori, the scope of rehabilitation for certain offences? To draw no distinction – in terms of consequences – between a gangland execution and a youthful burst of temper, even though that very difference was taken into account when the sentencing judge considered the appropriate tariff?'

There was no response.

Benson pushed on:

'The Inns of Court Conduct Committee routinely considers the gravity of declared convictions for public order offences, offences against the person, fraud, drug infractions and the like. Its deliberations are sometimes overturned by the Bar Standards Board Review precisely because the evaluation of a candidate is not subject to restriction. In the absence of a law, or a regulation or a guidance note regarding the exercise of discretion, it cannot be said that a candidate for the Bar is, de facto, eliminated from consideration because of an offence . . .'

Benson had lost his thread.

'Please continue,' said one of the judges.

But Benson couldn't remember the last thing he'd said. He started another sentence:

'If the exercise of discretion is not fettered, I respectfully urge your lordships to accept that in rare and perhaps unique circumstances . . .'

Benson's mouth carried on working, but he couldn't hear himself. Seeing the judges stop writing, and one of them glaring, he lost his way once more. He began speaking nonsense. A judge raised a hand:

'I think we've heard enough, Mr Benson.'

The judges looked at one another, nodded and retired.

When the tribunal reassembled, Benson stood up, swaying this time. The judge who'd glared began to speak:

'We've listened with interest to your submissions. We're troubled. It seems to us . . .'

Benson listened and nodded as if he understood what was being said, but, in truth, he was only catching snippets. Changing times . . . instant case . . . heinous crime . . . contemporary society . . . moral reconstruction. Moments later the judges were standing, too, and Benson bowed, thinking that's what you did in court. When he looked up, they'd gone. It took him a moment or two to realise what had just happened.

They'd agreed with him.

He turned around, expecting shouts of objection from the gallery. But it was empty. Save for one woman . . . but she turned before Benson could focus on her face. For a split second, he thought he'd seen her before.

On the way back to Denton Green, one of the guards bought him an egg and cress sandwich from the buffet car. Benson supposed this is what happens to people deemed fit and proper. He was ablaze with hope.

45

Elizabeth Benson had planted daffodils around the apple tree in the garden of the family home in Brancaster Staithe. Every year, when the first yellow petals began to unfurl – and there was always one flower ahead of the game – she'd get her camera out and take a picture. Winter was over, she'd say. The photographs all looked the same, but not for Lizzie. And she could tell you why. She'd point at the disparities, smiling, like a child doing a 'spot the difference' on the back of a packet of cornflakes.

Benson dreamed.

He was standing barefoot in the garden, dressed in his pyjamas. He was a boy. Over the wall he could see mist hiding the sea. His mum and dad were asleep in the house. And, somehow, Benson knew that Eddie wasn't there. His bed was cold. He'd gone. Benson looked down at the base of the apple tree. The daffodil that had begun to open was different from all the others. It stood alone. The stem was dark. The leaves were dark. The opening trumpet was even darker. The other daffodils, the ones circling the tree, were in tight bunches. They were green-stemmed with faint yellow heads, lowered towards the ground. And Benson panicked. His mother couldn't see this. She couldn't come into the garden with her camera. She couldn't find the black daffodil. He reached to tear it from the ground, knowing he'd have to uproot the bulb, and as he gripped the base and tugged, it suddenly gave . . .

And he woke.

Traddles was between his feet, his paws kneading the quilt.

Benson felt the itch of cooling sweat. He slid a foot onto the floor and pulled himself upright. In a daze, thinking of that strange daffodil, he didn't wash and he didn't shave and he didn't brush his teeth, he just got dressed, pulling on a pair of dirty jeans and a T-shirt, and wearing the same socks and pants as yesterday because they were on the floor and he couldn't be bothered to open a drawer. He fed Traddles, each movement releasing the fusty smell of old sweat, and then he made himself a cup of coffee. The cigarettes had dried out now, so he lit up and leaned on the Aga, wondering what had happened to those photos taken by his mother. She'd put them in a book, like some people keep school photographs. She'd stopped taking them the year after Eddie's accident. Eddie hit the car in July, and come February, when the daffodils opened, she'd—

Benson's doorbell rang.

He ignored it, but it rang again.

And again he ignored it, and again it rang.

He shoved his feet into his black work shoes, leaving the laces undone, and he went outside, crossing the landing stage. A path between trees led to a gate in high railings that fronted Seymour Road. Dragging his feet up the slight incline, he could see a figure standing on the pavement. Benson thought it was a woman. But he didn't get visitors, so he couldn't imagine who it was. Reaching the gate, he realised he'd forgotten his keys . . . but it didn't matter, because, last night, he'd forgotten to lock up. Rather than open up, though, he leaned on the railings, as if the bars would hide his smell, and the sight of him.

And then his heart stopped.

The woman had turned around.

Benson quickly looked left and right, wondering where the others might be.

'Don't worry, Mr Benson,' said the woman. 'I've come on my own.'

She came a step closer and grabbed one of the bars; Benson

stepped back, staring at the thick mascara and the eyes they seemed to magnify.

'I need to talk to you, Mr Benson. I need to know. Did you kill my son?'

It was Maureen Harbeton.

46

Tess dictated a letter to Jane Ryman and Danny Beaumont: a representative of the Hackney Council Housing Department's inspection and maintenance team would shortly be in contact to arrange a visit with a view to examining the state of the windows. She spoke in a drone, and quickly, watched by Sally, who'd come to Ely Place for a coffee prior to another morning of research into the Merrington family history. When Tess had finished, she turned off her dictation machine and said:

'I organised a background check on Annette.'

'And?'

'The results are interesting. And not just about her.'

Tess had wanted to call Sally immediately, yesterday evening, to tell her what she'd learned, but Sally had been out. Instead, knowing that they'd see each other the next morning, she'd left a cryptic message. Sally had turned up while Tess was dictating.

'We know from the photograph in the *Brighton Herald* that Annette is wearing the bracelet in May 1990,' said Tess. 'We know she must have inherited it.'

'Because her mother had died in 1979.'

'Exactly. So it's not borrowed. She's an only child. It's gone to her. The question is whether she was wearing it on the night Paul Harbeton was killed. And whether she was walking or driving on Powick Lane in Soho, some time between eleven and eleven-twenty-five p.m. If she was walking, then we pack up and go home. But if she was driving . . .'

The altercation between Benson and Paul Harbeton had occurred outside the Bricklayers Arms on Gresse Street at 10.45 p.m. Harbeton had then walked south, crossed Oxford Street, and ambled into Soho. His body had been found in the gutter on Powick Lane at 11.25 p.m. by Mickey Lever, the motorcycle despatch rider who'd called the police. The oaf who'd found a bracelet and slipped it into his pocket before they'd arrived. The bracelet that had ended up on the wrist of his girlfriend.

'What have you discovered, Tess?'

'Back in July '86 the police find Wilfred Baker's car in a hedge beside the Brighton Road in Lewes. There's a bottle of scotch in the passenger footwell. Wilfred pleads guilty to drink-driving at Lewes Magistrates' Court. Think about that while I make the coffee.'

When Tess came back, Sally had done:

'But I went through every local paper in Sussex. There's no report about Wilfred Baker being arrested, never mind appearing in court.'

'That's the interesting point,' said Tess, handing Sally a mug. 'It was covered up.'

Tess sat down behind her desk.

'At the time Wilfred was eighty-six. His wife had died seven years previously. He's retired, obviously, and he lives with Annette and Gilbert. It looks like the local press took pity on him. Point is, we might have discovered Annette's secret problem.'

'Annette's?'

'Yes.'

'But Wilfred is the one who got the conviction.'

'Wilfred is the one who pleaded guilty. No one knows who was driving that car. Annette could have borrowed it.'

Sally nodded uncertainly.

'And Wilfred could have taken the rap to protect his daughter, the vicar's wife, from a pasting. Not many journalists would have let that story go.'

'You're right,' said Sally. 'But how does that help us? Paul Harbeton was killed thirteen years later.'

'Drink problems don't go away that easily. Not when they're entrenched.'

'How do you know it was entrenched?'

'Because – assuming I'm right – the woman who went for a spin with a bottle of whisky was sixty years old. It's a Sunday night, Sally. This isn't a one-off episode.'

'Okay, Annette may have had a problem; and it may have endured. But we need something that ties her drinking into the night Harbeton was killed.'

'We might just have that something.'

Tess gave her mouse a shake, to find the cursor, and she opened up the email from Larry Pickering at EmCheck Ltd.

'Annette leaves Lewes in '93, after Gilbert died. She buys a flat in Hampstead.'

'Okay.'

'So Annette is now in London. Paul Harbeton is killed on the seventh of November 1998.'

'And?'

'Five days later, on the twelfth, Annette stops driving.'

'She informs the DVLA?'

'No.'

'So how do you know she stopped?'

'Because she opened an account with Raja's Taxis in Hampstead. She's been a client ever since. And the question, of course, is—'

'Why did she quit driving?'

'Yeah. And it's a big question. Because she was only seventy-three. She wasn't due a medical for another two years. There's no obvious reason for her to keep off the road.'

'Unless you've done a hit and run and you feel so bad you daren't get behind the wheel again.'

Tess nodded over her coffee.

'I'd call that a plausible explanation,' she said.

How had Paul Harbeton sustained a serious head injury? This had been the critical question during Benson's trial. The skull fracture was consistent with a blow from a hard object, but no such object had been found; and that allowed Camberley to point to the kerb, and a possible unreported hit and run . . . only there'd been no headlight glass on the ground, no recent skid marks, no transference of paint or oil on to Harbeton's clothing, no biological matter on the kerb near the body, only a bruise to the back of the right leg – from a kick, or a nudge from a car bumper. With respect to the injury, then, the jury had been left with competing accounts. But they'd also been left with Benson's lies to the taxi driver who'd taken him to hospital, the doctor who'd treated him, and the police officer who'd questioned him: he'd denied even fighting with Harbeton. Why had he lied? There were only two explanations: one – Benson's – he'd been ashamed of having got into a punch-up; two – the prosecutor's – he'd been terrified, because he'd killed someone. And Benson, dwarfed by guards in the dock, had certainly looked terrified.

'If the jury knew what we now know,' said Sally, 'Benson would have been acquitted.'

Tess shook her head.

'No, we're not there yet. There'd have been a wider investigation. And who knows . . . Benson might have been released without charge; and Annette may have found herself in the dock, with Benson giving evidence for the Crown.'

47

What could Benson do?

He invited the mother of the man he'd been convicted of murdering on to his boat for a cup of instant coffee. On board, with Maureen Harbeton sitting at the small dining table, he dropped and broke a mug, he fiddled with the kettle, he knocked over the coffee jar, he couldn't find a teaspoon, and he kept checking the fridge for milk . . . and while he flustered about, he was savagely aware of his own smell, his sharp odour, sharpening by the second, for he was sweating now, and it ran with the smudge of the night, which lay upon him like grease. Hot with humiliation and embarrassment and fear, he noticed his rumpled trousers on the sitting-room floor, the open tin of cat food on the counter, the plates and cutlery piled in the sink, the crammed ashtray, the door open to a toilet he hadn't cleaned in weeks, the used tissue by the telephone, the pedal bin, its lid raised by crushed trays and cardboard lids from a disgusting takeaway.

'Would you like sugar, Mrs Harbeton?'

'No, thank you.'

'I'm sorry, I don't think I've got biscuits or anything.'

'Don't worry.'

Don't worry? Benson had never been so worried in his life. What was he going to say? His eyes flashed towards the main door. She'd closed it. Even though Benson had let her enter first, she'd closed the door, and flipped the latch. But then he saw the open window . . . the small, circular window by the table. He could feel a current of air and sat near it.

'It's been eighteen years, Mr Benson,' she said.

'Yes, I know.'

'A very long time.'

'It is.'

Throughout the trial, eighteen years ago, Mrs Harbeton had sat in the public gallery with an expression of grief and incomprehension. She'd never shown anger as the evidence unfolded; or jubilation when Benson had been convicted. She'd sat still while her sons had sworn or shouted and, when the verdict had come, leapt in tribal ecstasy.

'I've followed you, Mr Benson,' she said.

She was seventy-one, now. Paul had been the eldest of three sons, the others being Stephen and Brian. Their father had been Kenny, who'd abandoned Maureen and the children when Paul was six. Stephen and Brian had both seen the inside of various young offender institutions, unlike Paul who'd quit school at fifteen to work on various building sites. Maureen had worked shifts in a clothing factory. Later, aged thirty-eight, she'd met Ron Chilton, and she'd had another son, Gary. But then Ron died of cancer and it had been Paul, now aged twenty-six, who'd come home to help out. He'd also started volunteering at the Lever Trauma Clinic in Finsbury and . . . Benson had researched Maureen's background. He knew everything about her, and her family.

'And it has been very difficult,' she said.

'I'm sorry.'

'No, don't say sorry . . . at least, not yet.'

She sat like Benson had seen people at a bus stop, waiting in hope. He'd seen the same patient attention in church, people sitting on the edge of a pew, straining forward.

'I know you wrote to the Parole Board, admitting your guilt, and I know there are lots of people who don't like you and think you should never have been allowed out, or become a lawyer and all that, but somehow you've got the reputation of being innocent.'

Benson had made no such public statement. But it was well known that he could never have come to the Bar unless he'd been rehabilitated. And admission of guilt had to be a preliminary step. Certain commentators had latched on to that. They'd mused in the pages of the legal press that maybe Benson had been a double victim: an innocent man condemned by a court, who'd then condemned himself, so he could fight for the innocence of others.

'It's difficult, Mr Benson, because it makes me wonder, you see . . . What if Mr Benson is innocent, I say to myself. That means there's someone out there who killed my Paul, and he's free. But I'm not free, Mr Benson. And neither are you.'

She looked around the boat; and for a scorching moment Benson feared she was going to pick up his tangled trousers or empty the ashtray, but she said:

'Two years ago, I received this letter.'

She reached into her shiny black handbag and took out a single sheet of paper, folded into a tight square. She opened it carefully, and slid it across the table towards Benson. The crease lines were brown. It had been folded and unfolded countless times. It had become fragile and Benson did not want to touch it. The writing slanted in irregular directions, straying off the lines. He leaned forward to read:

Your son was not a good man. He might have worked for charities in his spare time, but he had his reasons and I'm one of his reasons, right. I've got memory problems, right. And your son did bad things only I can't remember everything, can I, and I'm not sure of places and times and that, am I, and all I can tell yous is this. If William Benson hadn't done your son in then someone else would have. I'm sorry to tell you this, all right, because I'm sure you're a nice lady.

Benson leaned back.

'It was pushed through my door, Mr Benson. I've never showed it to no one else, not the boys and not the police, but I keep reading it and I keep asking myself why would someone send me something like this unless . . .'

Mrs Harbeton took the letter back. She folded it carefully and she placed it back in her handbag.

'You see, Mr Benson—'

But Benson had to speak and he interrupted her:

'I'm so very sorry you received something like this. I don't know who wrote it, and if I did, I would have told them . . .'

Benson stalled; and Mrs Harbeton nodded.

'What would you have said, Mr Benson? Not to say such horrible things? To let it drop, because that bad man is dead now? What's the point, you'll only upset his mum? Is that what you would have said, Mr Benson?'

Benson began to feel faint. His eyes were stinging with sweat. His back was soaking. His hair was tingling.

'May I open the door, Mrs Harbeton?'

'You're not going to do a runner on me, are you?'

'No, I'm just very hot . . . and I've problems with doors . . . when they're locked. Ever since I got out of prison, I can't—'

Mrs Harbeton stood up and went to the door and flipped over the latch. She then opened the door and came back and sat down.

'Is that better, Mr Benson?'

'Yes, thanks.'

She was staring at him with real feeling. Like a nurse. Someone you didn't know who'd stroke your hand while you died.

'You see, Mr Benson,' she said, after a pause. 'You wrote a letter to the Parole Board, saying you were guilty. But you didn't write to me. And you're a nice boy. I thought that during the trial. I was sat just along from your mum and I felt for her, because I said to myself, that could be me, that could, if one of my boys had gone too far . . . and all these years I've said to myself, if that nice boy had killed Paul, he'd have written to me, to say sorry. And you never did. Eighteen years. And no letter. And I think you didn't write one because you said to yourself, I can't lie to her . . . I can lie to the judges and the Parole Board and the newspapers, but I can't lie to his mother. You see, I don't think you're the lying kind, Mr Benson . . . it's not how you were brought up. But we all do things we shouldn't do. And people sometimes do things you'd never expect.'

Benson steadied himself, holding on to the table with both hands.

'I'm not too great these days, Mr Benson. I don't sleep well and I'm getting tired. But I'd find things easier if I knew the truth. I won't tell anyone what passes between us. But I do want to know . . . what does the letter mean? What really happened between you and my son?'

Benson had rehearsed many chance meetings with members of the Harbeton family, and they'd all ended in violence, with Benson on the ground, arms around his head, while boots shattered his rib cage and ruptured his spleen. But he'd never imagined a meeting with Maureen. He'd never imagined anything remotely like this, an encounter on his own boat, with doubt and tenderness. What was he going to say? The truth? How could he? He'd told no one. Not his father, not Helen, not Tess, not Archie . . . no one. Because it wasn't possible. There was too much at stake. But Benson was trapped. The door may as well have been locked and the window sealed. Mrs Harbeton was watching him, blinking slowly. And in her eyes he saw the same kind of hope that had kept him alive in prison; a hope other people had called madness.

'It all begins with Eddie, my brother,' he said at last.

48

'What now?' said Sally.

'We build a stronger case.'

'But how?'

'As Benson likes to say, by filling in the gaps.'

Unfortunately, said Tess, there are lots of them. EmCheck Ltd were a very efficient company. There would be nothing out there that they hadn't found. If Annette's car had been damaged when she hit Paul Harbeton, the evidence was now lost. That much was for sure: there'd been no insurance claim, either for her car, a Toyota Corolla, or the loss of a bracelet.

'And these are the sorts of gap we won't be able to fill.'

'Can't we just confront Annette? That would fill all the gaps in one go.'

'It would. And if she's innocent, then we'd get an innocent explanation. But if she's guilty, if she ran Harbeton down and drove off, she'll fill any gaps to her advantage.'

'How can you be so sure?'

'Assuming she's lied about what happened, if only to herself, then she's lied for nearly twenty years. She knows Benson is now a barrister. She must follow his cases. She's seen him rebuild a life. She's not going to suddenly admit that he was wrongly convicted. If we confront her, she'll explain everything away.'

'Why not go to the police?'

'We could, actually. But they would immediately interview Annette.'

'And?'

'Same result. Annette can still say she was walking down Powick Lane the day before the killing. Or the morning of the killing. No one can contradict her. Annette could be a recidivist drink-driver and it would still mean nothing in court if the police couldn't put her in a car, in Soho, at the time of the killing, wearing the bracelet.'

Tess and Sally had rehearsed this situation before. Annette could have lost her bracelet in Lewes or Shanghai and someone else, whoever found it, could have worn it and lost it in Soho.

'So how do we build a stronger case by filling in gaps that can't be filled?'

'We shift our angle of approach. There are other gaps.'

'Such as?'

'We put Annette to one side, and we go back to a coincidence. You're the one who found it.'

'The link with Camberley?'

'Yes, only it isn't a link. Not yet. But this is where the gaps lie.'

Sally's venture into the Merrington family history had uncovered the sort of coincidence that generates a conspiracy theory. A fantasy out of control. But with the evidence pointing towards Annette now in place, it was time, Tess felt, to find out whether chance or something more sinister was at work with respect to Benson's trial.

'It bothered me when you first told me, and it's bothered me since. The bracelet found at a crime scene belongs to a family with a professional connection – remote but real – to the woman who represented the person charged with the crime. It doesn't look good. And now's the time to find out how strong that connection might be.'

If connection was the right word.

Annette's father, Wilfred Baker, the barrister who'd soiled

his own doorstep, had been a member of Smollett Court Chambers. Another member of those chambers had been John Camberley. Jump forward to 1998, the year of Benson's trial, and John and his wife Vivien have a daughter, Helen, who'd become a big name at the Bar. Such are the antecedents. Annette's bracelet is found three or four yards from the body of Paul Harbeton and Helen Camberley is briefed to defend the young student charged with his murder. Tess said:

'It's not particularly remarkable that Richard Merrington's grandfather shared chambers with Helen Camberley's father. So maybe it means nothing that Camberley defends Benson and it just so happens that a Merrington has lost her bracelet in Soho. But this is the area we need to investigate. We need to know if there is any connection between the Merrington and Camberley families. Social or political. Some shared interest. Or something darker. A debt. Blackmail. Some crap between the two dads, played out through the kids. Anything.'

Sally was looking into her mug like a fortune teller reading tea leaves.

'Do you realise what we're talking about?' she said. 'What it would mean?'

Tess did. She couldn't shift it from her mind. It plagued her waking hours.

'Did you hear me?' said Sally. 'Can you get your head around what must have happened? It would mean Camberley knew Benson was innocent when she defended him.'

Sally's remark had brought the conversation to a sudden end. They'd each let their imaginations run, and finally Tess had spoken to herself as if she was her own client: forget what might have happened. Find out what did happen. Track down the evidence.

'Keep looking into the Merringtons,' she said. 'I'll deal with the Camberleys. Let's see if we meet in the middle.'

Sally nodded.

'Are you going to tell Benson?'

'No. Not until all the questions have been answered. And even then . . .'

'You won't tell him at all?'

'It depends what we find . . . if we find anything. Point is, Camberley is dying. Benson's losing the woman who rebuilt his identity. When's the right time to say . . . whatever it is we might have to say? While she's alive or after she's gone? This is why I stalled in the first place, Sally. Deciding to finish what we began is one thing; how we finish it is another.'

Sally rose and went to the window that looked on to Ely Place. She seemed to be talking to someone out there, or perhaps her own reflection.

'You sound much happier these days.'

Tess didn't reply. Sally went on:

'As we've got closer to the end of Benson's story, you seem less confused. As if you might know what you want.'

Tess had begun her investigation into Benson not because she'd felt driven to set right a miscarriage of justice, regardless of Benson's obscure objections. She'd done it because she needed to know if he'd lied to her all those years ago; whether he was lying to her now, every day; and because, aged thirty-five, she'd been struggling with a resurgence of high emotion, born from a haunting encounter when she'd been nineteen. It was Sally, astute Sally, who'd named Tess's problem and urged her to resolve it. Tess had quoted her to Fr Winsley. Was she experiencing a revival of compassion or had something new emerged: love? That first suggested friendship, deep and abiding and possibly unique; as for the second, well . . .

'You're right,' said Tess. 'I am less confused.'

And she blushed. Mercifully, Sally remained at the window, her eyes on the street below; or maybe staring at her likeness in the glass.

49

'We were playing in the grounds of the Lushmead Hotel,' said Benson. 'I was ten and Eddie was nine. A friend of mine was with us, Neil Reydon. He was eleven. We used to go to Lushmead's a lot because it wasn't far from home. A couple of miles or so. And there were these lanes winding through clumps of trees, and grassy slopes. And there was a lake. A big lake that used to freeze over. Anyway, we'd go there on our bikes and mess around until the gardener or the manager told us to clear off.'

Benson had only recounted the circumstances of the accident on four occasions. Once to his parents, once to the police, once to Abasiama and once to Tess. No, five occasions. He'd told the court welfare officer who'd prepared his pre-sentence report. She'd needed to know any significant family background information. No one, however, knew the full story. He'd very nearly told Tess, but Archie had crashed through the door like an overfed guardian angel. Benson took a breath. No one could save him now.

'We were daring each other to ride down this slope towards the lake. The idea was to bang your brakes on at the last minute, see how close you could get to the water's edge without getting soaking wet. It was Eddie's turn. I was by the lake, waiting, and watching, and suddenly Eddie heads off in another direction. Down a path towards the road. The B1153. He hit a red Citroën people carrier.'

Mrs Harbeton stopped herself from speaking. Benson understood what was happening. She was concerned. She wanted to know why this silly boy had done what he did, but she was sick to the stomach; wondering how Eddie's tragedy, and the Benson tragedy, fitted in with Paul's tragedy; her tragedy. She'd kept her coat on.

'He suffered a significant head injury,' said Benson. 'With paralysis. Affecting his legs. He's needed a wheelchair ever since.'

There were other consequences, but Benson didn't elaborate. For the purposes of this . . . what was it? Confession? . . . only one particular problem mattered.

'Eddie had difficulties with his memory. So he went to the Radwell Brain Trauma Clinic in Norwich.'

'Yes,' said Mrs Harbeton impulsively. She'd recognised the name. 'Paul was a volunteer there . . . for a while.'

'Yes. He was . . .'

Benson dried up. He looked away, too, because he couldn't endure the questioning in her eyes; and the fear of answers she didn't want to hear.

'Eddie went there for years, aged thirteen to eighteen. And he gradually recovered most of what he'd lost . . . except for the accident itself: he'd no idea why he did what he did, or what had happened.'

Benson paused. Then he went on.

'Just before I went to university I was with Eddie on the quay at Brancaster Staithe. We were sitting on this bench, looking at the fishing boats, and he suddenly said to me he needed more than the Radwell. He needed a different kind of help.'

Benson was looking at the coffee rings on the table. The grains of sugar scattered between the stained cork place mats. The smear of butter near Mrs Harbeton's elbow. He said:

'Eddie told me this volunteer had interfered with him. At the Radwell. When he was thirteen. This wasn't something he'd gradually remembered. He'd never forgotten it.'

Mrs Harbeton slowly took her arm off the table.

'He told me to say nothing. Especially to Mum and Dad. He wasn't ready to talk about, didn't want to talk about, might never talk about it . . . he was confused. But—'

'He told his big brother?'

'Yes, Mrs Harbeton. He trusted me. He needed someone to know . . . and that was me.'

Eddie had made Benson promise to never repeat what he'd told him. It was a secret between them. Like all the other secrets they'd shared. Only this one was so different from the others.

'I didn't know what to do. Eddie telling me not to do anything was like he'd stopped me breathing. I had to react. So I went back to the Radwell. Looking for your son. But he'd gone. A manager told me they'd asked him to leave. They'd been concerned about his relationships with the patients. Exploiting the fact they couldn't remember anything.'

Benson looked across the table. Mrs Harbeton's head had fallen to one side, as if she was examining a strange picture, wondering whether she had it the right way up.

'The next time I saw your son was on the seventh of November 1998. A Saturday night. I'd gone to the Bricklayers Arms on Gresse Street with my girlfriend, Jessica Buchanan. We were standing at the bar, waiting to order, when this man shoved his way between us . . . it was your son, Paul.'

Benson had been agitated; and so Jessica suggested they leave. But after they'd gone, and after saying goodnight to Jessica, Benson had doubled back and waited outside the pub. Waited for Paul Harbeton.

'He came outside at about ten forty-five p.m. and I called over to him. I think he thought I was out for a fight because of the scuffle at the bar, but I wasn't. I just wanted to say to him what I'd planned to say, if I'd found him at the Radwell.'

'What was that, Mr Benson?'

'That I knew what he'd done. That my brother remembered everything. And we weren't going to forget.'

Benson made an appeal. Not to Mrs Harbeton, but to history. For the truth that hadn't been told.

'I just wanted him to know that he could get away with it, but that someone knew what had happened . . . and that's what I said. I said, "Do you remember Eddie Benson? He remembers you. And what you did—" and at that point your son headbutted me.'

At his trial, Benson had lied. Obviously. He'd said the argument was about the shove at the bar.

'That's everything, Mrs Harbeton. I didn't follow your son into Soho. When I got off the ground my nose was bleeding and my cheek was broken and I was just in a daze. It just so happens that I, too, went into Soho. Your son was hit by a car, I'm sure of it. But there were no witnesses. I didn't touch him. I swear to you. When that despatch rider found him, I was sitting on the doorstep of a shoe shop five minutes away.'

A taxi driver stopped and offered to take him to hospital. Benson accepted. And he lied about what had happened. He said he'd tripped over some plastic packaging and fallen against a window. He gave the same story to the doctor at A&E. And the police after his arrest. He'd only admitted the fight when he'd been identified by a witness.

'I've been lying ever since, Mrs Harbeton. I couldn't tell the police what I'd said to your son because Eddie didn't want his story all over the papers. He wanted it told secretly, if ever, to a therapist . . . when he felt ready, and he still didn't feel ready, he still doesn't and maybe he never will, I don't know, because he won't speak to me now, but all that is irrelevant, the point is, I'd wrecked everything.'

'I don't understand, Mr Benson.'

'If I'd told the police what I'd said to your son that would have shown there was history between him and my brother. They'd have questioned Eddie, and if he confirmed what had happened that would have given the police what they were looking for, a motive for why I'd killed your son. So I couldn't tell the truth, not without putting Eddie in an impossible situation. Because if Eddie revealed his past, he'd put me in prison.'

'But why won't your brother talk to you? Because you broke your promise?'

'Partly. The main reason is he thinks I'm guilty. He's convinced I killed your son because of what your son did to him. The two are tied in his mind and I can't separate them. No one can. Not even my father . . . because, truth be told, he thinks I'm guilty, too.'

Benson's defence, then, rested upon a lie, that had spawned lie after lie, to create a coherent narrative. The first fiction? That he'd never met Paul Harbeton before. The next? That they'd squabbled over some bad manners in a pub. And after that? There were too many to count. Because each new situation had required a new twist on the truth. They'd finally come to an end when Benson wrote to the Parole Board to admit that he was guilty, but by that stage Benson had lost any hold on the truth. It just hadn't mattered any more.

'All I've got left is this promise to my brother, that I broke once before, and that I vowed I'd never to break again. And I haven't. Until now.'

After a very long silence, Mrs Harbeton stood up. She

hadn't touched her coffee, and she now took her cup to the sink and, seeing there was nowhere to put it, laid it down by the toaster, among crumbs, dried jam and a cotton bud. She looked around the boat slowly, drinking in Benson's world. Then she said:

'You've told so many lies, Mr Benson. So many lies.'

She walked towards the open door with even, marked steps.

'Why should I believe you now?'

50

Merrington took his mother to the highest restaurant in London. Or one of the highest. The Duck and Waffle on the fortieth floor of 110 Bishopsgate. The manager had proposed a window table with a eye-popping view onto the Gherkin, but Merrington chose another. With a view on to Spitalfields.

'It's not my birthday, Dicky, so I don't know why you're spoiling me.'

She looked over the twinkling lights of London.

'Actually, I do. I'm lying.'

'You, Mother?'

'Stop it. Yes, me. You're going to butter me up so I don't complain when you announce you're running to lead the party.'

'You're wrong. *Vox populi, vox Dei.* The voice of the people is the voice of—'

'Heavens, Dicky, I did go to school, you know.'

'I'm saying, unless called upon by the *vox*, I've no intention of putting myself forward. And there won't even be an *admurmuratio* . . . that's a murmur.'

'Be serious.'

'I am. It's *vale* to Number Ten.'

'What are you talking about?'

Annette reacted just like Pamela, though the transition from disbelief to jubilation took considerably longer. Her doubts were penetrating. She struggled, as if she had an itch she couldn't reach. But Merrington scratched it, so to speak. And, before so long, she was smiling, wanting more, moving her shoulder blades in time with his reassurances.

'It's a terrible workload, Dicky,' she said, demanding more claret. 'You'd never see Pamela. Or David. Now's the time to focus on that dear boy and guide his steps like only a father can. It's what your father did, you know. He was seen as a candidate for preferment, but he didn't want it. Lewes was enough for him. And you . . . talking to you.'

Merrington filled his mother's glass, for a moment abstracted. He missed his father. He'd admired him. He'd loved him. He'd been drawn to a certain loneliness in his habits. As Merrington had got older, he'd remembered, in alarming detail, father and son conversations to which he'd neither contributed nor paid attention. That they should return, unbidden, was unsettling, given that—

'So here's to all your tomorrows,' said Annette.

After they'd clinked glasses, Merrington said casually:

'Do you remember that bracelet you got from Granny?'

'Yes.'

'Why did you never wear it?'

'I did, Dicky, but not often, I agree. Why do you ask?'

'I saw it on your wrist in a photo. At Christmas.'

Annette nodded. She'd been leafing through an album; and she'd cried.

'I never liked what it stood for,' she said. 'What it represented.'

'What do you mean?'

245

'It had been given me on my eighteenth, but it was more of a reward. You see, I'd never wanted to leave London . . . Kensington. My life had been full. I'd had dreams – you must tell David to never stop dreaming; he's a dreamer, too, you know – and I let them go. I had to. And that bracelet,' – she took a large mouthful of wine (to Merrington's eye, a touch too enthusiastically) – 'I called it my manacle. Because it chained me to a life I'd never chosen for myself. A life I'd gone along with. These days, a girl my age would simply stay behind. Or run off with the window cleaner.'

Merrington laughed. Her mischief appealed to him.

'Then why did you wear the blasted thing at all?'

'Oh, for fun, Dicky. I'd wear it if ever I had to do something I didn't want to do. Or be with people I didn't like.'

This time they laughed together.

'But all that rebellion ended when I met your father. He's the reason I never wore it. Because I loved him so.' She caught her breath. 'He understood everything. He forgave everything . . .'

Annette was about to say more, but she stopped herself with another slug of claret.

'Well,' said Merrington. 'I don't feel too bad then.'

'Why would you feel bad?'

'Because I lost it.'

'Lost what?'

'Your bracelet.'

'You can't have done.'

'I did. You asked me to repair it. Week after week. I took it with me in the morning, and I brought it back with me in the evening. And at some point, somewhere, I dropped it. Don't know how, don't know where.'

Merrington went no further. To tell his mother that the bracelet had somehow become an item of evidence in a criminal investigation would only worry her. Now she just looked puzzled.

'That was years ago.'

'Yes. But I saw the photo. And I remembered. And I wanted to say sorry.'

Annette thought about her son's words as if they were lines delivered in a play. She waited until he'd finished and then she said her piece:

'Let's call it fate. I'm glad it's gone. And who knows, maybe someone nice is now wearing it.'

As if you weren't, thought Merrington, puzzled by the reply. He would have teased her on the point, but their meals arrived – duck confit on a waffle – so Merrington ordered another bottle of claret and he tugged her for detail on her abandoned life in Kensington. Relishing the memories, the person she spoke of was almost someone else. For he simply could not imagine his mother on stage. In *Chu Chin Chow*. Singing 'Any Time's Kissing Time'. When they moved on to dessert – rice pudding – Merrington had difficulty making his move. But the idea of someone who was not very nice now having the bracelet was on his mind.

'Are you following the Limehouse case?' he said.

'Awful business. That poor Spanish doctor. He worked in Calcutta. With Mother Teresa.'

'He didn't.'

'And why that silly judge let the woman off I'll never know.'

'Evidence, Mother. It wasn't strong enough.'

Annette sniffed. Then she smiled.

'The papers are saying Benson is doing it again.'

'Doing what again?'

'He's not just fighting for his clients. He's trying to find out the truth. That was in the *Telegraph*.'

'Admirable.'

'You should give him a chance, Dicky. Your—'

'Father would have. Yes, I know.'

Having completed the line, Merrington looked towards Spitalfields. Benson's chambers were over there, somewhere.

'Do you realise someone paid for Benson's law degree? The course?'

'Yes.'

'And his training for the Bar?'

'I know. Everyone does.'

'And a boat?'

'Yes, a barge.'

'Moored at Seymour Basin.' Merrington paused. 'And they gave him twenty thousand for a couple of years, so he could set himself up.'

This last nugget was not in the public domain. But Annette nodded.

'In all, that's something like one hundred and sixty thousand pounds.'

'That's an awful lot of money, isn't it, Dicky? Whoever paid the bills must believe in the boy.'

'He's not a boy.'

'No, I don't suppose he is. Not any more.'

'He never was.'

Annette concentrated on her rice pudding; and then Merrington changed his tone.

'I know, Mother.'

She looked up, as if ready to show confusion, shock and horror, with hands to her mouth, exit stage right, but she knew her son's voice and its layers of meaning. Instead she gathered her thoughts. And she waited. But Merrington didn't press her. He wasn't going to say anything else, so they just looked at each other, across the years of conspiracy, until Annette turned her blood-streaked eyes to the window. She drank in the extraordinary glitter – so many different kinds of shining – from buildings and streetlamps and vehicles and signs, spreading out as far as the eye could see. London was a wonder. And she said:

'Don't ask why. I did it for you.'

PART FOUR

The case for the defence

Benson was released from HMP Lindley on Monday the 26th of January 2010. His dad was there to meet him, in tears. He urged him to come home to Brancaster Staithe, but Benson said no, because he had a meeting with Gillian Thorpe, his probation officer, the next morning, and Mr Braithwaite wanted to see him in the afternoon. So Benson and his dad went on the town. All night.

Gillian wasn't impressed.

And neither was Mr Braithwaite, who took Benson by taxi to Seymour Basin, off the Albert Canal. Benson thought this was a hair of the dog outing, only there was no pub, just a gate in some railings, leading through some trees to a landing stage, and a barge called The Wooden Doll.

'She's yours, Will,' said Mr Braithwaite, holding out the keys.

Benson was speechless.

'You once observed you're not a landlubber. Your patron understands.'

Benson had lost the keys by nightfall. And he lost the replacement sets over the next few months. By the time he started the Bar Vocational Course at City University he'd managed to keep them within reach, only he struggled to remember where. He was always tapping his pockets or checking his briefcase. But his mind was sharp and clear, and he obtained a distinction in the final Bar examination.

After a celebratory meal at her home in Hampstead, Helen gave him a black gown, a circular leather collar box, a leather band case, a blue court bag – bearing his initials, WB, embroidered in white cotton – and a wig. Her grandfather's wig. He, too, had been a WB, and his initials were written in copperplate on the inside.

'Wear it with pride,' she said. 'He fought for both justice and truth.'

And so, on Friday the 7th of October 2011, Benson was called to the Bar at the Inner Temple. Standing among the Benchers was Rachel Glencoyne QC, who'd opposed, in the strongest possible terms, what was now happening. At the sound of Benson's name, she turned away.

She was not alone.

But for Helen, Benson was sure a pupillage would have been out of reach. No set of chambers would have granted him the mandatory sixth months' training with a master; no chambers would have granted him a second six, in which he received instructions and appeared in court on his own. In short, he'd never have completed the first year of formation required by the Bar Council if he was to practise at the independent Bar. But such opposition didn't matter. Helen was head of 14 King's Bench Walk. She offered Benson the full twelve months.

On his first day at 14 KBW, Benson took a chair opposite Helen's crowded desk. He was wearing a dark charcoal suit with a waistcoat, a white light twill shirt, and a yellow silk tie, the lot purchased from Ede & Ravenscroft the day before. He'd shaved twice. He'd patted some Dior aftershave onto his skin.

Helen peered over a heap of papers and said:

'I told you once before: I only had one lesson to teach. Do you remember?'

'Yes.'

'First I want to draw your attention to a lesson you've already learned. You just need to put it into practice. You must put someone else at the centre of your life.'

She allowed the sentence to settle.

'To do that, you must die to yourself. People concerned about the spiritual life spend a lifetime trying to do this. They go on retreat. They fast. They pray. They know that this is the only road to fulfilment and happiness. Some get there; many don't. And then there are those who don't even try.'

Again, Helen let the sentence bed down in Benson's mind.

'But we have travelled this journey, Will. Not by choice. And not because we think it's a noble pursuit. Which is why, for us, there's no virtue. And no fulfilment and no happiness. Not in the ordinary sense of those words. But we've reached the ultimate goal. We're dead to ourselves. The life we would have lived has been taken away. And this means we're free.'

After another pause, Helen said:

'We're free to put the client first. To make their case, our case. Their fears, our fears. Their struggle, our struggle. Their victory, our victory. We can weep with them; and we can rejoice with them. And that means, in court, believe me, you will suddenly find yourself fulfilled.'

Benson reflected on Helen's words. This is why she'd said there can be no looking back. No search for lost innocence. No resurrection. Not if he was to be an advocate . . . the kind of advocate that was now within his grasp. But what was this one lesson he had to learn? He daren't ask.

'I understand,' he said.

'Do you?'

Helen put the pencil down and fixed Benson with a long stare.

'It's no fun. Because even if we've arrived, there's the pain. The pain doesn't go away.'

255

51

'Where the hell is he?' said Tess.

Archie shook his head.

'I don't know. He didn't come into chambers this morning.'

'I've called him God knows how many times and there's no reply.'

'Me too. Same thing last night,' said Archie, still shaking his head. 'I called and called. No reply. He hasn't been himself, you know and I—'

'We have to find him, Archie.'

Tess put a hand to her head.

'You go back to chambers and I'll go to *The Wooden Doll.*' Then, moving away, she added, 'Check the hospitals. And police stations.'

Tess had arrived at the Old Bailey ready for the opening of John Lynwood's defence. She'd waited for Benson in a conference room with Karen and Mrs Tindale, making excuses, glancing anxiously at her watch. She'd called in Archie so she could go and see John. While talking about heavy traffic, they'd been called into court. Judge Stanfield had wondered where Benson might be. Neither the court nor Forde had been informed of any delay. Enquiries were to be made. The court would reconvene in an hour, or earlier if Mr Benson's whereabouts had been determined.

'Do you think he's okay?' said Archie, coming after her.

'Just get back to chambers. He might turn up. Or someone might call . . . someone who's found him.'

Tess, for once, had driven to work. Within fifteen minutes of turning the ignition she was parking on Seymour Road . . . and swearing because there was no reply at the gate, despite her pressing the buzzer over and over again. She tried the handle, and found it unlocked. Moments later, after a run down the path between the trees, and a leap on deck, she stumbled through the open aft door and came to a halt.

Benson, fully clothed, was splayed out on the sofa. Traddles was on the kitchen counter, licking the surface. She moved closer, her fears rising as she clocked the empty bottles and the spillage . . . of beer, whisky, wine . . . but then she heard him breathe, and she saw his chest rise. She glanced around with incomprehension at the chaos and squalor. And then, quite suddenly, she became angry. Regardless of whatever, he was meant to be in court. Calling his name, she grabbed a foot and shook it. She then shoved his shoulder, recoiling at the smell of . . . Hell, what was it? Vinegar and hops and armpit and smoke. She then grasped both ankles and pulled until Benson slid onto the floor. But he just rolled over, forcing his face into the darkness under the sofa. Looking around, Tess saw the sink, and the handle of a pan. She went over, and pulled the pan free, grimacing at the greasy water, and the floating beans. After hesitating for a moment, she threw it back into the sink. She then went over to Benson and slapped his face.

That worked.

'What's happening, Will?'

He'd showered, shaved and dressed for court. But he hadn't been able to remove the darkness in his skin, the deep blue around the eyes, so like bruising but evidently caused by a trauma in the mind, or somewhere deeper. He sat slumped in the passenger seat, staring into space.

'I'm finished, Tess.'

'You haven't even started. They've found Kilbride. She's at court.'

A message had been sent to Forde. Archie was dealing with the Lynwoods. An adjournment would be needed anyway, to assess whatever Kilbride might be ready to say, so no harm had been done. Tess dropped a gear.

'What do you mean, you're finished?'

'Maureen Harbeton came to see me yesterday . . . wanting answers. The answers you all want. And I told her the truth. Told her what I've never told anyone else. Not you, not Archie, no one. Not my parents. And she didn't believe me.'

There wasn't time to deal with this. She said:

'Think of Kilbride. Nothing else. We'll sort this later.'

'She'll go the media, Tess. She'll tell them everything. I'm finished.'

'You're not finished until you're finished.'

They'd arrived at the Bailey.

'Will, think of Kilbride. Think of John Lynwood. The defence opens now.'

52

The Bar is a family. Its members look out for each other. They support a colleague in crisis, without them having to explain what's happened. They make space for them. But Benson didn't belong. And had he been against anyone but Janet Forde that generosity – that affection – would not have been extended to him. But Forde was against Benson. And she rose to smooth over her opponent's breach of professionalism. Time had been put to good use, she said. Harriet Kilbride, whose evidence had been withheld from the defence by an error of the Crown, had been found by the police. A statement had been taken. It had been evaluated by both sides, and there would be no opposition to Mr Benson's application to call her as a witness for the defence. Judge Stanfield, sensing a delicate situation, didn't seek any further explanation. But he smiled at Benson.

Tess did, too. Hiding her concern. Would he be able to elicit the evidence needed from Kilbride? Or would he literally fall over? His voice was hoarse. But it evened out. There was an impression of subdued authority. Tess calmed down; and she listened.

Harriet Kilbride was aged seventy-one and a former actress. Her glory days had been the late sixties. She'd made the cast of *Hair*. It was painful listening because this proud, flamboyant woman, head tilted back, her voice loud to hit the back of a hall, was dressed in rags . . . colourful rags: a man's blue nylon trousers, a pink shirt, a green overcoat and a yellow crochet scarf. The sunglasses, she said, were to protect her eyes, Judge Stanfield had politely asked her to lower her voice.

But her narrative was crystal clear. Ordinarily, she slept on a bench on Caxton Green with a cat called Marbles, though sometimes she'd seek shelter indoors. Her beat was around Fenchurch Street Station. On the night of the murder – Monday the 5th of October 2015 – she'd been turned away from St Oswin's Nightshelter at 11.30 p.m. (The time had been confirmed by a log entry made by the manager.) She'd walked back to Caxton Green, arriving at roughly a quarter to one in the morning, which would be Tuesday the 6th of October. How did she know the time? Because she'd been walking that route for ten years. She'd counted the steps. And she knew it took her an hour and fifteen minutes.

'And as I approached the park, I saw a man coming out of Ropemaker's Way,' she declaimed.

'Would you describe his clothing, please?'

'He was a smart man. I notice these things. Black shoes

and beige trousers and a long brown overcoat. Shirt and tie. A silk paisley scarf. Purple. Cuff-links, no doubt. And cotton socks, too. Or a wool mix. He wore leather gloves. I'd say they were brown, the kind with three ribs on top. To match the coat. Black wouldn't have gone, not really.'

'Could you describe his gait? His way of walking.'

'I know the word "gait", thank you. He moved briskly, head down. Like he didn't want to be seen. Purposefully, I'd say. Like he was on his way to a meeting. Driven, like he'd been up to no good.'

'Miss Kilbride, there is a microphone,' said Judge Stanfield, 'and this is not the largest of rooms.'

'I know what I saw, sir,' she replied haughtily.

'For the moment, it's just a question of volume.'

'The police never took me seriously. I mean, do you blame them? Look at me. But I know what I saw. I've nothing else to do except look around, sir, and I remember things. Because it was once my job to remember. And not just my lines. I had to remember what people are doing, and where they're coming from, and what they'll do next, and why they did what they did. And I saw this man. He came out of Ropemaker's Way as if he shouldn't have been there. It's not easy to do, your honour, sir . . . it's not about skulking around or looking over your shoulder or tiptoeing and all that nonsense, it's in your step. Shall I show you?'

'No thank you, Miss Kilbride, I think we've got the message very clearly.'

'The policeman didn't. He yawned. He had better things to do.'

'Did the policeman arrange to take a statement from you?' said Benson.

'God, no. If he had done, I'd have told him everything.'

She spoke like she'd missed an audition for *Macbeth*. One of the witches.

In a strange way, Kilbride was absolutely credible. Amongst the contradictions and mish-mash of observation and assumption was something sharp and clear. She'd seen someone on the night of the murder near the crime scene. She'd seen into his character and his mood. She had the heightened perception of the artist.

'You mentioned gloved hands,' said Benson.

'Yes.'

'Were they empty?'

'One of them was. He held something in the other.'

'Did you see it?'

'No.'

'Then how do you know that—'

'It's like the walking trick, Mr Benson. You hold your shoulder slightly higher than the other and you keep your arm straight. It's how you hide something without putting it in your pocket . . . That's what the audience sees and they say to themselves, he's got something in his hand. Only this man wasn't acting, was he? He had something in his right hand.'

'Did you see his face?'

'No. He'd seen me.'

'How do you know?'

'He tilted his head to one side, like this.'

Kilbride turned away as if to evade Benson's gaze.

'I told all this to the police officer and he just looked at me as if I was half mad. Which I probably am. But that doesn't mean I couldn't witness something, does it?'

'No.'

'Can you put an age to the man you saw?'

'Sixty-two.'

'That's precise.'

'It's my answer.'

'In which direction was he walking?'

'Towards the Basin. Parallel to the Cut.'

53

Curiously, Benson didn't slip off to the advocates-only dining room. He stayed with Tess for lunch. But he ate nothing. They sat in a café near St Paul's. The same café, and the same table, at which he'd begged her to leave his past alone. Accept me as I am, he'd said. Accept my choices. She hadn't.

But what had he told Maureen Harbeton?

She couldn't ask; and he didn't want to say. All he wanted was company. He was like a man living his last hours. What was the point in going over anything? So, after Tess had eaten a ham sandwich in silence, with Benson glancing fearfully at a television screen showing breaking news on Sky – something was always breaking – they talked of Kilbride.

Calling her had been a difficult decision. On the one hand, she was demonstrably a fragile personality. But she had an arresting presence, and the sense of someone in command. Of having been shoved aside when she should have been listened to. And so Benson had taken a risk; but it had paid off, because he'd now secured what they'd needed for John Lynwood's limping defence: he could now point to someone – a he – who might have been with Dr Menderez throughout the evening of the 5th of October; who had the opportunity to kill him after the visit of John Lynwood; and who may have left by Ropemaker's Way when he'd thought it was safe to do so. Tess said:

'Archie's right, though.'

'About what?'

'There are so many mights and maybes.'

She signalled to the counter for two coffees.

'We're saying this man knew Menderez . . . and that he knew Menderez was seeing Karen Lynwood . . . and that he wanted to stop him from revealing his secret crime, either because he'd been paid to, or because he was a party to the offence.'

'Yes. That's John's case.'

'So the guy's a Spaniard. He's flown in to do the business.'

Benson was distracted by the shift of images on the screen. He'd recovered some colour; the darkness had lifted; but the tinge of dread remained. Tess continued:

'It just doesn't ring true. Like Archie said, what the hell had this guy been doing all evening, if he'd been in the house since Menderez got back from seeing Karen? Why didn't he kill him immediately? And why wait for John to come and go?'

A waiter brought the coffee and placed the chit under Benson's saucer. Tess said:

'And have you ever seen a hitman or whatever in a long brown overcoat with smart leather gloves?'

'Yes.'

'Where?'

'In films.'

Benson's remark said it all. Kilbride's evidence was helpful; but it was also theatrical. And whether the jury would be prepared to filter out the basics needed for the defence to succeed remained to be seen. It was a big ask.

'You have someone to point to,' said Tess, trying to be upbeat.

'I may have,' said Benson taking out his wallet. 'Forde is yet to cross-examine her.'

54

A lesser advocate would have exposed the scale of Kilbride's history of mental health issues; they'd have exploited her inability to separate what she'd seen from what she'd felt, using the confusion to undermine both elements; and they'd have reluctantly pointed out that she'd been refused entry to Saint Oswin's because of her rude and offensive behaviour.

But Forde did nothing of the kind.

First, because there was no need to. Second, she'd have lost the jury, because nothing would undo the entry in PC Rudge's notebook. And finally, because after decades in court she knew the meaning of economy. And its value. She simply enquired whether this businessman's conduct – he was a businessman, wasn't he? Oh yes – was consistent with someone being caught short in an area where there were no public toilets.

Archie had got it right again.

'That's exactly what he was like,' agreed Kilbride, striking the witness stand. 'Except . . .'

And she'd waited, as if to deliver a vital riposte.

'Except there was something in his right hand.'

Forde, in letting the matter go, appeared merciful. She'd let the actress go back to Caxton Green, or, if they would have her, St Oswin's, with something to hold on to: more dignity than she'd arrived with. Forde was a prosecutor you could trust. After Kilbride's departure the court rose for the day and Benson called a conference.

'We've got part of what we need,' said Benson.

Once more John sat between Karen and Mrs Tindale in the brightly lit room. And once more the tension between them, rooted in a complex family history, seemed to break into sound. Tess imagined a high-voltage humming.

'Yesterday the Crown could say no one had been seen near the crime scene shortly after the murder. That is no longer true. More to the point, we now have a man at the mouth of Ropemaker's Way, behaving suspiciously. That gives us an argument.'

'What else do you need, Mr Benson?' asked John.

'Evidence akin to what we heard from Harriet Kilbride. Not just facts, but a sense of atmosphere and purpose.'

'About what?'

'It's a who. Dr Menderez. We have Karen's notes, so we know he intended to reveal a secret of such significance he'd once wanted to kill himself. We know he proposed to tell his story first, to put everything in context. We know he never got there. But I need this to come alive.'

'How?'

'The jury need to hear what I have heard: the sense of accumulating tension, the build-up to a disclosure of import-ance – it would help the jury understand why you believe someone would want to silence him. This sense of emerging danger doesn't exist on the page. It can only come from Karen.'

John glanced at Karen and then said:

'We've spoken about this, Mr Benson. Obviously, Miss Forde will set out to show that Karen had become seriously involved with Dr Menderez?'

'Yes.'

'And there's no limit to the subjects she might raise?'

'None.'

'Well, Karen came to the prison yesterday. We've talked things over. And we've decided it would be better for Karen to keep out of the witness box. It's our choice, Mr Benson. We ask you to respect it.'

Tess wasn't surprised. Ever since their first meeting, Karen Lynwood had been wanting to hide. Either behind vague answers or that veil of hair that kept falling forward. That she'd agree to face Forde when she wouldn't face Tess or Benson was unimaginable. All that aside, Tess couldn't help but notice the slight nodding of Mrs Tindale. She might have been silenced by Karen; but she'd been consulted by John.

'You're sure, Karen?' said Benson.

'Yes.'

Benson watched her for a long while. And when her expression had hardened to the point of aggression, he asked Mrs Lynwood to endorse his brief, spelling out the decision she'd made. Then he stood up and said:

'Tomorrow you give evidence, Mr Lynwood. Think very carefully about the issues in the case. Think carefully about what you are going to say. This is the only chance you will ever have to explain yourself.'

'Was that an invitation to plead?' said Tess, when she and Benson were seated in the Gutting Room.

It was dark outside; the huge iron radiator was clinking and purring. Molly had closed the curtains and made tea. Archie was out front, troubled by a crossword.

'No. I told you, I think he's innocent.'

'Even now?'

'Crazy as it seems, yes.'

'What are you after, then?'

'The truth, Tess. Even now they're hiding something. With Karen out of reach and only John to save. I don't understand them.'

And saving him would be next to impossible. He was the last witness for the defence. He would enter the box unsupported by his wife. His fate was in the hands of a jury who knew he'd betrayed his wife by sleeping with her best friend. Forde's argument would be irresistible: this same man had then killed a man when his wife had dared to look in another direction.

'Maureen Harbeton,' said Tess, shifting her thoughts on to Benson's.

'I'm finished, Tess.'

Do I tell him, thought Tess. Do I tell him I tracked down the employee at the Radwell who sacked Paul Harbeton and who remembered Benson had come looking for him? Do I tell him that after the Hopton Yard killing a man with a scarred and dinted scalp had asked her to thank Benson for killing Paul Harbeton, because if he hadn't done someone else would have? Do I tell him that Sally and I had guessed Paul Harbeton, the charity volunteer, had exploited patients with memory problems, including Eddie? Do I tell him I know he lied during his trial, to hide Eddie's story, but that that trial may have been compromised in a way he couldn't begin to imagine, because there was an emerging connection between Helen Camberley and—'

'I told her everything, Tess, and she didn't believe me.'

'What did you say?'

Benson didn't hear; he was being pulled along by a stream of anxiety.

'She called me a liar. And soon it will be online. It'll be everywhere. She came looking for answers, and I filthied the name of her son, that's what she'll say. She'll say I made up stuff that I never mentioned during my trial, just to wound her, and it's—'

'Will, listen to me—'

'It's worse than that . . . she knows about my brother now, and she knows that I—'

'Will, just relax, and hear me out. There's something—'

Archie suddenly pushed open the door. In his hand was a copy of the *Standard*. He waved it frantically, like a bystander to an accident flagging down traffic:

'Have you seen this?'

Benson looked at Tess. And Tess turned to see Archie stride across the room. He dropped the paper on to Benson's desk.

'Do you know who just gave me this?'

Benson's eyes were on the large black lettering: 'WILLIAM BENSON IS INNOCENT'. Maureen Harbeton had told her story. But not the one he'd expected.

'Rizla?' said Archie, snapping his fingers.

'What?'

'Wake up. There's a bloody monk outside.'

'A monk?'

'Yes. He's the one who gave me the paper. And that's not all.'

Benson was in a daze.

'He's brought a witness from Spain.'

55

The monk was Fr Aelred Dunne from Lambton Abbey. Benson was intrigued by his story. He'd been a solicitor for twenty years, specialising in war crimes investigations. A quietly determined man, with a facility for languages, he'd tracked down culprits and witnesses alike, trying to substantiate the claims of victims left behind – to use his words – 'by the politics of convenience'. Perhaps it was the dearth of prosecutions that took away his taste for the law, or the sense of having let down his many trusting clients, but another sharp hunger had been growing, and he'd finally left the unresolved claims of history for the bustle and quiet of a Benedictine monastery in Suffolk.

But the person who most arrested Benson's attention was the dark-haired woman who'd come with him, seated now in an armchair. She had the extraordinary allure that comes from struggling year on year and never giving up. Benson had seen it a few times before, in the faces of mothers seated at tables in prison visiting rooms. He'd seen it in Helen Camberley's face, too. This woman was called Lucia Callasteros.

'Lucia doesn't speak English,' said Fr Aelred, 'so I'll explain her background and how I came to know her . . . and why she is here.'

Fr Aelred didn't look like a monk. His clothing – worn brown brogues, jeans and a shapeless blue jumper – had probably been retained from his days as a layman. He wore round glasses, and his eyes were a gentle brown.

'In 2005 I attended a conference in Madrid. When it was over a friend of mine suggested I visit a children's village a few miles outside the city. It's run by an NGO. Its purpose, to provide help and assistance to vulnerable children whose parents couldn't cope. Lucia has worked there since she was twenty-one. At the time I met her she'd been there fifteen years.'

'What was her job?'

'At first she was a volunteer in the kitchen of a villa. She then took a full-time job in the main day centre. She still works there.'

Benson's heart was beating fast; but he wouldn't let his eyes stray to the *Standard*.

'I met Lucia. And without going into why, she told me her story. A story she'd never told anyone before. Maybe she spoke to me because I'd be leaving that night and she'd never have to face me again, never have to look at me and say, "Oh God, he knows." Whatever the reason, it doesn't matter. She told me. And I came back to England with this shared memory. It created a bond. We stayed in touch. She is my friend.'

'So this was twelve years ago?'

'Yes. In time she found out I hadn't always been a monk. That I'd been a lawyer.'

Benson nodded.

'Last week the Limehouse case opened. Obviously, it's been covered by the media in the UK, but with Dr Menderez being a Spanish national the details were eventually reported by the press in Spain. Lucia was watching the news a few nights ago. She recognised Dr Menderez's name. She recognised his face. She knows him. She was once his patient.'

Benson glanced at Tess. She was noting everything down so as to prepare a witness statement, but like him she'd paused, to glance at Benson. Fr Aelred, seeing the exchange, said:

'Am I right in saying you're anticipating what I'm about to say?'

'I don't know, Father. All I can tell you is that from the moment I opened this brief I have been concerned to know the history of Dr Menderez. I've feared his story might not be entirely straightforward.'

Fr Aelred gave a nod of acknowledgement. He said:

'I think it's best if you listen to Lucia. She will speak, and I will translate.'

Until now, Lucia had sat absolutely still and silent, her gaze fixed upon the floor – like those mothers in the prison visiting rooms, hearing a language they could not understand, but resolved to be forever patient, to wait for their time to speak, hoping they might find the right words. And now, at a touch of the arm from Fr Aelred, she raised her eyes and looked directly at Benson. She had strong cheekbones and eyes as dark as water at night. But her gaze was so open that Benson flinched. He'd felt her need to speak; and the acceptance of despair. They'd cut him with the ease of a razor blade.

It was late when Lucia had finished. While the translating had been underway, Benson had watched her listening to the strange words in English, noting the expression of . . . what was it? Resolve? Endurance? Fatigue? They were all in play at different moments, like shadows moving across dry land.

'Thank you,' he said, incapable of finding an appropriate response.

Fr Aelred's slight nod implied thanks was about all you could say.

'There's much to be done,' said Benson, with a deep breath.

Another witness statement had to be taken, this time from Fr Winsley. Applications to admit late evidence and hearsay evidence and to amend the defence statement also needed to be prepared. An approved translator needed to be found. Forde had to be informed of developments, as did the court . . . and as Benson listed the tasks, Fr Aelred and Lucia rose and quietly left the room. Benson followed, to thank them once more, but they didn't want to linger, and Lucia was hiding her face; there was a sense she was already far away, inside herself, as Benson had often been; she carried on walking, opening the door and heading out on to the street; reluctantly, he let them go.

When Benson finally got home he immediately did the washing-up. He wiped down every surface. He gathered up the rubbish and filled a couple of green sacks and took them out to the bin on the landing stage. He sorted the recycling. He cleaned the toilet. He washed the floor. He did his laundry. He got out a clean suit – the charcoal one he'd worn the night he was called to the Bar – and he ironed a fresh white shirt. And then he did what he should have done at the outset: he propped the fore and aft doors wide open and he levered free the windows that had never swivelled on their hinges, along with those that did. And he paused.

A cold breeze blew through *The Wooden Doll* and Benson breathed in the air, slowly and deeply.

That Maureen Harbeton had told the *Standard* reporter she now believed Benson was obviously an important development. That she was also dropping her demand for 'Paul's Law' was stunning, because it meant she now endorsed him. But both these matters were as nothing compared to what was going to unfold in Number 3 Court the next morning. Because a woman had a story to tell, which, if true, would put Dr Jorge Luis Rafael Menderez, dead or alive, in the dock.

56

Forde agreed the witness statement of Fr Winsley (taken, by Tess, at midnight) so there was no need for him to be called. She would not, however, consent to the admission of evidence from Lucia Callasteros. There was a significant lack of verifiable fact, she'd argued, but Judge Stanfield, without calling on Benson, ruled against her: the evidence in question was relevant to the defence; how much weight to attach to it was a matter for the jury.

And with that the jury were summoned.

Word had evidently spread that evidence of significance was about to be given because the number of reporters had doubled. When the translator, Mrs Alvarez, was ready, Benson called his witness. While waiting for her arrival, he felt a tug on his gown from Tess. She tilted her head towards the public gallery. Fr Aelred was there. So was Karen Lynwood. And so was Mrs Tindale. Seated beside the grandmother he'd never had, was Simon Lynwood.

*   *   *

Benson looked at Lucia. Their eyes met. And with a slight nod of the head, Benson began guiding her through the most important day of her life.

'Please give the court your name.'

'Lucia Callasteros.'

'You were born in Madrid on the third of April 1968?'

'Yes.'

'You are now forty-eight years of age?'

'I am.'

Somehow Mrs Alvarez managed the triangle of question and answer without making herself the centre of attention. The light fell on Lucia and her deep, undulating voice. The only other sound was the pattering of fingers on the laptops of the press.

'Miss Callasteros, I would like you to begin by telling the jury about your childhood.'

Even as Benson drew out Lucia's narrative he was struck by her defencelessness. She hid nothing.

Lucia had been born into a violent home, made worse by alcohol abuse. She had little memory of her early years, save shouting and the intervention of neighbours and the police and social workers. She was eventually taken to a children's home, Santa Florentina, run by a community of sisters and lay people. Those days she recalled with clarity. And she'd been happy . . . or, more accurately, there'd been times when she was happy. She'd made friends. And one of the sisters – Sister Valentina – had been like a mother to her.

'But if you're damaged as a child, as I was, then the care and attention only helps you get by. When you're broken, inside, you're broken . . .'

Lucia absconded from Santa Florentina in 1985, when she was sixteen. Somehow being homeless felt . . . true to herself. The police came looking for her; and so did Sr Valentina – Lucia knew this from friends on the street.

Apparently, she'd drive around in a car at night, asking questions, leaving messages – but Lucia never got back in touch. Even now she didn't understand why she'd kept away from someone who cared for her. But she wouldn't turn to her; she wouldn't turn to anyone.

'I think it's because I knew I didn't belong anywhere . . . and I didn't want to pretend I belonged with people who were just being kind. I don't know why, but I thought I deserved to be harmed.'

Whether she did it herself, or whether others exploited her vulnerability, didn't really matter. Lucia felt drawn to a cycle of self-destruction, though, at the time, it had felt like a rush to be free.

'I moved around squats. I begged enough money to get a coach ticket and then I'd go somewhere new, and then I'd beg and come back again. Go to the same squats, and it was as though I'd come home. People were pleased to see me.'

'I got pregnant,' she said abruptly, not answering a question. 'I was seventeen.'

She'd looked at the test result, two pink lines in the window of a piece of plastic, and she'd panicked. The next day she'd knocked on the door of Santa Florentina, asking to see Sr Valentina, but she'd moved to run a homeless project in Cadiz. She'd left a letter for Lucia: with an address. She'd told her to write, to come and visit her.

'I still have that letter,' said Lucia. 'And after reading it I thought, no, I won't go there. Not yet. I decided that, the next time I saw her, I would be a different person.'

And so Lucia contacted a friend's social worker. She was placed in a hostel. And she was brought to the Clinica Lorenzo.

'When was this?'

'Some time in April 1986.'

'Who was your doctor?'

'Dr Menderez.'

Benson said:

'My lord, this is without doubt the same Dr Menderez with whose fate this court is now concerned.'

Judge Stanfield nodded, and Lucia continued with her evidence.

Dr Menderez had been very supportive. And there'd been a sister, too, who was also a nurse. But Lucia couldn't remember her name. She'd always been in the room, never saying much, just taking notes.

'I'd begun to sort myself out. But I'd no choice. I was carrying a life. And I knew I had to change . . . and I had the letter from Sister Valentina, and I wanted to go to Cadiz. I wanted to take a train, with my baby. I wanted to knock on the door and see Sister Valentina's face when I showed her my boy or my girl . . . and when I showed her how much I'd changed.'

Lucia now had her own social worker and she made scheduled visits to the Clinica Lorenzo, where she always saw Dr Menderez. The sister questioned her on her past and her plans. Everyone was concerned for the welfare of the coming baby.

'On the eleventh of October 1986, my waters broke. My daughter was born at seven p.m.'

It had been a forceps delivery and the child had immediately been taken away for tests. Lucia had been sedated and had no memory of the crisis that had accompanied the birth.

'In my mind, I'd named her Angela. But I wasn't allowed to see her. I kept asking, and I was told to get some sleep. That more tests had to be done. I never thought for one moment that anything was seriously wrong. But then, the next morning, the sister told me my little girl had died.'

Lucia seemed to be describing a headland seen from a ship, far, far from shore. She held her head back, eyes narrowed, as if to bring things into as tight a focus as possible.

'I wanted to see the body, just once, but the sister didn't think it was a good idea. I insisted, and so she sent for Dr Menderez, and he held my hand and he said the same thing. He was very, very kind. I saw pain in his eyes . . . and I was distraught, but he told me in the long run it would be harmful, to me . . . so I let Angela go.'

The funeral took place on the 12th of October 1986. A Friday morning. The coffin had been so small. That's what she'd kept thinking on the walk from the church to the cemetery. And the hole in the ground . . . it had been so deep. She'd watched, not daring to get close enough to touch the wood. The priest had waited for her to drop some earth into the grave, but Lucia had been unable to move; she could only watch.

Afterwards, she'd gone back to the hostel. All she could remember now – looking back – was sitting in her room listening to the traffic outside and the music from the room next door. She'd thought of her father, who was dead, and her mother, who was in prison. And she'd thought of Sr Valentina.

'I wanted to write to her. I wanted her to know . . . but I was too ashamed.

'Ashamed?' queried Benson.

Lucia looked towards the jury.

'I'd killed my own child. What other explanation could there be? I'd been on the street for two years. I'd eaten rubbish. I'd taken food out of bins. I'd poisoned my body . . . and I'd poisoned Angela.'

There was a very long silence following this declaration. Lucia had spoken slowly, like someone reading an inscription. Benson felt he was standing outside of time, until he heard a voice.

'We'll rise early for lunch,' said Judge Stanfield.

57

Tess and Benson went for a walk around the Barbican. They barely spoke. And Tess was sure that Benson, like her, was struggling to disentangle what he felt from what he had to think: the significance of Lucia's evidence for John Lynwood's defence. His troubled relationship with his wife, who'd become entangled with Dr Menderez, and his struggle to drive Dr Menderez away, seemed a world apart from what they'd heard. Further still, almost out of sight, was the dramatic development in Benson's private life. The mother of the man he'd allegedly killed had come to his defence. Nothing could have been more significant for Benson's future, save a hearing in the Court of Appeal. And yet it didn't seem to matter. Tess couldn't free her mind from what Lucia was about to say.

'I doubt if I will ever do anything as important as what I'm doing now,' said Benson, abruptly stopping.

'No,' said Tess. 'You won't.'

'Even if she's wrong about what happened, she has to speak out. You can't live with this kind of doubt. It has to be aired in a courtroom. A judge and jury have to hear it, even if there's no verdict.'

They walked back to the Bailey, falling into step, aware that they'd been overtaken by events; that they were privileged.

'What happened after the death of Angela?'

Benson resumed his questioning, discomfited once again

277

by Lucia's willingness to expose her history to the world, for those journalists were striking their laptops with something like a frenzy of anticipation.

'For the next few years I'd hand myself in to various police stations, saying I'd killed someone, and they'd lock me up for a while, and then after questioning they'd let me go. Before too long they knew me; and they knew what I was going to say. The officer on the desk had been told to send me away. But there was nowhere I could go . . . there was no one who'd punish me for what I'd done . . . so I thought of killing myself. It was the obvious thing to do. If I couldn't go to prison, then I'd end my life.'

'Why didn't you, Miss Callasteros?'

'Because Sister Valentina came to find me.'

She'd heard about the pregnancy and the death. And she'd scoured the streets once again, only this time Lucia wanted to be found. She wanted to tell this person who'd believed in her that she'd been wrong to do so.

'But Sister Valentina said something that changed everything. Not me, not the pain, not my guilt . . . but the light around me. That's what changed. And I saw things differently. She said Angela deserved a better epitaph than a ruined mother, that I could begin again, for her, like I'd done last time. That Angela could still be proud of me. That she still needed me.'

Sr Valentina had suggested Lucia work as a volunteer at a children's village she knew outside Madrid. A visit was organised, followed by an interview and . . . That had been twenty-seven years ago. Lucia looked down:

'Sister Valentina died that year, so she never knew that I settled down; that I have a very large family, now.'

Lucia spoke without a trace of sentimentality. She named a fact, nothing more. The loss of Angela had not been displaced; it had simply led Lucia towards a life she hadn't planned, sharing herself with other people's children.

'Did you talk of your past?'

'Only once, to a monk. From England. He'd come to visit the place where I worked. I never expected to talk about it again.'

'What changed your mind, Miss Callasteros? What brings you to this court today?'

'A phone call . . . in April 2014.'

It was from a man calling himself Gregorio. He refused to give his full name and Lucia suspected he wasn't even called Gregorio. He wheezed and coughed and Lucia was sure he'd been drinking. I'm ill, he said. Very ill. But I have to tell you something.

'He told me my daughter didn't die.'

The patter of the laptops ended at the same time, and the following silence was so absolute that Benson could hear Lucia breathe. Before he framed his next question, she said:

'I told him he was a bad man, and a cruel man to make up such a thing, but then he said he'd been there in the churchyard, on the day of the funeral, and that he'd worked for the undertaker. That he'd known me, Lucia Callasteros, before I'd gone to San Florentina's. He'd known my mother, Natalia. He'd buried my father.'

Benson took a sip of water, but Lucia continued of her own accord, her voice wavering.

'He'd felt guilty all his life, he said . . . and then I asked him about the coffin. I said there was a coffin. A small one. I hadn't wanted to touch it, but it had been there, and I'd seen it go into the ground. I'd seen the men lowering it with two white ropes. And Gregorio said he was one of those men, and he . . .'

Judge Stanfield addressed Mrs Alvarez, the interpreter. 'Would you please ask Miss Callasteros if she'd like to sit down, or have a glass of—'

But Lucia began speaking again, and for the first time Mrs Alvarez looked confused. She asked Lucia a question, slowly, and Lucia nodded, evidently repeating herself, also slowly. Frowning, and looking helpless, Mrs Alvarez translated:

'Gregorio said there was a dog in the coffin. He should know: he put it there.'

Judge Stanfield stopped taking notes. He was wondering how to formulate a response when Lucia went on:

'I asked him, why would anyone do that? And he said because my child had been sold . . . sold like fruit at the market.'

58

There'd been an arrangement, said Gregorio. The sister who'd worked with Dr Menderez was in touch with certain parishes. There'd been others, too. People who knew about the possibility of adopting outside the usual channels. And she'd kept a list of couples wanting to adopt a child. Her role was to identify an expectant mother who was unlikely to cope, and then arrange for the child to be collected within days of the birth. The undertaker's business where Gregorio worked had been part of the scheme. They'd get a call from the clinic and, for the customary fee, a funeral would be organised. All the usual paperwork would be filled out. The records would show a corpse had been collected on such a day and so on . . . and as a rule, stones would be put in the coffin, or some other kind of weight. On this occasion, however, the owner's dog happened to have died, and he'd saved money by not having to pay a vet to deal with the body.

'Did you act upon what you'd been told?' said Benson, after a pause.

'Yes, of course . . . but almost thirty years had passed. That's . . . a lifetime. I went to the undertaker's, but they'd closed down. I went to the Clinica Lorenzo and asked to see my medical records, but I was told they'd been moved, and anyway, most of the documents from that period had been destroyed, so I asked to see Dr Menderez, but he'd retired, they said, and so had the sister, the nurse who'd been there, writing everything down – I still don't know her name . . . but I knew which order she was from, so I wrote to their main house, to the head sister, but she didn't reply. So I went to see her – I turned up and knocked on the door – but she wouldn't talk to me, and when I told the sister at reception why I'd come, she looked at me as if I was completely mad . . . and that's when I thought I'd go and find Dr Menderez.'

This evidence had come in a rush, so Judge Stanfield paused to check his note. Then he gave a nod to Benson and Lucia continued her story.

She'd traced Dr Menderez easily enough and had gone to Candidar on the 1st of July 2014, turning up in his surgery unannounced.

'He listened to me very carefully. He didn't treat me as if I was mad. But he assured me that my child had died, that complications happen, and that if my problems had been in any way responsible, he would have remembered . . . and that I wasn't to blame myself in any way.'

'And what of Gregorio's disclosure?'

'He said it was incredible, obscene. And that no such thing could have happened.'

He asked Lucia lots of questions, trying to locate the period in his life when she'd come to the clinic. He'd been twenty-eight in 1986, he'd said. He'd worked out Lucia's

281

age, eighteen, and he'd tried to remember who else had been there . . . but no, sorry, he couldn't remember the sister's name . . . she'd come from Cantabria. And then he'd begun to wonder if he recalled Lucia. He'd asked about her life, after the loss of her child.

'I told him of my work in the children's village, and while he didn't say it, he was obviously amazed that someone like me could have changed so much. That made me feel nice . . . to think that the man who'd brought my child into the world saw me differently to the person he'd met so long ago.'

Lucia had been left with a stark choice. Who was she to believe? A drunk who'd only tell her he was called Gregorio, when he probably wasn't, or a respectable professional like Dr Menderez?

'Dr Menderez had to be right,' she said. 'If anyone had bought Angela, he would have known about it . . . and he'd come to see me at the time, he'd held my hand, he'd been compassionate. He'd never have been involved in something so . . . wrong . . . so evil as the theft of a child for money.'

Lucia had gone back to work. She'd tried to forget the memories raised by this Gregorio. She'd focused on her work, and the children in the village. And then, a few days ago, she'd seen a report of the trial on television. She'd recognised the name and face of Dr Menderez and she'd contacted her friend, the monk in England. He'd urged her to speak to the police or the defence. She'd chosen the defence because she'd been worried Mr Lynwood might have been wrongly accused.

'You see, if Dr Menderez lied to me, then he didn't work alone. There were these others involved in the scheme. And if he'd come to England, intending to reveal what he'd done, what he'd been a part of, because, like me, he'd changed . . . then I imagine someone might easily want to stop him.'

'Thank you, Miss Callasteros.'

Judge Stanfield thought it best to finish there. Miss Forde could cross-examine the next morning, he said, and then he addressed Benson:

'No doubt you'd like to remind the jury that Dr Menderez had become suicidal in July 2014? And since Miss Callasteros went to Candidar on the first of the month it's reasonable to conclude his rapid decline in mental health came after their meeting?'

'Yes, my lord. In terms of chronology, the one follows the other.'

59

It's likely, thought Tess, that most of the jury had no idea about the scale of the problem that lay behind Lucia's evidence. Tess hadn't known; and neither had Benson. It transpired Judge Stanfield and Forde hadn't known either. It was strange, in retrospect, that neither Lucia or Fr Aelred had mentioned it. Either way, everyone certainly knew by Friday morning, after Lucia's evidence had been reported by the media. Because investigative journalists and historians had placed Lucia's testimony in its wider context. In the light of that information Judge Stanfield had ordered counsel to locate an agreed expert in the field who might help the court with an authoritative summary of the issues involved. By late morning, Professor Matilde de Laranga from King's College London was in the witness box. Benson put the questions.

Reports in the media were broadly correct, she said.

In the aftermath of the Civil War, she explained, up to thirty thousand children had been stolen from individuals or families judged politically dangerous by the Franco regime. The children had been placed with approved couples who supported the values of the restored order, in effect making sure they were protected from threats seen, at the time, as potent as those of ISIS and its affiliates. Call it a form of eugenics, she said. The suppression of the red gene. The entire left was considered suspect, not just the communism of Stalin.

What began as a form of socio-political regulation, however, had gradually metamorphosed into something with a much wider remit: the removal of children from individuals or couples lacking financial resources or deemed morally wanting. The official, protracted process of adoption was circumvented, and would-be adoptive parents were put in direct contact with those working in hospitals and maternity clinics, who then identified appropriate children, without any discussion with the mother. And then, of course, there was the question of money. It had changed hands. How much? Estimates in today's money ranged between twelve hundred and eighteen thousand euros.

The adoption scheme – if that was what it was – had grown out of the purge, said Professor de Laranga. And like the purge, it had been unique.

There were no legal obligations to place a mother's name on a birth certificate or record the mother's name in the Civil Register. With respect to the Register, unmarried mothers would be protected from disapproval by the inherently unlikely phrase 'Mother not known'.

How long had this scheme been in operation?

It was thought to have lasted into the nineties.

How many children had been abducted?

According to lawyers instructed by the families seeking their children or children seeking their families, three hundred thousand.

Had a national inquiry been instigated by the government?

No, and none was expected. In the absence of a coordinated response, charitable associations had been formed to represent those affected. The first and most prominent was ANADIR.

'In what year was ANADIR founded?'

'2010.'

'Thank you.'

The judge had no questions for Professor de Laranga. Neither had Forde.

Forde began her cross-examination of Lucia in the afternoon.

'Miss Callasteros, have you contacted the police in Spain?'

'No.'

'Do you intend to?'

'No.'

'May I ask why?'

'Because the investigation would lead to closed door after closed door. I have the strength for the disappointment . . . but there's no point. Time has worked against me. I've been left behind.'

'Do you intend to apply for an order that would allow for the exhumation of Angela? So that you would know for sure if Gregorio had told you the truth?'

'No.'

'Again, may I ask why?'

'As I tried to say, it is too late now. If Angela is alive, she's now thirty. She'd have been taken, I hope, by a family who thought they were helping a mother who could never have coped . . . she may be married now, with children. They have a life . . . an identity . . . a self-understanding. How could I . . .'

Lucia paused.

'How could I present myself?' she said at last. 'I don't belong.'

Forde meditated on Lucia's answer; and then she said:
'How long did it take you to get from Madrid to Candidar?'
'It's a very long journey: eight hours or so.'
'You went by train?'
'To Granada, yes. And then a bus and taxi to the village.'
'You stayed in a hotel?'
'Yes, the night I saw Dr Menderez.'
Again, Forde thought about the answer; and then she spoke without emotion:
'Why have you been very careful – in this court – to limit yourself to suspicion?'
'Because I don't know the truth. I'll never know the truth.'
'Are you aware of anyone accusing Dr Menderez of involvement in a conspiracy to steal children?'
'No.'
'Thank you, Miss Callasteros. My lord, for the record – and I have discussed the matter with Mr Benson and he's agreed to me disclosing what I now say – those who instruct me have spoken to the Department of Justice in Spain. They confirm that allegations of this kind are taken with the utmost seriousness. No such contention has ever been made against Dr Menderez and no such case has ever been linked to the Clinica Lorenzo in Madrid.'

Forde had been as careful as Lucia herself. And it troubled Tess. She'd expected a meticulous and sustained interrogation demonstrating the weakness of Lucia's testimony; a concerted attempt to reinstate Dr Menderez as a morally inspiring figure. Instead she'd confined herself to a few brief points, leaving Lucia's story intact. This omission had nothing to do with compassion. Forde had done it because it suited her case. She'd left the horror in place because, ultimately, she'd decided to use it to her advantage . . . but Tess couldn't imagine how.

'I don't know what she's doing,' whispered Benson, after turning around.

'Neither do I.'

Tess watched Lucia leave the courtroom. She was pale and exhausted, barely able to hold herself upright. This had been her day and there'd been no fight.

'I don't like it.'

60

Benson read out the witness statement obtained from Fr Winsley. It contained, in effect, a single, now unsettling, admission from Dr Menderez: that the greatest mistake of his life had been to miss a course of lectures on medical ethics at Cambridge University. On that note, Benson asked for a short adjournment. Presently he and Tess were in the usual brightly lit conference room with Mr and Mrs Lynwood, their son, Simon, and the ever-present Mrs Tindale. The question was simple: who would next give evidence?

'It's extraordinary what's happened,' said Simon.

'It is,' replied Benson.

'I never could have foreseen this.'

'No one could.'

'Everything my parents said has turned out to be true. This man had a history. And it caught up with him.'

Simon spoke with deep relief, his dark eyes darting between his mother and father, and then between them and Mrs Tindale, and then between Tess and Benson. He was bringing everyone in on the good news: that his parents' marriage might have been in serious trouble but the unhappiness and betrayal hadn't led to a brutal murder. Simon had the fiery look of a recent convert. He said:

'I can't believe someone would come forward . . . all the way from Spain, and strip themselves down in public. Just because they're worried someone might be innocent. It's incredible.'

'It is.'

Benson's attention shifted to Karen. She looked as exhausted as Lucia. And like Lucia, she was staring at the ground. The effect of the trial on her had been profound. Upon first meeting, she'd been a precisely dressed woman with neatly cut dark hair; signs of age had begun to emerge in grey strands, gathered together like faint stripes. The effect, entirely natural, had been a conspicuous elegance. In the space of days these had turned white, and the contrast harsh. And as for her clothing, she'd worn the same black outfit every day. It was now creased: it had been thrown down before she'd gone to bed, and thrown on again in the morning. Benson said:

'If Miss Callasteros is right in what she fears, then Dr Menderez might well have been implicated in the sale of hundreds of children during his tenure at the Clinica Lorenzo.'

'It's inconceivable,' said Simon.

'I agree. But it happened; and times changed. And what had seemed acceptable back then may have gradually revealed itself for what it is: a crime against humanity. And if he tried to forget what he'd done, then I imagine he would have been shattered by the sudden arrival of a patient from the contaminated years of his life. I'd imagine he would want to run away from what he'd done. And I imagine he'd eventually want to confide in someone – and, conceivably, hand himself in to the police.'

Karen raised her eyes and said quietly:

'No, Mr Benson. I did not know. He gave me no hint that this was his secret . . . if it was his secret. Will you ever believe me?'

'I just have to know: did he ever mention anything that ties in with Miss Callasteros's evidence?'

'No, nothing at all. But why do you ask?'

'Because if he had, I would want you to reconsider your decision not to give evidence. At the moment, I can argue his involvement in child abduction may have been his secret. If you could add anything to—'

'Well I can't. And if you imagine I'd keep silent about something so horrific, then you must think I'm some kind of monster.'

She tugged at her hair – just like Simon, after his argument with Isabel Tindale – and she blurted out:

'Have you any idea what it feels like to be associated with this kind of abuse? Or to be seen as someone who could have fallen in love with such a man? Because that is what Miss Forde wants the jury to believe. It's in the papers. Don't you read what they're saying? They're saying I might have known, that—'

'I have read them. And while they're nothing to do with the trial, they can help us.'

'How?'

'They show us the mind of the jury. And the media, like the jury, are simply wondering if you knew what he'd done. It's a natural question. And it would make complete sense if you'd been overwhelmed by what you'd been told.'

'But that isn't what happened, and how on earth would it help John if it were true?'

'Because it would confirm Miss Callasteros's story. It would confirm that Dr Menderez was a man who other people might want to silence.'

'The nameless sister? Someone in her eighties?'

'Someone who knew the nameless sister,' replied Benson, ignoring her tone. 'Someone who knew an adoption could be arranged for a fee. A fixer, if you like. And then there are those who falsified medical records, birth certificates and death certificates. They're all deeply implicated. And they're all potential—'

'I understand, Mr Benson. But I'm in an impossible position. I can't make up what didn't happen. I know it would help John if I did, but all Dr Menderez said was that he wanted to claim back his integrity – it's all in my notes. He said nothing about . . .'

Her voice trailed off; and then Mr Lynwood said:

'Mr Benson, I wouldn't want Karen to go into the witness box. Miss Callasteros's evidence helps me, but it makes things worse for Karen. People are perverse. They want to believe she'd become involved with a monster. And that is what Miss Forde wants to show, too.'

Benson nodded.

'Karen handled the stalking badly,' continued Mr Lynwood sympathetically. 'She should have called the police when the texts and emails started coming, but she didn't. She shouldn't have met Dr Menderez in that pub. But she did, and Miss Forde is going to use this against her in order to get to me, to show why I'd charged over there and killed him, when I didn't.'

This was, in fact, the fundamental problem in the defence case. Mrs Lynwood's secret knowledge of Dr Menderez might well be central to a defence argument; but her relations with him were also central to the prosecution's case against her husband. She was needed by both sides.

'She can't go into the witness box,' said Mr Lynwood. 'You know that. Not if she can't add anything to Miss Callasteros's evidence. And I can't give evidence either. Because Miss Forde will question me about my marriage . . . about my relationship with Narinda Hassan. To show I can't be trusted. She'll quote Brian Unwin – that I wanted Dr Menderez to bugger off and die – and I can't contradict him. Because it's true. She'll put me in that house with Dr Menderez and ask why did I travel across London only to say something I'd already said on the phone. We'll lose the effect of Miss Callasteros's testimony. Miss Forde might argue he's still a selfless man who cared for the destitute, but I saw some of the jurors. They were nodding. I don't think anyone wants to think that somehow that poor woman has got it all wrong. They want to believe her.'

Benson was taken aback. Mr Lynwood the accountant had added up the numbers correctly with astonishing detachment. He'd not only assessed the evidence, he'd thought out a compelling tactical response. In the corner of his eye Benson saw Simon nodding. He was holding Mrs Tindale's hand. If Lucia Callasteros had achieved nothing else, she'd brought this family back together. She'd given them a shared purpose.

'It's my decision, Mr Benson. I won't change my mind.'

61

'Lucia Callasteros, ladies and gentlemen of the jury,' said Forde quietly.

That Benson had closed his case without calling the remaining defendant or his wife had surprised the jury. It was an unorthodox move. And, as Judge Stanfield pointed out, the decision exposed Mr Lynwood to adverse comment from the prosecution. What he didn't say, of course, was that he, and indeed Forde, were perfectly aware that husband and wife had more to gain than lose by refusing to answer any more questions. The case would now turn on the speeches.

'Lucia Callasteros.'

Forde wasn't so much savouring the name as reciting a password.

'She is the key to this case.'

There was a long pause, during which Forde nodded at the jury. She knew they were all agreed on this.

'Who could not pity her? Who could not weep with her? Who could not wish her peace of mind?'

When speaking, Lucia had frowned, drawing her eyebrows low, but raising them in the centre. She had the searching look of someone who'd never find the answers. Benson found her difficult to watch, because she reminded him of his mother.

'And who would dare suggest that this victim of tragedy would, in fact, share responsibility for a tragedy herself?'

Forde paused, and removed her half-moon glasses.

'I would. Dr Menderez led a blameless life. And one day a woman came to see him, all the way from Madrid . . . by train and bus and taxi. She'd sent no letter or email. There'd been no phone call. There'd been no warning. Because she'd wanted the element of surprise. Which showed the depth of her distrust. It matters not how careful she was with words, Dr Menderez was left in no doubt what was happening. He wasn't being asked to allay a troubling suspicion. He was being accused. Of a most terrible crime. One about which he must have heard. Heard about with indignation. And with compassion for the victims. And now he was being placed at the centre of a national scandal by a patient he was straining to remember.'

This is the age of public exposure, said Forde. Twitter. Facebook. Instagram. YouTube. You know the many unforgiving faces of social media. They are public courts that judge everything from unrest in the Middle East to a false arrest in Chicago to what you had for breakfast. There's no opportunity to reply. There are no rules of evidence to protect the innocent. And once a condemnation has been posted, you might as well kill yourself.

'Which is what Dr Menderez considered. I invite you to imagine his state of mind. He must have lived in absolute terror that his name would be appear on the internet. Because he wasn't to know that this patient who'd come to see him had in fact believed him. That she hadn't doubted his integrity. For all he knew, she'd gone back to Madrid intent on finding the nurse without a name, the quiet presence who'd written everything down. Who knew where Angela had gone, and with whom.'

Not surprisingly, continued Forde, he fled Spain. But he needed someone to talk to. And he found Karen Lynwood. A therapist with an understanding of Spanish culture and language. And he went back to the beginning. He told her how the Civil War had shattered his parents.

'He was planning to tell her that it had eventually shattered him, too. Because the legacy of those years had reached his door. But, in the end, he couldn't bring himself to name the crime with which he'd been associated. And we all know why. Because he'd fallen in love with her. And she had fallen in love with him. And he simply couldn't tell her about the storm that might one day break over his head.'

Forde polished the lenses of her reading glasses, still speaking.

'That, ladies and gentlemen, is what I thought until this morning. But I've now changed my mind.'

She placed her glasses back on her nose.

'I now think he told her about Lucia Callasteros. During their last session together. And Mrs Lynwood daren't enter the witness box for fear I will ask her if she recognises the name, a name she didn't note down; and that I will ask her to explain the profound hesitation which then seized her. Because that is exactly what happened. Reread the schedule of texts and emails. Dr Menderez had been urging her to tell John how she felt; for a month he'd begged her to find the courage to leave him. And on the day Dr Menderez was murdered, he'd given Mrs Lynwood an ultimatum: "Either you tell him, or I will."

'Tell him what?'

Forde raised a hand as if it contained the answer.

'That the marriage was over. But she was paralysed. The storm that might engulf the man she'd fallen in love with would also engulf her, and the family she was thinking of leaving. This is the one subject Karen Lynwood does not want to discuss. Not then, and not now. Not with Mr Benson and not with this court. And, I suspect, not with her husband . . . who won't enter the witness box either.'

Forde looked at the door that led out of Number 3 Court.

'Lucia Callasteros,' she said. 'What did she do? She spoke from a broken heart. But it drove Dr Menderez out of the country and into the arms of the one person he should have avoided: a lonely, unhappy woman with a husband who'd kill to keep the semblance of his family together.'

Forde smiled pityingly.

'A professional killing? On the instructions of someone involved in the abduction of children thirty years ago? Since when does a hitman spend hours with his victim before killing him? Since when does a hitman turn up for a job without his tools and, instead, borrows his victim's kitchen scissors? Since when does a hitman carefully place a body on its back, with arms folded on its chest, and a shroud placed over the upper torso? They don't, ladies and gentleman. There was no one with Dr Menderez for hours on end. The only person who came to see him that night was John Lynwood. He's the one who grabbed the scissors, he's the one who treated the body with respect, as an amateur might; as a decent man might, who's taken one momentous step too far.'

Forde moved towards Benson, and towards the jury.

'You must choose your coincidence. Is it a coincidence that Dr Menderez left maternity work in 2010, the year ANADIR was formed? I say it is. Alternatively, is it a coincidence that someone else should kill Dr Menderez on the very day John Lynwood should threaten to kill him, and actually be present, in the house, when John Lynwood arrives to have – what? Another pointless argument? I think not. The choice is yours.'

Benson was on his feet before Forde had sat down.

'And it is upon coincidence that many a man and woman has been taken from this court and led down a corridor in this building that gets narrower and narrower until they reached the gallows. With respect to my learned friend, weighing coincidences won't do.'

Benson couldn't shift the image of Lucia Callasteros from his mind. Or the recognition of what she'd done.

'Instead I offer you a woman who came all the way from Spain, by aircraft, train and the London Underground. She'd sent no letter or email. There'd been no phone call. There'd been no warning. She came because of the same suspicion, revived now, that had once brought her from Madrid to Candidar. A suspicion that has to be heard to be understood. Her concern this time was not for herself, but for a man who might have been wrongly accused. She had nothing to gain and everything to lose. She has now, in fact, lost everything. Because she gave up her dignity. Her anonymity. Her privacy.'

Benson, copying Forde, looked at the court door.

'Was it worth it?'

He let the question hang. Then he picked up the admitted

statement from Fr Winsley. And he read out the one line that mattered:

"'He told me the greatest mistake of his life had been to miss a course on medical ethics.'"

Benson pondered the line.

He was about to list the next steps in his argument: that this admission was decisive, because it linked Dr Menderez to the history he'd tried to escape; that in running he may have drawn attention to himself, and become a target – for the man seen at the mouth of Ropemaker's Way – but Benson seemed to hear Helen's voice.

Say nothing more. Let the jury join the dots.

Obedient to that instruction, Benson slowly sat down; and the court was thrown into silence.

62

Helen's voice.

It had come to Benson like a saving angel. But by Monday morning, when Judge Stanfield began his summing up, it was haunting him.

He'd spent the weekend sailing on the canal, keeping away from Seymour Basin. The press had assembled at his gate. Not to discuss the Limehouse case, but Mrs Harbeton's declaration of support for the man she believed had been wrongly convicted of the murder of her son. He'd turned his phone off, too, avoiding calls from Archie and Tess. The development – for want of a better word – had left him in turmoil. He couldn't celebrate. Because he remained deeply implicated in the events that had led to Paul Harbeton's death. He was part of a dead man's story; and a dead man was part of his. Nothing could ever shift that darkness. He'd gone to see Helen on Sunday, thinking she was the one person who'd understand the paradox of guilt seeping deeper into the mind than innocence, but she hadn't even raised the matter. As Judge Stanfield, well into the afternoon now, reminded the jury of what they'd heard, Benson stared ahead.

'You've been avoiding me,' said Helen, from inside her shining plastic helmet.

'I've just been busy. It's a difficult case. Have you read about—'

'Don't lie. Not to me. Not now.'

Turning to face her, Benson took one of her hands. It was soft and smooth from lack of use; and cool. The heat of life was slowly leaving her.

'You're breaking the rules,' said Benson awkwardly, 'and I don't know why. You want to talk about my trial, and it's painful. We left it behind. We've done something with the injustice.'

'I've no choice. I've run out of time. Tell me about Eddie.'

'Eddie?'

'Yes. How did the trial affect him?'

Benson took his hand back and knotted it into the other. So many years of silence were coming to an end, but for no reason, here in a hospital room, and without hope of change resulting from anything that he might say. It was pointless. But then, all at once, Benson had a confused epiphany. He saw Lucia Callasteros speaking from the witness stand; and he saw Maureen Harbeton listening in a filthy kitchen. Two victims, one of whom needn't say anything, and the other who'd forced Benson to reveal what Helen, this woman dying in front of him, had told him to keep secret: the truth about the night that had changed so many people's lives. Without understanding what was happening, Benson realised he was free. That he could speak without fear . . . that Maureen Harbeton had already pushed him through the door.

'I lied to you, Helen,' said Benson. He had to go back to the beginning.

'I knew Paul Harbeton. I'd gone looking for him. I can't tell you why, but I wanted to confront him. You see—'

'None of that is important now. Answer my question.'

Benson's emotions had been rising but Helen's indifference threw him. What could be more important than the truth behind his role in Paul Harbeton's death?

'The trial,' said Helen. 'How did it affect your brother?'

Benson had to repress the urge to speak about the fight with Paul Harbeton, and what had happened afterwards. Because he hadn't told his shattered mother everything . . . that would have been impossible; he'd been honest; he'd answered her question; but there was more, and he wanted to tell Helen; but Helen didn't want to know. Her eyes with their fading fire were focused exclusively on the trial and its consequences. Benson obeyed. There wasn't much to say.

'He got a life sentence, too.'

'How?'

'Because he's always believed I was guilty. When I wouldn't admit it, he cut me off; but in cutting me off he cut himself off from the help he needed. That's all I can say, because—'

'That's all I need to know. Thank you.'

Benson repositioned his chair so that it faced the bed, so that he could look at Helen directly; then, on the edge of his seat, he said:

'Helen, what's going on? You're going to leave me soon. Why do you want to trawl through the heartache we left behind?'

'I told you, Will, there are things you must tell me, and there are things I must say.'

'But I'm ready to speak. I lied. I didn't tell you what you needed to know if you were to defend me. I'm responsible for the conviction. I put myself in prison. I put Eddie in prison. I broke my father. I broke my mother. I'm—'

'Your lie made no difference.'

Helen's face was drawn and pale; she laboured to breathe.

'What do you mean?' said Benson, just above a whisper.

'There are things I must say, but not now. Not yet.'

The shiny blue plastic disc moved up and down, shivering and falling, shivering and falling.

'Will?'

Tess was at his side. Benson was standing. Judge Stanfield had finished his summing up. He'd given legal directions to the jury. The jury had retired to deliberate. The court had risen. The public gallery was empty. The stenographer who'd just got married was staring at him. So was the haggard usher.

'Are you okay?' said Tess.

Benson turned towards her. She'd always been there, by his side. She'd doubted him but opted for trust.

'Tess, I lied to you.'

'What?'

'I lied. From the beginning. To you, Archie, the Tuesday Club. I lied to you all. Because I was—'

'Stop, Will. Not here.'

Tess had whispered, reaching for his arm to pull him out of court. He followed her towards the heavy doors, and when they got outside, among the people milling around, waiting for verdicts, or to give evidence, or to support those who would, all of them anxious, she swung around and said:

'There are things I must say, but not now. Not yet.'

Benson couldn't believe it. He'd been silenced for almost twenty years. And when he'd finally been freed to speak, no one wanted to listen.

63

'Would the jury foreman please rise,' said the clerk.

A tall woman dressed in a red T-shirt and jeans stood up; and as she did so, she glanced towards the dock.

'Have you reached a verdict upon which you are all agreed?'

'Yes.'

The clerk looked at the indictment in his hands.

'Do you find the defendant, John Lynwood, guilty or not guilty of murder?'

The jury had only been out for an hour and a half. During that time, Benson had chatted to Forde. She'd never done a case like it, she'd said. There'd been something very peculiar about the evidence. The jury had been told everything they needed to know, but she'd had a sense that something vital was missing. Or perhaps it had been there, before her eyes, and she hadn't been able to see it.

The foreman cleared her throat, and as she spoke there came a shout from Mrs Tindale in the public gallery and again, for a moment, Benson was thrown out of time. The woman who'd been there to catch his mother, the woman he'd seen at the Royal Marsden . . . who was she? But the memory of her troubled face was shoved away by the commotion in the gallery and the detonation of energy among the press.

They'd found John Lynwood not guilty; and Judge

Stanfield was telling him he was free to go; and he was then thanking the jury, and Benson, obliged to interact, went through the motions until, finally, he was standing with Forde as she endorsed her brief. The judge had left the bench. The hum of a shock decision filled the room.

'I know what was missing,' said Forde with a smile. 'It's Father Winsley. He told us what he could. But I suspect he knew everything. He's the only one who ever knew everything.'

She'd read between the lines of the shortest statement in the trial, and guessed what must have happened.

'Well done, Will. Though it's a perverse verdict.'

Benson understood. On the evidence, John Lynwood was guilty. But the jury had joined the dots in such a way as to send Lucia Callasteros a message: Jorge Luis Rafael Menderez had not escaped justice. He'd been condemned to death.

'They're innocent, Janet,' said Benson.

'You think so?'

'It's a prison thing. You just know. John Lynwood didn't kill Dr Menderez. I know the evidence says he did, but, as you say, it's been a strange case.'

'Fought against a gentleman,' she said, holding out her hand. 'Look me up. We've a lot to discuss.'

And with that cryptic and completely unexpected invitation, Forde went over to the stenographer.

'Maggy, would you stop looking so damned contented,' she said.

To say Benson was mobbed would not be an exaggeration. When he came out of court, Mrs Tindale was the first to accost him. She grabbed both of Benson's arms and began tugging him towards John and Karen and Simon. Benson couldn't see the light between them. Their shoulders were joined as if they shared the same outlandish garment, woven to keep them forever warm. The only person who showed any discomfort was Karen, and even then it was well concealed. Benson recognised it, because he'd lived a contradiction: she was smiling and relieved and grateful, but there was a deeper rebellion that she'd never be able to express; that no one would ever understand. She remained a woman with a secret. The garment that bound her to her family was a straitjacket.

'I'm lost for words,' said John Lynwood, seizing Benson's hand.

There were tears in his eyes and his voice was strained.

'You've saved this family.'

At those words Simon came forward, drawing his mother with him.

'You have. We were falling apart, and now . . .'

He reached over to Mrs Tindale and pulled her towards the pack.

'We can put this nightmare behind us. We can start again, all of us. Because of what you've done. You've—'

Benson held up a hand, signalling the need for a correction.

'The person to thank is not me, but Lucia Callasteros. She's the one who saved you. Shall I find her? You really ought to speak to her.'

Mr Lynwood pulled an arm out of the huddle to place it around his wife.

'To be honest, I'd rather not. I'm worn out and I'll probably cry all over her, and I don't want to do that. I wouldn't know what to say, not after what she's been through. Forgive me, I just want to go home.'

'Of course.'

Benson understood. He'd felt the same after reading Mrs Harbeton's words in the *Standard*. Here was a woman who'd commanded national attention, attracting compassion and admiration, and she'd thrown it all away. For the sake of what she believed to be true. Putting the newspaper to one side, he'd slowly begun to realise what her support would mean for him; and he couldn't imagine speaking to her, because he knew he wouldn't find words adequate for the situation. For her suffering had begun afresh. He shook hands with John, Karen, Simon and the abnormally quiet Mrs Tindale, and as they walked away, tripping over their many feet, Benson noticed that Tess was with him. She was smiling.

'Say what you like about Lucia Callasteros, you've done it again, Mr Benson.'

Benson didn't go to the robing room. He went in search of Lucia and Fr Aelred. He'd seen them in the public gallery during the summing up. He'd seen them when the jury were called back into court by Judge Stanfield. They'd decided to wait for the verdict. Three days, braving cameras and microphones. Away from their attention, high in the gallery, Lucia had sat staring into space, not understanding what was going on around her, disengaged from the drama of her making, wanting to know, at least, its outcome.

The corridor outside the gallery was empty. So were the toilets. An usher told Benson everyone had left that part of the building, so he quickly ran down the stairs and out into the wet, bustling street, straining to spot them heading towards Newgate or Ludgate Hill. But they'd gone.

As mysteriously as they'd come.

64

'Here's to Archie Congreve,' said Tess, lining up four dispos-able plastic cups. For what they were about to drink, no other vessel was appropriate.

'What for?'

'You got it right and you got it wrong.'

'Eh?'

'The great Janet Forde QC borrowed all your arguments.'

'And what did I get wrong?'

'The verdict, Archie, the verdict.'

Tess, Benson, Archie and Molly were in the Gutting Room. Journalists were at the front and back, where they'd been left to wait. The phone had been ringing, too, and Archie had taken the thing off the hook. With the curtains tightly closed, he opened the jerrycan of prison hooch he'd made with Molly at the outset of the trial. Tess had watched with horror: Archie had taken the sock filled with breadcrumbs out of the warm water – 'I'm drawing out the yeast,' he'd said – and thrown it in the bin. He'd then mixed the yeasty water with a mountain of sugar, tipped into a bowl by Molly. And finally, he'd put the sweetened yeasty water in the can with lots of freshly squeezed orange juice.

'It's disgusting,' she said.

'You lack imagination, Miss de Vere,' said Archie. 'Think vodka and orange.'

'I can't. I can only think sock and dirt.'

Being a purist, Archie had dried the sliced bread on a radiator. A radiator that hadn't been dusted, Tess was sure, since the Congreves first came to Artillery Passage in 1893.

'Brings back those boring afternoons in HMP Lindley,' said Archie, lowering himself into an armchair. He gave a nod to Benson behind his desk. 'Have you seen the news?

Maureen Harbeton? She's asked for the investigation into her son's death to be reopened.'

'Yes, I saw that.'

'Says she'd got evidence that someone else might have wanted to kill him.'

'I know . . . it's incredible.'

'What the hell could it be? And how did she get her hands on it?'

Molly raised her cup.

'We'll find out soon enough.'

There was a hiatus, during which Tess felt the burning attention of Archie and Molly. Now that the pressure on Benson had eased, they expected Tess to pursue her lead and find out who might have dropped a bracelet by the body of Paul Harbeton. But they were also bemused, because they were both wondering how that someone might be connected to the other someone who wanted to kill him . . . it roused the image of an old woman with a cosh, which couldn't be right. Tess simply couldn't disabuse them. Smiling, she turned to Benson:

'Will we ever find out what happened with Menderez?'

Benson had his elbows propped on his desk, holding his plastic cup in both hands.

'We already know,' he said.

Tess smiled again, this time with admiration. Benson's insight into the Limehouse case had been extraordinary from the outset. He'd seen through a questionnaire into the troubled mind of a dead man. He'd seen into Karen Lynwood's relationship with her patient. He'd seen into John Lynwood's relationship with Narinda Hassan. He'd seen into Hassan's relationship with Karen. He'd seen into Karl Ambrose's relationship with Hayley Townsend – whose stepfather hadn't even thanked Tess for the urgent works order to replace all the windows in his flat. And, astonishingly, he'd seen into the mind of Lucia Callasteros before he knew she even existed, or before he knew what Dr Menderez had done. This was Benson's strong point: understanding troubled people, and how they relate to one another; how they hide and lie and suffer for what they do, and what they've done, and how they struggle with what has been done to them. He can see it on paper; and he can see it in the flicker of an eye. With such power – because that is what it is – he could devastate individuals and families. But he didn't. He entered their lives as if he'd been there before. In the context of a trial, where the truth was at stake, there was no judgement or condemnation; he just gave them the opportunity to be different.

'I'm afraid I agree with Mr Congreve,' said Molly. 'The only person who could have killed Dr Menderez was our client.'

Benson shook his head.

'This Gregorio who rang Lucia . . . that wasn't his only call. This man was trying to clear his conscience. He rang lots of people. They'd all been cheated and lied to and robbed. Most of them will have been decent, law-abiding citizens. But there will have been some – and for us it only takes one – who'd want to take the law into their own hands.'

'How can you be so sure?' said Tess.

'Because no justice is available to them. There's been no independent national inquiry, no appointment of a special prosecutor, no convictions, no opening of medical archives, no DNA database set up to permit cross-referencing. Nothing of substance. All these thousands of victims have is solidarity, and lawyers who won't give up. And it's possible at least one of them wanted something more tangible. And paid someone to do it.'

Archie was shaking his head.

'Forde got it right, Archie,' said Benson. 'And so did John Lynwood. This case was about coincidence. Whoever killed Menderez knew Lynwood was coming. They were in the house waiting to choose their moment. And then they heard the call. It was a stroke of luck. They waited some more. And when Lynwood had gone, they did a professional job.'

Professionals don't bring tool kits, he said. When they can, they improvise, to hide their professionalism. They make things look like a burglary gone wrong. So that people like Karl Ambrose get arrested. Or John Lynwood. Their mistake, for Benson, was the manner of the killing. The single stab to the head, striking a specific part of the brainstem, was the one fact Benson refused to put down to chance. That was the key to the rest of the evidence; and from the moment Benson had opened the brief, he'd been sure this was the one decisive fact around which all the others had to be interpreted.

'John Lynwood could never have done that.'

Archie accepted that last point, but he remained uneasy.

'A professional killing is always an unsatisfactory explanation,' acknowledged Benson. 'Because there's no anger or hatred or resentment. All we've got is a cold contract.'

'And what about Karen?' said Tess. 'Was she stalked, or was that just a lie?'

Tess had her own view; she just enjoyed listening to Benson; watching him weave himself into someone's hidden life; wanting him to look at her and see what was written all over her face.

'Forde got that right, too,' he said, looking out of the window. 'Along with the great Archie Congreve, of course. Karen found herself in the most difficult situation imaginable. She'd fallen in love with someone who was good and kind and gentle and sensitive . . . and yet he'd done something unimaginably bad.' Benson gave a resigned shrug. 'And he'd fallen in love with her. He'd come to a therapist to try and make amends, but he felt different now. Something new was underway.'

Benson threw a glance at Archie.

'It's easier for us to understand this, because we've met people inside who've . . . killed their own children . . . their brothers . . . their best friends . . . and sometimes the people they've become, afterwards . . . do you remember Larry, Archie? He just wasn't the same man who'd killed his wife, was he? Remorse can do that. It can change your cells. That's why Karen will never be able to tell John the truth, or Simon. Or anyone. She has to lie. Fact is, she'd forgiven him. She just daren't admit it. But she couldn't condemn the man who sat on the other side of the table, she couldn't call the police. He'd changed, and she loved him.'

When Tess got home, it was late. But not too late to ring her best friend. Now that the Limehouse case was finally over, Tess was free to think of nothing but her investigation into Benson, which, until now, had been reserved for late in the evening. The hooch had made her heady in a way she'd never been before. She was about to pick up her phone, when it rang.

'I was just about to call you,' she said.

Sally spoke quickly.

'I think I've found something.'

'So have I.'

'And what's that?'

After years of self-disclosure over cut glass and expensive cocktails, Tess had learnt when to put the brakes on. Thing is, she hadn't had an expensive cocktail served in Dartington crystal. Throwing caution to the wind, she'd had plastic cup after plastic cup of something brewed in the mind of the desperate. Tess, slumped on the sofa, stretched out her foot as if to find that brake pedal, but she missed and hit the accelerator.

'I love him, Sally,' she said.

'Who?'

'Benson . . . William Benson. I love his eyes, his nose, his mouth, his lips, his teeth, and his hair.'

'You sound like an ENT surgeon. Isn't there anything else?'

'Yes.' Tess let go of the wheel. 'His past.'

PART FIVE

Ubi jus ibi remedium

Where there is a wrong there must be a remedy

'Always look for the truth,' said Helen. 'And the truth will lead you to the evidence.'

Benson wondered whether he should write that down, but reaching for pen and paper would have annoyed her.

'People out there, in the street, they think it's the other way around, that evidence leads to the truth. But they're mistaken. And in these chambers, there are counsel who think the truth doesn't matter, because it's a court of evidence. They're mistaken, too. Avoid these two pitfalls – trusting the evidence and not caring about the truth. Instead, as soon as you open a brief, search for the one fact that you think is incontrovertibly true, and build your defence from there.'

Benson was amazed by her aplomb. He'd completed his pupillage. Tonight, the members of 14 King's Bench Walk would vote on whether or not to offer Benson a tenancy. By tradition, a pupil master opens the proceedings with a speech in favour of the pupil. In Benson's case that speech would be given not by some middle-ranking barrister with at least seven years' call under their belt – the prerequisite to become a pupil master – but by Helen, not only Head of Chambers, but a QC with a national reputation. The entire arrangement was unique. QCs don't have pupils. In taking Benson on, Helen had said to her colleagues, I'm standing by this man. And the day will come when I will ask you to do the same.

That day had come.

And the rebellion was already underway. One after the other, counsel had come sheepishly to Helen's room to tell her they couldn't support Benson. With each knock on the door, Benson had been obliged to step outside. When someone had left, he'd go back in again, waiting for another knock and another short departure. And between times, Helen extemporised on the relationship between evidence and truth.

'I said I had only one lesson to teach, and this is it. Always look for the truth. And the truth will lead you to the evidence.'

Benson committed the words to memory. Helen frowned.

'Aren't you going to write that down?'

Benson did so, on the back of a receipt from Marks & Spencer. Then he said:

'Helen, all hell's letting loose. It's breaking over your head.'

Even before Benson had begun his pupillage two Lord Justices of Appeal and the Master of the Rolls had warned her not to get involved with him; that association with his name was harming her standing at the Bar and before the Bench. She'd ignored them. And now her own chambers were in mutiny.

'Let me go. I'll fend for myself.'

'You won't survive. As long as you are in these chambers, you'll work.'

'But they don't want me.'

'Let's see how people actually vote.'

Benson wondered about the thickness of Helen's skin, marvelling at her commitment to him.

'Why are you helping me, Helen?' he said.

For the first time she looked troubled by what was happening. There'd been another knock on the door.

'Because I know you were innocent. I knew it before I'd opened the brief.'

65

Tess went to Sally's house first thing in the morning. They went into the drawing room. The old paint had been stripped away; the walls had been repapered; the plasterwork had been repaired; the wood had been oiled; the brass fittings were shining: the old room had become a new room. All that was needed now were the furnishings, the pictures and the ornaments. There were, as yet, no curtains, net or cloth, so morning sunshine spilled into the room bringing the shifting lustre that comes from light falling on trees and a river. In the centre of the room was a paint-spattered trestle table. On it were Sally's notes.

'I did as you said,' Sally began. She was tense with antici-pation. 'I took the material you gave me, and I drew up a chronology.'

Tess's research into the social and political life of the Camberleys had produced a list of dates and names and places, and these had all been emailed to Sally with a sugges-tion that they be paired with everything she knew about the Merringtons.

'Annette's family were very close to the Camberleys. Prior to 1942, Wilfred Baker and John Camberley were members of the same Inn and the same golf club. But, interestingly, Wilfred and Vivien Camberley are on the boards of the same three charities and the same three schools. They're organising a dance at the Hammersmith Palais to raise money for HMS *Manchester*. He's the Labour candidate for Kensington North. She's the secretary. They're on the hustings together. Wilfred must have spent more time with Vivien that he did with his own wife, and Vivien must have spent more time with him than she did with her own husband. There are weeks when they saw each other every night. Not a month goes by without them being involved in something together.'

Sally pointed at a date, written in her annoyingly small handwriting.

'1942 is the inexplicable year in the life of Wilfred Baker. He leaves the Bar and the Labour Party. He resigns from six boards. He drops golf and he never goes back to his Inn. The attraction that kept him away? Inquests in a coroner's court? Look what else happens in 1942.'

Tess read the entry: 'Birth of Helen Camberley.'

'After 1942,' said Sally, 'there is no contact between the Camberleys and the Bakers. Most family events for the Camberleys took place at Gray's Inn. There's a magazine for members: *Graya*. It lists who was present for what. With photos. The Bakers didn't go to Helen's christening. They didn't go to any of the days marking Helen's personal or professional life. They didn't go to any of the events organ- ised to attract members who lived outside London. John had been there, but not Wilfred. When Vivien died, the Bakers didn't go to the funeral. I could go on. There was zero contact.'

'What does this mean?' whispered Tess.

'Do I need to spell it out?'

'No.'

Wilfred Baker had left the Bar because he'd had an affair with Vivien Camberley. He'd got the wife of a colleague in chambers pregnant. A woman who also happened to be the daughter of his Head of Chambers. And Vivien had elected to keep the child. Had she ever told John? Or had John thought this wonderful, precocious girl was his own? Had he watched her grow seeing something of himself in Helen's glances, or something of Wilfred, the friend who'd betrayed him, and who'd quite properly vanished from the streets of London?

Poor Annette. She'd been obliged to share the consequences.

'Wilfred must have confessed to his wife and daughter what he'd done,' said Tess. 'How else could he persuade Annette that he had to take up the job in Lewes? In effect, the future was decided for them all. Annette and her mother didn't have a choice. They'd gone with him into exile.'

And something else had been born in 1942, added Sally. A lifelong resentment. Annette had lost her opportunities and she'd seen Helen, from afar, thrive on hers. Seen her become a barrister and then a QC. She'd lived the life that had been rightfully hers.

'It wasn't easy for Wilfred, either.' Sally pointed at another date. 'He must have seen Helen taking off, knowing that Annette had been grounded. He'd have been proud of Helen and unable to utter a word of praise, feeling guilty about Annette.'

Sally had drawn Tess's attention to Wilfred's conviction for drink-driving. The date of the offence was Sunday the 6th of July 1986.

'Look at what happened two days earlier, the previous Friday.'

'Camberley's son committed suicide.'

Tess already knew about this tragedy. Christopher had done four months in a young offender institution for possession of cannabis with intent to supply. He'd dreamed of becoming a barrister. He'd blown his chances. He'd no longer been a 'fit and proper person'.

'Camberley was already well known,' said Sally. 'Reports of her son's death were in the papers by that Sunday.'

'And on Sunday night, Wilfred tries to hide what he feels. He gets drunk out of his mind and then goes out for a drive.'

Sally nodded. 'But when he staggers back home, it's Annette

who comforts him. He's lost a grandson he never knew, and he can't mourn with the grieving mother because he never knew her either.'

Tess fell quiet, subdued by these mingled histories of secret pain.

Sally broke the reverie:

'After Annette ran down Paul Harbeton, she turned to the person who owed her one. She rang up her half-sister.'

'No,' said Tess. 'This doesn't work.'

'Why not?'

'You're saying Camberley asked for the brief, knowing that Annette was guilty?'

'Yes.'

'Well, that's the flaw. Because Camberley doesn't pick and choose her cases. She's not allowed to. It's sent to her. By people like me. That's how it works.'

Tess felt the sunlight on her back. Sweat was running between her shoulder blades. Stepping into a shadow she took out her phone and made a call. After a few rings, she cut the line.

'I want to see his face,' she said. 'I need to look into his eyes.'

66

'These eggs are free range, darling. They're from a woman who lives by a river in Sussex and she only feeds her chickens peelings and lettuce and corn. They walk about all day singing their little hearts out and I'm told you can only eat two of these whoppers at a time, otherwise you won't be hungry for the rest of the week. So that's your lot. Sausage? From that farm in Norfolk?'

'Yes, dear.'

Pamela busied herself at the Aga and Merrington went into the dining room. He sat down and tried to do the *Telegraph* crossword. But he'd been troubled by a front-page article, which was continued on page 11. Paul Harbeton's mother had gone to the police with evidence implicating her son in grave wrongdoing. Her own murdered son, would you believe. And she was calling upon the police to enlarge the pool of potential suspects. In effect, she was insisting on a new investigation. She'd written to Merrington, too. Saying she could no longer support 'Paul's Law'. Merrington looked at four down. Then two across. Then he gave up.

'Here you are, Richard,' said Pamela, laying the plate in front of him. 'Those tomatoes are from Mr Grimshaw's allotment.'

'Bugger Mr Grimshaw's allotment.'

'I beg your pardon?'

'I said bugger his allotment. And Grimshaw, too, if you like.'

'What on earth for? He gives them to me for nothing. They'd cost a—'

'I confronted my mother about her spending on Benson.'

'You what?'

'You heard.'

Pamela sat down.

'When?'

'Last week.'

'That explains it.'

'Explains what?'

'Her endless crying. And the low mood. Haven't you noticed?'

Merrington had. His mother had refused to come round for lunch on Sunday. And she'd refused to go for her eye

319

injections. She'd said, 'I'll be dead soon, so what's the point?'

Pamela stamped a foot and the table shook.

'Why confront her?'

'Necessity, my love.'

'Necessity? You've rubbed her face in it and now she's lost her strength.'

'Pamela, my mother may hail from Kensington, but believe me, she was put together with rivets from Glasgow. She's tougher than anyone I know.'

'But there was no damned reason.'

'There was every damned reason.'

Merrington held up the *Telegraph*.

'You'll have seen this, darling?'

'I have.'

'I bet you've read it, with little shivers of excitement.'

'I've read it, darling.'

'What you won't know is that running in tandem with this curious development is a secret enquiry.'

'Secret enquiry?'

'You and I are turning into parrots, my love. Every time one of us says something, the other—'

'Get on with it. What secret enquiry?'

'That of Tess de Vere into the whereabouts of my grandmother's bracelet.'

Pamela blinked slowly, her eyes shifting around as if she'd heard a burglar in the room next door.

'You're still on about that bracelet?'

'Did you hear me? Tess de Vere – and probably Benson – are interested in the bracelet. In fact, I've misled you. They've found the bracelet, and—'

'What do you mean they've found it?'

'I cannot express myself with greater clarity. You should also know that Miss de Vere has not only found the bracelet, she's taken photographs of it. And she's been to Shipton's, who made it, asking them to preserve all records regarding its manufacture. And do you know why?'

Pamela smoothed a wrinkle in the tablecloth.

'No.'

'Because she is gathering evidence. The bracelet, it would seem, is of supreme significance to an enquiry that she has described as being criminal in nature.'

'Criminal in nature?'

'There we go again. Yes, criminal in nature. Which is why I thought it prudent to speak to my poor mother. You see, I'm the fool who lost the damned thing, so it seemed prudent, in my eyes, to enlighten her myself rather than hand the opportunity to Miss de Vere – who, I assume, will one day turn up with questions to ask.'

'Questions?'

'Questions. Though she may not, of course, follow that route. She may well leave the interrogation of a ninety-two-year-old woman who happens to be the mother of the Secretary of State for Justice to the police.'

'The police?'

Merrington smiled woodenly. Pamela was staring out of the window towards the faithful perennials.

'None other. Can we try and cut the echoes?'

Merrington looked at his breakfast. Pamela always laid out the different elements with inordinate care. The plate was always a delight to the eye. But today he laughed bitterly. A profound sympathetic resonance had taken place between his temper and Pamela's doings in the kitchen. The result was a wonder of metaphysics. The eggs were like two wide eyes. The tomatoes made two red cheeks and the sausage from Norfolk formed a curved, sad mouth.

'And do you know what my mother said, when I laid bare

her many sins – you could call it one, if you like, but I've upped the count given the amount of money involved.'

'No. How could I?'

'It's just an expression, darling. She said, "I did it for you."'

With his knife, Merrington popped both eyes and they bled a thick cooling yolk onto Mr Grimshaw's bright red tomatoes.

'Did it for me? What the hell does that mean?'

'Did she say?'

'No. And she refused to explain herself.'

Merrington sliced the unhappy mouth in two.

'Speaking as a lawyer, the problem with the right to silence is that you're at the mercy of the evidence. And if my mother thinks that she only has to answer to me, then she's very much mistaken. Someone else is out there with more questions than I can dream of. Absolutely delicious, my love. On second thoughts, leave Mr Grimshaw well alone: I'd hate to lose his favour. His tomatoes really are exceptional.'

67

'How very nice to see you, Miss de Vere,' said George Braithwaite. 'And this is?'

'Sally Martindale, an old friend.'

'I hope not a troubled friend, but if you are, I'm at your disposal.'

Braithwaite closed one eye and nodded at Mrs Purdy, his secretary. The gesture had a secret meaning. He then folded his hands together and said:

'What a bloody win. I mean the Limehouse case. How does the blighter do it? All the evidence was against those frightful people – they don't come across well, do they? I don't mean the husband's dirty secret, I mean them, as a couple, they seem so . . . contrived. Do you know what I mean? But all that's by the by. Benson's done it again. Anybody else would have given a speech that lasted all day. But he did *exactly* what Helen Camberley would have done. Insinuation. That's the key. Let the jury think they've worked it out for themselves. Sheer bloody cheek, of course, but—'

'Mr Braithwaite, you handled the payments to Benson, didn't you? The disbursements from his benefactor.'

Braithwaite had never become George to Tess. Or, indeed, anyone else. He belonged roughly in the late nineteenth century. Though fashions had changed, he'd done his best to retain the starched white collar and heavy-suited importance of a London criminal solicitor. His college tie was so tight it threatened the flow of blood to his head.

'I did.'

'Is Benson's patron Annette Merrington?'

Braithwaite didn't move. Then his red cheeks sucked in even more colour.

'You know I can't talk about that, Miss de Vere.'

'Thank you, Mr Braithwaite. You've said enough. Next—'

The door opened and Mrs Purdy brought in a tray with a pot of coffee and three cups.

'She's a wonder,' said Braithwaite, trying to find his balance. 'Did you notice? I didn't need to ask. How many years have we been together, Mrs Purdy?'

'Thirty-four, Mr Braithwaite.'

'She knows my mind inside out,' he said to Tess, still recovering his composure. 'All I have to do is think something, and she's on to it. I trust these are Walker's shortbreads?'

'Yes, Mr Braithwaite.'

She was proud; and after she'd poured and served she moved silently out of the room. Then Tess said:

'Mr Braithwaite, for the past two years I have been

investigating Benson's conviction. I've been helped by a friend. This friend. And we've uncovered information that may well lead to an application in the Court of Appeal.'

Tess recognised in Braithwaite's frozen expression a mixture of foreboding and relief. This very proper gentleman had been compromised. Tess knew it. He'd been trapped. Either by complicity or suspicion. Tess needed to find out which.

'I see, Miss de Vere. Does your investigation relate to the recent announcement of Mrs Harbeton?'

'No. Her speaking out is pure coincidence.'

'I'd call that a good omen.'

'I'd call it meaningless unless you're prepared to be absolutely honest with me.'

Braithwaite opened his tightened mouth and then mastered his indignation.

'It's because of our long history and our shared association with Mr Benson that I will ignore the implications of that remark.'

'I'm here for him, Mr Braithwaite. I believe he's innocent. And I'll say anything to anyone and risk causing any amount of offence if it will get me closer to the truth.'

'What do you want to know?'

On the way to Braithwaite's office in Field Court, Tess had ordered her thoughts. They'd now fallen apart. Seeing Braithwaite's discomfort, she'd become unsettled. This was the man who'd introduced her to criminal law, and he was hiding something.

'You were the duty solicitor on the day Benson was arrested?'

'I was.'

'Did anybody apart from the desk sergeant tell you to come to the station?'

'No.'

324

'It was by chance you came to represent him.'

'Totally.'

'When you'd taken instructions from Benson, did he say he wanted a particular barrister?'

'No.'

'So once you'd prepared the brief for counsel, you then instructed Helen Camberley?'

'No, Miss de Vere, I did not. I instructed Roddy Kemble QC.'

Braithwaite loosened his stiff white collar with a thick, shaking finger.

'The brief was ready to be delivered to his chambers when I received a call.'

'From Miss Camberley's clerk?'

'No. From Miss Camberley herself. She asked for the Benson brief.'

'That's unheard of.'

'It is, and it was the last thing I expected from Miss Camberley.'

'Did she say why?'

'She apologised profusely for the impropriety. She said she'd never done it before and would never do it again, but there was something about the Benson case that had gripped her sensibilities. She said he'd made her think of her son. She'd seen his picture in the paper and she'd thought of Christopher.'

For a long time Tess and Braithwaite regarded each other.

'That's moral blackmail,' said Tess eventually. 'She was forcing your hand.'

'Whatever it was, I didn't feel I could refuse. She was most upset.'

Braithwaite had readdressed the brief. Mrs Purdy had called Mr Kemble's clerk to apologise for the mistake and the case had gone to Camberley.

'And after Benson had been convicted,' said Tess, 'an individual came to this office with an offer to finance his rehabilitation?'

'They did.'

'Binding you to secrecy?'

'The utmost secrecy, Miss de Vere.'

'And forbidding Will ever to try and establish their identity?'

'Precisely.'

Braithwaite raised a finger to identify a point of law and personal honour.

'You must appreciate, Miss de Vere, there was nothing whatsoever in this arrangement that suggested criminal conduct of any kind was being concealed.'

Tess now understood the delicacy of Braithwaite's circumstances. These two events linked to Benson – a QC asking for the brief and the mother of an MP offering him money – will have roused Braithwaite's unease. And it could only have grown over the years, becoming profound, as Camberley had become Benson's guide, risking her own reputation, while the MP had made his, finally becoming a government minister. And all the while, Annette had been writing out the cheques for the client account.

'What have you discovered, Miss de Vere?'

Tess was sure Braithwaite knew nothing more. That he'd been a pawn. Something he'd always wondered, anxiously. For his relations with Benson, the centrepiece of the game, had continued year on year. He longed to know the connection between Helen Camberley's distress and Annette Merrington's generosity. This was his moment of truth. Only he would have to wait.

'I'd rather not say, Mr Braithwaite.'

'Because you don't trust me?'

'Because I don't have the time.'

68

'You were right, Sally,' said Tess, driving towards Hampstead. 'Annette went to Camberley and Camberley went to Braithwaite. Camberley knew Benson was innocent, and she knew Annette was guilty.'

'But why did she take on the case?'

'I've no idea.'

'Annette told her she'd killed someone. Why didn't Camberley call the police?'

'I don't know, and it doesn't make sense.'

'They both knew that Benson had been arrested.'

Tess tried to imagine the conversation. Annette must have told Camberley they shared a father. And that she was her half-sister. And that her son was an MP, who was married and had a young child. Maybe she'd spoken of the personal cost, her sacrifice, London for Lewes . . . but the outcome still didn't make sense. Camberley hadn't called the police. She'd called Braithwaite.

'She must have felt obligated,' said Tess, without conviction.

'What? To break the law? To gamble with Benson's life?'

'I don't have any answers, Sally.'

Tess focused on the road, thinking of Benson being spat on; of the rubbish piled by his gate; of the beating he'd been given. She thought of the petition to shut him down. She thought of the brother he never saw, the mother who'd died while he was inside, and the father who'd been widowed. She saw Benson looking for his keys, sucking on a cigarette, avoiding eye contact. She heard his voice from the other side of the wall he'd started building in HMP Kensal Green. He was locked away . . . except in court. In court he was free. Because of Helen Camberley.

'I do,' said Sally.

'Do what?'

'I have the answer.'

'Tell me.'

'Annette blackmailed Camberley, and not morally.'

'How?'

'She called in a favour. The threat? To tell John Camberley he wasn't the father of his only child. That her mother had been shagging Wilfred Baker. Which forced Camberley to blackmail Braithwaite.'

Sally hit the dashboard.

'What a nasty, dreadful piece of work she'd become. I feel for her, Tess, I really do, but look at it from Camberley's perspective. This woman turns up out of nowhere, a vicar's wife, and after she leaves, Camberley throws away her integrity.'

For a long moment they shared unspoken confusion. Then Sally said:

'There's not much time, you know. Annette's ninety-two. She could die this afternoon. And Camberley could be dead as we speak. If either of them goes, we lose our leverage. Because that's our only hope, isn't it? Playing one off against the other.'

'Yes. Which is why we're going to confront Annette.'

They'd reached Hampstead Heath. Once Tess had parked, she said:

'Annette killed Paul Harbeton. That's one secret. But the secret that matters most to her, and the one she'd never want her son to know, is her link to Camberley. That's our lever.'

'What are you suggesting?'

'The time of secrets is over. And like Benson said to John Lynwood, Annette will have to choose which of the two she wants to keep. Only one of them has to be told.'

According to EmCheck Ltd, Annette lived at 32a Cranbourne

Gardens. When Tess and Sally reached a gate in front of a large Victorian house, recently pointed, but with old windows that needed a clean, they looked at each other. This meeting was their one chance to change Benson's future. With that thought, Tess walked up the driveway, anger rising in her throat. She poked the bell as if to start a fight. But when the door opened, she was stung with compassion. Annette had been weeping. Her eyes were reddened with blood. She was defeated already.

'Mrs Merrington?' said Tess.

'Yes, my dear?'

'I'm Tess de Vere, a solicitor, and I represent William Benson.'

'Oh yes.' Annette made a weak smile. 'I know all about him.'

'And we know all about you. And your relationship to Helen, who did her best to set him free, and failed. And your mother's bracelet, which was found by the body of Paul Harbeton.'

Annette asked if they might go for a short walk. The rain had held off, and she didn't like going out on her own, and, well, it wasn't every day that two strangers who knew more about you than anyone else came knocking on your door. Tess took one arm, and Sally the other. But she was a strong and purposeful woman, and she led them along a path to a bench on the Heath. To one side was a row of Georgian houses, one of which had wisteria entwined around the windows. Ahead, the wintry grass sloped away, into a light fog. In the distance central London seemed afloat, an armada of stranded buildings.

'I met Hugh Dawley at the Hammersmith Palais in March 1942,' she said. 'He was a sailor on HMS *Manchester*. Five months later he was killed, during Operation Pedestal.

Supplying Malta, which was under siege. Did you know that?'

'No,' said Tess.

'Have you heard of HMS *Manchester*?'

'No, I'm sorry.'

'Don't worry, dear, not many people have. Yes, he was killed. I don't know how. I mean, it's not the sort of thing you ask, is it? Poor chap never knew I was pregnant.'

Tess gave a start, and turned to catch Sally's astonishment, but Annette carried on talking, her eyes on the fog and the floating city.

'I only met him that one night. It had been a fundraiser, organised by my father, because the ship had been damaged, and money was needed to help defray the costs of repair. Hugh took me home, while my parents gave speeches.'

The ship had been in Portsmouth since February, getting readied for sea – she'd been torpedoed the previous July. Repairs had been carried out in Gibraltar and somewhere else. Annette couldn't recall.

'You said you were pregnant?'

'Yes, dear, with Helen.'

The possibility of keeping the baby hadn't even been considered. Not that Annette knew what she'd wanted – she'd been so confused – but she'd have liked to be involved in the discussions. The birth itself had been handled under guise of a TB infection.

'I was whisked off to a home for girls in difficulty. Outside Glasgow. I've never touched porridge since. Meanwhile, in Kensington, all the preparations for the adoption took place. I didn't even know who the couple were, not until thirty odd years later. In 1978. Just before my mother died, she cracked and told me that John Camberley had been sterile, and he'd been terribly ashamed. Didn't want it known he was short of lead. And that meant people thought, well,

there must be something wrong with skinny Vivien. So when
I got pregnant, they were thrilled to bits: I was seen as some
kind of gift horse. They just unpacked my saddlebag and
them slapped my backside. I solved everybody's problems.'
She paused. 'Except my own. I never quite solved my own.'

She turned her streaked eyes to Tess.

'It's not easy keeping this kind of secret, my dear. Not
easy at all. Richard would never understand. You've got
me there.'

Annette never went back to Kensington. She'd moved
directly from Glasgow to Lewes. And for months afterwards,
Annette kept receiving get well soon cards and enquiries
about her lungs.

'A month or so later, on my eighteenth birthday, my
mother gave me a bracelet. Given to her by her mother, so
this was a mother-to-daughter moment. It was beautiful.
Platinum with nine small diamonds. And do you know –
this wasn't said, of course – but the wretched thing was a
reward. I'd lost something . . . and I got something in return,
and I was accepted back into the family. You see, she's the
one who said we had to leave London, not my father. I've
often asked myself if things would have been different if
Hugh had been an officer. Anyway, I hated the damn thing.
Saw it as a manacle with an invisible chain tied to the hull
of HMS *Manchester*.'

Annette pointed to the house with the wisteria.

'That's where Helen lived,' she said. 'After my mother died
I'd come here, with my father. I'd look out for my daughter,
and he'd look out for his granddaughter. By the time I told
her who I was, we already knew each other.'

Annette looked first at Tess and then at Sally.

'My grandson committed suicide. Did you know that?'

Tess nodded sympathetically.

'That's when I got in touch with Helen. I found out because

331

of a picture in the *Sunday Mirror*. I was in the newsagent's. Fancied a Fry's Chocolate Cream, and I looked at this stand and saw Helen's name . . . When we met, I gave her my father's wig. And she gave it to Benson. He wears it in court, you know.'

Annette was honoured. She sighed and gently slapped her thighs.

'Well, there we are. I've never told anyone my story before. Except Helen, of course. Would you take me home now, please?'

When they reached Cranbourne Gardens, Annette fished out her house keys and said, 'Thank you both very much for listening.'

She fiddled a key into the lock, her other hand flat against the door.

'On this other matter, the reason why you're here . . . the doctor tells me it's unlikely Helen will survive the night.'

She turned, as if to face her jailors, and her bloodied eyes were filled with tears.

'Do you mind if I wait until my daughter has died before I come clean?'

Tess could barely find her voice. She managed an 'of course', and then added, 'Please rest assured, your story will remain a secret.'

'I know, Miss de Vere. I'm perfectly aware you've offered me a deal. I accept the terms.'

The door needed a shove to open fully; then Annette stepped inside without even a look over her shoulder.

Tess sat staring through the windscreen at fog lifting from the Heath. Sally did the same. Neither of them could think of anything to say. There was so much that Annette might have said about her role in a great injustice; but she'd said none of it. Instead she'd spoken of another great injustice, unknown to the law, not even recognising that she'd been a victim. Annette's parents had committed no crime: they'd just done what they'd thought was right; they'd found a good home for a child, born to a minor. Not considering the wishes of the mother was neither here nor there. So there was no legal remedy. And there would be no sympathy, because this was the secret she'd chosen to keep. Only, it hadn't been a choice. Not really. Either she owned up to the hit and run, or . . .

Tess put the key in the ignition, and her stomach turned with the moan of the engine.

This is what a blackmailer must feel like, she thought.

69

Solicitors organise information. Barristers determine its flow. They choose the witness order. It's a question of tactics. And so it was with Helen's dying, though she'd fulfilled both functions. Knowing the moment was drawing near, she'd chosen who she was going to see, and when. Benson had been told to come to her room at 9 p.m. He went along the empty corridor, breathing in the antiseptic, his shoes squeaking on the gleaming lino. Perhaps it was because of Helen's organisation of the information – this enquiry into the effect of Benson's trial upon his family – but as he approached her open door he had a sense that another trial was almost over, and that he was about to enter the public gallery of a courtroom. A verdict was about to be given.

Propped up between pillows, she was grumbling about her breathing helmet to a nurse. There were flowers of every colour and size on the table and bedside cabinet. Still more had been lined up on the floor. Letters were stacked between the vases. Messages from colleagues and clients and friends. Those she'd decided not to see.

'Take a seat, Will,' she said wearily, when the nurse had left the room.

Benson sat down and took her hand. She seemed far away, in a universe circumscribed by PVC.

'How are you?' he said uselessly.

'I'm frightened.'

'So am I.'

She gave a slight shake of her head.

'I've asked Forde to look after you. She'll be there for you from now on. You can trust her.'

Forde? The room seemed to tilt; and Benson felt himself sliding back in time, into his cell at HMP Codrington and the heavy smell of slop. A screw had just told him his mother had died . . . The floor lifted and he slid back into Helen's room, and she was passing him on to someone else.

'No one can replace you, Helen, no one.'

Helen breathed in and out several times, like someone about to plunge into cold water. The blue plastic disc rose, fluttered, and fell.

'Thank you for telling me about Jim,' she began, tentatively, 'and Lizzie and Eddie.' She closed her eyes. 'I'd planned to ask about you, how the trial had affected you, but I've run out of time, and anyway, I think I know already . . . There's not much I don't know about you.'

'You know all there is to know, Helen.'

Benson had spilled out the words; he couldn't hold back the rising panic: Helen was going. Benson had been last on the list.

'And I just want to thank you for everything you've done for me. Anyone else would have turned away, but you didn't. You've stood by me. We both got the abuse, only you didn't deserve it. You took it . . . and you've given meaning to my life. Every day, I do something I believe in. Every day, I help someone who might as well be me, because I live for them, and their case, and . . . you gave me this. I'm sorry, I didn't mean to upset you, but . . .'

Helen was crying. Benson didn't want to look. Her face had folded, like a frightened child with nowhere to turn, and again Benson found himself sliding back into a cell, for this is how prisoners cry. Something of their childhood appears like a ghost; something ruined. It's an agony to see. Because they can never get back what they have lost. Benson welled up.

'I'm sorry, but I've got to say it now, otherwise, it'll never be said. You have meant so much to me. You always will. And I hope . . . I hope you've been proud of me.'

'There is something I must say,' said Helen, opening her eyes. 'I told you, before we began this journey together. You've spoken to me, and now I must speak to you. Help me get this damned thing off.'

She was tugging at the yellow straps that held her breathing helmet in place.

'Don't worry, I won't die, just get me out of this prison. I can't have any barrier between us.'

Benson unhooked the straps, but then thought better of what he was doing. He called the nurse, who sanctioned the move. She transferred some tulips from the table to the floor and then removed the helmet, placing it where the flowers had been. The thing seemed to watch over them, hissing air, as Helen, with a wheeze, said:

'Do you remember when I came to see you just after you'd been sentenced? I told you the story of a woman who'd lost her son?'

'Yes, I remember.'

She took back her hand and laid it on something he hadn't quite noticed. An A4 manila envelope.

'Now I'd like to tell you another story. About a woman who found her mother.'

70

Merrington's mother might have decided she wouldn't be having any more injections, but she'd certainly not given up on a decent supper – the event that would ordinarily mark the end of an otherwise unpleasant day. On this occasion she'd come, on her own initiative, to Pond Square. Pamela had put on some soothing music. She'd cooked something simple – macaroni cheese, by the smell of it. And she'd got the Scrabble out for later.

'The blurred vision has gone,' said Annette. 'Along with the crooked lines. So I don't see the point.'

'I completely agree.'

Merrington was glad she'd come over. Is this what we're brought to, by old age, he thought, with a wink at his mother. Sadness? Regret? Needles in the eye so we can see a little better? He thought she could do with a few compliments. She did, in fact, look oddly different.

'You might feel wretched, Mater, but you look ten years younger.'

Annette didn't even smile. She was seated on the large sofa, a small figure dwarfed by cushions.

'I think you've been a real sport about the bracelet,' he said, having another go. 'It shows, if I might say so, a spirit of detachment usually associated with a life of penance and—'

'Shut up, Dicky.'

'Certainly.'

If she refused to smile, Merrington would. And he did.

His own mood had improved greatly since discussing things with Pamela. He'd called Bradley Hilmarton to outline his fears, and Bradley had smoothed out an important wrinkle. He'd stated the obvious, to which Merrington had been blinded by anxiety. The bracelet must have been found at a recent crime scene. But there was no way it could be linked to Merrington. Not unless—

'You mustn't worry about the bracelet, Dicky.'

'I don't. Not any more.'

'Good. Because you didn't lose it.'

'I assure you I did.'

'You didn't, because I took it back.'

'You what?'

'I took it back.'

'Why?'

'You didn't do as I'd asked. I'd wanted it repaired. You kept forgetting.'

'I said I was sorry.'

'You did. But it doesn't matter. What matters is that I wore and lost it. More than that . . . it was found at the scene of a crime.'

Merrington had a premonition he would now make his mother smile. He would pass on Bradley's wisdom as his own. But his mind fogged, because he was wondering how his mother knew a link had been made between the bracelet and a crime. He was about to ask, when Annette said:

'I killed Paul Harbeton.'

Merrington thought about the idea for a moment.

'I'm all for a laugh, Mother,' he said, 'but—'

'I'm serious, Dicky. I'd attended a fundraiser at Spellow and Hardy. Organised by Pamela. I'd had one too many. I turned into Powick Lane, fiddling with the radio. Didn't even see him.'

'See who?'

'Paul Harbeton. He was in the middle of the road.'

'What are you—?'

'I'd hit him. But he got up. And he staggered down the street a few yards . . . and he fell, near the kerb. Then he got up again . . . walking as if he was asleep, his arms by his side . . . looking up at the sky . . . and then he just dropped down onto the ground.'

'Paul Harbeton?'

'Paul Harbeton. And I got out of the car and walked over to him . . . and he was snoring. Breathing oddly.'

Merrington stared at his mother. She seemed even smaller now. She'd been shrinking as she spoke.

'This is a bad dream. You're not saying this.'

Annette shook her head.

'I thought of you, a well-known journalist. And now an MP. And I looked at the man on the road. I thought, he'll come round and go home . . . so I went back to my car. But I must have dropped my bracelet. Because it was found. And somehow, all these years later, it's surfaced. In the hands of—'

'Tess de Vere.'

Merrington spoke like an automaton.

'Yes, Dicky. We had a chat just after lunch.'

'*À table*. That's what they say in France.' Pamela had appeared, her hands joined by flowery oven gloves, the material looping underneath like bunting. She was holding up a Pyrex dish of bubbling macaroni cheese, smiling sweetly.

'Is there anything wrong?' she said.

Merrington frowned at the question. Wrong? Could that little word encompass what he'd just been told, and what had happened as a result? The devastation? Mysteries were popping in his mind like bubbles of acid: her frown when he'd first become a minister; her suggestions that he retire and get away from Westminster; her enthusiasm for the salvation of William Benson. Snap, crackle and pop. She'd lived in fear that one day her link to an innocent man just might surface in the scum.

'Is it because David's still here?'

'No, my love.'

'He's heading back first thing in the morning.'

'Right-o.'

The swirl of emotion was so fast it jarred with the pace of the music. The choir was . . . searching, not soaring. The melody was like a wave constantly opening on to an immense shore in the mind.

'What the hell is this?'

'What?'

'This bloody awful music.'

'It's from Sarah, darling. It's a psalm or something.'

'Oh my God.'

The CD, *Da Pacem*, had arrived that morning. With a note. 'Track three. For a humble man.' He'd looked. It was a setting of Psalm 131. O Lord, my heart is not proud . . . The prayer had soured in his mouth. And now the fight was on. Sarah had been told the required number of letters had been received by the 1922 Committee. The PM was finished. The only question was who would take over the flame. While Sarah and Rex burned. Merrington fumbled for his mobile and rang Jos Fowler.

'Jos, it's Richard.

'Good news, isn't it?'

'Can't talk. Just a warning. If anything appears in the press about Rex, I'll personally finish you. Think Riyadh and an export licence.'

He cut the call. Pamela was still standing there, holding the macaroni cheese, though she'd lowered her arms.

'What's wrong with Rex?'

'Absolutely nothing, my love.'

The front door slammed and a thud of air reached Merrington's ear. David came in to the room, red-faced and breathing hard.

'Dad, have you seen? The Prime Minister's—'

'Yes. Not interested. Will someone please turn this infernal racket off.'

'But it's all spiritual, darling.'

Merrington couldn't think because of the noise in his head. He turned on his mother, who'd made it all. The diminutive figure sat there, slowly blinking, not quite present. She'd thought forking out compensation was enough.

Merrington jabbed his phone and looked up a number.

'What's going on, darling?'

'Just a moment, dear,' – he waited for the voicemail to kick in – 'This is Richard Merrington, Minister of State for Justice. A message for George Braithwaite. You have an assistant. The Dreadful Purdy. You can't trust her as far as you can throw her. Quiz her. If she plays dumb, do call back.'

Pamela put the macaroni cheese on the table and came back into the sitting room, the oven gloves slung over her shoulder.

'Richard, have you gone barking mad? What's happened?'

Merrington walked over to the window and looked into his garden. He couldn't see a thing. Just his reflection. The perennials were out there, doing what perennials do . . . the same thing, year in, year out. Blooming and seeming to die, and then coming back again as if nothing had happened. The room was deathly quiet. David had stopped that maddening music. They were ready to hang on his every word.

'What's happened?' Pamela repeated.

He turned around, sickened by his own image.

'I don't know where to begin. I haven't the wit.'

'Nonsense, darling. You always know what to say. It's why you got to where you are.'

Merrington went into the hallway and shrugged on his overcoat; then he peeped around the sitting-room door. His mother, Pamela and David were perfectly still, like ornamental statues pilfered from a stately home.

'Not this time, my love. Not this time.'

71

'She didn't know what to do,' said Helen.

Benson had moved his chair away from the bed. Just a few inches, as if he'd got too close to a fire. His elbows were on his knees, and his hands hung between his legs.

'She found out he was dead. And she came to see me straight away. In Hampstead.'

'Had I been arrested?'

'No.'

Helen's face was turned slightly away from Benson, as if she was talking to the crowd of flowers.

'She wanted me to go to the police station with her, but it was complicated. They'd want to know why she'd turned to me. There was no known connection between us, and I couldn't tell them, I couldn't tell anyone. John Camberley, the man I thought had been my father, was still alive. He was eighty-six, I couldn't tell him I'd found my real mother. So she said she'd go on her own and I stopped her.'

Benson got up and went across the room to the dimmer switch; he lowered it and Helen's face relaxed in a kind of dusk.

'I hesitated. Because if we did nothing, no one would be any the wiser. If she admitted what she'd done she'd go to prison. And Richard's career would be over.'

Helen spoke in spurts of desperate, dogged energy and then rested, gathering her strength for the next step. This was the last journey. All day, maybe all week, she'd saved herself for this final stretch.

'I looked up the Harbetons. Two of the brothers had a criminal record. Violence and dishonesty. Harbeton himself had been charged with sexual assault. Twice. And twice the CPS had said there wasn't enough evidence. Off the record, the witnesses had been scared away. The lot of them were on benefits. None had ever worked. Except the mother. Paul's bit-work was all cash in hand. And I thought . . .'

Her voice faded with self-contempt.

She'd thought why should my mother go to prison for having killed a tax-fiddling pervert who'd just headbutted a student for no reason? Why should Richard lose his future by default, and his family suffer loss, so that another family of scroungers can gain some justice – and probably start a civil action for damages? Make something out of it. With a fictitious loss of earnings claim, and a lump sum to cover the imaginary house-hold services the dead son would have provided.

'The hesitation became a decision,' she said.

Her face edged further away, into the crease of a pillow.

'I was winning cases that everyone thought couldn't be won. Colleagues came into court to hear my cross-exami-nations. They talked about a witness being Camberleyed. Same for my speeches. They'd say, get into Number One Court, she's doing a Camberley. I'd won six trials in a row, all of them difficult, all of them dramatic. And then you were arrested And that's when my hesitation tipped over.'

Into a decision? Or was it arrogance? Could evil so disguise itself that it didn't look too bad? Camberley's hand crawled like a spider from the manila envelope towards Benson; it was halted by a ruck in the bedsheet.

'I thought I could interfere with the workings of justice . . . that I could do something that was, in the round, the right thing, and bring about a fair outcome . . . something a court could never do . . . because it never knows the complete picture. I thought I was bigger than the law. Did Mrs Harbeton really need to know who'd run over her son? Would it change her life to know, as much as it would change my mother's life to confess? It didn't seem right . . . and all I needed to do was Camberley the witnesses and the jury . . .'

Why not? Paul Harbeton might not have been convicted, but he'd harmed a boy and a girl. His brothers had harmed pensioners, a teacher, a traffic warden and a lollipop lady. They were harming the benefit system. Why should these harmers not experience a little harm themselves – harm they wouldn't even know about?

'I thought I could pull it off. I thought I could save you and save my mother, and I failed.'

Her hand began crawling back the way it had come, back to the envelope.

'I injured you. I injured your family. I injured all who know you. And I injured the Harbetons.'

So much injury. So much anguish. Because Helen thought she could do a Camberley.

Benson no longer felt he was sitting on a chair, in a room, in a hospital. He was adrift, hearing words from another world.

'My mother paid for your rehabilitation, not me. She took

the money from a trust fund for Richard: if he was to benefit from your conviction, then . . .'

More harm. More dishonesty.

'I've prepared an affidavit, witnessed by George Braithwaite. He knows everything now.'

Helen picked up the envelope and raised it in the air; and Benson took it, not because he wanted it, but because it was too heavy for Helen to carry on holding.

'And so does Tess de Vere.'

Benson's feet seemed to find the floor.

'Tess?'

'Yes. I found out this afternoon, when I saw my mother for the last time.'

Helen's face was still averted, seeking further refuge into the crease.

'Tess took the step I failed to take: she's proved your innocence.'

'How?'

'She found the bracelet. She traced it to my mother. She's forced her to confess . . . in exchange for not revealing that I am her daughter; and that I did what I did.'

Benson's eyes flickered suddenly. He looked at the envelope. In his hands was Helen's confession. But it was something else, too. It was a weapon. A blunt instrument.

Annette's confession would lead to Benson's exoneration.

Helen's would go further. It would, of course, ruin her reputation. And expose her to criminal charges. But Benson knew that honour and good character were hardly in issue, for she would shortly die. No, the real casualties would be Richard Merrington and his family. Helen had empowered him to go further than Annette wanted. She'd given him a choice.

'I'm so very sorry, Will,' said Helen quietly. 'I don't seek . . .'

She couldn't bring herself to say the word. And neither

could Benson. Forgiveness? That was a delicate flower, and it didn't always grow, no matter how much you watched and waited and watered. And all at once, Benson noticed the scent in the room. It was a riot of sensation. The different perfumes almost had colours of their own, and sounds, and even texture and taste . . . and they ought to have collided, producing the very incarnation of confusion, but they hadn't. They'd formed something absolutely unique to this time and place, for Helen, and its strange harmony would vanish when they faded, or when the nurses threw them in the bin, because, sooner or later, they'd begin to stink. But for this moment, here and now, they were like a burst of unearthly sunshine, something you could hold on to, and bring to your lips.

Benson sat by the bed for a long time. He didn't want to leave, and he didn't want to stay. His mind retraced his steps, all the way back to HMP Kensal Green, when he'd been on remand, and when this almost alarming presence had swept into the room. She'd never looked him in the eye, which made her seem remote and majestic. But then she'd agreed to help him; she'd come down from on high and told him he could call her Helen, and their eyes had met. It had been a burning moment of privilege and anticipation. He thought of the hours they'd spent together, playing billiards, smoking, drinking, laughing, and falling quiet; always falling quiet, and enjoying that steady pulse which seemed to fill the room, beating between them. He thought of Helen sitting in her study, Benson with his feet crossed on her table, as they tried to find the one fact upon which to build a defence. And he thought of the photograph – there was only one, a formal shot – of Christopher on the wall. He was in his school uniform, smiling. He'd seemed to watch them, feeling left out.

345

'Helen?'

Benson had to speak. He had to put together a few words from the heap in his mind. He had to give her something to take away.

'Maybe I'd never have become what I am, without this. Never have represented people the way I do, without . . . Helen?'

She didn't move from her crease.

Benson dropped the envelope, and he reached over and touched her hand. It was soft and warm, but there was no reaction. Her chest wasn't moving. Her eyes, still open, were looking towards the bank of flowers.

'Helen?'

He wanted her to face him, so she might see the confusion and torment that wasn't in the room; the withered possibilities and expectations and hopes and relationships and . . . these other flowers that had all been within his grasp, ready to be picked and enjoyed. To see the barren ground that was his private life. And the stones. There weren't any weeds because nothing grew there. But she didn't move. He watched, blinking erratically . . . and then something childlike seemed to escape the darkness in his mind, rising like a balloon, with its string trailing in a breeze. He wanted to say goodbye. But she'd gone.

72

Not so long ago, Tess had sat parked in this very spot on Seymour Road.

It had been a late evening like this one. Darkness had fallen quickly. A misty orange light had hovered around the streetlamps. She'd been waiting for Benson.

And once more it was dark, with the sparkle of orange against the night sky, and her eyes were on the road, looking out for Benson.

Back then, she'd come, nervously, to offer her help. She'd heard two solicitors guffawing over lunch in a Chinese restaurant about the murderer who'd just opened his own chambers from an old fishmonger's in Spitalfields. The clown couldn't possibly survive, they'd said.

Again, Tess had come with an offer of help. She was nervous.

And there he was . . . walking – just like back then – head down, not looking where he was going. In his hands was an envelope.

That night, she'd seen a man cross the street, gather mucus in his mouth and spit into Benson's face, inviting retaliation. But he'd just looked up at the black sky, still tapping his pockets, looking for a tissue. Tess had thrown open the car door and reached him in seconds, holding out a handkerchief.

Tess opened the door. This time she walked slowly; and when she reached him, they just fell into step. He said nothing, and Tess, attaching far too much to his silence, hoped he'd expected her to be waiting; as she'd always been.

After a search for his keys, Benson unlocked the gate in the railings and, followed by Tess, went down the path between the trees that led to the landing stage and *The Wooden Doll*. There, he opened the cabin door, and Tess followed him on board.

The boat moved gently, up and down, barely noticeably, but enough for Tess to feel she'd left dry land behind. They were in the dark, but she could tell the place was clean and tidy, in a blokeish sort of way. Without a word passing between them, Tess gingerly walked the length of the sitting room. She was feeling her way, past the shelves packed

with books until, at the far end, she went into Benson's
bedroom. She threw her coat on a chair, kicked off her
shoes, and lay on the bed. Through the window, she could
see the sky, its darkness flushed with an excess of light
from London's sleepless life. Benson's shape appeared in
the doorway. He took off his jacket and tie and put them
on a hanger. Sitting on the edge of the bed, he untied his
laces, and threw each shoe to one side. Then he lay down
beside her.

They were silent in the dark, shoulder to shoulder.

'Tess?'

'Yes?'

Benson didn't move. He was thinking.

'Helen's told me everything. She's prepared an affidavit.
It's on the table in the kitchen. You can read it.'

'Okay.'

He pulled some air through his nose and said:

'Thank you.'

'What for?'

'For ignoring me. For breaking your promise.'

He joined his hands on his stomach; then he swallowed
and said:

'Tess?'

'Yes?'

'The night Paul Harbeton was killed.'

'Yes.'

'There's something you need to know.'

He was quiet again.

'I was walking down Stafford Passage . . . it leads into
Powick Lane.'

'Yes, I know it.'

'My cheekbone was broken. My nose was bleeding. I
was totally disorientated . . . I was stumbling along, and
I looked up . . . and there, in Powick Lane – I was about

twenty yards away – I saw Paul Harbeton. Framed by the buildings at the end of the road.'

Tess held her breath. She didn't want this. She thought about her coat, her shoes.

'He was on the pavement, and then it happened. He just walked into the road, and out of my line of vision, sort of exit stage right. Seconds later a car came past, coming from behind . . . and I heard this noise, not a screech, but skid, and a bang.'

Tess sat up, looking down at Benson's dark shape on the bed. Her hands were joined, too.

'When I reached Powick Lane, I saw him . . . lying on the ground. The car had gone. And I walked over to him.'

Benson was breathing almost silently, and watching Tess out of his darkness.

'He was coughing. And twitching. And I took my phone out. And I dialled 999. And I just looked at him, lying there. I didn't think of the searing pain in my face, I only thought of Eddie, at thirteen, and now at nineteen, and what had happened in between . . . and I cut the call. I walked away. I walked back into Stafford Passage. And I was about ten yards in when I heard this motorbike behind me. It stopped, but I just carried on walking. Until I found a doorstep in the next street. And I sat down . . . and I thought, I hope he dies. I hope he bloody dies, for what he did, and for who he is, and for what he hasn't done yet . . .'

There's no obligation in English law to help anyone. Tess knew this; as did Benson. There's no duty to rescue. You can walk away from the dying and no court has the power to condemn you. That belongs to the conscience alone.

'I still feel I killed him, Tess. Because I left him to die. I did that. I made that choice. I walked away . . . I'm no different to some of the people I represent. Not really.

They went that one step further, the one that matters, and they got caught. But, believe me, I willed him dead.'

Tess lay back down and gazed at the glamour of the night sky. The boat moved lightly. She was like flotsam on the surface of Seymour Basin. After about half an hour, she felt Benson's shoulder juddering. He was holding his breath, not wanting to let it out. She turned on her side, propped up on her elbow. She wanted to lean over and place a hand behind his head, and draw him towards her. But now wasn't the time. Perhaps the time would never come. But this time had. She reached into her pocket and took out a handkerchief.

PART SIX

Unfinished business

The members of 14 King's Bench Walk weren't swayed by Helen's speech. They wouldn't offer Benson a tenancy. So Helen got on the phone to an old friend, and she begged. She secured Benson a couple of months in another set of chambers.

This sequence of events became a pattern. Benson worked for a few months, then he was shown the door, then Helen got on the phone again. One of London's most high-profile silks was on her knees seeking favours. She did that for three years.

And at the end of three years – to the day – Benson did what no one had been expecting.

The big hope had been that a soul-destroying itinerant existence would sap the resolve of Helen's protégé. They'd been certain that, given time, he'd eventually pack his bags and go. Their mistake had been to give him even a morning's work.

Because Benson had been waiting. He'd been counting the days. And when he reached 1095, scratched into the hull of The Wooden Doll, he made an announcement (that very morning) in the legal pages of The Times.

William Benson Esq is pleased to announce that he intends to establish Congreve Chambers at 9B Artillery Passage, Spitalfields, London E1. He will specialise in criminal defence work. Instructions are invited from anyone seeking a distinctive personal service. He wishes to thank all those colleagues who worked tirelessly to make this possible.

None of his detractors had thought of the obvious: that Benson was clocking up flying time to meet the Bar Council's minimum requirement for a barrister to operate on his own.

'You clever boy,' said Helen, lighting another cigar and coughing. 'Why didn't you tell me?'

'I wanted to surprise you.'

'You have. How did you secure the premises?'

Benson had been faithfully attending Archie Congreve's Tuesday Club, a private members' club for those with hands-on experience of HMP No-Matter-Where, convened each week at the Pride of Spitalfields on Heneage Street. And Archie, who'd presided over the decline of a family business – people weren't prepared to pay the price of a fresh catch, not any more, they'd gone frozen, or to a supermarket, and his wife had been dying of cancer, and to get by he'd fiddled the books, and then the Inland Revenue had turned up – good old Archie had suggested Benson take over the good old shop.

'Wonderful,' said Helen. 'Just wonderful.'

Archie secured some favourable coverage in the Guardian. *But then the* Sun *hit back, with a petition to close Benson down. The next morning, the Rt. Hon. Richard Merrington MP, Minister of State for Justice, weighed in, promising legislation to reflect the public's very proper sense of outrage. By Wednesday morning – which is to say after a rousing meeting of the Tuesday Club the night before – Benson had a brain-shaking hangover.*

And then the phone rang.

It was from Sarah Collingstone. She stood accused of murder. She'd sacked her solicitor and barrister. The trial was due to start in four days. She wanted Benson.

'I'm afraid I've never done a Crown Court trial, Miss Collingstone.'

'I don't care.'

'My experience is limited to the magistrates' court, injunctions in the county court, and what you need is—'

'Mr Benson, I want you. You're the only person I'm prepared to trust. Everyone else thinks I must be guilty. They won't listen to me.'

Two days prior to trial, a Monday, Benson was walking home along Seymour Road. He couldn't find his damned keys, but that was the least of his worries. He was heading back to the Old Bailey. Number 1 Court. The very court in which he'd been convicted. He didn't know what to do then, and he didn't know what to do now. He felt like a grade 2 piano student being asked to play Rachmaninov's second piano concerto. How the hell was he going to . . .

He looked up, and there was a man in front of him, wide-shouldered, jaw protruding, eyes laughing, and he spat right in Benson's face.

He was so shocked that, at first, he could only feel the warmth of hatred on his cheeks. Then, the outrage began to move in his guts, like a wall falling down, only there was another, and Benson was standing behind it. He looked up, unable to see over the top course, and peered at the night sky.

Would this ever stop? Would someone ever turn up who didn't want to bring him down?

Benson heard the sound of running feet, and when he lowered his gaze there was a hand in front of him, holding a pure white handkerchief with a lace trim. His eyes ran over the fine wrist, a peeping cuff, and up the arm, to the face of a woman wearing a green velvet hat.

There was something familiar about that look of anxiety and concern. He'd seen her before . . . before he'd been sent down.

73

Benson sat bolt upright.

Tess had gone. He glanced at his bedside clock. It was 10.32 a.m. He hadn't slept this late since he was a teenager. Only he had no recollection of having slept at all. He thought he'd lain awake all night going over the process Helen had begun at the start of the Lynwood trial. She'd put herself in the dock. She'd insisted on hearing evidence about the individuals she'd damaged, and he'd thought Tess was there, silent and unmoving, asleep. He'd no idea when she'd slipped out. And he felt her absence as if part of his body had disappeared.

But the amputation was of no importance.

Benson had experienced one of those intuitions, which, despite their brief passage across the mind, are peculiarly violent. It was why he had shot up, as if jolted awake by a crash in a dream, or one of those falls from a cliff, when you lose your footing on a grassy lip and suddenly you're falling—

There was something wrong with the Lynwood verdicts.

While reliving his last moments with Helen, overwhelmed by recollections of their previous meetings, he recognised she'd been heading remorselessly towards a declaration of who she really was; who she'd really been . . . and Benson, thinking he was awake, thinking Tess was breathing quietly beside him, had suddenly realised this was exactly what Menderez had been doing with Karen Lynwood.

He'd controlled the entire therapeutic process, right from the outset.

He'd gradually told her what he wanted her to know, in stages moving methodically from what he'd heard as a child to what he'd done as a man. He'd begun with the effect of the Red Terror on his parents, which explained their fear of communists and the left, whose children had been stolen as a kind of 'benign' social intervention; and he'd ended with his own involvement in the theft of children from women like Lucia, who'd been judged as inadequate when it came to the heavy responsibility of parenting. He'd come to see that his intervention wasn't so benign after all. That it had been criminal. And he'd fled Spain . . .

To escape his conscience?

Or to attend to 'unfinished business'?

Benson had a quick shower and dressed. All the while, fragments of the trial bounced around his mind, unattached, like electrons that had lost their nucleus. Menderez had insisted on a property in Limehouse, nowhere else. He'd chosen a therapist who specialised in the management of midlife crises. He'd arrived home at roughly 7 p.m. but he'd still been wearing his coat when he was killed, some two and a half hours later. John Lynwood had come up with an answer to the riddle: whoever killed Menderez had been in the property all the time. There were problems in the Lynwood marriage, but then Menderez had turned up, speaking a language Karen understood. Karen had told Narinda Hassan all her secrets, save one. She'd said nothing of Menderez's crime. Mrs Tindale – Isabel Delegado – writer for *El Testigo*, had been a supporter of the Franco regime. Bob Graynor had served five years in the Royal London Rifles. Menderez had bombarded Karen with emails and texts. 'We have to do what's right for everyone.' Black Iberian pigs fed on acorns. Along with roots and olives and herbs and grass. More CCTV cameras were needed in the Limehouse area. Menderez had made a call using the landline. His mobile phone had been found in his coat pocket, without the SIM card. The Lynwoods had never fully cooperated. Not Karen and not John. They'd both refused to give evidence. Heart of Spain (Imports) Ltd had been formed in 1971. Menderez had purchased a Canon EOS M5 with a telephoto lens. At the time of the stabbing, his head was angled downwards as if to make a telephone call.

'They controlled the trial,' said Benson, reaching for his duffel coat.

Opening the door, he saw a Tesco bag on the outside doormat. He'd left the gate unlocked, and someone must have made a hasty delivery that morning. He looked inside, and found a bundle of photographs. For a long moment, he stared at the pictures of a man and his wife, and their child. In a park. By a swing. Walking home. Then, confused, he put them in his pocket.

74

Tess was at home, cleaning the windows.

She'd been thinking of Benson sleeping at her side. How he'd shifted and turned, moaning occasionally. And she'd thought of him standing over Paul Harbeton like an executioner. That savouring of revenge, only for a matter of seconds, while half-drunk and bleeding, had still poisoned him. The half-deaf Fr Kennedy had been right: what we would do, if we got the chance, can be as harmful as what we actually do. So don't judge. And she hadn't judged Benson. She'd just been grateful a motorcycle despatch rider had turned up with a mobile, if not a conscience.

And Tess had been thinking of her investigation into Benson, which was now complete.

She'd been waiting, anxiously, for news of Annette's arrest, so the next step could be taken towards the restoration of Benson's good character: an application to appeal his conviction and sentence. The prospect of Annette changing her mind, challenging Tess to fulfil her threat, had plagued her imagination. As did her attempts to enter Benson's experience of vindication, for it had come at the cost of Camberley's unmasking. How could he survive the shock?

To escape that question, she'd grabbed a bucket and cloth, but then suffered a shock of her own. As soon as the hot water touched the glass, the surface turned murky and she couldn't understand how she'd ever looked out at the world without noticing the grime inside. But she had done, and that made—

Her phone rang. Flipping open the cover, she saw the name on the screen and was immediately worried. Was he all right? Should she have stayed with him? Had he done something stupid?

'Tess, meet me at Limehouse Basin. The marina. Linfield House.'

Benson hadn't even said hello.

'Why?'

'Menderez wasn't just confessing. He was confronting.'

'What do you mean?'

'The Lynwood trial was a sham. We were played.'

Benson was speaking nonsense. There was no connection between his sentences, and Tess feared some vital inner thread that held his personality together might have snapped. Which is why she threw her wet rag into the bucket and drove at speed to an address she'd never heard of. He was waiting for her on the pavement, pacing the short distance between a row of parked cars and the grand entrance to a luxurious residential block evoking the prow of a ship, with a gleaming glass façade, and balconies overlooking the twinkling, wind-tossed marina.

As soon as he heard her footsteps, Benson turned and pressed the buzzer of one of the apartments.

'You've got me worried,' said Tess. 'Are you okay?'

'No. And I doubt if I ever will be again.'

'I couldn't leave you as you were.'

'And I can't stay as I am.'

'What are you doing?' said Tess. 'Is this because of what I've done?'

Far from being dissociated, Benson was supremely self-possessed; his expression was grave, but it was the anger that frightened Tess. The sort of wild rage he must have bottled up since the day he'd been sent down.

'I can't prove anything, Tess.'

'Prove what?'

'Just give the impression we know everything.'

75

The Graynor family were in a flap.

They'd just had a board meeting. Joy, Bob's rosy-cheeked wife, had a talk to give at the London Spanish Society, whereas the twins, Nicola and Sophie, were both attending a presentation in Westminster for small businesses preparing for Brexit.

'Though we're not that small,' said Joy sunnily. 'Not any more.'

She nodded at her daughters.

'They moved the business onto the internet. Bob had to travel all over Spain; now these two get up when they want and send an email.'

'Hey, Mum, less of it,' said Nicola grabbing her Barbour raincoat – she was tall, with long black hair, like her sister – 'C'mon Fi-fi.'

'That's Sophie's nickname,' explained Joy with a magenta smile. 'We call Nicola Knick-knack.'

The two women went over to their father, who was seated, legs crossed, in a leather armchair. Playing out a family ritual as if it was obligatory, Knick-knack went to one side of her father and Fi-fi went to the other, and then, as if on a signal, they both bowed to kiss his forehead, reminding Tess of birds that come out of a cuckoo clock to perform a synchronised action. It was the sort of thing friends would watch and wait for, and maybe applaud. With a smile and wave, the directors of Heart of Spain (Imports) Ltd left the apartment. The company secretary, Joy, bustled into the kitchen to check the percolator.

'Do they have any idea?' said Benson in a low voice.

'About what?' said Graynor.

Joy appeared.

'Would you like a snack?'

'No thank you,' said Benson with a smile; and when she'd gone, he whispered, 'Does she know?'

'Know what?'

'The name of the nursing sister from Cantabria?'

'I don't know what you're talking about.'

Graynor was wearing a white shirt with thick blue stripes. His silk tie, with its crossed muskets, or whatever they were – thought Tess – had to be regimental.

'You said you wanted to discuss the importance of CCTV cameras,' he said, standing up. 'And since you—'

'All right, we will,' said Benson. 'Is that how you got home without being picked up? You knew all the camera placements.'

'Look . . . I don't know what are you playing at, but—'

'You also knew that John Lynwood would be caught coming and going to his car. That he'd get arrested.'

'The girls have been an absolute wonder,' said Joy, coming into the room with a tray. 'Do sit down. We're old-school, Bobby and I. We're face-to-face people. Names. Addresses. Telephone numbers. Handshakes. Christmas cards. We got to know our clients. These days, like I said, they just don't have to put the miles in. Bobby there,' – she gave a short nod – 'he's covered every inch of Spain. Every valley. Every track. To get the best cheeses from Navarra, the finest ham from the Alpujarra, the most . . . bloomin' 'eck I'm sorry: I'm in gear already. You won't have a snack? From Barcelona?'

'Leave us for a moment, Joy.'

'No need to ask, Bobby, I can't stay for long.'

She went into another room, plump reddish hands untying her apron.

'Unlike you,' said Benson. 'You stayed. You arrived at 3.30 p.m. And you didn't leave. Because you were waiting to find out if Karen Lynwood – I suppose we ought to call her your client – if your client was going to give in. Menderez had been pushing her and pushing her, trying to get her to own up to what she'd done. Trying to get John to agree, but he wouldn't.'

Tess frowned at Benson. Giving the impression she knew everything was beyond her capability. It was clear from the looks between Benson and Graynor that they were the only ones who understood what Benson was talking about.

'My guess is that back in the seventies you visited a client you knew to be childless, only now they had a boy or a girl. You knew they'd never adopt, and in those days IVF wasn't available, so you wondered how the miracle had happened. Maybe this client was proud. Maybe they told you they'd saved a baby from a life of hell. And because it was passed off as a natural birth, no one had to admit they were barren or sterile. Everyone was a winner.'

'Have you seen my watch, Bobby?'

'Try the bathroom.'

'I don't think you saw a business opportunity,' said Benson. 'I think you saw the answer to someone's crisis. Maybe a relative's. Maybe a friend's.' He paused. 'Maybe your own,

Mr Graynor. So you got back in touch with your client. Who put you in touch with the sister without a name.'

Joy came back into the room.

'Not there.'

'By the bed,' said Graynor. 'On the floor.'

'I doubt you gave the matter much thought,' said Benson. 'Like others sucked into this business, you didn't think beyond the economics. You didn't think of the human cost. You didn't think unknown wrongs might just matter.'

'I'm going to have to get one of those clip watches that you fit on a pocket, like nurses have. Bobby, you big lump, you haven't served the refreshments.'

Shaking her head, Joy began pouring, spilling coffee in the saucers and on the tray. After dashing in and out with paper towels, she said:

'I'll just have to retrace my steps,' – adding – 'How are you getting along? About the CCTV question, I mean? Bobby's right, we need lots more.'

She didn't wait for the answer; and Benson didn't wait for Graynor.

'And then Isabel Tindale contacted you. Why? Because you're known on the circuit, here and in Spain – because Isabel's heard about this most delicate type of social work; she approves – and you're then brought into the childless sitting room of the Lynwoods. You're the fixer. You're the man who's done the business countless times before. Importing cheese from Navarra, ham from the Alpujarra, and babies from—'

'I don't have to listen to this,' said Graynor. 'If you want to make such allegations, then—'

'Dr Menderez came to you first. For three months he courted you. And then he told you who he was and why he was in London. He wanted you on board. Before he approached Karen.'

'You're leaving. Now.'

'You panicked. You thought, God Almighty, this guy wants to blow the lid off everything. So you played along, as if you'd seen the light, gambling Karen would never agree to this crazy attempt to make amends.'

Graynor stood up swiftly, as if his commanding officer had entered the room. He pointed towards the door, and Tess thought of those fascist salutes made by men with very short hair. He looked utterly ridiculous.

'Go.'

Benson sipped his coffee. He was the only one to have touched his cup.

'Menderez courted Karen for three months. And when he finally revealed his crime – their crime – and his purpose, her world came crashing down, because the abduction of Simon had been her secret torment, especially since she'd gone into therapy, only she was confused, because Menderez was holding out more than the promise of redemption. There was the tricky question of damnation. It had to come first.'

'If you don't leave, I'll call the police.'

'Like you, John wouldn't agree,' continued Benson, unabashed. 'So you thought you were safe. But then Dr Menderez came home. You discussed it some more. He was devastated, because he'd heard nothing from Karen. She'd gone to the bloody theatre.'

Benson sneered.

'He thought you were on board. And when he turned around to call the police—'

'Found it!'

Joy was triumphant. She came into the sitting room holding out her watch as if she'd caught a goldfish by its tail.

'Guess where it was? In the toilet. Well, not in it: on the paper holder. Not that you need to know, Mr Benson. Oops. Don't you want your coffee, Miss de . . . what is it?'

'De Vere. No thank you.'

'They're leaving,' said Graynor, striding towards the door of the apartment.

Tess followed Benson out of the sitting room, unable to process what had just happened, where she was, where they were going, and what had taken place during the Lynwood trial.

'So, are you going to back a move to get more CCTV cameras?' sang Joy, now fiddling with a pearl necklace.

Benson paused in the doorway. There was something about his manner that said he knew he'd never be back here. That he'd never speak to the Graynors again. He held out his hand, but not to the man he'd just accused of murder. His attention had shifted to Joy, and when she took it, Benson tugged her closer:

'Are the girls well settled?'

Joy glanced at her husband, the necklace knotted around her hand.

'They're both happily married, if that's what you mean.'

'You have grandchildren?'

'Yes. Four.'

'Get out,' said Graynor.

Benson let Joy go.

'You must be very proud, both of you. Very proud indeed.'

76

'Those two girls,' said Tess. 'Knick-knack and Fi-fi . . . they're from—'

'Salamanca, Seville, Bilbao, who knows.'

'Do you think Joy's in on it?'

'Tess, that is an extraordinary question.'

Tess just couldn't imagine the process. Heading off to Spain full of excitement. Taking the plane and then a taxi and then, ten grand poorer, taking someone else's child. Or children, in the case of the Graynors.

'Menderez was involved?'

'No. This was before his time.'

'I need a drink, but not here.'

Tess had to get away from Limehouse, from the air around the ship-like building, and once she and Benson were in her Mini she drove aimlessly, but at speed, finally pulling up outside a small café in Whitechapel. They found a table towards the back, away from the busy street and the brightness of the morning light. Tess needed shadow.

'What happened, Will?' she said.

'In leaving Madrid for Candidar, Menderez was running away from the idea of what he'd done. A national movement was underway. Women were protesting outside court houses, seeking justice. In meeting Lucia, he faced the reality. And he had a breakdown. She was inspiring; and he'd taken her child away from her. He hadn't given her a chance.'

'So he came to London . . . I still don't get it.'

'If this child theft went on into the nineties, then Menderez was involved for ten years. He wouldn't even remember how many children he'd signed over to Graynor, or someone else. But I'll bet you he'd remember the first – and the date. The eleventh of October 1986.'

Tess thought about Menderez filling out a false death certificate for the first time, and then comforting the mother, holding her hand. Yes, he'd remember the performance: it can't have been easy, even if you thought this was somehow a good thing to do. Only . . .

'Lucia's child was a girl,' she said. 'She'd named her Angela.'

'Tess, this whole scheme rests on lies. It rests on deceit.

Menderez and this nameless sister misled Lucia. Told her she'd had a girl when she'd had a boy. It's all part of erasing any possible connection between a child and its mother.'

Tess stared into space.

'So Menderez set out to restore one child to its mother . . . the first theft. As some kind of symbol?'

'To start a new process,' said Benson. 'Menderez wanted to bring the police into the equation. He wanted everyone involved – Graynor, himself, the Lynwoods and, I imagine, Isabel Tindale – to come together and admit what they'd done. The vulnerable party here, of course, is Simon. He couldn't just be told he'd been bought from a clinic in Madrid. The whole situation is crying out for highly trained specialist intervention, in tandem with any criminal proceedings, and that, for Menderez, would only be the beginning. He'd then admit there were others. Many others.'

'And that would trigger the process. Former patients would start coming forward, women who'd been told their child had died.'

'Yes.'

'And the exhumations would begin.'

'Opening a moral challenge.'

Tess thought about that, too. Any investigation would be hopeless if the documentary trail had been falsified, destroyed or concealed. The process could only succeed if the thousands of Lynwoods – in the UK, or Spain, or wherever – decided to admit what they'd been involved in. In seeking the cooperation of the Lynwoods, Menderez had been trying to set an example. He'd hoped to persuade the others, whom he didn't know, or couldn't remember, to come forward. To become part of a voluntary process that would return stolen children to their mothers, to their fathers. That was the moral challenge.

It was a big ask.

And the Lynwoods hadn't cooperated.

And neither had the fixer, Mr Graynor.

'And when Menderez decided to call the police,' said Benson, who'd followed Tess's thoughts, 'still in his coat, because his evening was just beginning – he'd expected to be arrested – Graynor grabbed a pair of scissors and did what a trained solider would never forget. He went for the most vulnerable exposed part of his enemy.'

Tess didn't even ask herself why. It was obvious. He, of all people, had most to lose. Knick-knack and Fi-fi would never understand. They'd look at the import figures, and then the confusion would begin. These beloved parents, the cheery Joy and Colonel Mustard, would change instantly before their eyes. So many happy memories, so much kindness and tenderness, devotion, guidance and love, real love, given and received, would boil to the surface, only to cool down, forever transformed.

Graynor hadn't had a murderous thought in his head, until Menderez turned around and got out his mobile phone.

'He took the SIM card,' said Tess.

'Yes. To cover the traffic between himself and Menderez.'

Tess recalled a schedule of texts and emails.

'So there was no affair between Menderez and Karen?'

'No. Just moral pressure.'

'Then why did he ring John Lynwood at eight thirty-one? On the landline?'

'He didn't. Menderez was already dead. The call was made by Graynor. Think that through.'

John Lynwood got a call out of the blue from a man he'd last seen in 1986. Twenty-nine years had passed. John had been dealing with Menderez, and now Graynor was back on the scene. Graynor, who knew everything. Graynor must have told John to get himself over to Limehouse Cut, and he'd obeyed, wondering what the hell for . . . not knowing that he'd be picked up by the CCTV cameras on Upper North Street. He'd walked into a murder scene.

'That's why John told us he'd been framed,' said Tess.

'Yes.'

'He'd helped move the body, and then he'd run for his life.'

Benson was sitting back in his chair, arms folded as if he were cold. He said:

'When Graynor was in the witness box, all the conspirators were in court. These traffickers of children. They were together, the Lynwoods unable to expose Graynor because that would bounce back on Simon, and Graynor unable to confess because that would bounce back on Nicola and Sophie. They were all gambling that we'd get John Lynwood off. And we did – which is just as well, because he was innocent. But they were all conspiring to pervert the course of justice. One of them was a murderer. And they were all guilty of a crime against humanity.'

77

A crime against humanity that would never find its way onto an indictment.

And as regards a conspiracy to pervert the course of justice, Tess disagreed with Benson on the law.

'Agreement,' says Blackstone's, 'is the essence of conspiracy.' It can be explicit or inferred. In all likelihood, these parties had never sat down and worked out what they were going to do. There was no chain, either, whereby John agreed with Graynor, and then Karen agreed with John. And there was no wheel where Graynor was the hub, recruiting first John and then Karen. They were party to a common design without having to agree to anything. Each party had a secret to hide; each was dependent on the other. As soon as John had been arrested, they'd each known what to do: keep quiet.

And they had done.

Even as Lucia Callasteros, the victim, described her loss.

The Lynwoods had sat there listening, seeing the mother of their son for the first time. A woman whose evidence was slowly opening the door of Number 3 Court, so John could walk free. John, who hadn't wanted to thank her afterwards, because he'd been overwhelmed by her story; who'd just wanted to go home, with his arm around Simon.

Lucia Callasteros had no idea what she'd just done.

Driving out of Whitechapel, Tess couldn't shake these thoughts off. Worse, she felt drawn into this silent world of grotesque indifference and criminality, as if she and Benson had been part of the wider plan that had never been spoken about. For they'd been the agents of the Lynwoods' exoneration. Vital players in an undeclared strategy.

She was sure Benson felt the same; and like him she didn't want to put into words what they'd done. Instead she turned to other unfinished business.

'I'd expected to tell you about Helen myself. I'd no idea she was planning to—'

'I can't talk about her. Not yet. Maybe not ever. Look at these.'

Benson reached into the pocket of his duffel coat and took out some photographs. He held one up, so Tess could take a quick glance.

'That's Simon Lynwood . . . and his family.'

'Looks like Hayley's stepdad kept the camera after all.'

Tess frowned.

'But why give them to you?'

'He knew they might be important. And he owed you for the windows.'

'Then why not call me?'

'Because that would involve admitting he's got the camera. And he wants to keep it. My question is, why did Menderez take the pictures at all?'

Tess turned into Bishopsgate, heading up towards Congreve Chambers.

'To remind himself of what he'd set out to do?' she ventured.

'Why? He couldn't possibly forget.'

'In case he lost his nerve?'

Benson put the photos away, shaking his head.

'So what do you think?' said Tess.

'I don't know. Except this: they're all that's left of a bid for justice. Printed off by a handler of stolen goods.'

As soon as Benson entered chambers, both Archie and Molly came towards him, expressing their condolences; Tess stepped back, thinking she'd best leave. She felt compromised. They'd no conception of the scale of his grief, or its true content. Whether they'd ever know was Benson's prerogative. For he might decide to leave Camberley's reputation intact, keeping, in effect, her secret. Similarly, neither Archie nor Molly – low-voiced and tiptoeing around now – had the remotest idea that Annette Merrington's name would shortly appear all over the press. And when it did happen, if Benson buried Camberley's story, they'd be mystified by his subdued reaction. He'd remain, in some strange way, prisoner AC1963. Even as Archie tried valiantly to change the subject, he was approaching its heart.

'Have you heard the news, Rizla?'

'No, Archie, I have not.'

'There's to be a vote of no confidence today. In the Prime Minister.'

'Can't we have a vote of no confidence in all of them?'

'Good one, Rizla, good one. Point is, those who want the driving seat are lining up already.'

'I see.'

'And guess who says he isn't interested when he is?'

'I've no idea.'

'The most right honourable git Richard Merrington.'

Who appeared in paragraph 16 of Camberley's sworn affidavit as her half-brother, named also in paragraph 17 as a blind beneficiary of her decision to pervert the course of justice with their shared mother.

There was a sudden pause, because Benson had glanced at Tess and Archie had seen their eyes lock in mutual understanding, but thankfully the phone rang in the clerk's room. When Archie came back into the Gutting Room, he was smiling broadly.

'You've both been invited to a party.'

'Who by?' said Benson, again looking at Tess; this time with foreboding.

'Simon Lynwood. To celebrate the acquittal of his parents.'

78

For years – when it came to clothes – Tess had only ever wondered if one colour went with another. Now she asked herself if Benson would like the match. The result was that what should have taken ten minutes took half an hour, and completely messed up her bedroom, because, with all the trying on and throwing aside, she'd literally taken out everything she possessed. When she picked up Benson at his gate on Seymour Road she was wearing ordinary work clothes.

'Where've you been?' she said, pulling away from the kerb.

After insisting they attend this God-awful party, Benson had booked himself out of court for a week. Archie didn't know where he'd gone, and he hadn't answered Tess's calls. She'd fretted, too, that he'd been running away from the threat of intimacy between them. Sailed away, actually, because she'd gone to Seymour Basin and *The Wooden Doll* hadn't been there. He'd been hiding somewhere on the Albert Canal.

'I can't keep still.'

He, too, had dressed for work. In the suit he'd worn for the trial.

'You could answer my bloody calls.'

'I'm sorry.'

'And don't give me any of that "I was a prisoner, I'm all messed up" crap. You can be decent. I've been worried.'

'Honestly, I'm sorry. I just needed to get away. I still do. And it's not simply because of Helen.'

He seemed to try to get an unpleasant taste out of his mouth.

'I keep reliving Lucia's evidence-in-chief. I brought her story out, I put it on the court record. It's perverse. And it's perverse that the Lynwoods could hear someone recount what they've endured, because of them, and not . . . be changed.'

'My thoughts exactly. We might have shared them. Changed into what, though?'

'Themselves. Back to who they once were, before they found themselves doing something that was so obviously wrong.'

Tess wanted to reach over and take Benson's clenched hand but she didn't dare. He might pull away; and she wanted this, at least: the shared disgust.

'Why are we here, Will? We didn't have to come. And I don't want—'

'Because we have to do something.'

'They're out of reach.'

'Not completely.'

Tess parked up, a few doors down from the Lynwoods' home on Cornfield Road. Benson said:

'If they have any peace of mind, it rests upon the belief that no one knows what they did. Even Karen, unhappy as she is, takes consolation in the fact that she suffers in private.'

'What are you going to do?'

'Take it away.'

On reaching the property, they saw it was for sale; which was hardly surprising given that two of their neighbours had given evidence for the prosecution. But what struck Tess most was the sight of the family, seen through the window.

Simon was beaming. So was Isabel Tindale. But John's wide smile was wooden, and Karen wasn't smiling at all, and they were on different sides of the room. They hadn't wanted this party any more than Tess and Benson had wanted to attend it. People were milling between them, talking and laughing, wholly unaware of the hell these two had made for themselves. There were canapés and quiches and sausage rolls and salads and flutes of champagne, along with glasses of wine, and cans of beer. The feast might as well have been so much sewage. These two winners weren't going to enjoy the taste of anything. Tess and Benson had got it wrong, their clients had been changed: John had caught up with Karen, and Karen, seeing further, was dragging John deeper into the pit of self-knowledge, deeper than he could ever have imagined. Opening a joint present, they understood each other now. It had just taken a few days' reflection on the words of Lucia Callasteros. People were chanting 'Speech!

Speech!' but John, turning to the window, saw Tess and immediately came to the door, carving up a fresh smile. When it opened, Benson spoke:

'We know, John.'

John kept the hideous grin in place, as if it might ward off the devil.

'We know why Menderez died. We know who killed him. We know what he was hoping to achieve. We know why you and Karen were scared, and what you both stood to lose. You can tell that to your wife and godmother. And here is something specifically for you: we know you refused to listen. And that's why Menderez is dead.'

If this had been a first date, it didn't bode well. First, what a place to go. And secondly, having spoken his mind, Benson had turned around and walked off, leaving Tess to chase after him. Back in the car, she'd roasted him, and again he'd said sorry, and again she'd told him to keep any prison crap out of his explanation, which, as it happened, hadn't been forthcoming. He'd wanted to go home. He'd forgotten to feed the cat.

79

Benson had to get away. There was too much on his mind. The death of Helen, her . . . what was it? Her betrayal? The term was too narrow, because, following her grand deception, she'd devoted what was left of her life to him. He'd become something he wanted to be and perhaps wouldn't have become without the destruction he'd undergone. But that couldn't alleviate the loss of years and family, or his anger, or his confusion, all of which complicated primitive feelings of grief for the going of someone he'd loved; and still loved. But what was he to do with the memories of what they'd shared? Those hours spent in Hampstead?

Benson didn't know.

At the same time, he possessed an affidavit that, if released, would destroy Richard Merrington's self-understanding. What was he to do with it?

Benson didn't know.

There was also Tess, who'd worked to prove his innocence: an innocence that would shortly be declared. When she'd lain there beside him in the darkness he'd realised, even as he struggled to understand Helen's duplicity, there was no longer any obstacle between them. But he felt suddenly naked. He was used to the loneliness that had crippled him for so many years. He couldn't admit it, but he quite liked it now. What was he to do?

Benson didn't know.

And then there was the Limehouse case. He couldn't escape the sense of complicity; of having been controlled. What could he do now?

Benson didn't know.

These thoughts kept him quiet all the way from Islington to Seymour Road. And after Tess had left, angrily, because he'd given her some nonsense about Traddles, he went back on board. Turning the light on, his eyes fell on the photographs of Simon Lynwood's family, laid out on the kitchen table. And with the same speed it had taken for the switch to banish the darkness Benson knew what Menderez had been planning.

He knew what he had to do; and where he had to go.

80

Lambton Abbey was situated at the end of a long winding lane among low green hills in Suffolk. Driving the Tuesday Club's members-only battered Fiesta, Benson slowed down, gripped by the sight of red-tiled roofs, pink-washed buildings, a wave of dense woodland, and, sharp against the horizon, the pale, worn stone of a large bell tower. Having arranged his visit, he parked as instructed on a patch of grass between a herb garden and an orchard of apple trees. Enchanted, he made his way to reception where a large, red-faced monk looked him up and down.

'Have you had a decent breakfast?'

'No.'

The monk's watery eyes were severe.

'A pity. There's no meat on you. Are you hungry?'

'Well, I—'

'When did you last eat? I used to be a cook, and—'

'God almighty . . .'

The voice belonged to Fr Aelred, dressed not in jeans this time, but a shabby black habit with another length of black cloth running down the front . . . just like the other monk, in fact, save the former cook had a length of garden twine around his waist in place of a leather belt. He'd emerged from an arched door.

'Gilbert, he doesn't want any bacon. Or black pudding. Or sausages.'

Shaking his head in mock despair, he smiled at Benson and drew him outside.

'Are you interested in bees?'

'Actually, I'm interested in the sausages.'

'Really? I'm going to show you my hives.'

I'm in a crazy place, thought Benson.

They walked beside a rippling stream towards a cluster of poplars, and Benson explained what had happened during the trial. How Menderez had set out to change history. How he'd first approached Graynor. And then, thinking he had an ally, he'd sat with Karen Lynwood as if he was just another patient, before finally revealing his identity and his plan, for by then he'd drawn her into understanding why he'd done what he'd done; thereby thrusting the same question onto her. He'd trapped her with her own ethics policy.

'I can't prove anything. I just know this is what happened.'

Fr Aelred listened, nodding and shuffling through the grass.

'I can't sleep, thinking Lucia came into court wanting to help the very people who'd robbed her, not knowing that the man in the public gallery was her son.'

They were approaching the shivering poplars, and Benson could see white crosses leaning amongst the slender trunks. It was unheard of. A graveyard in a copse. The dead among live roots.

'And she helped people who've chosen to lie. Their past rests on lies, and their future is built on lies. They're otherwise good people, leading good lives; they just can't see clearly. And they aren't on their own. Governments and institutions developed the policies. And none of them dare do what is necessary to bring the truth to light. Because the cost is too high, and yet people like Lucia have to pay the price twice over. First they're robbed as mothers, and then they're robbed as victims. They lose their own blood and there's no justice afterwards. That's what I'm a part of. And I can't forgive myself, even though I did nothing wrong, even though I didn't know what I was doing.'

Fr Aelred led the way into the trees, along a narrow, worn path. Benson felt he was among a sleeping crowd, for there were graves everywhere, their crosses leaning and peering in the undergrowth. In spring, there would be a carpet of wild flowers, bluebells, maybe.

'I think Dr Menderez thought this might happen; that he might fail,' said Benson. 'Because he took photographs of Simon and his family. And I think he wanted to give them to Lucia.'

Fr Aelred turned around.

'Is that why you are here?'

'Yes. I thought you might send them on. She deserves to know the truth, no matter what the fallout might be.'

'You can give them to her yourself.'

'What do you mean?'

Fr Aelred walked up some steps cut from railway sleepers, set into a gentle incline. Ahead was a fence that had become a trellis for brambles and thorns.

'She's still here. But I think there is something you should know.'

He lifted a loop of rope off a post and dragged open a broken gate. Standing like a benign jailor, he said:

'Lucia knew exactly what she was doing. Before she even left Spain. She hadn't been fooled. And when she got here . . . well, a mother knows her son. They were beside each other in the public gallery for the verdict.'

Benson saw Lucia picking her way towards him. Behind her was a weathered pew among a circle of hives, all slightly askew on their stone platforms. The trees were like witnesses.

'To be honest, I wouldn't mind heading back for those sausages.'

But it was too late. Lucia was standing in front of him. Fr Aelred spoke to her, his appearance itself seeming to change as he switched to the warm, melodic sounds of Spanish. And as he was speaking, her face was transformed. Light seemed to shine from around her eyes. Benson held out the photographs. She took them gratefully. And then, quite suddenly, and shyly, she kissed Benson on the cheek.

Benson drove away from the red-tiled roofs unable to forget the image of Lucia, curled up on that pew among the hives, studying her son, her daughter-in-law and her grandson. He was appalled by her sacrifice. She'd not dared disturb Simon's world. And even if she'd been minded to, she'd no confidence he'd want to know her, or make space for her in his life. All she knew was that if John Lynwood was convicted, the repercussions for Simon and his family would be significant; and the family that had given him a home would probably fall apart.

Benson had learnt all this from Fr Aelred, walking back on the other bank of the stream. They'd spoken of the Church, martyred and then saved, becoming an integral part of the social services in Franco's Spain. How do we judge that epoch? Governments, institutions and individuals? How did anyone ever come to think that the secret removal of children from their parents was in the best interests of everyone concerned? How could people do something bad, thinking they were doing something good? Only a national inquiry could answer those types of questions. And that wasn't going to happen. On reaching the Fiesta parked beneath the plum trees, Fr Aelred had paused to think; then he'd said:

'People can learn to live without justice, but not without the truth. Living without the truth . . . that's unbearable.'

81

The last thing Benson wanted was a party, not after seeing the Lynwoods gathered with glasses in hand. Not after seeing Lucia clutching those photographs. And he wasn't inclined to gloat over an old woman's encounter with judicial retribution. But Tess wouldn't listen. She'd insisted on a gathering, in chambers, the place where Benson's career had sunk its foundations. She'd insisted on a minimum of invitees, apart from Archie and Molly: Braithwaite, Sally, Abasiama, CJ Congreve, and, of course, the four Congreve girls. The Few. The ones who'd stood by him.

'What about your dad, Will?'

'No . . . I can't see him without seeing my brother.'

And Benson had decided to tear down the wall between himself and Eddie. It had been there since the day of Eddie's accident and Benson couldn't endure the separation any longer; and he couldn't imagine accepting Eddie's apologies for having condemned him over a murder he hadn't committed, when he stood condemned of an offence Eddie didn't even know about. No, the wall had to come down, regardless of the consequences. Having given Tess his conditions, Benson had rung his father:

'Dad, get *Dalston's Girl* ready. We're going out to sea. The three of us. Me, you and Eddie.'

In all other respects, Benson did he as he was told: at the appointed time he arrived at chambers and braved the Gutting Room.

The chambers television set, used for video-link hearings and conferences, had been wheeled in front of Benson's desk. He looked at the opaque screen and the dark reflection of the restive crowd, wondering what he was going to say to them. But then Tess pressed the remote control and

Big Ben appeared to the sound of trumpets. It was time for the evening news.

The lead item came as no surprise.

Annette Merrington, aged ninety-two, had presented herself at West Hampstead Police Station in the presence of her son, the Rt. Hon. Richard Merrington MP, the Lord Chancellor and Secretary of State for Justice. As a result of a voluntary confession in relation to the death of Paul Harbeton in 1998, she'd been charged with causing death by careless driving, and failing to stop and failing to report an accident. Given her age, she'd been released on bail.

There was no mention of her conspiring with Helen Camberley QC to pervert the course of justice. Annette was well aware that Benson had in his possession an affidavit that would prove the offence, but she, like Helen, had left Benson to decide what to do. And Benson, his vision blurred, marvelled at the double cheek: even after all that had happened to him, for which they were alone responsible, Helen and Annette had both thought they could rely on Benson's cooperation . . . to hold back the truth, for the benefit of someone they wished to protect: Richard, the son who didn't need to know the true reasons for why his mother had driven off. It was incredible. They wanted to perpetuate the rationale for their offending in the first place.

Well, Benson had a surprise for both of them. He intended to judge the living and the dead. The affidavit would be published. The only—

Tess elbowed him in the ribs.

'Are you watching?'

'I'm glued. Look – something's up.'

The newsreader had paused to announce breaking news. Richard Merrington was about to give a statement from outside his home in Highgate. Transmission shifted from the studio to the street, and after the usual checking of an earpiece by a reporter in the field, followed by a repetition of what had already been said, the Secretary of State for Justice emerged from behind a shining black door to face the cameras and microphones. At his elbow, brave-faced but mortified, was his wife, Pamela.

'Honour is a family tradition. Without saying more, I trust you will understand why, then, I have today tendered my resignation. I have further decided to withdraw from political life with immediate effect. This is the shortest statement I have ever given, and I don't propose to expand upon it at any stage in the future. I do, however, have one final remark to make. And it is this: William Benson spent eleven years in prison for an offence he did not commit. I set out to finish his career. Thankfully, I failed. I owe him an apology. In the circumstances, the term is hopelessly inadequate. But I offer it nonetheless, without reservation, here and now.'

With a nod, he turned on his heel and went back into the house.

Tess had cut the transmission before the reporter could repeat what Merrington had just said. And Archie stepped into the silence, large, baggy-trousered, and nervous. As a sort of father of the house, he thought he had to say something. He expanded his chest with a huge gulp of air.

'I always said you were innocent, Rizla.'

That was all he could muster and Benson realised he had to fill the void. But with what? It was immense.

'My life is words, and how to use them,' he said. 'But I don't have any that I can draw on to say what needs to be said.'

He looked first at Abasiama, who'd done her best to unlock so many doors; and then Braithwaite, who'd believed that one day they'd open; and then at CJ, who'd nodded off . . . And then Dot, Betsy, Joyce and Eileen, clustered and sniffing, who'd given him a home after he'd lost his own; and then Sally, a total stranger who'd still believed in him; and then, as if finally, Archie and Molly, who'd always been there, and would always be there.

'All I can say is thank you . . .'

He'd dried up already; and his eyes had moved on to Tess. She was on the other side of the room but he could still feel the warmth of her against his shoulder.

'And as for you, if you get the Merrington brief . . . don't turn to me.'

It wasn't that good a joke, but it released the tension in the room, for everyone laughed. And everyone wanted to make a speech, and they did, and while Molly handed round the Victoria sponge and the napkins and the cups of tea, Benson listened gratefully, but from afar.

He'd been struck by the harrowed face of the woman beside the Secretary of State for Justice. Pamela Merrington had attended every day of Benson's trial. She'd sat beside his mother. And when the verdict had been given, she'd been there to catch her when she lost consciousness.

82

Sally said she had to leave, so Tess walked her through the clerk's room and out onto Artillery Passage. It was dark and cold. The sound of muffled conversation came from Grapeshots Wine Bar, further down the alley. A siren sounded from Bishopsgate, becoming loud, and then rapidly fading. When it had gone, and the warming hum of the night had been restored, Tess spoke:

'You know what Archie and Molly just told me?'

'Go on.'

'That we saved Benson's life. That's he's free now.'

Sally nodded, then, almost rushing her words, she said: 'This is it, Tess. It's time for me to go.'

'I understand – you said.'

'No. I mean move on . . . or at least move aside.'

'What are you talking about?'

'You really don't know?'

'I really don't know.'

'Get back inside. Take control. Stop hanging around.'

'Take control of what?'

'Benson. He needs help. That is a man who will never take the initiative.'

Avoiding Tess's enquiring gaze, Sally leaned back, looking up the passage towards Sandy's Row as if to hail a stray taxi. And Tess felt the threat of loss that comes with change. And she felt an odd kind of guilt, too, as if she was about to snatch something before anyone noticed it was there.

Sally was still eyeing Sandy's Row.

'He's someone special, Tess. Don't let him slip out of the back door. You never know who might be there, waiting.'

Tess hadn't seen what had been happening. Between chasing down a bracelet and reconstructing the owner's secret history, Sally had slowly become involved with someone she hadn't even met.

'Seriously, Tess. Get back inside.'

And with that instruction, Sally quickly marched away, her heels striking the ground. But with every yard of separation Tess felt a longing to run after her, to keep what they had, two thirty-somethings with more scars than wounds, worldly wise, and with a taste for ridiculously expensive cocktails. To get to where they were, they'd done all sorts . . . like dragging a restaurant table from Paris to London, and getting arrested in Vienna . . . a long ride that had begun with a bottle of Bulgarian plonk when they'd been teenagers on the Isis. The journey couldn't be over.

'Get back inside,' hollered Sally, like a British Army officer – schooled at Eton – on the streets of Belfast. She'd reached the bright mouth of the alley. 'That's an order.'

She'd wheeled into Sandy's Row and vanished before Tess could tell her nothing could part them . . . nothing.

Feeling smaller, Tess returned through the clerk's room, and pushed open the Gutting Room door, only to see Benson literally exiting through another door at the back of chambers. As it shut, she said:

'Where's he going?'

'To feed his cat,' said Abasiama, glancing at the clump of Congreve girls, who, as one, gave a go-get-him nod.

Archie, with a clerk's bow, pulled open the door; and Braithwaite, who'd once warned her not to have any further contact with Benson – the Benson who'd just been sentenced to life in prison – gave her a red-faced push.

'Will?' she called . . . and Benson turned.

The door closed behind her, and Tess went down a couple of steps into the enclosed cobbled yard where the fresh fish had once been delivered to Congreves'. A long rectangle of light fell on Benson from the Gutting Room window, his face caught in the cross-hairs of a shadow.

'There's something I forgot to mention,' he said in a businesslike voice, one hand smoothing his hair.

'Yes?'

'I know why Menderez took those photos.'

'You do?'

Tess came up to him, feeling more unsteady than curious.

'Yes. He wanted them to go to Lucia.'

Tess nodded, feeling her heart beat against her ribs as if it was a fist.

'So I went to that Lambton place and gave them to Father Aelred . . . and – this is extraordinary – Lucia was still there, and I spoke to her, and I—'

'You went to Lambton Abbey?'

'Yes.'

'Without me?'

Benson thought.

'I suppose not.'

Tess's heart, that fist, seemed to grab a rib.

'You didn't even consider telling me you were going?'

Benson frowned to think about that.

'I'm sorry, you see—'

Tess snapped.

'Look, I really don't want to hear any bollocks about what prison does to you—'

'But it's true, you sort of end up locked in, and awkward, and—'

'Seriously, stop, don't go there.'

She looked at him, his hands thrust into the pockets of his duffel coat, and something inside her cracked. She advanced on him, pushing his shoulder. Benson stumbled back, and Tess shoved him again, and again, until he'd reached the back wall, out of the box of light.

'You're incredible,' she said.

Tess thought of the fish laid out in trays of ice, coming through the gate. And the crabs. And the prawns. And the lobsters. None of them wanted to be caught. They'd been as happy as Larry beneath the waves until someone like Benson's father yanked them to the surface.

'Tess, let me tell you what eleven—'

Benson didn't get to 'years' because Tess had landed a kiss on his mouth, meant for his eyes, his nose, his lips, his teeth, his hair. When she eventually let go of him, he almost fell over, but she caught him, with a hand around his neck.

'I've got a confession to make,' she managed, her breath racing.

'Yes?'

'I've wanted to do that since I was nineteen.'

Benson's eyes flickered in the shadow.

'That'll be five Hail Marys.'

83

Benson did, in fact, need to feed the cat.

Feeling Tess upon him, he'd lost sense of his own shape. He'd been transported by the awakening of sensation, all over his body which, for so long, had been cold. He'd never realised just how cold – with the coldness of the cell and the recreation yard – until he stumbled down the lane behind chambers, enveloped in a fire that he thought might never go out, all-consuming but leaving him still intact. The heat was still there when he reached his gate in the railings, and took the path home. He didn't know why he was running away from the flickering and the flashing and the snapping . . . they were life-giving. They were good. Why had he tried to put them out? The cat could wait. Colours had been—

Benson came to a sudden halt on the landing stage.

On board *The Wooden Doll* Benson had installed a bench and a herb garden. He liked to sit there and read poetry, hoping to recover the kind of sensations he'd just tried to extinguish. Which was a problem for another day. Sitting on the bench in a heavy overcoat was Helen's half-brother and Annette's first son. Richard Merrington.

He'd come with a large manila envelope.

It was the usual kind, just like the one Braithwaite had

used for Helen's affidavit. Both envelopes were now on Benson's small kitchen table. He'd done what men do when they sit down together to be serious: he'd got out the hard stuff. All that was left of the prison hooch. And a couple of glasses.

'It's all I've got,' said Benson.

'And you can keep it.'

Merrington looked around the boat, taking in the round windows, the wooden beams, the brass fittings, and, at last, the Aga.

'How like my blessed mother,' he said. 'We have the same model.'

Changing his mind about the hooch, he gave his glass a light shove.

'When my mother confessed, I went out for a walk. I just couldn't stay in the room.'

'I understand.'

'Oh, you don't, Mr Benson. Believe you me. I went out because I was stunned by her ability to lie. I just couldn't join in the next . . . charade.'

He tasted the hooch and gave a wince of approval.

'You of all people deserve to know the truth, and that's partly why I'm here. But the dear old fool is taking the fall for my darling wife, who really is an extraordinary woman – you should meet, come to think of it. She's one of your most ardent fans. Honestly. But she's the one who was driving. Trying to get home in time because she was late, as usual, for the babysitter. She was probably looking for her phone.'

Benson's frown only added to Merrington's anguished delight.

'It really is a remarkable story. You see, my dear mother had always planned to give that damned bracelet to Pamela . . . she's my wife. But it was broken. Something wrong with

the catch, and she kept asking me to get it fixed, and like
an eejit, as the Irish say, I kept forgetting. In the end, she
took it back. Well, she must have given it to Pamela as is.
Without any repair. And Pamela, like an eejit, wore it. And
she was obviously wearing it the night of that fundraiser
at Spellow and Hardy.'

Benson, an instinctive defender, couldn't restrain himself:

'You can't be sure.'

'Oh yes I can.'

'Why?'

'Because my mother can't have been there. She never
went near cocktail parties, not after my father died. And
she never drove in central London. Ever. She must think
I'm stupid . . . or at least ready to believe anything which
is to my advantage. Which is a terrible thing to say, don't
you think? This is good stuff.'

He nodded at his glass.

'It's all so bloody *involved*. You see, my wonderful mother
says she did it for me. For my career. Which is absolutely
credible. But it's just another lie, bless her. All those years
ago, when Pamela knocked that dreadful Harbeton fellow
over, they weren't keeping schtum for me: it was for David.
He was two years old at the time. His mother would have
spent his third birthday in Holloway. He'd have grown up
with a mother who'd killed someone. That's why they said
nothing. And that's why you got eleven years.'

Benson nodded slowly, but not at Merrington's disclosure.
He'd understood what had really taken place between
Annette and Helen. For Helen, facing death, had told Benson
what she believed to be the truth – that her mother had got
herself into a terrible situation. But Annette had misled her
own daughter with a calculated fabrication. She'd rightly
concluded that Helen was far more likely to offer help if
she believed Annette was in danger, as opposed to Annette's

daughter-in-law. Even as Helen died wanting to tell the truth, she didn't know it. And neither did Merrington. He thought he'd seen through his mother, but he hadn't.

'You deserve the right scalp, after all you've been through,' Merrington said, eyeing the sludge at the bottom of his glass.

'I don't want any scalp.'

'Yes, you do. You just don't want an old one.'

Merrington humphed.

'This isn't easy for me, and damn it, I can't do it, but . . . if you push the police to look beyond my mother's admissions, Pamela will crack. She's not a natural-born liar, my wife. She's just got used to it. And having got used to it, she can't get back to where she started from . . . in prep school, I suppose . . . that was the last time I told the truth without thinking about it. Except for now, of course. Feels odd. You know, this is really rather good, in an unpleasant sort of way.'

Benson topped up his glass.

'Now, this next bit should please you,' said Merrington and he leaned forward confidentially.

'Everyone thinks I knew all along – which I assure you I didn't. So my future is your past. I'm on your boat and in your shoes. I'm saying I'm innocent and nobody believes me. Isn't that wonderful?'

'Not really.'

Benson glanced at the envelope containing Helen's affidavit. The truth about Merrington's family was right in front of him and he just didn't know it. Just like Benson had been wearing Wilfred Baker's wig, not knowing the answer to his situation was on top of his head. Benson poured himself what was left of the hooch and then placed the jerrycan on the floor.

'There's something else,' said Merrington, raising his glass.

'Yes?'

'My boy, David. He applied to spend a week with you.'

'Yes. I turned him down.'

'And that was very gentlemanly of you. Speaking of your shoes, if I'd been wearing them, I'd've rolled out the red carpet, just to get at me. Thing is, he's the one who put that petition on the net . . . Everyone Deserves a Second Chance . . . it was bloody well him. Launched in my own bloody house. Now, when it comes to shopping his mother, don't let that stand in your way. I just thought the lad deserves some moral credit. He's the only Merrington not to have harmed you. Which brings me to this.'

Merrington tapped the envelope in front of him.

'I ordered by devious means the rifling of your abandoned property.'

Benson frowned.

'Going through your bins.'

'Why?'

'Seeking evidence with which to destroy you, professionally and morally.'

'I see.'

'I'm sure you can guess why. Success in politics, as in life, is made up of countless assassinations. Don't let anyone ever tell you anything different . . . though your good self may be a shining, solitary exception. Either way, that is why I got hold of these.'

He shoved the envelope across the table. Benson reached inside and pulled out a sheaf of photocopies . . . of his handwritten confessions. He'd put them in a shredder. Someone with a software package had put the pieces back together again.

'If I were you, I'd go in for burning,' said Merrington.

Benson's eyes flicked across the front page. He'd no need to look any further. He knew what was there. Each page had been a foray into guilt, guilt unknown to any jury.

'May I offer you some advice, Benson?'

'Sure.'

'Spilling your guts out isn't always a good idea.'

'Okay.'

'I'm being serious. And in present circumstances, what with my mother pretending to tell the truth, and me actually telling you the truth, and my dear wife not daring to tell the truth, you could easily conclude that one should always tell the truth. And that's not so.'

Benson glanced at his own envelope.

'Your brother, Eddie,' said Merrington, by way of example.

'What about him?'

'He doesn't need to know the truth. To find out what you did won't change his lot one bit. It will, in fact, make things considerably worse. You may be tempted to get things off your chest, and maybe you would feel better. But he wouldn't. Whatever nightmares you still have . . . just put up with them. You owe him your silence.'

Merrington stood up and examined his surroundings once more.

'It's nice to know my mother bought you this.'

He held out his hand.

'I'm sorry, Benson. Truly.'

As he took it, Benson had some kind of synaptic malfunction, because he thought of Lucia.

'I'll represent your mother,' he said. 'It's her only chance of keeping out of prison. There aren't many judges out there who'd ignore my plea.'

Benson sat on deck, trying to get the barbecue going. He'd used an inordinate number of firelighters. The breeze that had been his enemy finally became his friend, and soon the coals were red and raging, turning white at their edges. Benson prodded them with an old umbrella, trying to make sense of what he'd just done. He'd joined the scheme after all. He'd go into court to represent Annette Merrington in the full knowledge that she was innocent, claiming to be guilty, while Pamela would be back in the public gallery, squirming as she'd squirmed once before. And they'd all do this, as it was done at the outset, for David Merrington, who believed everyone deserved a second chance.

When the blaze had died down, Benson dropped Helen's affidavit, still in its envelope, on the white-hot coals. Shortly, the edges turned black and buckled, bursting into flame. The smoke stung Benson's eyes and he jerked away, unable to see properly, feeling tears gather in protest.

84

Dalston's Girl danced with the lilt of the waves. There was a rising wind, and spray was landing in the boat as if corks were being popped.

'I thought we'd come and say goodbye to the Wash,' said Jim, cutting the engine.

He nodded out to sea, smiling.

'I've spent most of my life around here.'

Jim had got his boys out of bed early. He'd thrown dark blue ganseys at the two of them, knitted by their mother. He'd shouted a captain's shout when they'd both rolled over, two brothers back in their bunks, groaning. There'd been no breakfast, and the three of them had gone down the jetty at the end of the garden, Benson and his dad trudging on either side of Eddie, as his strong arms propelled his wheelchair over the rasping planks. They'd set a course for Race Bank, and the indigo darkness of morning had quickly disappeared.

Jim lit the Primus and got the bacon sizzling. He was in his element.

'In a few months' time there'll be ninety-one turbines out there, and—'

'The sand will disappear,' said Benson.

'And once the sand's gone,' added Eddie, 'the crabs'll go too.'

'It's a cemetery in the making,' they all said together.

They laughed. Though Jim had never before said that phrase with a smile. He'd fought against the planned wind farm and lost. So there was nothing to laugh about. But this time he didn't care. He'd got his boys back. Both of them, even if they'd never work these waters, or any waters. He was at sea, with Will and Eddie.

'Sausage?'

'Aye,' they said.

'Beans?'

'Aye.'

It would be an unholy mess served up in a tin bowl. And the boys would eat, swaying between the upsurge and the stomach-turning dip, for they'd both lost their sea legs. Only Jim would stand there, feeling nothing.

'Does it get any better than this?' he said, winking.

'No,' replied Eddie.

He'd been strapped into a chair bolted to the deck. He looked at Benson, waiting. But Benson couldn't give him the answer he expected and wanted. Not yet.

'I'll answer that one if I keep anything down.'

Their dad had kept it vague. He couldn't say his son's vindication was the best thing in life, because his other son would never walk again, at least not easily, and he'd lost his wife, their mother. These were part of any review he'd ever make. He'd learned, instead, to take the fullest satisfaction in small moments, like breakfast at sea. With his boys.

'Down there,' – Jim indicated overboard – 'there's tons of unexploded ordnance. Bombs from the War. There'll be no moving forward, not until they've cleared 'em away.'

This was a new fact. And Benson thought about it while he ate his breakfast, leaning on the rail, looking into the sea. Eddie was quiet, too. When they'd finished eating, Jim took the bowls and went below deck. Turning to look at Eddie, Benson suddenly remembered a question Abasiama had asked him long ago, when he'd first told her how much he thought about his brother; how he couldn't see a wheel-chair without thinking of him. She'd said: 'What would you say to Eddie if he rose from that chair? If he stood up, his legs restored, and he walked towards you?' Benson had been slain. And he felt sick now, because Eddie was unbuckling the harness that kept him in the chair.

'What are you doing?'

'I want to say sorry.'

'What for?'

'Because I didn't believe in you.'

The day before Benson's trial, Eddie had stared at a gash of crimson cloud above the sea and told him if he didn't plead guilty, he'd never speak to him again. That had been eighteen years ago. Apart from one meeting – only last year, when Benson had resolved to be honest, and lost his nerve – Eddie had kept his word.

'There's something wrong with me, Will,' he said, struggling with a clip.

He paused to pat his head on both sides.

'I can't see things clearly . . . not any more, and back then I couldn't see that you'd told me the truth.'

He was tugging at the strap again.

'Help me, will you?'

But Benson couldn't move. A wave hit the side of the boat and it broke over them like a gust of rain. When Benson had rubbed the salt out of his eyes, he saw Eddie rising. *Dalston's Girl* tilted starboard, the prow rising, and her ropes whistled in the wind. Eddie was up, stepping towards him, but the deck swung port-side and he lost control. As Eddie threw out his arms, Benson caught him. They gripped each other as another wave turned into spray.

'Can we get back?' said Eddie. 'Back to where we were?'

It was all Benson wanted, but his route to the old simplicity lay in the wooded grounds of the Lushmead Hotel. Along a path that led to the main road. Do I tell him? Do I explain why he hit that red people carrier?

'Say something, Will, please. I'm sorry. So sorry.'

'Eddie, you need to understand something.'

'I'll understand anything.'

Benson closed his eyes, hearing Merrington; and he opened them to see his father emerging from below deck, turning away, unable to believe that his boys were reconciled. *Dalston's Girl* was on the rise again.

'What is it, Will?'

'Nothing's changed, Eddie. I promise,' said Benson. 'We're back to where we started.'

85

Benson couldn't cope. And neither could Archie.

Congreve Chambers was completely inundated with work. Sent by the many solicitors who had once reviled him. Benson was the most in-demand counsel in London. Because he was good? Oh dear, yes, said Archie. But also because Benson's gown had the sheen of the suffering servant who'd risen humbly and without fuss from the ashes, leaving his doubters to rend their garments. So said Braithwaite.

Whatever the explanation, Benson was the man of the moment, because the prevailing view was that if Benson told the jury it was Friday when it was actually Monday, they'd stop to think.

The question then arose as to whether chambers should expand. Should they take on other counsel? Again, this was a question that imposed itself as much from without as within. People were applying for vacancies that hadn't even been advertised. Benson received emails every week from barristers telling him their life stories – how they'd always been misunderstood, by their parents and their colleagues – and how much they'd always wanted to work in a small set with a reputation for fearless advocacy . . . Benson put them in a folder, with the same reply attached. For the present, Congreve Chambers did not envisage an expansion of service provision.

There were other communications of a legal character.

One was an email from Bancroft & Lewis, the solicitors representing Annette Merrington. Benson's services would not be required for the simple reason their client had died peacefully at home in Hampstead.

Benson just stared at the screen. Mother and daughter had played their cards with consummate skill. They'd lived their lives with chosen discomfort. They'd picked their suffering. And, when it was too late for anyone to impose on them what they'd didn't want, they'd died, Helen having cleared her conscience, and Annette having pretended to. As game plans to manage life's vicissitudes, they'd been masterful conceptions. Benson pressed delete lightly, and with relief for, having offered to help Annette – like Lucia had helped the Lynwoods – he'd realised afterwards that the comparison didn't hold. Only Maureen Harbeton could make such a decision. Victims alone could intervene with a species of forgiveness . . . and had Benson appeared in court representing Annette Merrington, he'd have joined himself to the workings of another deception on an already deceived woman. This time, Annette's card-laying had, for once, saved Benson from the one condemnation he would have deserved.

The same day, Benson got an email from the Court of Appeal Criminal Division. He deleted that one without reading it, because he knew its contents. It was an acknowledgement of receipt for his online NG application. Benson's innocence might be beyond dispute, but it would take months, perhaps over a year, for the court to formally quash his conviction . . . and then invite him to prove, beyond reasonable doubt, his innocence. That was the only way to win compensation, which, in fact, Benson didn't want. Not after receiving direct payment from Annette. But an anomaly of the system, designed to save money, was that a quashed conviction didn't restore the presumption of innocence. And Benson wanted his character back. All of it. So, frustrated, he'd hit that delete button with something like a thump.

A few days later, Benson received a parcel.

The sender was Janet Forde QC, who'd agreed to represent him in the Court of Appeal. She'd sent him her own verdict, and quickly. QCs who lead junior counsel in a case have in their gift the right to award a red bag – in place of the usual blue – to hold their gown, wig and other courtroom paraphernalia. It was a way of saying the bearer has potential. Only Benson hadn't been led by Forde. He'd been against her. But that didn't stop her breaking with tradition. Written on the parchment inside were these words:

To William Benson, a fit and proper person.

And then, a week or so later, another email arrived from Bancroft & Lewis. It transpired that the firm were also acting for the estate of Helen Camberley. And by the terms of her last will and testament, Benson was the sole beneficiary. The residential property in Hampstead had been valued at £3.6 million. Other assets – goods, chattels, investments and cash – came to approximately £1.2 million. The total, a sum of £4.8 million, would, of course, be subject to the usual charges and tax provisions, but it was thought—

Benson pressed delete again. It was a payoff. An apology in pounds, shillings and pence. She'd taken away his home, and now she was giving him one he could never have afforded. Then, after an hour's staring into space, he restored it to his inbox. He'd sell the house, and the rest, and set up the More than One Chance Foundation. A resource for those who couldn't get legal aid . . . and for ex-prisoners who couldn't get a break.

It was a time of gifts, in every sense.

But Benson was worried. Tess had dropped off the horizon. After the encounter with shared flame in the back yard – it really did feel like a tale from school, now – she had not been in touch. Benson couldn't sleep, for fear he'd crossed a line, only he hadn't. But for his consent, he'd been vigorously assaulted pursuant to section 3 of the Sexual Offences Act 2003. Something wonderful had happened between them, something that didn't happen with first loves, or between adolescents grappling at a bus stop. It had been inevitable. A coming together of so much hope and expectation. The sensations in Benson's body, the pinpricks of yellow and green and gold and blue and purple and orange and magenta, weren't just the atoms of desire, colliding and splitting, they were the elements of longing, breaking down, at last . . .

But Tess wasn't answering her phone. She hadn't responded to texts. She hadn't replied to his emails. After two weeks' silence, he'd rung Coker & Dale, only to be told Miss de Vere had taken a few days off work.

After a troubled weekend, Benson came into chambers resolved to lose himself in a case management hearing at the Bailey. He was leafing through the papers when Archie came into the Gutting Room. In his hand was a letter.

Benson opened the envelope wondering who might still write with pen and ink. It was postmarked Sudbury, in Suffolk. And it was from Fr Aelred. Benson read it and then dropped his hands onto his desk.

'Simon Lynwood went to Spain,' he said at last.

Archie raised a so-what eyebrow.

'He checked the date on his birth certificate . . . and it was the same as that belonging to Angela.'

Had Karen Lynwood broken down? Had John? Had they told Simon the truth? Or had Simon just thought again about that woman sitting beside him in the public gallery; the woman his parents kept avoiding.

'They're setting up a centre.'

'Who are?'

'Simon and his mother, Lucia. They're opening a centre to offer confidential support and guidance to parents who want to come forward and admit what they'd done, years back, but don't know how to handle the fallout . . .'

Benson swung his chair around and looked at the sky. Lucia got her child back . . . Angela's grave was empty. And now they were going to rouse more of the dead. The thought so arrested Benson that he didn't notice Archie leave the room, though he'd vaguely heard the insistent jangle of the phone. He only noticed his clerk when he lumbered back in again, thumbs in his waistcoat.

'That was Miss de Vere,' he announced.

Benson dropped his gaze to the yard where the wall had collapsed between them. It was as though the dull bricks had been covered with bright tints of paint, thrown on with buckets and then mixed around with a floor brush.

'You've been instructed in the Nine Elms killing,' said Molly.

Benson turned back. The two of them were standing side by side like proud parents. But there was nothing to celebrate. Someone was dead. Someone else had been accused. There'd be grief on both sides of the equation. There'd be no consolation for anyone. In a way, no one came out of a murder trial alive. You couldn't involve yourself in the trauma without losing something vital. But this, thought Benson, is my world. Helen prepared me for this. She showed me how to survive; and how to accompany those who are about to die.

'Book a conference, please, Archie,' he said. 'There's work to be done.'

Acknowledgements

I warmly thank: Clare Smith, Zoe Gullen and Grace Vincent at Little, Brown; Victoria Hobbs at A.M. Heath; Ursula Mackenzie, Elizabeth Dobson, Her Honour Judge Penny Moreland, Françoise Koetschet, and Sabine Guyard. And, as always, Anne.

Representations regarding the law, criminal procedure and the prison system are mine.

About the Author

John Fairfax is the pen name of William Brodrick, who practised as a barrister before becoming a full-time novelist. Under his own name he is a previous winner of the Crime Writers' Association Gold Dagger Award and his first novel, *The Sixth Lamentation*, was a Richard and Judy selection.